The Power of the Stallion Queen

Sepul drew his sword and insisted they couldn't leave in the dark. "You'll start a stampede."

Hengst stared them down. "I've a task given by the Stallion Queen. If you keep us from leaving, I promise there will be a stampede of the like you've never seen in all your days upon the Saquave. There is no horse that does not obey *her*."

One of Sepul's group spat on the ground in front of Hengst's boots. "No Stallion Queen perhaps, but a witch. A witch can command the rains and the buffalo herds, send them to her lackeys, and keep them from those who refuse to bend a knee."

D0802628

Ace Books by Constance Ash

THE HORSEGIRL
THE STALKING HORSE
THE STALLION QUEEN

THE STALLION QUEEN

CONSTANCE ASH

ACE BOOKS, NEW YORK

THE STALLION QUEEN

An Ace Book / published by arrangement with
the author

PRINTING HISTORY
Ace edition / August 1992

In memory of my sister,
whose soul was stolen.

As I step down from my long,
rewarding tenure as Headmaster
of our scholarly community, I
am honored that my esteemed
colleagues have requested I speak
on the subject of my own studies—
the history of that heroine, too
much doubted, too little understood,
the Stallion Queen.

From: *Farewell Address* presented
by Edwin Muran, Headmaster
of Seven Universities, on the
occasion of his retirement
banquet.

·One·

IN THE BRIEF hour between false dawn and sunrise a very young man lay submerged in sleep. The banked fire, the main defense against the great predators that ruled the night, popped. The youth's limbs were pulled in upon himself, like a snake's coils, against the cold of air and earth.

By degrees the sun crested the Rain Shadow Mountains to the northeast. The first radiance touching the broken thornscrub lands below was a deceptively gentle warm bath. Leon's arms and legs straightened and relaxed.

As the sun's strength waxed he rolled over on his back. The hide-blanket fell away, and the brief clout covering the nakedness of his narrow, hollowed loins was disturbed.

He was still growing into the stature promised by the breadth of his shoulders, thickness of collarbone, the length of thigh and calf, and the size of hand and foot. Gut-tied leggings shielded him, hip to ankle, against thorn and spine, fang and claw. Crude buskins had rubbed his heels and toes raw. The hair on the hides that made his garments was mangy, and the skins stank.

Thick golden lashes edged delicately blue-veined lids that concealed large green-flecked, wide-spaced eyes. The high cheekbones were sharp as axe blades in the unhealthy gauntness of his face. A fledgling beard gleamed red and gold along the strong lines of his jaw. The fierce elements of this harsh land in which he and his companion were lost had bleached his greasy hair to a bitter orange. However, the new growth at the hairline of his broad forehead glowed with the same richness as the garnet studded in his left earlobe.

Leon sighed and stretched. The sunlight exposed the grimed skin and showed up his bones. It pitilessly highlighted each tear, scrape, and puncture in the fine-pored flesh that nature had intended to be unblemished. His arms and chest were a weltered map of scores made by teeth and claws of his quarry, and the larger beasts which disputed possession of his prey and hunted him.

His hands were blistered and bruised from fire and stone. His hands, along with fire, knife, and the devotion of the older man, were the only faithful weapons fortune had given him leave to keep.

His escape had been a long one, and carefully prepared. But at the pass which was to lead them to the Rain Shadow Crossing and down into the Wilderness Lands, his train had been ambushed. The supplies and weapons for all landscapes and enemies had been stolen, the guides, guardian escort, and the horses, every one, slaughtered. These two sleepers alone had been able to flee.

They'd been hunted relentlessly over the mountain range where they'd been ambushed. Only after they'd climbed a crag outside of the maps memorized by the older man did their harriers drop away.

Leon was of a lineage that identified prowess with riding to the hunt and to war. He believed that all his losses could have been remedied, if he only had a horse.

His eyelids quivered. He was awake, but not ready to accept another day in this endless series of days, alike in weariness, pain, and peril.

One hand groped in the shallow depression scooped out next to the uncured hide upon which he rested. There, within immediate reach, were his sparkstones, three knives, a pile of rocks, and a few odds and ends. By feel he found the small pouch of rancid goose grease.

His fingers, slick and glistening in the sun, reached between his thighs and touched his stiff member. The erect phallus was smooth as ivory, and the sensitive tip was soft as the velvets he used to wear. His hands had been made by this wild country, and what they grasped now seemed to belong to another time, another place, one of easier living, but fraught with dangers more cruel than those of the Wilderness.

His own fingers transformed into the cool, fair, long fingers of Thurlow, his Uncle Roald's raven-haired mistress, his Uncle who was husband to his mother. She was his mother Sharissa's unwavering enemy which, luck save him, had only added to the hold her beauty had on him. He thrust through the images that formed behind his eyelids, of his mother and the other members of the court, and banished them. He penetrated into the only private place this Wilderness permitted him to possess, there where his vitality had another focus other than the overwhelming one of his belly.

The rich creamy swell of Thurlow's breasts framed by the crimson satin of her ballgown heaved with impatient, overwhelming desire for him. She whispered in her silken voice. She begged him to use his hands, tear away the confining satin, and grasp the fine, soft, taut flesh that strained for his touch. In a moment he was released.

He opened his eyes. As every morning, the sky was a brilliant turquoise. The emptiness was marred by the same watchful circling of vultures.

However, the vibration that they'd felt under their feet as they traveled, and under their bodies as they rested, had ceased. And last night wolves and lions hadn't come visiting. He speculated on what connection there might be between the earth's shaking and the absence of hunting animals. The Saquave Wilderness abounded in volcanoes living and dead, as well as predators. Earthquakes were frequent, as were sandstorms.

He got up, rinsed his mouth several times, and spit out the water. It was deep pleasure to use, without giving a thought to conserving. At the bottom of the ravine making one line of their camp's defense ran a streamlet of pure, sweet water, the first that they'd come upon in many days. After drinking deeply of the alkali-free water, he shuffled around the banked fire and pissed.

His tutor, Edwin Muran, remained as deep in his sleep as the overhanging boulders were rooted in their foundation rock under the shallow, gritty soil. The formation had provided a natural backline defense. He looked up into the sky again. The vultures had gone. His spirits lifted.

His belly rumbled. He gauged the intensity of the sun shining upon the tablelands and the thornscrub through which they'd crept since leaving the huge upthrust of the Rain Shadows. It was warm enough now for the small life that refuged underground during the cool of night to be up and about.

He scrambled down, and then up the other side of the ravine, heading for one of the bits of grassland pocking the thornscrub. His shuffle became a lithe, noiseless tread, learned through inborn instinct and utter necessity.

It was a good town. Its residents were doing their business early, no doubt because the usual night spoor of coyote and wolf wasn't present. Consequently the young dogs standing periphery sentinel were less wary. Beside the dogs he also caught a brace of burrowing owls and a rattlesnake. The snake provided a lagniappe, the unexpected, free extra of its own undigested meal. One tiny step at a time he moved to the center of the town. Here was the largest, fattest meat his unaided hands could take.

Light and warmth beckoned at the porches of the King's citadel. Food must be gathered. The little Queen, their offspring, and the aunties of his household wouldn't leave the burrow until they heard the Sire's short, sharp barks.

Like a terrier Leon crouched at the threshold of the funnel-shaped mound. His hands were ready, perfectly still, pulsing with the true hunter's power that compels life to approach that his own might continue.

He felt the minute vibration of the little King's claws skittering on the sand of his tunnel floor. Leon's blood coursed in sympathetic rhythm with the shifts in the currents made by the wind soughing across the entrance.

His hands snared its neck tightly. One slipped down and grabbed the haunches. The prairie dog's teeth tore at his hands. It writhed and twisted, claws opening tracks like new veins in his forearms. Its life beat wild, vital determination against the man's.

I am sorry, the hunter thought, holding firm. Please grant me your life, for me and mine are under necessity to take it.

The hunter's eyes bored into those of the little King for a moment that held all the power of monarchy within it. The hunter's animating force was immeasurably greater than that of the animal's. The body went slack.

The vertebrae, tendons, and ligaments were elastically resistent. It took skill, rather than strength, to snap its spine.

He felt an immense gratitude to what he'd killed this morning. On one knee, head bowed, the prairie dog King's lifeless body in his hands, he reflected for a short moment on how even the humblest of creation was animated by a sense of entitlement to live out its natural span of days. This wasn't a thought he'd entertained previously in his existence. But in his struggle to survive there was no time to examine such an interesting, if disturbing, idea.

He gathered the nine brace of dog, brace of owl, and the rattlesnake and headed back to camp in an unaccustomed state of hopefulness. Three nights without fighting off large meat-eating animals had given him much-needed rest. His bowels were uncramped after drinking good water. And he had provisions in hand ample for the day.

His eyes were working all the way to the ravine, scanning the ground for sign of horse or man, other game, or threatening creatures. He constantly checked the horizons, all four of the cardinal directions, and the sky, which, out here, made a fifth cardinal point.

Edwin Muran spotted him from the far side of the ravine. The tutor raised an arm as a signal that all was well. Scholar, clerk, tutor to a King-in-waiting, a traitor to the cause for which he'd been carefully selected and paid, he put down the journal in which he'd been writing. As if they were jewels beyond price Muran put the notebook, a nearly empty jar of ink, and a tiny leather case holding metal pen nibs into the larger one dangling from his neck by a slim chain. The fine-grained, tooled leather was in ludicrous contrast to the uncured, unworked skins that clothed and sheltered him.

Muran built up the fire of brambles knife-hacked out of the bottom of the ravine. Dry fewmets served as tinder. Earlier, he'd rolled up the elk hide which was their camp awning, and the two small bearskins on which they slept, ready to be back-carried. In the space of a few days late in the spring, they'd stumbled upon these animals, fresh-killed, a piece of luck they'd valued so highly that they were able to steal them from the beasts that had hunted them down. Close to Muran's hand were the poles they'd cut in the Mountains, which were walking staffs by day, and when necessary, armed with two of their knives, spears.

Muran carried nearly fifty years. His head was covered with

coarse, cascading black hair which no sun could lighten. More hair curled on his back, breast, and legs, poking through the rents and gaps of his garments. His frame was intended to carry comfortably a good deal of weight. The emaciation consequent to their diet had proceeded more slowly with him.

The tutor was of an even disposition, and his curiosity about everything that came his way was keen. These characteristics, coupled with the amount of learning and literature packed into his round head, saved him from the high-strung outbursts which afflicted Leon, so young and born into entitled power.

Muran's quick intelligence and retentive memory had allowed him to rise out of the impoverished, illiterate class into which he'd been born. His life's experience had taught him what his companion had not needed to learn, which was never to waste substance fighting against what he couldn't change. Muran also possessed in the highest degree the peasant's ability to recognize opportunity and seize it. His employers, of high pedigree and lofty degree, hadn't recognized that a peasant's intellect could provide him with a strong sense of honor. Ordered to administer a slow poison to the heir of Nolan's throne, the tutor had sought clandestine paths of audience with Queen Sharissa.

His honor had awarded him an endless wandering in the Saquave Wilderness, which he'd never had any desire to see, far away from his community of scholarly peers, and the studies which gave purpose to his life.

Muran gave the boy a short bow as Leon dropped a wealth of provisions by the fire. There was even a rabbit, caught in the snare he'd set last night in the ravine. Between the heavy beard and mustache, the tutor's chapped lips grinned.

In St. Lucien cheers of multitudes had greeted Leon whenever he rode the avenues with his mother, the Queen. Those cheers had been in memory of his father, dead before his son was born, whom the crowd had loved, and for what it hoped he, when he reached his majority and was crowned, would become. A wicked gleam of teeth and a wisp of genuflection, given him here because he fed his people, though only one man, provided a greater refreshment than all the adulation of Nolan.

They prepared their sorry repast for immediate dining and for later in the day. The meat was accompanied by wild onion bulbs growing close to the streamlet. The roots of some stubby, low-growing thistles they'd discovered, out of desperation, were palatable, gave satisfaction to their guts, and didn't make them sick afterwards.

Leon was presented with the entire prairie dog King for himself. He swallowed the liver whole, without putting it in the fire first. They shared the rabbit equally between them.

After eating Leon said, "Back in Nolan we were always taught that this land created our horses, and us too. I still have seen no sign that horses ever ran this land, either wild, hunted, or herded. Cactus brakes are too thick, too continuous, and the grass too sparse and infrequent. The little swards we come across are too holed by ground rodents to be good horse footing, and the grass is so eaten down a horse can't get but a mouthful."

Muran said, "The spine and thorn groves are thinning out. We've hit some sweet water. The daylight hours are getting shorter. Hard to calculate seasons without leaves turning and the stars where we're used to having them, yet it seems summer's waning. I'd like to take a day or two and use this water to flush out the poisons from the piss we've been drinking. But it's probably best to keep moving."

Leon nodded and got up to refill the water skins. The new hides, wet and reeking, were divided among them, to patch buskins and clothes. The snakeskin was wrapped inner side out around Muran's staff.

Following as best they could determine the country's vague downward gradient west, they set out. The ravine was their guide until the water disappeared and its bed turned into a gully, then a crack in the earth that closed at an exposed, windswept expanse of rock. Somewhere ahead, always ahead, they had to strike the Snake River Valley, the headquarters of the Saquave Settlement Company.

The tough roots of Ironbush pushing through the shallow topsoil tripped their feet. Washes opened without warning, tumbling them into cactus that came in varieties as countless as the ants.

Some of the cacti had tiny flowers that opened in the early and late hours of the day. These hosted swarms of bees, wasps, and flocks of ruby-throated humming birds, nearly as hard to see as the flowers. Bloodthirsty flies hung about them. Leon's

new beard and sleek eyebrows provided scant protection to his
face and eyes.

Monumental features, steep at the sides, and flat at the
top, like tables furnishing the dining halls of giants, forced
them into detours. All around them, deceptively near in the
clear, dry air, were spurs calved off the titanic shield wall
that barricaded the Saquave Wilderness from Nolan, the Rain
Shadow Mountains.

The next two nights of their journey were quiet. The daylight's heat lacked the scrotum-frying quality they'd suffered
from previously, but it was still powerful. On the third day
after they'd left the sweet water ravine behind they stopped as
usual at midday. They sprawled in the shade of a giant's table
and devoured the remains of another rabbit. Before falling into
their rest the last thing they saw was a Bee Eater dart by, its
long beak and plumage of gold and turquoise sharply etched
against a tower of white cloud.

The "who-cooks-for-you" call of White Wing Doves, a chorus of "wichity-coicity-wichity" from Yellowthroats, and the
trills of Canyon Wrens provided a reassuring lullaby while
they slept.

A sudden interjection, "brrruuutt," was a harsh, dissonant
note among the melodious voices of the other birds. It startled
Muran awake. He sat up and saw a long-tailed Ground Cuckoo
running only a short distance away. He sucked on a piece of
rabbit cranium for the sake of bringing up saliva into his dry
mouth. He gazed meditatively upon the emptiness before him.
Then he roused Leon.

"Take a look. Is that a clear route down there? Doesn't it
look to you as if it's going downslope? It twists fair for sure,
but ain't it a clear trail that has an object of destination?"

Leon stood up to better sniff the wind currents. He squinted,
moved to a different point of view, and then another. He mut-
tered, "Likely only another demon trick devised by Saquave
out of light and shadow."

He put his palms up as blinders at the sides of his eyes,
examining each field of vision as he slowly turned his head.
Excitement thickened his dry tongue.

"We've been blind. This is grassland, true rolling prairie!
Not the little plots of gophers and dogs. The earth shook on
our backtrail. Winter is on its way and the buffalo are coming

together in their migration herds. I can smell their droppings from up here. They've got to be heading to winter grounds around the Snake River, and there's got to be water on the way there. Our luck's turned at last!"

Muran panted like a dog to release the heat of hope building in him. Carefully, he said, "After we strike the River, Albany Town will be child's play to find. We'll be entering territory I know from my memory of our lost maps. Let's go, boy. The sooner we start, the sooner we come."

Leon didn't move. When he finally put foot down to what they thought was the final stage of their journey, his accompanying words were those of an embittered, only child, who was used to being spoiled after hurting himself.

"Maybe there is a Stallion Queen reigning over this bloody hole of the Saquave Wilderness after all, and she's finally reached out the assisting hand she owes me in fealty."

Muran said, "It's not diplomatic to speak rudely of a land when you are in it seeking refuge and assistance."

Together they moved out, on the way to a Queen that another far away had promised would help put a King on his rightful throne, following the trail of the buffalo.

· Two ·

BEHIND THE PALISADE that crowned Hometown's watchtower, two young rangers kept careful vigilance over the Saquave Settlement Company's headquarters in the Snake River Valley.

Below Hometown's stockades the Snake was a contracted ribbon within the wide, looping channels which overflowed during good springs. Late afternoon sunlight glinted on the surface currents and wind riffles. Irrigation ditches twined through terraces of tawny mulch built up between the stockades and the River. Red dirt, containing much sand, whirled and eddied in the ditches now that the sluice gates were closed. In spring the terraces would be the various greens of gardens and crops.

The scents of juniper, cedar, and creosote burning on Hometown's hearths mingled with the mouth-watering aroma of peanuts and hot peppers roasting in the outdoor mudbrick stoves while supper's cornbread baked. Smoke from homesteads further down the Valley, outside the tumble of Hometown within its stockades, plumed peacefully southward.

Inside the River's toils were bosky dells and marsh. Flocks of wild ducks and geese quacked and honked, lifting now and again into a whir of flight. Hunters, with their retriever dogs, disturbed them, as the day's harvest of game was brought down.

Above Hometown's cleared meridian, where the dwarf pine groves protected the Settlement from the front line wind and storm assault, sounded the furious roars of swine. Today they'd been rounded up from their free, foraging life and penned to put on flesh until the week of Winter Solstice. Then, the whole

Settlement would have gathered, working together. The results of butchering, rendering lard, making sausage and soap, and smoking hams would be shared out during Yule Jubilee. Rat terriers, sight hounds, guard and herd dogs added to the din up there, anticipating their share of the coming feast.

These were the sights, smells, and sounds of home, for Cameron and Sky could remember only dimly any other. The tasks for this time of day, on the verge of winter, were intimately familiar, for they too had put their backs to them in the past, and expected to do so forever. Down below was comfort and security. These days their work was learning the knowledge and tasks of Rangers. They were honored by their community's trust. Rangers carried arms to defend the SSC, and if necessary, to attack its enemies.

"It's your turn for these," said Sky, handing over one of the SSC's precious spyglasses to Cameron. "Screw it into one of your lovely eyes."

She accepted the vision-expanding glass.

Children attended the poultry runs. Older ones brought up water barrels from the River to replenish the tanks in the Big House's common Hall and kitchen. Some worked in private gardens behind their homes, swept the courtyards, along with adults who might be either their birth or foster parents. Many, like Cameron herself, had been orphaned before coming to the Saquave, and accident and illness took a toll on the mature and strong, as well as the young and the weak.

Rooks and crows scratched and pecked on the compost fields where the honeypot brigade had dug in the latest accumulation from the latrines. Those who'd drawn that unpopular duty were heard bathing with the dyeworkers and tanners in the Hot Springs hidden in the rocky defile among the pines.

Cameron found no danger signs no matter how diligently she looked. She searched most carefully to the north, training the glass on the Hammers, a spur of mountains under the Rain Shadow peak named the Claw. In the Hammers perched Silver City, aerie of the Alaminites, who claimed all this country by divine right granted by their Lord God, Alam. Most of all they coveted the prospering Valley, nurtured by the Snake River, the only year-round dependable source of water in the Saquave. The Alaminite leaders hadn't foreseen that all the wealth of their silver mines would be for nothing in the Mountains, where there was nothing to buy. They couldn't eat silver.

Winter was a time of fear in the Valley. Blizzards stormed out of the Mountains, filling the chasms and passes with snow, at times filling the Valley too, when the wind chased the Snake. Then, on ski, toboggan, and snow shoes, came the Alaminite Coals of the Lord, for snow and cold were their natural elements. They murdered whom they would, stole what they could carry, burned what they could not, and raced back to their fastness, over the deep snow, through which neither horse nor mule could pursue.

The greatest prizes rended out of the SSC were females—animal or human. In the rigid Alaminite hierarchy, a man needed several wives and numerous male progeny to prove his leadership and right to power. Women labored in field, hearth, mine, and childbed. Life in the Mountains for women was as short and brutish as it was for the SSC's stolen mares, mated continuously with the vicious mountain ass-sires. The abducted women provided the sons Alaminite men had to have. The mares gave them mules upon which Alaminites depended.

The snowline had been creeping steadily down from the upper ranges of the Hammers for weeks. But winter hadn't arrived in the Valley, not yet.

A blast of northern wind seized Cameron's neck veil. She tucked the ends securely inside her poncho. She pulled up the hood and drew the strings tightly under her chin.

Down in the Valley, though, it was still warm from the sun. It was a blazing wheel, revolving orange and red, its burning rim slicing out a giant arc above the horizon. The cone of an ancient volcano in the southwest quadrant glowed violet. Three tables, features called kurgans by the nomadic native tribes, cast long, blue shadows over the empty grasslands.

By the Governor's decision the Valley's herds and flocks were fostered among the Wilderness tribes, in exchange for the SSC's yarns and woven cloth, a tithing of the year's lambs and foals, grain, and alliance against the Alaminites. This allowed the Valley to preserve its own fragile meadows for the times when drought and sandstorms blasted life while still in the womb.

The harsh glare of day softened by degrees. The land was revealed in the Saquave palette of dusty reds and oranges, smoky blues and purples, corn yellow, and slate greys.

Cameron leaned over the palisade. The leather-lashed logs gave a bit to her weight with a creak. Her long, supple back made a fine, straight line from neck to the angle of her hips. The wide, silver-trimmed belt pulled her poncho snugly around the narrow waist that flowered out of her round hips. This characteristic pose of Cameron with an object of study pulled her breeches tight over the low-slung, perfectly inverted heart of her buttocks.

She stood up abruptly, aware that Sky was studying her rump, not the area.

The end of their watch was closing in. She made another sweep with the glass. From their view at the top of the watch-tower, they could see over the willows and cottonwoods on the riverbanks into the bosky. The night patrol riders were having a time getting their chosen mounts in hand.

The horses gathered in a tight, warding bunch. They sidled away from the men they usually yielded to easily. They pre-ferred giving their attention to something else, and the rid-ers were an interfering nuisance. Some presented their hind-quarters and kicked. It was going to have to be rope and noose if the patrol was to ride. No doubt there was some fine swearing going on down there.

Cameron and Sky made delighted rude comments as they passed the glass back and forth. It was good entertainment when it was someone else's horse who decided to break the pact between rider and ridden.

The horses moved deeper into the bosky, in good position now for a bolt into the snarl of trees and slippery marsh. Then all of them, as with one mind, came to a standstill, heads up and ears pricked to the southwest.

"Whoa, take a peek at this, will ya!" Sky yelled.

Cameron grabbed the glass. A cloud of dust burgeoned on the horizon.

All the fibers of Cameron's being dilated. On the threshold of the meadows, where the bosky dried up, a human figure materialized.

"It's the Governor," Sky commented unnecessarily. The dis-tance made her tiny, but that figure was the largest object in Hometown.

The swath of her poncho blew around her. Long hair, held back by the flash of her silver fillet, swirled over her shoulders.

The dust cloud skimmed the ground, moving in upon Hometown as inexorably as a tornado. The cloud beat with drumming thunder. Then it hung in a rolling suspension over the grass.

A shadow leaped through the dust curtain. It ran over the grass, sharp and swift, shot into existence upon the earth through the mysteries of mutability.

The stallion blew his virile, silver carillon. The music was so high and clear it cut through the air cleanly up to the dwarf pines. "You called me, and I have come, from out of the Wilderness land that is our own."

All of Hometown put down its occupations. People climbed roofs or ran down to the River to see what was going on. Brecca bugled once, twice and three times. He announced to the bosky's horses and all other lesser beings that Saquave's King was present. He raced in a wide, serpentine loop around Glennys Eve, Governor of the SSC, Stallion Queen to the native Wilderness tribes. He danced in and out of the rays of sundown.

He approached the windblown, motionless woman waiting for him, then retreated with a prancing toss of mane and plumed tail.

It was an equine choreography that spoke of their bargain. I have my freedom and my mares, except when you are in most need of me, the greatest of all horses in the land.

The woman was a statue. She remained still when Brecca's lengthened stride took him behind her, to charge the horses of Hometown. They were gathered closely behind their herd leader, an eight-year-old bay stallion.

The bay herd master gave ground. The others behind him broke up into small bunches and singletons, turned tail, and raced to the River's edge. There they gave themselves up to the night patrol riders.

His sovereignty established, Brecca's progress contracted about the point of his regard. Finally, his race concluded, he came to his consort. One fidgety step at a time he closed in, until his heavy head rested on her shoulder, his black muzzle whiskers tickled her neck, and his nostrils snorted heat into her ear.

Glennys groomed his tangled mane with her fingers, pulling out burrs, twigs, clumps of dirt. A tick swelled under his neck skin. She rubbed behind his ears, stroked his neck, and scratched the damp point between his withers. His quarters were dry, and when she slapped them, dust flew.

His body quivered, a consequence of driving his mares and their foals over such a long distance, fighting their need to rest and graze. Her demand had pushed him hard, and the herd more so, but like their master, they'd recover quickly.

Brecca leaned into his mistress, yielding to the pleasure of touch that he so loved, yet would never accept at any hands but hers.

The sun sank like a stone into the coming night. As it dropped out of sight, so did the woman and stallion. In sunset's afterglow the thrill from Saquave's display of sovereignty lingered. Brecca's arrival had made a change in routine, given Hometown a demonstration that reminded them that in all ways life here differed significantly from life in Nolan, across the Rain Shadow Mountains, where life for anyone unentitled was made small or nothing. Here, everything carried the potential to be bigger than life.

"I guess they've gone to her cave in the Sandbank," Cameron said.

Then, the exhilaration was replaced by a rising tide of grumbles that she could sense, if not hear, from the top of the watchtower. All Hometown knew Glennys was different. Because she was different, she gave early warning of Alaminite raids and weather changes extraordinary even for the Saquave, mother of extreme weathers. She could find game when crops and gardens failed, and discover nourishment in Saquave plants that no one else noticed. The SSC understood that Brecca, three-quarters native to Saquave, was part of what she was. Her bond with Brecca made the Wilderness tribes their allies, and not implacable enemies.

Glennys was Governor, by virtue of the fabled, dead Nolanese Duke Albany. She was mistress to them all. In exchange for her gifts they gave her trust, respect, and obedience.

If Glennys wasn't with them, then neither were her guardianship and provision. When Glennys separated Brecca from his mares, she meant to ride out of the Valley. Alone.

"Blow the all clear on the ram's horn," Cameron prodded Sky. "Maybe that will shut up the gossipers down there. More important, it'll get the attention of our relief so we can go down to supper."

Sky grumbled like the rest of them below. "Old Nolan's stopped her civil wars, and now that she's putting herself back in order the cutthroats that preyed on Nolan's riches are showing up out here. We've been fighting them more than Alaminites. If *she's* got to get out of the Valley, she should go with some tribespeople, if *she's* that sick of our faces. She'd have help then if there's trouble."

Cameron made no comment.

After the new watch relieved them, Cameron and Sky climbed down the ladders, then threaded through the Rambles to the Big House barracks, where they'd wash up for supper. The barracks were the oldest part of the Big House, since they were built originally as a hunting lodge for Duke Albany and the first Rangers. The passage between men's and women's quarters smelled agreeably of freshly applied gesso on the sun-dried bricks out of which all of Hometown was built.

"Save a place for me next to you at table if you sit down first?" Sky requested.

Inwardly, Cameron sighed. She spent hours every day in his company. But off-duty she wanted the look of someone else, the conversation of someone different. Sky had nothing fresh to say.

"I'll see what I can do," Cameron said, hoping he understood that was a kind refusal, but suspecting he didn't. Just as he preferred the daylight hours, he only heard the words that were said, not the meanings in between.

Sky was only one of the SSC's young men, and there were older ones too, who were on her tail whenever an opportunity presented itself. Cameron liked them all, but none of them interested her in the way she interested them.

Other SSC women her age seemed to find effortlessly one face among those they'd always known upon which to settle, either for good, or in sequence. But none of the others had chosen Glennys Eve, the Governor of SSC, Brecca's consort, to be their adopted mother. Lately, Cameron had begun to speculate that was the heart of *her* difference from the others.

· Three ·

"MY RULE IS is no dogs in the House, and you know it, Michaela!"

"Leave the pup be, Debbie. How else will your sister's new watchdog get housebroke, if she's not trained inside? She can't hurt this dirt floor. Since this is Rangers' quarters I clean up her accidents, so it's none of your mind anyhow."

"My name's Deborah, and I'll thank you to remember that! Barracks or not, this is part of the Big House. I'll remove the creature myself since you're too lazy."

"Touch Grinner, I swear, Governor's sister or not, *Deborah*, you'll wish you hadn't."

Cameron pushed aside the heavy wool drapes over the entry and stepped down into the dimly lighted barracks. Most of Hometown's floors were dirt, made hard by frequent water sprinklings, followed by sandstone rubbings. The chambers of the Big House, added on as needed, were not aligned square. Some were higher than the passages opening into them, some were lower than the doors leading out. But for all of the haphazardness involved with mudbrick architecture, the structures, in such arid country, were easy to heat in cold weather, and remained cool during the blazing heat.

"Deborah, I'm so glad you're here," Cameron trilled. "Hatice needs your advice, she says."

Hatice was in charge of the Big House and the SSC's stores of everything from flour to blankets. She welcomed Deborah's advice as much as she welcomed lice.

Cameron slipped between the two women. Their heads were lowered, like rams about to engage. She gave the puppy, whose mouth was hanging open in the grin that provided her name, a quick fondle, then made for the latrine alcove. She peed hard, embellishing the function with so much noise that Deborah's deep prudishness was mortified.

"I must go where I'm needed," Deborah said. She bustled out of the barracks, as much as anyone possessing such a wide stride could bustle. "All day long, all night, it's Deborah, you're wanted here, Deborah, you must go there. I run from pillar to post, never any rest, never any consideration, never any thanks."

Behind her back Cameron dropped a wink to Michaela, and Michaela prominently stuck her tongue in her cheek. After Deborah's plaints had faded safely away, Michaela said, "Very wicked, Ronnie, but tactically effective. I was ready to slap her, which since she's not a Ranger would have made a lot of trouble."

Cameron stripped off the outdoor poncho and hung it on the peg over her pallet. She undid the drawstring around the collarless neck of the homespun shirt, then pulled it down around her waist. While she washed, Michaela tossed a round leather sack stuffed with turquoise stones, feathers, and silver nuggets among the pallets for Grinner to play with.

"It's either my conceit, or the Gov's sister is more impossible than usual," Michaela said.

"Damn dirty up on the tower this afternoon. I could sprout corn on my neck, judging by the state of this water," Cameron observed. She poured out the first washing into a slop jar and refilled the pottery basin with rinse water from a matching pottery pitcher glazed an earthen tone of red.

"Deb was born to be difficult, I think. The only time she's supported the Governor in anything was during our Goat's Run winter-over previous to the Rain Shadow Crossing. I'd decided Glenn was my new mother, and Glenn was doing everything to persuade me otherwise. Deb would take me aside and shake me, all the while telling me that this was so I'd understand that Glennys Eve was never, ever going to be anybody's mother. Made no sense to me then."

Cameron's bare shoulders and back shrugged. "That was . . . fourteen years ago already? I wonder how old I was then?"

"No way of knowing certainly the ages of any of the youngest orphans out of the coffles. Like so many of the other women, your mother was sick before the pressers picked us up. I guessed you were about four, but you'd never had enough to eat so you might have been older," Michaela said.

"I've never remembered anything before Goat's Run, except being scared, and angry, and always hungry. Then all that stopped the night Glennys Eve and her Rangers rode out of the dark. The men I hated and feared so much were killed or they ran away. We were freed from the chains, and I was never hungry again," Cameron said.

She took down her hair, bent over, and shook out the tresses. If a filly had the color of Cameron's hair, she'd be called a bright bay. The young woman scratched her scalp luxuriously.

"Not a one of us has got a fond memory of Old Nolan," Michaela said. "I'll brush your hair and do it up for you in a new way."

"Blessings on your own head," Cameron said, yielding up the brush and wood combs.

"You did us a favor that Goat's Run winter, while we waited to leave Nolan forever, and anxious we were going from the frying pan into the fire. We learned a lot about the nature of that complete stranger that we'd given ourselves to. You were as stubborn as a kitten. She'd tell you, nicely, but clearly wanting to swat you away, that she was the Governor and that meant she couldn't be anybody's mother, and put you back with the other orphans. And you'd come cat-footing right back and tell her that she was your new mother. Soon enough, like a kitten, there you were, curled up in her lap, getting stroked and fed tidbits. The next thing she was teaching you to sit a horse, and we knew you'd got your way. It was *Brecca's* back she put you on," Michaela reminisced.

She added, "It was a good thing you got your way since she was so different from the rest of us. It was reassuring to see that the Gov was as susceptible to new human affections as we were then, indentured and taken away from everyone and everything we knew, and then rescued out of hell."

Cameron laughed. "Good thing I was young enough that I couldn't understand anything but what *I* wanted. Otherwise,

I'd never have forced myself on her. I'd have been too scared, because since those days, some people, you among them, have taught me better manners."

"I wouldn't bet on that," Michaela said. "Since then, when you got what you wanted, you haven't wanted anything that much. You and the Gov have a lot in common. When you've decided you want something, or that something should be done, that's it, until you get your way."

Cameron pulled a fresh shirt over her hair, now looped in thick rolls over her ears by Michaela's deft fingers. "What do you think put such a big burr under our Glenn that she's gone calling Brecca?"

Michaela said, "Shoot, if I knew, I could barter the news for a pair of Jeremy's boots and one of Rebecca's silver and turquoise belts, instead of going to the trouble of training them a new watch bitch in exchange."

The grey-haired woman rolled the leather ball filled with the sort of items Grinner would be guarding in the workshop kept by Glennys's youngest sister and her husband across the floor for the puppy. "Everybody's going to ask *you*, since big Chief Hengst's up at Fort Cloud until he comes in for Jubilee to blow off, and Thea's down Valley with the Gov's mother."

Cameron interrupted to ask, "Who's dying? If Stella's gone with Thea it's got to be bad."

Michaela answered, "The Calbert homestead's youngest pulled a pot of boiling laundry water over herself. There's no skin left on Essie that's not blistered up they say. The little girl needs all the numbing healing Thea can give and her parents every bit of comfort Stella's mother-goddess provides to those who must face the death of their own."

Cameron's own skin quivered in sickening empathy. "Poor, poor Essie. And Nedda and Rance, how much they'll blame themselves. It was just a little while ago we mourned our reckoning on the Day of the Dead. Too soon to add to it."

The two women murmured together, "What diminishes one diminishes us all." As soon as they could, they'd ride to the Calbert homestead and weep with the family.

The roar of supper in the common dining hall could be heard in the twisting, up-and-down, empty corridors between barracks and hall. Cameron found herself without stomach to participate.

"Go on, Michaela. I'm going to Hatice and get some supper for my foster mother. Grooming Brecca for the first time since last spring is one hard job. Whether she notices or not, Glenn will be hungry out there on the Sandbank," Cameron said.

"Give her my respects," Michaela said. "But you're not let off from geometry. Wheatly Lubbock and I expect you and Sky at the schoolhouse later. There's a lot you novice Rangers have to learn before we allow you to spend the winter building our new bridge down the Valley."

Cameron groaned, because it was expected. "Yes, Captain." Everyone knew Cameron enjoyed the studies that went into engineering roads and bridges. Everyone knew she hated the labor.

The Rangers were responsible for the SSC's lines of communications. The rawest Rangers did most of the real, finger-, hand-, arm- and back-breaking parts of it.

The building began by gathering the stone for the abutments and logging the trees for the beams and girders. Stone and log had to be skidded off mountainside, through the Wilderness and down to the Valley. The seasoning of timber, before and after sawing it into board and beam, was Ranger responsibility, as well as the mule teams that hauled the loads. All the work was done under threat of attack by Alaminites or outlaws, which made it sensible of the SSC to give it over to Rangers, who were particularly trained in arms.

The platters and bowls had been placed on the boards and those eating in the Hall tonight were on the benches. Cameron and Hatice's helpers waited silently in the cavernous kitchen while Hatice spoke briefly of the sad accident at the Calbert homestead. After a common moment of silent sympathy, Hatice limped into the kitchen to the accompaniment of hungry clatter.

Hatice's bad back and leg, like her missing teeth, were legacies of beatings she'd suffered while in a Nolanese work gang. A tall woman, the large hump on her shoulders forced her to stoop. Her black hair, streaked with grey, was in a tight bun.

"Deborah, my dear beekeeper, you're certain then there are twenty-seven honeypots and not twenty-six in the pantry? My eyes must be going as bad as my back. Please, sit down and eat."

Hatice twitched a thick eyebrow at Cameron. "Thanks, Ron, for finding Deborah. Certainly, I'll throw together something for the Governor. But are you sure it's wanted? Standing orders are that no one's supposed to bother her at the Sandbank."

Swiftly she cut wedges of cornbread and filled a jar with vegetable stew thickened with cornmeal. "Your face is wind-burned. Use some of Thea's sage salve on it. You'll find a jar on the third shelf from the bottom at the end wall of the pantry."

Obediently, Cameron did as she was told. "Hatice, that's more food than Glenn's going to eat. How am I to carry it all?" she asked.

"Some of it's for you, darlin'. You'll carry it in mule pan-niers strapped to your back over my own poncho. It's cold out there now."

Rapidly she fitted the jars with lids. "Be careful of the River with this awkward load. Find out from her how many days,' journey food she wants me to put up for her. That's a good girl, Ronnie. Off with you."

Feeling a slothful, untidy, greedy child, as most people did around Hatice, Cameron climbed out of the kitchen.

Outside, the darkness was lit uncertainly by torches of creo-sote wands. A flood of dogs heaved and receded up and down the main Ramble, and puddled around the broad veranda out-side the Hall.

Several of the oldest male settlers, well wrapped against the cold, were already stationed there. More hobbled as fast as they could to the Hall, swearing at the dogs, laying about with their walking sticks, to get to their accustomed benches against the wall.

They'd gobbled the evening meal in their own houses. Now they were going to have to wait for the common supper to be cleared away before Hatice opened the Hall to everybody looking for a card game, gossip, a jug of the Valley's date wine or, more likely, a warming thimble or two of Sidewinder.

The SSC couldn't afford to use any of its precious corn for liquor. The date wine tended to run out before the next vintage came in, and as the Valley didn't have hops, there was no beer either.

Sidewinder was plentiful, since it was made from the pads of Scale Cactus, which grew everywhere. Even before the SSC settlers arrived, the earlier Albany Rangers had learned to make Sidewinder from the tribes.

Cameron heard the common toast that began and ended common meals, "Confusion to Nolan!" On the veranda the wheezers, as the younger residents called the gossip-mongering oldsters behind their backs, were clucking their disapproval over Glennys riding off on Brecca.

She paused to look over the dogs. The terriers were already at work in the corncribs, hunting rats, mice, rabbits and the other creatures that wanted a share of the SSC's basic foodstuff. The hunters and retrievers were either kenneled or snoozing on their owner's hearths.

Like Rangers, watchdogs had assigned duty rosters. Some were at the foot of the watchtower ladder or at the stockade gates. Hatice had several warding the Company storehouses, and one that stayed in the Big House's pantry after supper since, sadly, pilferage did happen. The rest had the run of Hometown, inside and out, at night.

"Rastil, let's go." She whistled twice, high and sharp.

Momentarily a huge dog, looking much like a grey wolf, but heavier, came out from under the veranda. Though Glennys would never take a dog for her own, she wanted everyone else to have one, and she'd picked Rastil out for Cameron. Cameron had trained him herself, with help and advice from both Michaela, who was gifted at the business, and Glennys.

Cameron wasn't afraid of the dark, but neither were wolves, coyotes and lions. Fourteen years of Valley settlement was nothing to the vastness of the Saquave Wilderness. The SSC was an attractive larder to the Wilderness natives. If she were to encounter one of them, Cameron preferred to have a set of fangs on her side.

· Four ·

AT THE RIVERSIDE Gate Cameron paused, to test her night vision. There was a cold slide of moonlight within the Snake's deepest channel. The sky was a clear black sea studded with starry islands, archipelagoes of constellations, and the lunar continent.

She'd never seen an ocean, but Chief Hengst and the Ranger officers out of Nolan's old cavalry had often described their campaign voyage over the Majis Sea. Sometimes Cameron felt wild to see such things with her own eyes. Then came nights like this, in which she knew that everything she'd ever need to see was in the Saquave sky, the sky of home.

A cat leaped from the Gate's top crossbeam. She landed with a soft thud and twined herself around Cameron's ankles. Boxer had a tawny coat dappled with dark rings, marking her a cross between the small Wilderness felines and the domestic ones who'd come with the settlers on the Crossing.

Rastil walked over to greet the Gate watchdogs. All the canines pointedly ignored Boxer. She yowled into the thin, chill air to provoke them, but they knew better. Boxer had whipped them all soundly as puppies. One day, no doubt, one of their progeny would avenge them, but for now the cat was in her arrogant prime, too fast and too cunning.

Tail erect, the cat padded over the Planks, a swaying, suspended rope bridge that connected the two banks of the Snake's largest loop. Cameron and Rastil followed. Regarding the weight strapped on her back, considering its effect on her balance, respectful of the Planks' fluctuating shimmy, Cameron used the knotted handholds. After the spring floods the inconvenient thing would have to be constructed anew. The prickly, fresh hemp knots would score wherever hands and fingers were unprotected by calluses.

The horses in the Bosky lifted their heads. Snorting with suspicion, as one, they whirled away downstream, manes and tails floating like cloud scraps under the moon. Brecca's herd was still off on the farther range, not yet secure enough to go for the water they needed. But the Hometown horses resented them so close to their own territory, so were spooky themselves in revenge.

The trail to the Sandbank was narrow, twisting and twining through thickets of river willows and cottonwoods. When Cameron was a child she and the others used to come here to play during the hottest part of summer afternoons, while the adults rested. Sometimes the flies were bad, but the River here moved too fast and the air was too dry for mosquitos. The shade protected the children's play from the sun, the place itself from adult eyes.

Hometown's density enforced daily intimacy, so privacy was as unavailable to Glennys as to anyone else. The Governor had taken, within recent seasons, to hiding out in a large, abandoned animal den in the upper Sandbank when she wanted to be undisturbed. That had been, in Cameron's childhood, their favorite place to play.

Now, children came here on a dare, to thrill themselves into delicious, shrieking terror, pretending this was where the bogeyman laired, and maybe a witch too. Cameron, occupied by new things as she got older, hadn't walked here in a long time.

The trail was more overgrown than she recollected, as though it was used only by fox, muskrat, and the other wild creatures who denned in the Sandbank. The supple willows spanged against her body with each step. They stung her face, arms, and legs, caught at the pack on her back. The canopy of branches blocked out the moonlight. The dead leaves were rough and rasping as flint saws, opening cuts and scratches on her neck and hands. Spider webs stuck to her eyes, nose and mouth.

She should have brought a torch, Cameron thought. But that extra thing to carry seemed unnecessary back within the stockade. All of this land was her home. She knew it like she knew the back of her hand.

By now she should have come to the beach beneath the Sandbank. A dead branch tripped her. A cottonwood root caught her foot. Her weight came down wrongly on the root. That queer, shocking tingle of pain ran up from the sole of her foot, to her knee, and then up her spine. Where her neck met the back of her skull the pain concussed, divided and fountained into her eyes.

As the pain receded, she was left blind and terrified.

Cameron groped for a tree branch to take the weight off her twisted foot. She lifted her leg, straightened it from the knee to relieve the pressure on the ligaments that pulled the little bones of her toes askew.

When she could walk again, her sight had returned. But she didn't know where she was.

She never got lost, not even riding between Fort Cloud and the Valley with others as new to Rangering as herself. She was never afraid either. Now she was both.

The night was empty of everything by which she could gauge her bearing. She was chilled all the way through. There was no reason to be so cold, not even next to the River on the hindquarters of the year.

The hackles on her neck were up.

Boxer can get me out of this, she thought. Cats are my creatures. All of Hometown has always said so. Didn't Michaela call me a kitten before supper? Boxer can see where I can't.

Fear trapped the last breath she'd taken inside her breast. If she didn't exhale her chest would burst. She called Boxer. What came out was an agonized wail with no resemblance to the bururrlurrpt, bururrlurrpt of cat calls.

But she could breathe again. With breath in her she could run away.

She blundered through bushes, over roots. She felt mud under her feet and heard the rattle that meant she'd come to a stand of bulrushes. She had stumbled into the marsh, far from the Sandbank. She ran again, under a spell of primitive, unreasoning terror.

The force, from out of which the terror had risen, seized her. It was the Wilderness, where there was little quarter and less mercy, where life had no future and no past, for it was night, and whatever moved upon the Saquave moved to feed or evade being food.

She was snared in the center of a great web, spinning under the moon in wider and wider circumference, lifting higher and higher. One silvery spinneret after another was thrown in an immeasurably powerful trajectory out into the night, out of the Valley, out of the community of humanity, into the Wild.

The driving velocity was incredibly strong. The force searched for an attachment that allowed for another propulsive leap. It anchored itself within the sweeping hunt of the great horned owl. A cottontail rocked across a bare patch of ground. The owl prepared to drop. It was of no further use to what accelerated this quest.

Like a spinning top whipped up by a child's cord, Cameron's self was one among a flock of migrating geese.

For a time there was nothing but the vast, unrolling quilt of landscape between the Valley and the thornscrub flowing beneath the timed beating of mighty pinions. The desire that had captured her was not interested in the southern Wilderness.

She was loosed from the geese. Vertiginously she was settled upon a she-lion, nose open to a meaty, salty-sweet, yet off-putting scent. There was more of carrion stench in it than of blood. Fastidious, mature, healthy, the lioness rejected the scent with a sneeze and shake of paw. She searched the air in another direction for living meat. But the direction rejected by the lioness was where the decision-maker chose to go.

Choking clouds of dust rolled in the night. The buffalo moved unstoppable, determined to merge with the pouring rivulets of their own kind and claim the winter feeding grounds that called them. At the periphery of the lordly, thundering migration loped the eager hungers of meat eaters.

The mote that was Cameron hung in a pack of lithe, grey wolves, inebriated with the nearness of blood and meat. But this small herd of bulls, cows and calves were well fed, uninjured, without disease. The pack could wait.

In the pack were those older, no longer the leaders. One of these sat on his haunches, lifted muzzle to the moon, and howled. His nose wrinkled back, opening nostrils to their widest, exposing the moist, inner, scent sensitive membranes. By drinking the wind through nostril and mouth he found what the lioness had turned from, among a host of other smells. His ears heard the booming of buffalo hooves, his pads interpreted the vibration the animals drummed upon the grass-veiled hard body of Saquave.

She was too small to survive this welter of sensation alone. Even scents she knew to be innocent of harm like sage, mesquite, creosote, were too thick, too full. Gagging, hearing imploded, she was drowning as surely as though she'd fallen from the Planks and been caught in the implacable center current of the Snake.

She flailed against the undertow of smell, sight and sound that tossed her from winged life to that with fangs to that with hooves. She fought against the driving current that dragged her through wind and over earth.

It was so strong, so swift, she tumbled over and over, never catching her breath. She was going under for the last time.

She was noticed.

At the last possible moment she was noosed as securely as though a champion roper standing on the Planks had caught her. She was played slowly and carefully, the roper advancing up his line as he pulled her back to the center from which the web was spun.

She had been rescued, but she was without her own body still. Then she felt hands, and then she could see the little beach under the Sandbank. The moon made the gravel and stones bright as day. Bile rose. She choked. Tenderly she was lowered to the sand, face toward the Snake's winding waters. Her neck and shoulders were supported, so that in her weakness she'd not strangle on her own effluvia. The panniers strapped to her back were removed.

Cameron was lifted to a sitting position by the same hands that had caught her. She tried to turn her head to see behind her, but her neck was very sore and resisted with a sharp stab of pain.

She saw Brecca.

The hair under his belly curled thick and coarse as a billy goat's. The moon in his eyes made them flat, baleful, silver disks. He was so close she could see the three sets of lashes on those eyes, the first the longest, good for whisking away insects and guarding against windblown debris, while allowing sight. Those eyes regarded her as a captor, a predator, and an intruder between him and what was his. There was nothing in those eyes of recognition of the little girl who had ridden on his back, nothing of the community of humanity, whether of the settled Valley or the nomadic Wilderness folk. His long, thick neck and big head reached out. Cameron flinched away.

Brecca nuzzled the woman who was holding her.

Cameron's body quaked like aspen leaves in the breeze. She still felt ill, as though she'd eaten bad meat. Rastil burst out of the willows and, barking, ran up to her. Weakly Cameron pushed away the supporting embrace to cling to her dog who smelled of Hometown.

Glennys put out a hand to Rastil. Without a warning growl, his fangs slashed her hand.

Glennys's hair was cold and stringy, wet with her own sweat and Brecca's. She reeked of the stallion and his odor of the Wild.

Boxer appeared. She touched noses with Brecca, before investigating the panniers. As nothing opened to her probing paws she picked a dainty path to Cameron, prepared to use her lap as a warm resting place before food appeared.

Cameron flung the cat across the beach.

"Witch familiars, all witch familiars!" she cried. "Only dogs, only dogs!" She hugged Rastil to herself desperately, and hid her face in the ruff around his neck, breathing in his domestic doggy smell.

When she looked up again, Glennys was kneeling before her, face full of bewildered pain. She tried to touch the girl but Cameron skittered away in a flurry of sand, still shaking in the aftermath of her experience.

"I am very sorry," Glennys said softly. "You were caught in the Stallion Queen's Weirding Ride. I had no idea you were about. No one comes here when I'm alone. Even so, I can't think why our hunt caught you."

Cameron's mouth twisted in humanity's fear of what is not like itself. "It's so animal!"

Glennys said, "Are we not animals? Like the beasts we kill to feed ourselves and our young, we guard our territory against those who would prey upon us as we prey upon others. To learn what occurs in the Wilderness, to guard the Valley, I must do this sometimes. The Saquave is vast, we have many enemies and we are too few to watch every point, to patrol everywhere."

Glennys busied herself with the panniers. Everything inside was jumbled and many of the pots and flagons were broken, but Hatice's jar of sun tea was intact.

She offered the tea first to Cameron. "Rinse out the dregs of the weird, spit out your fear. It's the only way you'll start to feel better again."

After rinsing and drinking, Cameron did feel as though her balance would return after all. Glennys had to have lived successfully with a great deal of fear to know that would happen. With that she felt a spinneret of warm connection to the woman she'd thought of as her mother for so long.

Then, faintly surprising herself, deliberately, Cameron broke the thread. She preferred revulsion, separation.

"How did I get here?" Cameron asked.

Brecca was pulling up great drafts out of the River. The Weirding Ride had dehydrated the stallion as much as it had Glennys and Cameron. The Wild, the greater part of his nature, prevented him from drinking too much at one time.

"It's not easy to talk when pulled off the Weirding Ride before its natural conclusion. I learned you were with us and we, Brecca and I, went looking for you down our back trail. It is very dangerous to come out of such a deep matching suddenly. The last time I did that, when younger than you are now, I lost all my Horse Sense for several years. Now it's even more dangerous."

Cameron spat, "You like it! You like running with the hunters, feeling all they feel, knowing all they know with the senses they possess."

Glennys offered the jar of sun tea again to Cameron. She refused it. Glennys picked through the broken pottery and found something that would serve as a drinking vessel. She cleaned it in the River and poured in the tea. This time Cameron accepted the tea.

Glennys sighed. "This was a big ride. I needed Brecca, who has the sovereignty of the Saquave, to go so far. He can get me out of the Valley and into the Wild. Once I'm out of humanity, Saquave lends its own power to my quests. Brecca, born here, with most of his pedigree out of the wild horses, is part of this land. He regards me as part of him. I'm his old boss mare, the most dominant, who is unencumbered by breeding. The boss mare helps the stallion continue his blood line by guiding and guarding his breeding mares in his absence, taking them to water and grass while he drives off other stallions and predators."

Cameron said, "It's hideous for a human to descend into such bestiality. And it's a lie. You are not the subordinate one, not even to Brecca. That's really why the tribes call you Stallion Queen, isn't it? Because you're boss mare and stallion, holding the power of both in yourself."

Glennys seemed to catch every word of Cameron's, to turn them over and sort them, as she was doing with the broken pottery out of Hatice's panniers. Then she fit them together in their proper patterns.

Very gently she said, "Cameron, I know how frightened you must have been to be taken with no warning on a Weirding Ride, but you're acting so strangely, not like yourself at all."

Cameron said, "Anyone human would be the same!"

Glennys said, "But surely you can imagine that a Weirding Ride is not always like this, for the Wilderness does know its own affections and its own delights. There must be something within you that allowed participation, even so unwillingly. You must understand that I was hunting. Someone has been looking for the Valley for a long time. It's not Alaminite, nor is it outlaws and raiders. I have a hunch it's more dangerous than either of those. But I've discovered something more important than what hunts us, and far more wonderful. *You have Horse Sense of your own, Cameron*! We can ride together, mother and daughter, throughout Saquave. You can be my companion in this, the first I've ever had."

Cameron pushed herself to her knees, and then to her feet. She could walk.

"You're a Nolanese Aristo witch, not my mother. My mother is dead, a long time dead. Your Aristo Nolanese relatives killed her, making sure that I'd never live in my mother's own country!"

Again, Cameron was surprised. She didn't know she would say those words until they dripped like poison off her tongue.

Glennys recoiled in pain.

Cameron was leaving her, walking steadily on her feet, Rastil at her side.

"Let me help you back to the stockade," Glennys cried.

"I don't need your help. Leave me alone," Cameron said.

There were few lights in Hometown by the time Cameron returned. She had missed her class. Though Michaela and Wheatly Lubbock gave her the opportunity to plead duty to Governor and mother, Cameron wouldn't give them an explanatory reason, other than to say it was her own fault.

That was insubordination. There was no choice but to put Cameron into solitary confinement on bread and water.

Solitary provided Cameron with ample time to reflect upon the confusion of feeling in her breast that had gathered with no warning about the person of the one she'd thought she loved and honored more than any other.

There was no one to hear her. Over and over again Cameron found herself saying the words, "I won't be treated like a child for the rest my life. I won't, I won't."

There were other words beating hot and deep within her. "I want, I want, I want."

Cameron had no idea what it was that she wanted. Or perhaps, she refused to admit what it was because what she wanted seemed too impossibly out of her reach, out here, on the edge of the world.

· Five ·

THEIR SPIRITS WERE higher on the buffalo trail than at any time since the Prince and his tutor had realized they were the only ones who had survived the Rain Shadow pass ambush. The buffalo had broken down all obstacles, or else opened new routes around anything standing in the herd's way. Every day or two they hit stands of water, roiled with buffalo excrement, muddy, but water for all of that. The country seemed less hostile, and they made good time.

The two of them shared the anticipation of an ending to this journey, with a homecoming, and a laying down of their burdens.

So it was a confident Leon who yodeled from scouting up the trail. "Muran, now! Bring all the gear. Dinner, Muran. Steaks!"

Leon stalked a young bull crowned with two sharp horns. His left front leg was broken. For all that he had the use of only three legs instead of four, he moved very fast. Both his back legs were whole so he could put a powerful charge behind his youthful, needle-sharp horns aimed at the men's vulnerable middles.

They played him throughout the afternoon, but couldn't get close enough to hamstring him without seriously risking themselves. Though they now expected rescue, in their current condition they couldn't afford to have either of them disabled. The hide over the buffalo's ribs was tough, and his flesh was thick. The knife blades substituting for spearheads on their walking staves didn't have the length or heft to make a killing thrust.

The sun sat between two buttes on the distant horizon. They heard a wolf howl. Another joined, making a duet. Soon an entire pack was in cry, hunger howling on four legs in choral harmony.

Their faces were covered in red dust raised by the bull. Their limbs were coated with dirt from the falls suffered while darting at the bull's hocks with their makeshift spears. Muran thought their appearance was likely as bestial as that of the wolves which had most certainly scented them and their quarry.

"It's early for the packs to be out," Muran said between pants.

The bull had taken a stand within a cluster of honey mesquites. Slobber dribbled off his hanging tongue. Blood and red mud puddled in the socket where his left eye had been. Leon had taken it out with one of his jabs.

"He's my meat," Leon growled. "Gimme some water. You keep in front of him. Dance, yell, fart, keep him on you, no matter what."

While Muran dug out their water bag, Leon unwrapped the thongs that secured the haft of his biggest knife to the lance of his walking staff.

Before Muran understood what Leon was up to, the Prince dropped out sight.

The tutor cavorted at the edge of the mesquites. He dug his feet into the dirt, kicking dust all around. He rained clods and stones on the bull. A tuneless hunger song came out of his belly.

"Oh, dinner mine, dinner mine, fall on my plate of gold, dinner mine, dinner mine, slide your fat into my belly's cup, dinner mine, dinner mine."

Muran grabbed up one of the skins in which they bundled their gear. He twirled it around his head, swirled it around his thighs. He waggled his hips, turned his back and presented his ass, waving the skin in mesmerizing patterns before the bull's remaining eye.

The bull tracked every movement he made. They were in a trance, the boundaries of which were each other, connected as surely as by a cord.

Then Leon, who had snaked his way upwind among the mesquite trunks on his elbows and knees, the knife between his teeth, intruded upon Muran's hunting dance. Muran saw himself from the outside as a lumbering, twitching, jerking old fool. Momentarily, he resented the Prince as if he were an outsider, a stranger coming between him and his object of devotion. As quickly as that sensation entered his breast it was replaced by a choking fear for the Prince's life.

The Prince closed in upon their quarry's blind side. He slashed at one of the hind legs. With the bull crippled in his rear, it was an easier maneuver to hamstring the remaining hind leg. Then he was on the bull. The long blade went in, between the shoulders. It rose up, plunged down, flashing several times in the long rays of the sun. Leon's arms and chest were bloodied. He leaned over and dug the blade into the other eye up to the hilt.

It was several more minutes before the young buffalo bull's life was absolutely extinguished.

He was the best meal they ever ate. Though he was young and had been harried for hours, there remained several pounds of fat and tallow on his ribs and shoulders. Their shrunken bellies regurgitated the unaccustomed richness of meat and fat. After vomiting they crawled back to the fire and ate more slowly.

The wolves they'd heard earlier never materialized. Evidently they'd been diverted by business closer than the two men.

"Muran, our luck has definitely turned," Leon said. "We're almost out of this."

Meat doesn't last forever, and the trail went ever onwards. The day after the buffalo kill, one of Muran's sandals went to pieces all at once. As the improvised sole separated into various parts, his foot was impaled upon a large cactus segment. At that place the trail had been driven through a cactus stand. Entire arms of spined cactus had been trampled into the dirt and buffalo shit.

One long spine broke off deep in the ball of Muran's foc They cleared the muck as best they could from the area, and probed carefully. The tools they had at their command were powerless to remove the deeply embedded spine.

"It's a trifle. I can easily walk," Muran insisted.

They fashioned another sandal and reinforced the other. Muran walked. They didn't make as good time as previously. Muran suggested more rest periods, and over the next couple of days they moved more and more slowly.

During one of their halts Leon went scouting for water. Watching Muran without appearing to do so, he saw his tutor drop to the ground, attempting to disguise his grunt of relief as a sneeze.

When Leon returned he described the water hole he'd found. "It's big, really a small lake, probably fed by underground springs. The shores have been torn up by the buffalo, but the water's settled. The bottom's sand, not mud. It's good, potable water. And, best of all, there are some trees. A good place to camp. I think we should move down there and call it quits for today, maybe even rest all of tomorrow. We can wash your foot in hot water. Shoot, we can even take a bath."

Muran said, "My boy, why ever would we want to do something as silly as take a bath? We'd smell funny."

It was a feeble jest, but the first one Muran had made since the cactus spine had broken off in his foot. He hadn't recited poetry or old Nolanese chronicles at the end of their days. He hadn't written in his journal either.

Leon built a fire with the dead branches fallen from the cottonwoods. Soaking Muran's foot was the first priority, even before food. He hummed to himself as he worked. It was good to have a fire out of wood, instead of dry dung.

Then he saw the foot.

It was swollen twice its normal size. What really scared him was seeing the pus oozing out from around the toenails, and touching the hot, swollen flesh.

By morning Muran couldn't walk even as far as the lake for a bath.

By noon, the vultures, absent since they'd hit the buffalo trail, lazed above the cottonwoods.

The hovering, black scavengers made Leon's guts twist and squirm with fear, as the buffalo droppings did with maggots and flies. Not even during the ambush had it been like this.

He threw dirt at the sky where the vultures glided in tighter, lower circles than he'd ever seen before. Leon tore up the ground with his hands, fell over, kicked against the earth.

"You Saquave bitch, give me some luck for a change! I've been looking for you and your help forever. I demand your help, you whore! My mother said you'd help me!"

Leon collapsed. Tears scalded his eyes, shutting out the haunting hunters of dead meat.

Muran sat up from his pallet with a groan.

"My King, you can't afford to lose that much moisture in this dry climate. Please, for the sake of Nolan, compose yourself. Let us take council."

Muran invoked the vengeance the Prince would take upon the enemies who'd driven him from his rightful throne. His run of stout words were a hash of Nolan's history, snatches of poetry, opera lyrics, and ballet librettos, all colliding aimlessly.

The tutor was off his head with fever.

Leon bathed him with lake water until the afternoon waned. Then he went to hunt the crows that hunted what lived in buffalo manure.

The hunt failed. What was left of the buffalo they'd killed five days ago was green and crawling with maggots. He looked for frogs along the lake's edge but never heard a croak. There were no prairie dog towns here. He dared not leave Muran alone for even a little while. He set rabbit snares on what, earlier in the year, had been a grassy verge beyond the little grove of trees where they camped. But rabbits, or buffalo, had already eaten every grassy clump down to its dry, brown roots.

The night was cold enough to be called frigid. He kept the fire roaring. The dead wood came from young pines, choked out by the cottonwoods' longer, deeper tap roots. The branches caught instantly, the resins popping in the heat, burning out soon after it ignited. His firewood wasn't going to last more than a couple more nights like this one.

Through the dark hours he alternately bathed Muran to bring down the fever, and made him as hot as possible with fire and their skins, hoping that would sweat out the fever.

His animal cunning, highly developed by his struggle to survive the Saquave, knew the fever was only a symptom. The cause of all their evil was the cactus spine in Muran's foot.

But the activity created a necessary illusion that he was doing something for his fellow creature trapped, by loyalty, not choice, with him here on the face of the Wilderness. Leon knew he'd never have gotten this far without his tutor's love, and what he carried in his retentive, reflective intelligence.

Bathing Muran, rubbing his limbs, heating his skin, helped Leon ignore the hunger gnawing in his guts.

Morning appeared as a sparkle of rose and mauve upon the still waters of the lake. At the rim there was a slender, fragile lace of ice. In the center a few ducks bobbed. He thought of swimming out, beneath the surface, and snaring their webbed feet. It wasn't his lack of practice at such a skill that dissuaded him. It was his sure instinct that he didn't have the strength to go so far, even above the water. The sandy bottom grew none of the water plants, and what they hosted, to give ducks breakfast. They flew off seeking better stocked larders. Leon saw no signs of fish.

Numbly, the Prince picked out the maggots from the rotting buffalo meat. He shaved the trimmings as thin as possible with his knife and put them to a boil. The maggots and rejected meat he piled in the center of a snare for the interest of the vultures.

They stayed in the air.

He gagged down the smallest share of the broth, saving the rest for Muran, if he should emerge from the comalike sleep into which he'd fallen. That happened around midday.

Muran managed to down a few swallows.

"I think you must go on, my King, without me. Otherwise you will die here, and all I've suffered will have been for nothing."

"I command you, as your King, never to suggest I leave you. We are in this together, through no fault of yours. We will survive together or die together."

"So Romantic, Leon, so young," the tutor murmured before slipping into a hot doze.

During the daylight hours, between catnaps, Leon tried one useless device after another to draw out the infectious fluids, and with them, the broken cactus spine. The swelling had not spread up from the foot. So far, no red or black streaks had appeared on the leg. That was all that put heart into him for the futile task. The nails of the first three toes were loose. They'd be off in another day or two.

Soon after sunset he heard the wolves. Fire was all he had to hold them off—fire, his blades, and his two hands. He'd rather leave the world as a meal for beasts than as a solitary starvation victim. With that resolve, the strength that had deserted him at the prospect of swimming the cold lake waters that morning returned.

He split the fire in two smaller parts that he moved to either side of Muran's pallet. The Wild feared fire, but the Wild was also patient, curious, hungry. Wolf senses were keener, but Leon's were sharp too, honed by months of Saquave survival. He smelled them coming on the clean wind blowing over the lake.

A hunting couple of two old males materialized, slinking toward the fires, tails tight against their testicles, eyes hotly aglow. Saliva drooled between worn-down fangs and missing renders. They were less fleet and agile than they'd been even last winter. After the turn of the year they'd be starved enough they'd press an attack immediately, presented with such helpless prey.

But tonight, at the end of autumn, they weren't as ravenous as Prince Leon. He'd killed wolves before, though never without Muran at his back. The wolves had never stalked a man.

Hunting was their instinct. To be hunted themselves as food had no part in their experience, though if Saquave turned hard on the pack, the old and weak were legitimate food. These two hadn't been on that side of things yet.

Spear in one hand, his knife in the other, he dropped from the cottonwood branch where he'd perched in the cold wind, waiting. His dead weight landed, the wolf beneath him. He stabbed between the shoulders and rolled off between the fires.

The wounded wolf recovered, circled behind him, while the other crouched to spring. Its jaws opened wide, preparation for the snap which, two years ago, was backed by enough power to break a buffalo's vertebrae. Leon shoved his spear between the fangs. Instinctively they closed down like a trap. He twisted his spear, ripping through the side of its mouth, and into its jowls, staking its face to the ground.

The second wolf, head down, leaped into the killing zone slightly behind and to his side. He streaked for Leon's legs, for the slashing, in-and-out hamstringing strike.

Leon grabbed a burning branch from the fire closest to him. His knuckles blistered from his short grip. He thrust the burning brand in a sharp, vicious arc across the wolf's face. Its lips, whiskers and muzzle hair seared and burned.

He scorched its nostrils, and saw the black, scaly skin blister in its turn. He boiled the eyes.

The roar was hideous, out of beasts, out of man.

The agonized convulsions of the first opponent tore the walking staff from the hilt of the knife. The wolf scrabbled his paws, his head and neck at an impossible angle on the earth, seeking purchase, to tear himself free. Leon was on him with his knife. Into the eye, up into the brain.

He yanked the blade out, seeking the second wolf. But it was gone, running blind up its own death trail. Maybe he could find it in the morning before the vultures got it.

Muran groaned in pain. He half-raised himself on one elbow. "What's all this?" He sank down again into unconsciousness.

Leon had never heard even the hard-bitten cavalry veterans boast of a battle like this one. Without someone to witness, someone with whom it could be relived, he felt none of the elation rightfully his. All he felt was weary unto death. And hungry.

He set about cooking the wolf's liver. The heart was a tough, grainy mass. He boiled it up for Muran's broth. He could get a couple more meals, of sorts, out of his latest kill.

He stabbed a few morsels off the wolf's shoulders into the fire and devoured them barely warm. The blood he mixed with water and drank. He wondered if this was how men became transformed and werewolves stalked the world.

He went down to the lake to wash himself. Even beasts cleaned themselves after feeding.

·Six·

IN SPITE OF exhaustion he slept badly. He ached everywhere. For once, the rising sun was hidden under clouds. It was very cold. Mist came off the deepest, warmest part of the lake. Streamers of vapor curled around his legs as he stumbled to the water's edge to drink. He splashed his face several times. It didn't help. He remained completely snared within the toils of enervation.

This was a watering hole. Animals should be coming to drink. He needed to set snares, look for trails leading to drinking places. He couldn't make himself move.

He watched the water dripping through his fingers as he knelt. The drops in this grey light reminded him of pearls. His mother had many of them, strung into necklaces and hanging from earrings.

When very young he had spent hours playing with the contents of her jewel boxes. He particularly enjoyed the sensation of the smooth ovoid pearls slipping through his hands, spilling between his fingers to rest in their velvet-lined cases.

"Dear heart, isn't this emerald pretty? Wouldn't you like to play with something that sparkles green, instead of pearls that go dull when much handled?"

He must be asleep and lost within a dream. Words signifying tenderness and luxury were as meaningless as a garnet in an earlobe.

His face tipped closer and closer to the water's surface. He could fall over, his face in the water. It was only inches deep here, but that was enough to drown in if he didn't get up.

He felt the last of his vitality retreating, like a ripple flattening into finality.

Leon dug deep, seeking a power that would get him to his feet. It would be cowardly, traitorous, to take the easy way out and leave Muran to suffer the death torments of gangrene and starvation alone.

Rage was all that was left to him. He tapped it, forcing the furious white heat into his legs, his arms, his head. It warmed him so he could feel again. Every strain and sprain, every cut, slash, and puncture burned.

"I make an oath here," he whispered. "If Muran dies, and still I somehow survive, I will find you, Stallion Queen. I will take my vengeance upon one that is as dear to you as that man is to me, whose only bed is pain, and only covering a bare tree. Then, though my tower has fallen and my star has died, the usurpers of my throne will feel my weight. I do swear."

His fingers fell upon a hefty stone. He grasped it, and got to his feet. "You hear me, Stallion Queen?" he shouted.

He aimed the stone at the middle of the lake and hurled it. His violent eruption shredded the silent mist.

The head of a horse thrust through the parted fog. The horse was the same insubstantial hue as the ethers out of which it came soundlessly, as though it moved upon the shallow shore water, not through it.

A horse! He'd given up believing in them.

Its mane hung thick and shaggy down one side of the curved neck. A single rein hung slack. The rein tightened against the horse's neck. It altered course to a point on Leon's near side. Leon startled, trembled as if touched by lightning.

A rider!

It had been so long since he'd seen a person, except for Muran, that the most elementary notice of the other, male or female, failed him. He saw only parts and pieces, not the whole.

The horse reached the shore, swiped water from the end of a long, full tail, where it had dragged in the lake. Pivoting lightly from the quarters, it came to a stand downwind of Leon. It snorted and blew, not liking his odor.

A slender leg, foot encased in a trim, tooled boot, swung out of a silver-chased leather stirrup and crossed over the horse's withers.

"Boots!" Leon croaked.

The horse's head lowered, hooves scraped stones, nostrils snuffed. Leon's instinctive response was to kill it for food.

Canted slightly over the crossed leg, a dark face peered down at him. There was a long parted fall of golden hair. On the hair was a silver band, like a slim crown.

A brown hand touched the silvery grey neck of the horse. Long fringes, beaded with blue nuggets, hung from the worked leather of the sleeve out of which the hand appeared.

The rider straightened. The boot went into the stirrup. The horse headed up from the lake.

"Don't go!"

Leon caught a fresh scent that utterly jolted him after living so deeply within male fetor for so long. It was the pungent attar of female.

"Woman, stay!" he cried.

It was as if they were in two different worlds. He couldn't affect her at all.

He ran after them. He was terrified horse and woman were hallucinations.

She observed the raddled hides and skins, the paltry fire, the knives, the butchered wolf.

She was so exquisitely clean, so well fed. She was an order of being entirely out of his world.

"I am Prince Leon, heir apparent to the throne of Nolan," he said.

A very long forefinger pointed at the butchered remains of the wolf.

"I killed it. There were two. The other ran away before I could finish it off, but it's surely dead too," Leon said.

"Such a doughty deed is nearly an unimaginable performance from royalty."

Her first words to him flayed his sensibilities like a whip. He wanted her admiration. He deserved it. He needed her help even more.

"This is Edwin Muran, my dear tutor. He's going to die unless you can save him."

A hint of animation appeared for the first time upon her face, or perhaps he was getting used to looking at a new one. She dismounted. Her horse faded into the outlying landscape.

She knelt by Muran. While she examined his tutor, Leon

poured out their history together, beginning with the Crossing ambush.

She said. "The Schoolmaster *must* be saved."

He had never heard anyone call Muran "Schoolmaster." She used the title with an awkward familiarity.

She turned to the lake. In a little while two fine horses, the same color as the one she'd ridden, appeared, laden with gear.

Leon leaped for the horses.

They squealed at his approach.

"They'll attack you, if you touch them," she warned.

She unlashed the tarps over the horses. Two wicker baskets hung from the sides of one.

"Pigeons! Roast pigeons!"

He grabbed for the baskets. The horse on which they were carried kicked away from him, then butted him to the ground with its head.

"There will be food, and soon, I swear. But we must get this spine out of the Schoolmaster's foot at once. There isn't a moment to lose."

Leon went for water. There was an honest pot to put to boil. She had a case that was as neatly equipped with delicate probes, scalpels, pinchers, and tweezers as any field medical kit Nolanese cavalry carried into battle. She was riches incarnate.

He braced Muran's ankle, moving it as she instructed. Her investigation into the puncture was painstakingly patient. She concentrated upon the foot for long minutes at a time before cutting away another sliver of the dessicated upper layers of sloughing skin. A bit at a time she sliced away the putrescent tissue on the ball of the foot.

"Are you going to amputate?" Leon asked.

"If the operation is necessary to save the Schoolmaster's life," she answered, "someone must."

She got up and brought Leon a pouch. "You need steadier hands. Soak the fruit in water first and drink off the juice. These are dates and dried apricots."

Fruit!

A little later she brought him some flat cornbread to sop up the fruit juice.

The clouds had burned away. In the broad sunlight she seemed less substantial even than in the dawn mist.

Her surgery inflicted pain. The pain brought Muran to

shrieking semiconsciousness. "Don't let him move!" she warned.

She added several pinches of a powder to water. "Schoolmaster Muran, dear Schoolmaster, drink this, please," she coaxed. He went back under.

Leon saw clearly that Muran was the object of her interest, and that she regarded him only as the sick man's adjunct.

The sway of breasts under the embroidered, homespun tunic, the swell of buttocks when she leaned into her work, the curve of hip and thigh in the suede trousers made Leon as dizzy with lust as all her other possessions.

Finally she'd trimmed away enough of the decaying, infected flesh. There was the broken end of the spine, wedged between the exposed ligments and white ball and socket. With a tweezers she pulled it out.

Leon watched the medical case jealously, but it disappeared among her clothes. She was wise enough, he saw, to know it was too precious to chance to the pack horses. But he wanted it, like he wanted everything of hers.

As she promised, food appeared. There wasn't a scrap of meat, though.

"I seldom eat it," she said. "But the Schoolmaster will need a good meat broth."

She unloaded the pack horse carrying the pigeons. Leon's mouth watered at the prospect of roasted squab. Instead of cooking them, however, she slid out a tray from under one of the cages. While the birds ate, she drew cryptic signs on two squares of supple leather with a fine feather dipped into a tiny jar of blue paint. The leather scraps were rolled into small tubes and attached to a pair of the birds. These were messenger pigeons, Leon learned.

There was a one-person tent, which Leon was able to set up easily. They moved Muran into the tent, settled him upon a rich, fine fur pelt and covered him with a wool blanket.

"When you wake up, boil water. Before changing the Schoolmaster's bandages, soak the fresh wrappings with a handful of this bark," she instructed.

"I won't sleep," Leon insisted.

The silver stallion reappeared. A bow case and quiver hung from his saddle. There was a spear as well. She took both of the pack horses with her.

Leon had a famished rapture with the food. He nibbled a
tiny portion of each dried item he found, before hiding part
of it. His belly visibly swelled out of its shrunken concavity
long before he'd made noticeable inroads upon the supplies.
It seemed to him there was a mountain of food, and it was
there, to hand, without his doing. Snitching part of her supplies
came as unthinkingly to him as hoarding seeds did to ground
squirrels in the fall.

He gloated over the treasures she'd left behind. A hatchet!
While determining where he'd dig the hole to secret the tinder
box, he glanced up into the sky.

There were no vultures.

He fell over where he crouched, into a well of sleep so deep
not even dreams were able to follow.

He woke late in the afternoon, cramped and confused, but
with a new vitality running clear and hot in his veins. Immediately he shoved more food into himself.

He took the hatchet from where he'd hidden it and chopped
off some of the larger branches from a cottonwood. After the fire
was built up he attended to Muran in the way she'd told him.

Then she returned, a fat antelope doe on the second pack
horse. He noticed now that the two pack horses were mares
and that she rode a stallion.

Soon after, Muran woke to such a degree he could drink
some antelope broth.

"You feed him. A new face would be too much of a shock
to our Schoolmaster, weak as he is. If the infection's on the
run, he'll ask questions. Tell him you've been rescued, and the
quieter he is the sooner he'll recover, and the sooner he'll get
answers. Be sure to tell him there is enough to eat, as much
as he wants. It's astonishing he's lived through all this. What a
man the Schoolmaster is."

"What about me?" Leon demanded.

"You say you're to be a King. Survival is royalty's greatest
talent," she answered.

"And what are you? Who are you?"

She said, "Saquave's first law is don't tell all you know to
a stranger on two legs. Attend to your companion."

She'd hung the antelope carcass in the tree from which he'd
cut firewoood while he'd been with Muran.

She was with the horses. Some corn was spilled on the

ground in front of each of them.

"You said you've rescued me. Surely I'm entitled to know to whom I owe my gratitude," he told her. He tore off another mouthful of antelope haunch.

The moon was bright and full. Her flanks tightened and swelled as she squatted to look at the hooves of a mare.

"Royalty believes its entitlement is the first law of the whole world." She stood up and faced him. "You've stolen the property Saquave generously intended as gifts. You chopped from a tree with life in it, stealing it from others who might come here in need as great as your own. Saquave's second law is do not steal."

The moon, his full stomach, her smell. He closed his eyes. They opened, his hands opened. The meat fell unheeded to the ground. His senses swam, his temples pounded. He grabbed her.

She broke his hold and pushed him away. A blade, like the loops of a snake, slithered from under her sleeve into her hand.

He gasped.

The stallion raised his head from the corn.

"You can't steal from me," she said, in a voice as glittering and deadly as her blade.

"I can run you down," he groaned, hating his words. "I've killed wolves."

The stallion was there.

"So has he, without a knife or fire."

"I am to be King in Nolan. I was born in the Saquave. By charter all this land is in my hand."

"Royalty's charter has nothing to do with Saquave's sovereignty. Saquave only grants charter to what lives with respect, above, on, and below the land," she said.

She threw the saddle blanket on the stallion.

"Attend to Muran," she said.

Leon dropped to one knee. "I don't understand this Saquave sovereignty."

"Learn quickly, then. Other people will arrive soon, to conduct you where there are many other people. Some of them have lived on Saquave all their lives, and the lives of all their pedigrees, which are far longer than that of Nolanese royalty."

When he came out of the tent, there were new treasures spread on the ground where the horses had been.

She, and the horses, were gone.

· Seven ·

"THANKS, LAD, BUT we've had enough. You can have the rest of it," Chief Hengst said.

The Elk boy hugged the platter of roasted buffalo hump close to his belly and backed out of the tent. The two men inside heard him calling his friends to pick over their leavings.

Hengst belched. He uncrossed his long legs and leaned back against cushions stuffed with aromatic herbs. Underneath him were thick carpets, fleeces and furs. Like the tent and its contents, the meal had been provided by Kazimir, Chief of the Badgers.

The Elk Chief, Sepul, received Kazimir's buffalo as an insult to his own tribe, though such provision had been correct behavior. Within the loose confederacy of Wilderness tribes, it was common knowledge that the Elks were having a run of bad luck.

Sepul refused their "gift of salt" by pleading an indisposition of the guts that kept him from eating. Therefore the Elk Chief wasn't bound by the ancient laws of hospitality by which those who have eaten together are pledged to one another's safety until they part company.

Kazimir filled the bowl of a long-stemmed pipe. "I wonder if Sepul has an indisposition of his wind too, and will refuse my tobacco. Their luck has been so poor these last Rains they can't trade for tobacco, or anything else."

Kazimir had been Badger Chief only four Rains, or in Valley reckoning, two years. Usually the Badger women chose a much older man for the position. Kazimir was under thirty.

His height, the length and fullness of his shining plaits of hair, and the frequency of his infectious laughter had surely entered into the decision of the women's council. The wealth of his mother, proving an inheritance of good luck, his prowess as a hunter, and his even temperament had also weighed heavily in their choice.

The women's council had judged most significant his friendship with Chief Hengst, brother to the Valley's Stallion Queen, and the Queen's own approval of his stand against trading with Alaminites.

In this cycle the Badgers were most favored by Saquave, and the dominant of the twelve Wilderness tribes. The Badgers' numbers were ample for defense, but not too many for their traditional grounds to make them and their herds fat. The graze lands for their own animals, and those for the wandering wild beasts they hunted, had received rains in season. Unless it was their own choice, the Badgers' nubile population was able to pair within the tribe, rather than seek more expensive partners in another. With so many of the younger generation remaining close to their birth parents and siblings, the Badgers' bands and clans were closely woven together. They presented a strong, united front to any threat from without.

Tribes to which Saquave had recently shown its hard face, such as the Elks, didn't share the Badgers' Alaminite policy.

Hengst blew out the sweet smoke with a contented sigh. "How will you introduce to Sepul these rumors you brought to Fort Cloud that Elk women have been sold by their own to Alaminites?"

Kazimir grinned. His strong teeth were blindingly white against the darkness of his close-shaven face.

"By allowing Sepul to prove it without asking him one question about it. He's a man compelled to flaunt everything he knows, as an elk stag must shake his antlers in your face," Kazimir answered.

One of Kazimir's pozeem stepped inside. "Sepul invites you to his kurgan for an exchange of news over pipes."

Hengst quirked an eyebrow at Kazimir. "So much for Sepul's lack of tobacco."

Kazimir's pozeem grouped themselves behind the two Chiefs. He'd brought only three members with him on this journey. Deliberately, he'd chosen the oldest Badger warrior-hunters for this business.

Though much the older, Hengst carried himself as lithely as Kazimir, and had as much hair. Like their own Chief, Hengst enjoyed laughter and an easy companionship with other men.

The fires of the Elks' bands dotted the uplands of their summer territory. When the rains had failed over their winter ranges again, they were forced to graze over the same routes they'd followed in the summer.

Favorite mounts were being led to spend the night close to their owners' kurgans. Children peered at them curiously.

While keeping his face straight ahead, following the Elk leading them, Kazimir's eyes darted here and there. They had come by easy stages from Fort Cloud, and had arrived shortly before sunset. It would have been most impolite for either Kazimir or his pozeem to have walked about, exhibiting curiosity, before being formally welcomed by Chief Sepul.

Softly, so that his remark would be heard only by his companions, Kazimir said, "We have lost our good looks, boys, or else the Elk men have turned into such great lovers their young women no longer have any curiosity to look upon fresh conquests."

Kazimir's eyes and ears missed nothing, including what should have been part of their progress to Sepul's kurgan. Where were the unpaired women, playing their drums, tambourines, flutes, and ouds, dancing, singing, and throwing out suggestive taunts to the visitors, challenging their prowess as lovers?

The young women in evidence stayed close to their mothers' fires, instead of gathering in front of the kurgans shared by unpartnered, sexually active women. Their appearance was so unlike a young tribeswoman's bold confidence that only Kazimir had noticed them.

Sepul's kurgan was palisaded by racks of elk antlers. Kazimir instructed his pozeem to stay outside Sepul's kurgan, which was the correct behavior, as he was the visiting Chief.

Hengst was familiar with Sepul, as he was with all the important figures of the twelve tribes. The Elk Chief was older than Hengst, much older than Kazimir, with braids and mustache turning grey. He did not rise from his cushion when he invited them to sit before him. That way he indicated as much disdain for Kazimir's age as his own appearance of robust good health showed for his refusal of the young fellow chief's gift of salt.

He flaunted possession of prodigal amounts of tobacco, further offending good manners. Instead of ensuring the bowl was tamped, lit adequately, and drawing well, Sepul gave Kazimir the first draw upon the pipe. This was insolent in the extreme.

Kazimir's pozeem would have reacted rashly to Sepul's series of rudenesses, as the Elk Chief no doubt had intended. However, Kazimir did not rise to the bait. He simply narrowed his eyes against the smoke and counted, as he knew Hengst was doing, the number of pozeem ranged behind Sepul. Each man prominently displayed his weapons. That too, was impolite.

"Very fine tobacco, Sepul. I congratulate you. It must have been difficult to come by, as Saquave valued the Elks so little this year you were unable to contribute goods for the winter trading caravan. We had expected, of course, under the circumstances, you'd be with the caravan yourself."

Then Kazimir coughed, showing his low opinion of the tobacco.

The cough was the final insult of three. First Kazimir had spoken of the Elks' bad luck. Second, he mentioned the caravan. Only cowardly men, when the tribe's luck was bad, refused to join the annual, dangerous caravan that traveled through the Dead Lands to that of the Green People, where tobacco and other good things came from.

Without shares in the annual trading, a poor tribe became, of course, even poorer.

Hengst arranged himself against his backrest, feeling the silky kikkuli fibers conform comfortably to him. This was tedious. Why was Sepul ranking Kazimir? The Elk Chief, possessing neither ingenuity nor fast wit, never showed well at that game.

In truth, Hengst thought, puffing the pipe in turn, the tobacco wasn't the well-cured sweet leaf of the Green People. It bit hard and had a whiff of mold about it, and perhaps, old corn shucks. Either Sepul was insulting them beyond belief, or he'd licked the wrong end of the bargaining stick.

Kazimir said, "You recognize the face of the Stallion Queen's Chief."

Sepul jerked his chin in Hengst's direction, acknowledging his existence. Barely.

Such blatant hostility put all of Hengst's senses alert. If things turned actively nasty, he was going to wish he hadn't eaten so well at supper.

"The Elks have heard you made the Valley man an honorary pozeem of the Badgers," Sepul said.

A girl, not older than five, brought a bowl of acorns, without the crackers to open the shells, instead of the usual bowl of dried fruit and peanuts. There was no jug of Sidewinder either.

Hengst said, "As the Badgers have done me honor with the respect of a place in their pozeem, the Valley has honored Kazimir. He's one of our Rangers."

Sepul rocked side to side, guffawing heartily. "Better him than me, taking service under a woman!"

His pozeem hee-hawed behind their Chief. There seemed to be authentic amusement in their harsh laughter, as if they shared a joke they knew the two visitors too dim to understand.

After the laughter died away, Kazimir offered the Elks, as well as the Owls, a share in grazing rights on parts of the winter ranges claimed by Badgers, Wolves, and the Rabbits. "I bring this suggestion from our women's councils. They remind us we are all people of the horse, Tongue Kindred, and Saquave's children. You and the Owls have suffered drought, and the grass used by our three tribes has flourished these past Rains. So you aren't embarrassed, we ask for one foal, and one lamb, out of each seven that are born on our grass in the spring."

It was a generous offer, which took Hengst by surprise.

Sepul made a chin. His lower lip protruded. "Elk herds don't follow the same trail as Rabbits. Owls don't fly after the leavings of Wolves. And wherever the Badger makes his set, there are holes to snap the legs of an honest pozeem's stallion. I am sure you understand. The signs are for heavy snows in the Rain Shadows this winter. By this time next year our grass will have recovered. And who knows? Badgers, and the Valley too, may come asking for assistance from Elks. Things happen."

Sepul's words were the same as a slap in the face. But Kazimir spread his hands. "For the sake of your horses and your children I truly hope your grass will be good in the spring Rain. Yet we all know that double-grazing pasturage without allowing seasonal rest and recovery leads to destruction. What does your council say to the offer from ours? Is your mother ill, your aunts, and all the wise women of your people? Surely they should have joined us by now?"

Sepul stood up. "This is not women's business. Now you will excuse me, for I have matters that need my attention. I will see you again tomorrow."

The Elks' Chief disappeared behind a richly painted hanging into the private quarters of his kurgan.

There was nothing for it but to return to their tent.

They squatted around the fire in front of the entrance to their tent. Their breath steamed in the cold air in spite of the heat of the flames.

Kazimir's three pozeem were thunderstruck when he gave them an account. "To say provision for the herds and children is not women's business? Whoever heard of such a thing?"

Kazimir said thoughtfully, "No one has heard such a thing since before the Stallion Queens sacrificed themselves by leading the spoiled part of Saquave's people across the Mountains. Next the Elks will bring back slavery. The ancient division between the Tongue Kindred begins once again."

Now that was interesting, Hengst thought. He must remember Kazimir's words for Glenn. The tribes seldom brought up the Crossing, or the events that led up to it a thousand years ago, and the subsequent disappearance of Stallion Queens, even to her whom they recognized as another.

Hengst said, "More to the point, it's Alaminites working to divide Valley from Wilderness, and additionally, turn the Wilderness upon itself. Sepul never used to have a mustache. As he went behind the hanging I caught a glimpse of one standing there, with a long beard, the very sign of an Alaminite."

Kazimir said, "What is Sepul getting that is worth losing the Elks' women? It certainly isn't food. The boy who served us was gaunt and famished. The Alaminites barely feed their own."

Hengst said, "Weapons, of course. Most likely the firearms about which I've told you, against which no horse or palisade can stand."

All five agreed that being set upon in the night, or at breakfast, was all too likely.

"At best, Sepul will hold us hostage. I have every intention of dancing with the Stallion Queen's foster daughter, Cameron, at Hometown's Solstice Jubilee," Kazimir declared.

Upon arrival they politely had tethered their own horses by Kazimir's tent, giving them a small ration of grain, so they wouldn't forage upon the Elks' overgrazed pasturage. They had to have a reason for leaving in the night, however, if only to save the face of Kazimir's tribal authority.

Pairs of pozeem strutted past their fire, flourishing knives and lances, their bows hanging uncased from their shoulders. Kazimir's own pozeem reassured themselves that the extra bow strings tied into their hair were still securely fastened.

"For all the swaggering," Hengst said, "I've never seen such a miserable camp of the Tongue Kindred."

Kazimir agreed. "Except for Sepul's pozeem, the people look as if they've been hit by lightning, stunned somehow. None of that makes them regard us with any more friendliness, though."

Far off upon the ridge came a yodel. A relay Ranger, mounted upon one of Brecca's swiftest progeny, was coming in at a hard gallop, identifying himself as upon Ranger business for his Chief. His appearance was so sudden that the old forms of agreement between Rangers and the Elks held, and way was made open for him to Hengst.

"A messenger pigeon came for you, Sir, from the Governor," he panted as soon as he slid out of the saddle. He handed over the small bag hanging under his coat, then immediately attended to his horse.

Hengst unrolled the little tube holding a bit of leather covered in blue-painted signs.

He pushed back the hair that always fell into his eyes. "I don't believe it. My sister, our Stallion Queen, has sent an order. I'm to take myself, two extra horses and many supplies to that water hole we in the Valley call Spring Lake. What I find there I'm to deliver to Hometown. I'm to make for Spring Lake faster than yesterday. We're already on our way to Hometown. We've got the horses and our gear. Let's go now."

Two of Kazimir's pozeem began dismantling the tent, the other to pack their things. "Your horse has to make more miles tonight," Hengst told the Ranger. "You can't stay here. The Elks have a burr up their tail."

Sepul's pozeem drew swords and insisted they couldn't leave in the dark. "You'll start a stampede."

Hengst stared them down. "I've a task given by the Stallion Queen. If you keep us from leaving, I promise there will be a stampede of the like you've never seen in all your days upon the Saquave. There is no horse that does not obey *her*."

One of Sepul's pozeem spat on the ground in front of Hengst's boots. "Perhaps she is not a Stallion Queen, but a witch from Nolan. A witch can command the rains and the buffalo herds, send them to her lackeys, and keep them from those like the Elks, who refuse to bend a knee."

The Ranger relay rider clenched his fist and swung. Hengst pulled him back before the blow could connect. He put the reins of his horse in the relay rider's fingers.

"Head out."

Once clear of the Elks' fires Kazimir asked, "Is it true that your sister can control the buffalo and the rain clouds?"

Hengst said, "I can't say. Maybe buffalo. But who can stop the rain if it wishes to fall? She's a Stallion Queen and no witch. That is Alaminite talk if I ever heard it, and I'm sorry to say, I've heard it all too much in my life already."

A little later, after they'd settled into a steady rhythm under the stars, Hengst diplomatically brought up the witch accusation against Glennys.

"This isn't the first time Alaminites have tried to use accusations of witchcraft against Glenn. The second time I saw her, long, long before we learned we shared the same sire, she was still a little girl. She'd been abused all day by Alaminites. Their excuse was that women who made men angry were witches, or about to become witches, or something equally foolish. That was the extent of it. Some Alaminite men were angry, first at Stella, Glennys's mother, who, as you all know, has never hurt anyone, and then Glenn, because she was loyal to her mother, as a daughter will be."

Kazimir nearly pulled up his horse in astonishment. "There likely are witches in the world, but if a witch is a woman who has a man angry with her, well then, there isn't a woman born who is not witch! The more I learn of Alaminites, the more proof I have that they are loco, sports of nature."

Hengst laughed. "Shoot. As my old dad, the Baron Fulk, used to say, 'There ain't nothing in the world so bad that Alaminites can't make worse.'"

· Eight ·

THE MEN PRESSED their horses throughout the night. At sunrise the country sparkled like a diamond. Frost had fallen upon the Saquave, a sure sign in this dry land that winter and its Black Blizzards were on their way.

When they got up from their sleep four hours later, the frost had evaporated and the air was warm enough that they rolled the outer layers of their clothing behind the saddles. The relay rider sheered off, to return himself, and Wings, his brilliantly speedy mount, to Windgate, a posting of Flying Company Rangers, whose duty was communications, below Fort Cloud.

Goaded from behind by the possibility of pursuit by Elk pozeem, drawn ahead by curiosity over the Stallion Queen's message, the others flew across the miles separating them from Spring Lake. By the middle of the afternoon they picked their way through the Arches, a tumble of red sandstone standing pillars and broken columns lying on a stone floor between two buttes. On the other side, directly east, they saw the forlorn trees that marked Spring Lake.

Hulaff, the oldest of Kazimir's pozeem, said, "In my childhood that was an oasis rimmed round by trees and grass. Dates grew, fish lived in the water, and ducks and geese too. But in those days the Elks didn't summer goats and sheep there."

Hengst said, "At least the water's fit to drink. I wonder what we'll find under those trees. No goats, I'll bet."

The shortening days brought cold with them. The men shrugged into their outwear.

Hengst chirruped to his stallion, this one named Catclaw, holding him back. He, like the other horses, was thirsty, and scented water.

"Should we wait for dark?" Hengst asked. "Scout first?"

Hulaff volunteered to make a ground crossing while the light remained, to study what might be found some furlongs between the Arches and the oasis.

Hulaff returned, dragging the bones of a wolf in his noose. "The winged scavengers took what they wanted. This was left for the ants, who never sleep except during the blizzards. What's left of the head fur has been burned. You can still smell it. That is the work of what goes on two legs."

Kazimir exclaimed, "Whoa! The man who did this must be your baggage, Hengst. Let us not ride upon him in an arrogant manner."

Hulaff severed the wolf's skull from the vertebrae. "He was an old one. See his teeth? Nevertheless, his opponent will be pleased to see the evidence of his work."

Darkness approached the oasis more rapidly than they. Only a tiny tongue of flame showed through the trees.

They drew up the horses beyond bowshot behind the trees. "Ho!" shouted Hengst. "Friends come to water their horses. We are ready to share the gift of salt and news."

They waited. Finally a voice, uncertainly placed, replied. "Let the horses drink their fill, as we have drunk ours."

They split their forces, Kazimir with two pozeem to the left and Hengst and Hulaff to the right. Holding themselves upright, as if a stiff backbone could deflect an arrow, they gave their mounts free rein to the lake.

Hengst dismounted. One of his skills was that other men trusted him quickly and easily. He walked up to the little fire among the trees, arms loose at his sides.

"Many thanks for your hospitality. We will be most honored if you join us in our trail meal."

The small fire revealed two figures. One of them had a strung bow, with an arrow hanging loosely from thumb and two fingers. The other was seated behind him, nursing his foot. A knife was close at his hand.

Hengst proceeded into the edge of the firelight as though he expected no hostility. He stood alert but at ease.

Wordless communication passed between the two strangers.

Then they both stared at his face as though drawn by an irresistible attraction, or, as Hengst finally realized, as though a face other than their own was an astounding miracle.

Hengst said, "As we said, we are friends meaning no harm."

The one holding the bow looked like nothing Hengst had ever seen, even during the long-ago evil days of the Nolanese cavalry campaign in the Nemourian Mountains. He was nearly naked. He was nothing but skin and bones, scars and wounds. His eyes were as steady as his hands upon the bow. He wasn't going to speak until something else happened, that was clear.

"Ho! Wolf-slayer! I bring proof of your kill!"

Hulaff came into range of the small fire, carrying the wolf skull. "Now tell us, while we eat, how you fired a wolf!"

Uncertainly the youth with the bow said, "There were two wolves. Between two appetites, little enough remains of the other who didn't run away."

Hulaff walked over to where the youth pointed. Sure enough, another wolf skull swung from a tree, hanging from threads twisted from the youth's own hair.

Hulaff sat down by the fire and crossed his legs. "The story. How did you, singlehanded, kill a pair of wolves? Talk while your friends prepare our gift of salt. Bring the food, Kazimir!"

"This camp is very strange," Kazimir said quietly to Hengst, while going about the tasks of preparing a supper for seven men.

"Orangehair, and everything about him, except for that bow, and these other things I see from the Valley, is indecently primitive. The two of them smell of disease," Kazimir added.

"Only one of them is sick," Hengst said.

"They smell like Sepul," Kazimir said.

The strangeness seemed to have rubbed off on Kazimir, Hengst thought. The Chief kept himself unobtrusive, while his men wove the threads of campfire amiability. Orangehair haltingly began his hunter's tale. The pozeem's expression of admiration encouraged him. Soon Orangehair became excited as he relived what had happened. He strung more and more words together, instead of using only one or two.

Orangehair described sitting in the tree, the cold wind whipping about his bare body, bringing the scent of the wolves intent upon hunting him. His audience was completely in his hand.

"Hah! Ho!" The pozeem beat their fists upon their thighs. "And then, what comes next!"

Orangehair looked about wildly, words failing him. He leaped for the tree. He acted out his own story, as himself, now one wolf, then the other. When he finished, the pozeem demanded to see the makeshift weapons with which he'd accomplished such a deed.

Kazimir's head was down throughout the story. He refused participation in the drama. Now he looked up, and used his tone of command. "Orangehair, all of us here have done as much. Tell us, what is the most dangerous quarry a man can face?"

Kazimir stood up to his full height. He was young, strong, healthy, clean, and filled with the power of leadership. The youth saw the Badger Chief now for the first time because Kazimir had chosen that moment to be noticed.

The stranger's eyes flashed. He was no more used to interruption than Kazimir. His companion, who, except to express his gratitude when passed food, had also been silent, reached over and lightly touched the storyteller's thigh.

Hulaff said, "Kazimir, he's only a boy, and he's Tongue Kindred. We all understand each other here. And none in our own company have ever been so hungry!"

"Speak for yourself, Hulaff. I was but a boy when drought came to our territory, and obeying the Rain Laws, I went to the Elk orphan wagons," Kazimir said.

The stranger youth swallowed. "I have killed lions too, but only because, then, my friend was at my back. Now I am your guest, and my place is to be taught which animal is the most difficult to kill."

Hengst and Hulaff exchanged a quick glance. Orangehair's courtesy had scored off Kazimir's ranking.

Kazimir said, "A man is the most dangerous prey of all, for he is the only animal that knows treachery."

Stiff-legged as a cat smelling something disagreeable, the Badger Chief walked away from the fire to the horses.

Hulaff laughed. "Our Badger Chief is so little your elder, Orangehair, that his admiration for another's deeds can still choke him."

Hulaff got up. "Where should we relieve ourselves?"

Orangehair said, "I'll show you."

All of them, except the one with the hurt foot, got up. Outside the trees, under the stars, the men opened their clothes and made water in fraternity.

Back at the fire Hengst walked about the strangers' camp. He looked at the tent, the carcass of the antelope hanging in the tree, and the other things neatly stowed. It was all from Hometown. Glennys had been here. Clearly, from the language used by the youth, and its inflections, when he'd gotten excited, he was Nolanese, and an Aristo. Hengst thought about the garnet in Orangehair's earlobe.

Orangehair helped his friend change the dressings on his foot. Leaning upon him, the other man hopped to the piss ground.

Hengst took a skin of Sidewinder out of his gear. Tears started at the corners of the strangers' eyes after their turns.

Hengst said, "May we learn with whom we are sharing salt, fire, and tales?"

Orangehair said, "Saquave's first law is not to tell all you know to strangers, even those who feed you." He sounded bitter.

Hengst's heart warmed toward this young wolf. "If there were more light I think I might make some good guesses."

Orangehair said, "Saquave's second law is be sparing of what you use, for others with need as great or greater may come after you."

Hengst laughed. "You've mastered Saquave's basic lessons for sure, and none better than the hardest one of all, how to survive alone. You are one I'd far prefer to have at my side, or at my back, than face as a foe. Fortunately, for us here, there's no question of foe."

The youth's mouth and eyes worked queerly. He scratched at his meager facial hair. Hengst realized Orangehair had forgotten how to smile. That brought home more clearly than the youth's scars the ordeals by which he'd been tested.

The youth said, "There was a visitor before you. She brought us food, medicine, a hatchet, and all the other wonderful Saquave gifts you see here. She said others were coming to take us away."

Hengst said, "She was the one who told me to come get you, and bring you home."

"Home. Humans and beasts have homes. I am neither and without one. But we'll gladly go with you to yours. Yes?" The garnet in his ear flashed in the dying fire as he turned to his friend.

The two of them clasped hands.

The youth stood up suddenly and rushed into the dark. Shortly they heard an agitation of the lake waters. It wasn't enough to mask the wracking violence of a man's sobs erupting from relief and thanksgiving.

Hengst said, "Many Rains ago, across the Mountains, in another country, a Master took a young, untried, lonely boy to rescue a girl, even younger and more lonely. I think you were that man."

The injured man said, "A good teacher never forgets a student, particularly one as bad as you were, Hengst. What took you so bloody long to rescue me, Hengst?" Muran asked, good naturedly.

"I am Hulaff. A Master teaches. You taught Orangehair excellent hunting skills."

Muran shook Hulaff's hand. "Please, may I?" He took another swallow of Sidewinder and shuddered. "Saquave taught him to hunt. What I'd give for a mug of ale."

Those last words carried no meaning in this land without hops.

"I am Kazimir, Chief of the Badgers, one of Saquave's twelve tribes. Who is he?" the Badger demanded, pointing with his chin to the lake.

"A man who possesses loyalty, courage, and strength without limit, and one who learns his lessons. He is Leon, my best student, and my King," Muran said.

Kazimir turned to Hengst. "I do not hear the Master's words, Tongue Kindred though he be. Only a Herdmaster, consorted with a Stallion Queen, has sovereignty upon Saquave. Where her chosen stallion runs, there the Queen's word runs, for the delight and good of all Saquave's children. Brecca is King, as your sister is Queen. There are no others."

Hengst pushed the hair that had escaped his braids out of his eyes.

"Over the Mountains, as you know, they have other ways. Our Stallion Queen requested I bring home what I found at Spring Lake," Hengst said. "That is what I will do. Saquave has supported these persons. They have not harmed Saquave. They need other persons. Taking them home is what a person does for those in this condition," Hengst said.

Hulaff said, "We should sleep now. I'm cold. There's no more wood for a fire unless we use these living trees. We should ride early, as our rides must be short. This Master is not strong enough for more. And the one he teaches, he needs lots of fat before he learns to laugh."

Hengst helped Muran into the tent. Then, like the others, he listened, waiting for Orangehair to roll into the stiff hides at the tent's foot. Though Hengst had known the youth's father, the assassinated King Leon, Hengst thought of the young man by the name Kazimir had bestowed, Orangehair.

Hometown's Chief found sleep elusive. He tried to think of Hometown's bridge building project. Instead, the knowledge that his assassinated King's son had lived through Nolan's bloody civil wars inserted itself and demanded all of his attention. A nearly buried part of him was glad. But that was the past, he told himself. His loyalty was pledged to the life he, and all the rest of the settlers, had made here.

Alaminites and Aristos. Religion and royalty, that was what everyone in Hometown had risked their lives to escape. Nolan's young King *here*. Uncrowned and disputed most likely, why else would royalty be wandering in the Wilderness? Why do pretenders to thrones leave home? They were forced out. Then they quested for money and armies. Behind them plots followed.

But for all that, young Leon impressed him deeply. Once, long ago, when he'd dreamed of the sort of man he might be, Hengst had thought of himself in deep adventure, hard up against it. For all of the adventure he'd experienced in his own life, nothing matched what Leon had accomplished.

He listened for some time to Kazimir shifting restlessly in his sleep furs.

Hengst reached out his hand and put it on Kazimir's chest. "Friend, let's go down to the lake and see how drunk two Chiefs can get on one shrunken skin of Sidewinder."

· Nine ·

As THE CONSEQUENCE of drinking Sidewinder instead of sleeping, Kazimir edged sideways into the new day. As his pozeem knew well, when in that condition Kazimir wanted only to be left alone. Hengst was famed throughout the Saquave for his strong head where liquor was concerned. He and Hulaff helped Leon pack what the Governor had brought to the camp. They also helped him decide what to throw away of the few things he and Muran had brought with them into the Saquave.

"My blades," said Leon. "I will keep them all my life. Only death will separate us."

Hulaff said, "The pair of skulls, young Wolf. You must keep them all your life also, may it be long, mounted at the entrance of your kurgan, when you have your own household. Your children will be proud to see them there."

With the exception of Kazimir, all the rest outfitted Muran and Leon in contributions from their own clothing. What no one had on hand was a remedy for the fleas and lice with which the two were infested.

Hengst reluctantly decided not to share his shaving kit. "For all our sakes, I hope you don't have to keep all that hair until we're in Hometown. Facing wolves might have you prepared, barely, for Hatice and Deborah, confronted by someone bringing fleas into the House."

All the frost hadn't melted under the sun's assault before the party was ready. Hulaff clearly entertained suspicions, despite having been told differently, that Muran possessed profound secrets of the hunt, and might be persuaded to give them up.

He helped the Schoolmaster, whose injury made it impossible to ride alone, up behind him on Banner.

Among tribespeople only a sick person and a caretaker, parents and children, or sexual partners rode double. The extra horse among the company carried Kazimir's tent furnishings and the strangers' few things.

If a thing must be done, as friendly a face as possible should be put on it. Hengst said, "This is Catclaw, named for the way he fights, and for his manner of hanging on the flanks of the horse ahead of him in a race. There's a cactus here with the same name. How about you get in the saddle? I'll pull up behind you."

Born among horses as they all were, it would have been difficult for the tribespeople to have understood how someone could not know his way around a horse. It never occurred to any of them that Leon wasn't able to ride or didn't know that horses can be a pain in the neck, and other places as well.

But his haste to snatch the reins offered him out of Hengst's hands, and the greediness in his eyes fixed upon the light-boned, flossy-maned, grey stallion shocked them all.

Then he caught hold of himself, slowed down, and talked to Catclaw before stroking the horse's neck and scratching his ears. The trim-hocked stallion blew against his hand.

Catclaw tossed his head and preened like a parrot. Hengst said, "I say, Leon, there's something else you should know about that horse, and that is he's more vain than a pozeem with braids full of flowers, who thinks he's Saquave's greatest gift to women. You're letting Catclaw believe that he's finally met someone who recognizes him as Saquave's greatest gift to the world."

Leon turned to Hengst and said, "If your legs could feel even a part of how far mine have carried me, you'd understand that Catclaw is the most wonderful being upon the face of the entire world!"

They took it in short jogs, with many rests. Neither of the two newcomers had any riding muscles left, and Muran's strength hadn't returned. Hulaff's horse's gaits were smooth and even, but their short rides made Muran's foot ache sorely.

There was lots of time to talk, listen, and ask questions, while riding and resting. By gradual degrees the dust of overgrazed land settled down to that normal to grasslands before winter.

"This is SSC grass, the only area Brecca chose for us on this side of the Snake River Valley," Hengst said.

There was a lot to see in these swales of rich grass, gently humping and rolling down to the Snake River Valley. Family groups of buffalo grazed. Antelope soared out of the shoulder-high grass. A cougar lioness sunned herself at the highest point of the day on an eruption of red rocks.

"Brecca chose this?" Leon asked.

Hengst explained. "His claim run for the SSC lasted six days and six nights. He outlasted every witness horse and rider, and all the relays, except Glennys. She was still with Brecca when he stopped. The womens' councils were agreed that Saquave had granted sovereignty, and Glennys Eve was Stallion Queen. Before that we were only Tongue Kindred and New Persons. Now we're the thirteenth tribe, the Snakes, named for the River, of course."

"King, or Brecca, or whatever *She* calls him, he's a monster. Once you look at him, the less semblance he has to any horse you've ever seen," Leon said.

Hengst was quiet for a while. Then he said, "Whatever embodies sovereignty tends toward the monstrous."

They reached the SSC sheep station. It also doubled as a Flying Company post, and thus was doubly supplied. First thing Leon and Muran were taken off to be sheared, shaved and doused in a solution of creosote and sulphur for the fleas and lice.

Muran and Leon emerged to hoots. Hulaff pointed at the tutor. "If you do not tell me now your secrets of the hunt, Master, you will forever be known as the Black Lamb!"

Hairy as Muran was, he'd fared much worse than Leon. He hardly appeared the same person without his pelt. His face was nearly white in contrast to the darkness of whatever skin had been exposed to the sun. The shearers hadn't even allowed him to keep his heavy eyebrows.

A wide space was made for them at the rough plank supper board. They reeked of the lanolin rubbed all over their bodies to soothe their skin after razors and dipping.

"How long before we reach Albany, I mean, Hometown?" Leon asked.

"Hard to say at the rate we're going. But soon," Hengst said.

Leon scraped away a layer of splinters and lewd carvings from the table with his knife.

"The Saquave Settlement Company makes headquarters in Hometown, here, at this confluence of Snake River channels. From this point *She* controls the whole of the Snake River Valley. And tonight we are somewhere way over here? And the redrock Arches, the buttes and Spring Lake, are over there, generally speaking?" Leon asked.

Hengst scratched his head. "Your map is serviceable. But your understanding of Hometown and the Valley, not on the mark. You've left out the tribes, who have been here for thousands of years. And it leaves out Brecca. He's Saquave's King. And, perhaps, for your purposes, you've left out the most important element, Hometown's people, the settlers."

Hengst had noted the young Royal always said *She* when referring to Glenn. Not for him the tribesmen's title, Stallion Queen, spoken with easy, familiar, respect, or his own use of Glenn, Glennys, and Gov or Governor.

Everyone who was going to eat supper at the SSC sheep station was seated, except for the three relay riders of the Flying Company. They were the cooks unless there was a mission or an alert.

Leon's knife speared toward a platter of steaming, dripping roast mutton put down a couple of seats away. Muran's hand pulled his student's back.

"Service here is rough and ready, but it has its own courtesy," the tutor said.

All his scraggly facial hair gone, the Royal's blush was easily visible in the flickering firelight.

The Rangers, two women and a man, came out of the kitchen. The sheepherders' eyes glowed. The Rangers were carrying date wine.

Beakers were poured all around.

"In honor of the Rangers' Blood Chief! To Hengst! His honored brothers, Blood Chief Kazimir and his pozeem!"

Another beaker was poured. "To the strangers in our land. Welcome and refuge!"

At the end of the meal there was one more round. "Confusion to Nolan!"

After the board was cleared, those who weren't sleeping with the flocks that night stayed at the table for a little while before going to their beds.

The SSC settlers congratulated Leon and Muran upon their escape over the Mountains from "the crushing weight of Aristos and Wheels."

Questions came thick and fast about the condition of Nolan, and others that were more personal, which, to Hengst's eyes, seemed to make the newcomers uncomfortable. They'd gotten used to the courteous reticence of the Badgers. Hengst himself preferred to find out what he needed to know by paying attention, rather than by direct interrogation.

Evidently the young Royal, whatever his problems had been in Nolan, found the open, loud, pointed expressions of derision and hatred directed toward Nolan's ruling class hard to handle. He was further confused by the casual assumption that he shared these attitudes.

A herder by name of Breevor was inspired to retell his own tale of how he'd become a refugee to the SSC. It included the familiar themes of unfair taxation, extortion, eviction, and forced labor in a textile factory. One winter night, while he and his family huddled together in the mountains of lint trying to stay warm, a woman sneaked into the factory.

"Whoever heard of sneaking into one of those death houses? If she'd been caught the Wheel bosses would have killed her faster than a rat. She told us about the SSC, and how to get to a place where we'd be helped. My wife didn't want to try it. It was awful cold and the children were sick."

By the time spring came around they had all died. Caring about nothing then, Breevor took off.

"I'm still a weaver, but now I also raise the wool out of which my goods are made," Breevor concluded.

Hengst felt like shaking poor old Breevor. The weaver's tale had been long and prolix. Leon had regained his composure, and Muran had collected his formidable wits.

"What made you two decide your luck had to be better here than in old Nolan?" another herder asked.

Muran answered smoothly, "Leon's lost his father and two half-brothers. The Wheels want him killed too."

Hengst hoped someone else would ask the questions so he wouldn't have to.

"Who was your contact? Who pointed you in the right direction?" Breevor inquired, winking at Hengst.

"My mother and a Fortune House justiciar named Justin Sharp. Between the two of them we had a good outfit, maps, and guides. Then we lost everything in an ambush," Leon said.

Involuntarily Hengst pursed his lips. Justin Sharp! That old fox still alive! How many more lived of that old bunch fighting among themselves to determine which of them had the right to plunder Nolan? He was ready to sit here all night, if people would keep asking questions.

But Muran indicated his injury had left him exhausted, and he needed Leon's help for the latrine before bed.

Sleep called everyone else too. "Once more, welcome and refuge. We'll see you soon in Hometown, during Solstice Jubilee."

Perhaps Leon would return when his tutor no longer needed his assistance. Hengst listened hard to the doors opening and closing.

Then he heard Muran crow from the bunk room, "Beds! And pillows!"

Hengst went outside to look at Catclaw again. The grazing had been poor until they'd hit the SSC pastures. The stallion was getting worn down from carrying a double load. He'd been working hard even before reaching the outlanders' camp at Spring Lake.

So, Hengst noted to himself, I think of the young Royal and his tutor as outlanders, not refugees or settlers. They're not here to stay but to drag Glenn into whatever troubles Leon's running from. I wonder though, why she didn't bring them in herself.

Kazimir hooked his toes behind the corral rail next to Hengst. "What is on your mind?"

"Which two horses I'm going to borrow from the Flying Company here for the rest of our journey. I've big plans for Catclaw in the Solstice Jubilee races. I'm thinking he might could beat your Dervish, if Catclaw gets some rest between now and then. He's been working his butt off, and doing well too. But see, his quarters are getting some deep hollows."

Kazimir lit his pipe and passed it to Hengst.

"The Master can't stand on his own two legs alone, so Hulaff doesn't mind. But your second rider has no injury. Two then, and leading Catclaw. Three horses for you to take care of alone," Kazimir said.

Hengst said, "After such an ordeal both need, and deserve, a rest. And with races coming up I prefer keeping everything about Catclaw in my own hands."

Kazimir responded, "My friend, you keep everything concerning Catclaw to yourself, except the reins. Those you have given to Orangehair."

They smoked together. After a while, without exchanging words, they knew what was troubling their friendship.

"I know he's trouble, big trouble," Hengst said. "Yet I'm drawn to him. The trouble he causes isn't by his intention or even by his fault."

Kazimir said, "Choose three horses, not two. Tomorrow the Badgers ride at speed for Hometown. Burdened with Orangehair's Master, you will not be able to keep up with us."

Hengst laughed. "If I'd guessed you were that much in a hurry to see Cameron, I'd have sent you ahead long ago."

Kazimir grinned for a moment. "I've been impatient for that, for so long, that I can certainly wait longer. That isn't the reason I'm leaving my friend behind."

Hengst asked, "Why, then?"

"I won't play escort to Orangehair's entrance into Hometown."

·Ten·

MURAN SCRATCHED HIS groin, belly, and chest furiously. Leon joined in, rather less violently.

"You all haven't acquired a new infestation of lice already?" Hengst drawled. Then he sneezed. "You still stink of sheep dip."

Muran laughed. "It's our hair growing back. For every action, there's a reaction."

He sniffed at his armpits. "We don't smell much either. Leon insisting we jump into the Snake last night took care of that."

Leon said, "I'm never going to be filthy again."

Muran's itching subsided. He pulled his buffalo robe closer around his shoulders. He warmed his fingers around the cup of sage tea Hengst passed to him. A fine wood fire, hot food, a snug campsite, the tissue restoring itself over the ball of his foot, he felt more secure than anytime since he'd received the summons to become Leon's tutor in St. Lucien.

"Well, I smell something," Hengst said. He got up, leaves crackling under his boots, as he walked away from the fire. He peered through a thick tangle of bank willows.

"Our fire," Muran suggested lazily, from the depths of his robe.

"Hengst's right, Muran," Leon said, standing at the edge of the River, sniffing the cold air. Dawn had barely broken. He squatted and scooped up a palm of water, holding it to his nose. He snorted and blew, clearing his nostrils of their campfire smoke, dust of wood and leaves.

"From up the canyon," Leon said. "It's smoke, but a different wood than our fire's burning. Moisture pulls a lot of the dust out of the air, so you can smell it more clearly when you get by the water."

Hengst said, troubled, "I don't think there's any homesteading so far down from Hometown. This is canyon country, not properly the valley at all. During summer the River runs out of itself, and during the other seasons, like now, it's shallow or intermittent. For about another day there's nowhere soil's deep enough or gentle enough even for a garden. But I don't spend enough time in the valley these days to know everything."

The canyon trail was relatively wide and straight forward. The gullies and washes steeply falling down to the river channel appeared to have been dry for years. The landscape was ruggedly picturesque rather than imposing. Thick clusters of evergreens, birches, and aspens hung along the trail above the bank willows and cottonwoods. As late in the year as it was, brown, yellow, and red leaves still rustled on branches, and jays, brilliantly blue as falling pieces of sky, swooped before their eyes in raucous territorial warning. A fox froze and stared, before slinking into the bush.

Muran's belly was full. There was fresh water close by. His riding muscles had come back. His foot only throbbed when his horse misstepped, which was infrequent. In another day or two he thought he would try wearing the other boot of the pair he'd been given at the SSC sheep station. By mid-day the air was pleasantly warm.

Hengst, leading Catclaw, and Leon after him, went up another bend in the trail. Muran halted his horse to take the heel of his injured foot out of the leather cup he used on that side instead of a stirrup. He felt quite unlike himself. He examined this, attempting to determine what was out of balance here.

It was him. He realized there was a possibility of falling passionately in love with such a country.

He was alive. They'd made it. He felt good!

He shouted. "Hengst, do you have paper and ink in Hometown?"

He rode around the bend.

Catclaw, his lead cut through, squatted on his quarters, tearing with his front hooves at a figure with a skull instead of a face.

Several more Skulls capered among trees, thrown out at crazy angles by a recent rockslide, letting loose a rain of arrows.

Leon was streaking toward him, yelling his name, zigging to the side. "Get off the trail, Muran! That way, down there!"

Hengst's sabre flashed down and sidewise, sliced into the neck of the Skull at the shoulder of his buckskin riding horse.

Catclaw drove down on all fours in an explosion of arched back and kicking hooves. The Skull leaped for the grey stallion's neck. The stallion sunfished, shoulder knocking the Skull off his legs. Catclaw twisted east and west. He reared, and stomped the Skull into the ground. He sprang clear, head low, driving like a spearhead through the Skulls on the barricade. He leaped over a fallen tree, skimmed over the rocks, and galloped up the trail on the other side.

Muran's mare folded her legs underneath him as neatly as a lady snaps her fan shut. He sprawled on the ground, staring at the arrow which sprouted from the mare's head.

"Roll, Schoolmaster. Behind you. Roll!"

He rolled, smashed through thick brush, landed at the bottom of a rocky dry wash. His right cheek was stabbed by stickers of a ground-hugging, thick-padded cactus. He saw exposed roots of the short junipers densely clustered around the wash. Down here the sunlight was already cut off by the trees and the canyon walls. It was cold. The wash wall at his back was sheer rock far above his head, with no provision for climbing out.

Cautiously, Muran crawled a way farther up the wash, ignoring the pain burning in his foot where the new flesh had ripped open. Lucky his bad one couldn't take much of a stirrup. He'd only had his heel in it for balance. Otherwise he'd probably be caught under the dead weight of the mare.

The others were ahead of him, here on this side, the one falling to the River. He knew Leon's mind almost as well as his own, and Leon expected him to join them, not the other way around.

He heard a horse first, snorting with alarm on its tether, unable to find secure footing upon the rocky incline. Hengst had just finished off the buckskin who had broken both knees in their dive off the trail.

"What in the world is up there?" Muran whispered.

"Outlaws, wearing masks, calling themselves the Skulls, twisting the tribes' custom, since none of us will have them. Thieves, murderers, and thugs, no persons. Maybe Alaminite converts who changed their mind. Or just any of the other trash the conditions over there have been sending us. They like the Valley because it's richest pickings. We patrol but we can't be everywhere all the time."

Leon said, "So much for the Stallion Queen who sees all, hears all, and knows all."

Hengst snapped, "What were you expecting? A sorceress draped in stars riding air, the fingers of one hand shooting fire, the other waving a magic wand? You've spent too much time at the opera, boy."

He crawled up the wash wall to peer at the rockslide. An arrow zipped past his cheek. He dropped down the wall like a rock.

"My brains went out the door. I didn't even send a messenger pigeon to Hometown, giving our location and general expectation of arrival. Saquave's only law is don't be stupid! Shit with hair in it for choosing the shortcut instead of the safest way!"

When a man like Hengst talked like that in a situation like this, Muran knew there was less chance of getting out of it alive than anything he'd been through before.

Hengst sat back against the wall, fingers drumming on his drawn-up knee. The other made a fist at his mouth. He blew through it, spread the fingers wide. They'd stopped shaking.

He went to the horses. The one still alive had froth hanging off its bit. He put his hands on the horse, soothing it down.

He pulled bundles and weapons off the dead and living. "Leon, one hunting bow. Me, hunting and battle. Two quivers hunting, one battle. My sabre, my spear, and knives. Leon's knives on him. Muran, you wearing one, right?"

Leon said, "Do the Skulls have horses?"

"Often they do, but in country where they're not so useful as their own two legs they eat 'em."

Hengst brought the weapons up to the wall, momentarily brightening. "Did you see Cat take one of 'em out before he hightailed out of here? Glennys trained him herself. He's so fast he's probably halfway to Hometown by now. My sabre got one. Now it's seven to three, I think."

He became somber instantly. "We are outnumbered, friends. All we can do is attack."

Leon swallowed hard, fastening meal and water bags to himself, stringing his bow. After all the terrors he'd faced, here was a churning in his guts like he'd never known.

The Skulls were trying to move behind them. Leon's stomach settled down.

"They're no hunters. They can't move without the deaf hearing them."

Hengst said quietly, "Keep in mind that your Equine Academy training was with guns, sabres, arrows, used from the back of a horse. The killing skills you learned on Saquave's open ground were directed against what couldn't think of their quarry sitting in a tree."

Leon said stubbornly, "My ears say four of them coming down behind us."

After a moment Hengst said, "If you say so, all right. That means a match for the three of us up at the barricade. And for all my stupidity I know this place. We're going to move. Everything now depends on the two of you remembering everything I say and doing what I tell you, without question. That will be difficult, one of you a Royal and one a teacher."

The other two said nothing, asked no questions.

"Behind the barricade, on our off side, this gully wash wall gentles out. Moth, our horse, can get back up there. The ground levels out for about four strides, then there's a slope made of runoff and fallen trash. Three old spruces push out of the canyon to the sky, which still holds light, dark as it is down here. Three big trees. A bat cave opens at the top of the trash. Lots of boulders in front of it, a good place for us to hold. Like some others, these ass eggs thought the cave would make them a winter camp, which is why the barricade. Go over what I said in your minds now. Think of three trees."

Hengst took Moth, the Flying Company relay gelding loaned from the SSC Sheep Station, off his tether. The day faded rapidly above them.

"Muran, hang your knife sheath around your neck. You'll carry my two bows and a quiver of hunting arrows on your back."

Hengst boosted him up to Moth's saddle.

"Lay over Moth's neck and use your thighs and knees. Hit him with your fists, anything to force him to the three trees. Moth's job is shock. Yours is shoving Moth to those trees. Three trees, Muran, three trees."

Hengst touched Leon's shoulder.

"You're rear defense. When I say shoot, you lay down a fire to our rear. Don't take considered aim. Those behind us can't see any better than you and probably worse, going by what you've proved so far. Listen always for my voice and obey whatever it tells you, instantly."

They moved, Moth's noise covered by the blundering search of their hunters.

"Muran, I'm counting three. On three you kick with your heels and hang on with everything you've got. Three trees!"

Hengst pulled back the gelding's tail. On three he struck its anal vent with a cactus arm, and Muran lay down and kicked.

Moth charged up the slope, faltered at the top. Muran's long arms had the reins close to Moth's bit. He yanked the gelding's head up as his own raised from Moth's neck, sighting for three trees.

Far out of the past something stirred in his chest. A cry burst out of Muran. "Three Trees! Fulk and Three Trees!"

The rocks and boulders under the cave surged into his vision and fell behind. Moth went down, screaming and thrashing.

On elbows and knees, he dug with his fingernails. Stones and debris slid under him. Inch by inch Muran furrowed up to the yawning cavern. His nails broke, his fingers split, nose hurt, banged into his knife sheath. One set of fingers scrabbled, the other closed upon the hilt of his knife. The knife helped him the rest of the way, digging into the shifting ground under him.

Hengst struck down and slashed with sabre in one hand, knife in another, over and over again. There was blood. Strike, slash, pull out, cut and run.

Arrows showered over the slope, thrumming like wasps bigger than the world. His shoulder struck something hard and sharp as he went down.

A Skull fell on top of him and his knife, waiting to meet flesh. His arm went numb from the impact, then hurt. His sabre was on the ground, there.

He grabbed the blade, choked up and smashed the hilt into the nose hidden behind the skull mask. His knife ripped open a gut, blood and stench gushing over the blade.

"Run, Leon. For Three Trees and Fulk! Run!"

Leon's nose, ears, eyes, fingers, hands, his arms, were one. One arrow after another zinged through the air. The others couldn't smell, see, or hear over the walking wall that was Leon, holding the ground between the hunters and the persons that were his.

Muran pulled himself into the blackness of the cave. He could stop now. A hand grabbed his bad foot. Pain stung up his leg like a horde of fire ants. Muran's leg retracted against the agony, kicked in all directions at once to shake it off, while his intelligence twisted feverishly to get his opponent in sight. The knife in his hand thrust into a maskless face.

Muran hung on all fours, gasping and panting. He bowled over, struck by the force of Hengst's arrival. He crawled to the edge of the cave looking for Leon. Moth floundered in unending spasms, gut-shot three times.

Hengst clawed Muran's back, getting bow and quiver into his hands. He shouted to be heard over the ugly uproar surging at the foot of the slope.

"Leon, hold on to your weapons! Head to bottom, on your belly now! Muran, pull him in."

Under the cover of Hengst's bow work Muran dragged Leon, face down, into the cave. Moth continued to scream until Hengst silenced him by an arrow to his brain.

There was no more sunlight.

"Muran, kill that fire," Hengst yelled. Until that moment Muran hadn't been aware there was a fire.

"How many arrows you got left?" Hengst demanded of Leon.

"Six hunting, one quiver battle," Leon answered, on his knees behind the boulders and Moth's dead body.

"That's good, because the battle's about to begin. Our only advantages are that they and we know now our weapons are superior and we've got the high ground."

Leon said, "Chief, Sir, you took out their entire front. The intact rear's fallen back to regroup. Shall I hold my fire, Sir?"

"Hold your fire, Sir," Hengst said, falling upon his back, arms outspread, his lungs gasping in big breaths of foul-smelling air.

Flexing his fingers, he learned he was still grasping both sabre and knife.

Inside the cave and out, it was dark as death's pit.

"Drink," Hengst said. "Eat whatever you've got."

Voices raised in altercation below them. Such beings could live with each other no more than they could live with persons or animals, which made them more dangerous than either.

Breath back, Hengst said, "We're still pinned down, but the odds are better. It's going to get really nasty now."

The smell in the cave was nauseating and their noses couldn't get used to it, not even Muran's and Leon's, which had lived with the scent of carrion for so long. Hengst thought it was more than the funk of bat guano and a dead man's bowels.

Muran thought, I've killed. I've killed a man.

Leon thought, I missed every time.

Hengst thought, the young Royal performed royally.

Hengst felt around for tinder and kindling. Crouching, he cautiously moved back to where the cave turned and widened. There he struck a light. Very quickly it went out.

"I think what we're smelling was female once," he said.

Muran's strong arms hefted the carrion Skull at the front of the cave and threw it downslope. It landed below Moth, as he intended. It was that or throw himself upon the dead body and tear it to pieces with his own hands.

They stood watch in turns. It was bloody cold.

Some arrows flew back and forth during the morning.

"Why don't they leave?"

"The Skulls know their fate if the Valley gets on their backtrail any time soon. They're unhorsed. Rangers will run them down, and any left after that will hang," Hengst said.

"Hanging's too good for them," Muran said.

"There's plenty who agree with you, but that's the Governor's rule. It's public, and they have an opportunity to plead whatever they can plead. Hometown judges," Hengst said.

Leon was on watch. "Sir, the Skulls have brought reinforcements. Sir, if you can count flies around a latrine, that's how many."

The cave was rushed twice.

Leon thought about how few arrows they had left, not about how many his arrows had taken out.

The stink from the back of the cave made them sick. They worried about water. They were hungry beyond what rations they possessed. Muran's foot oozed fluid. Leon first, Hengst second, found a reason to brush a hand across the School-master's face. The fever was back.

The sun was cut off from the canyon like a head by an executioner's axe.

"Sir," Leon said, "Wolves are wolves. But I can't leave Muran alive for the sport of what's down there."

What was down there was confident enough to set fires for its comfort at the edge of the gully. It shouted descriptions of what was going to happen to the cave stealers. It wasn't reckless enough to get in front of the fires and make a target.

The wind in the trees, at such a place, might be eerie, but in such a time minds would be occupied by other considerations than nature.

The air filled with wails, sobs, moans, laments, all ending in a shrieking whine.

The whine became a screech, not once, twice, or thrice. Over and over again. Then the howls and gibbers started.

The moon was half full.

Leon's hairs stood on end and stayed that way. Sticky sweat turned the grime on his face greasy. Muran huddled into himself, sometimes shaking with heat and cold simultaneously. Hengst stayed on watch, and totally silent. But the weirdness never stopped. It was like nails ripping over tin. His nerves were about to snap.

Leon crept next to Hengst. He strained his eyes against the darkness, for once wishing his ears weren't so acute. In spite of himself Leon thought he was hearing words in all that excruciating groaning.

"Our brother. My brother, where are you? Brother, we want you. My brother, I want you."

One by one the fires in the crescent between trail and gully went out. Leon tried to find some satisfaction in seeing that the Skulls found this gibbering as hideous as he did.

After the fires went out it gradually became silent. Leon's eyes ached trying to make out anything, anything at all in the night.

Hengst stretched cautiously. Leon heard the Chief get out his tinder box. He groped to the pile of firewood that the Skulls

had put into the cave. He set one small piece burning, and
tossed it a short way outside, where it gave off a small, gentle
light, before going out with a pop.

The sky filled with fires that dropped like falcons behind the
Skulls' lines. They fed upon dry, dead needles and wood. They
licked with ferocious appetite upon the oils of spruce, juniper,
and pine, exploding in their greed, dividing and beginning
again in another place.

The Skulls were driven up to the trail.

Leon would cheerfully have given his left ball for more
arrows. He could have taken out a dozen, outlined so clearly against the fires. The Skulls' retreat from the fire was
forced toward the cave because the wind spread it in the
other direction.

A silver shape, another wind, a materialized piece of air,
dropped from the stars. Fire came from one hand, the other
carried a bow.

"My grandma's big tits," Leon said, the favorite oath of his
Academy class.

She flew across the Skull line, shooting one fire arrow after
another. A fire outlined her, and Leon saw it was Brecca she
rode, not the wind.

There were others now, jimming their horses down the canyon, sabres flashing, spears thrusting, holding the ground in
front of them before the Skulls' desperation rushed the cave
and took that strong defense.

"Leon, do what I tell you. Side to side we go downslope.
After the arrows are gone, the knife, and stay at my back. And
careful. Let's not be stupid now."

Between them, Hengst and Leon saw to it there were none
to be hung in Hometown.

Glennys sadly placed a buffalo robe over the dead woman
at the back of the cave. A tight rock cairn was built on top
of that.

They all held hands while Rance Calbert said, "Goodbye,
Nedda. The Governor's mother will say that you and little
Essie are together again. But don't forget Rance, Essie's dad.
Now he's got two to mourn, not one."

Rance turned to Glennys. "At least we got them as kid-
napped a poor, wandering grieving woman. And we don't

have any left to hang. That's my comfort right now."

The Stallion Queen and the Rangers had gone hunting the Skulls as soon as Rance read the signs of his wife's kidnapping. Nedda, careless with exhaustion and grief in the wake of Essie's prolonged, agonizing death, had taken a ride to be alone and think of her daughter.

Along the track they'd found Catclaw.

Hengst clapped Leon on the back. "See, still no magic."

Leon wasn't so sure. He'd never seen anything like that leap down the canyon to the trail in his life.

· Eleven ·

THE MUSIC WAS fiddles and lively tambourines. The case was banged and battered, held together with rope, but impossibly the SSC even had a bass viol and a tiny man who knew how to play his instrument. A small girl, hair fine and nearly white, hung about the stage made from table trestles at the back of the Big House's Hall. She watched everything the bass player did while he tuned the big thing. Leon had seen hand drums and kettles, and flutes, heard them too, during the daytime. Tonight this lineup seemed to be all that was wanted.

Early in the morning a bazaar had gone up in Hometown's dusty Rambles. Rugs, boots, jewelry, shirts, riding gear, hides, all sorts of items of utter fascination to one who couldn't claim as his own even the clothes he stood up in, were for trade and barter between tribes and the SSC.

He'd been told that tomorrow afternoon, when the qualifying heats finished, horse trading would start. The breed stock exchange for domestic animals other than the horses was already in effect. There'd be more of that after the twelve tribes' representatives received their shares from SSC's flocks and herds. Then Wilderness and Valley would have a better idea how to value various lines.

Members of the twelve tribes, and the Snakes, milled about the Hall, eating a little of this, a little of that, squirting Sidewinder into any passing mouth hanging open. The younger males clutched jugs of MaMa Milk. They waved their jugs derisively at those who had none.

Leon and Muran sat together in a dark corner. "MaMa Milk

is date wine mixed with goat milk yogurt and honey. The girls like it far better than Sidewinder," Muran whispered in Leon's ear.

"How do you know everything?" Leon asked, wishing for a jug of his own, repellent as MaMa sounded.

"I use my ears and my eyes. They seem better than yours, oh great hunter, when it comes to another sort of hunt, in which the quarry wants to be caught," Muran said affectionately.

The bass viol finished tuning. The music began, cheerful and fast. People began tapping time. Children bounced to the middle of the cleared Hall, grabbing a chance to kick up their heels before those who were serious about their dancing, and the courting couples, mixed it up.

Little by little the Hall began to divide. The old folks, who felt their dancing days were over, gathered in groups, finding places where they could get a good eyeful of who did what with whom tonight. The fiddles were playing something soft and sweet. One of the players was singing.

"When you and I were young and the moon of summer rose over the Sea . . ."

A couple went to the middle of the floor. The woman's fair hair was rolled away from her face in thick, golden plaits. The man swept her into his arms. Her eyes closed in a face full of dreams, as if she were an alien in this world of flesh and material things, but the music, and the man leading her through it, warded her so safely she could, for the music's moment, inhabit her true home. Her full blue skirt flared and twirled around them both in graceful waves.

"They're waltzing," Leon said in amazement.

Muran said, "That's Rebecca, Glennys's baby sister, and her husband, Jeremy. They do beautiful leather work together. Jewelry too."

Leon peered around. Bustling among the tables at the back of the Hall, he saw a tall, severely braided woman. That was Deborah, Glennys's second sister. Unlike Becky, the youngest, she appeared completely knowledgeable of the world's conflicting desires of the flesh. She also radiated her contempt for such desires.

"Deborah's an Alaminite in her heart, in spite of raids and kidnappings on the Valley. Alaminites think dancing and musical instruments are from the Devil," Muran said.

Leon had figured out very quickly that in the Saquave, Alaminites were no more liked or trusted than in Nolan.

The walls were togged out with mistletoe, evergreens, and hanging blankets worked in a variety of patterns. Their dyes glowed richly in the light from tallow candles interspersed with big pottery jars holding thick wicks fired with creosote. All the best weavers of tribe and Valley had their work up there. At some point a prize was to be awarded of one of Brecca's children for the blanket judged the best. Stuck up next to each entry was a flat clay tablet inscribed with the weaver's characteristic mark. Voters painted a copy of their favorite's mark on a smaller stone out of a box at the end of the hall, dropped it into a jar, guarded by a group of weavers, Wilderness and Valley, who weren't competing this year.

Unpaired women floated into the Hall, in groups, arm in arm with a best friend, or alone. Their finery took many forms, from leggings to skirts. No velvets, satins, silks, or lace.

Long twists of silver and turquoise dangled bewitchingly from their ears, ending in feathers brushing bare necks. Turquoise hung between swelling breasts. Beaded belts showed off supple waists, silver worn low pulled attention to pelvis and buttocks. Their hair was elaborately dressed in braids, tails, and rolls, or in curled enchantment about their faces. Their footgear was made for dancing long and vigorously.

Leon's blood moved between his legs, making his scrotum high and tight, and his member swell. He wanted to seize them. He wanted to run his tongue across their eyelids and cheeks, rip open their clothes, spread their legs, fall upon them then and there, regardless of eyes. He'd deck whoever got in his way. He wanted them all.

But he was a person, and he knew how to behave as one. The memory of the grab he'd made for Glennys out in the desert, and her reaction, shamed the fire in his blood. Unlike her, these carried knives openly, some from their necks, some at hips, others over their navels, and those had bare midriffs.

He drew his knees together, upon the bench, sitting next to Muran, drunk from the cornucopia of female plenitude.

The women displaying themselves bunched in drifts and eddies during their progress through the Hall, stopping here and there to chat, add new members to their ranks. They made a flower garden near the stage, thick, hothouse bouquets, an intimidating prospect for someone shy wanting a partner, who had to go up under the eyes of the entire floor to tender an invitation to dance.

Before the available women appeared, everything already was more daunting than Leon had anticipated. There were so many people in one place, which he'd quite lost the habit of. All of them knew each other well, or, at least, knew of each other. Leon hardly knew the names of more than a dozen. No one seemed to want to know him, which had never happened in his life. In Nolan, though he was without real power, at any time luck might pass power off to him. He was the heir apparent to the throne. People at court were used to playing both sides against the middle, and they'd made a point of being friendly to his face. Here, people acted as though they preferred to escape his notice all together.

Muran, sick though he'd been when they'd arrived in Hometown, already had a huge acquaintance. The SSC had shown Muran enthusiastic hospitality when it learned a University certified Schoolmaster had arrived. Hometown possessed a schoolhouse. It started building an addition on it for Muran's living quarters immediately. People stopped by the bed where the teacher was recovering, to visit and introduce their children. He was brought gifts of food, promises of furniture, utensils, help with a garden.

Pozeem and Rangers, other men, SSC and tribe, penetrated into the forbidden garden. Greetings and conversation passed back and forth. Sips of MaMa were accepted graciously. The dancing began in earnest.

For all their capacity to enjoy themselves, Leon was impressed by their pacing and discipline. The big blowout was still two nights away. No one, dancers or musicians, pushed all out.

The only person, seemingly, without particular duties was Leon. Early this morning he'd dropped in upon the Governor's meeting with the pozeem and the Rangers. Outside watches were kept and patrols ridden in sobriety. Others, both Wilderness and Valley, had been tagged. Their responsibility was to keep brawls from starting. They'd been drilled on the correct manner and timing of breaking up private fights that were inevitable, and without which such a Jubilee would be remembered as dull.

He wished he were keeping watch or riding a patrol instead of sitting here hunched over his futile lust. He didn't know the steps to the vigorous pattern dances that had taken over from the brief waltz.

Jeremy conducted his wife to Muran's corner. "Welcome to the Valley, Schoolmaster Muran," she said.

Then she gasped and stuttered. "You as well, Sir." She was red to her hairline. She didn't have any idea how to address Leon.

Leon stood. He took her hand, bent to kiss it. She snatched it back and hid it between her breasts as if a scorpion had touched her. Feeling stung himself, he sat back down.

"Call me Orangehair, like Kazimir, the Badger Chief does," he suggested, releasing the bitter poison of rejection he felt on all sides.

"Please, call me Becky," she said. With a great big breath she turned back to Muran.

"I was too young to know you, but Glennys has always spoken with affection about Schoolmaster Muran, on those rare occasions when she has time to sit together and remember that long ago time over there, in Soudaka County."

Her eyes were huge, and appeared perpetually startled, like a deer's. Her mother, Stella, paused to brush her daughter's cheek, before floating away on the tide of her own visions.

Yet, as lost to the world as Stella seemed, her arms shot out and firmly took two little boys by the scruff of their necks and gave them smacks. They'd been keeping other kids their age from the food tables.

Leon heard her say, "Little birds in their nests know how to agree, so why don't you?"

One of them twisted in her grasp. "You hit us, hit them too. They started it!"

Stella said, "I'm your grandmother and have the right to clobber you when you deserve it, especially when your own mother doesn't see you misbehave."

Leon was interested to see Becky blush again.

"This food is for everybody. Remember, the Bogeyman will be out on Solstice Eve, and bad children get acorns and swats, not honey sweets."

Stella let them go. One of the two she'd cuffed stuck out

his tongue at her retreating back, but the other covered it up with a grimy hand. They both began to giggle.

They ran to their parents. "Mama, does the Bogeyman live in the witch's cave down in the Sandbank?"

"Nonsense, that's your aunt's cave, where the Governor goes to be alone and think without little boys to pester her," Becky said.

The tallest one said doubtfully, "I heard Cousin Cameron tell Thea *she* thought it was a witch cave."

Becky said, obviously confused, "You're not supposed to listen to what little boys shouldn't hear. You'll get as many sweeties as anybody, my darlings."

The two ran off to cause more trouble.

Stella and her daughters, Deborah and Becky, had many features in common, Leon thought, but they weren't the same. Stella and Deborah shared the sense of properness, Stella and Becky the visionary aspect of their eyes.

Out of the corners of those big eyes Becky sneaked wary peeks at Leon, as if she feared he was to demonstrate immediately in his own person every evil for which the SSC had claimed royalty and Nolan responsible.

Jeremy said, "Those two threatened with the Bogeyman, and he's real, you'll see, are Becky's and mine. Sadly, they seem to resemble their Aunt Glennys in paying heed to no one but themselves more than they take after either of their parents. What can we expect? They were born here. But they've both had two winters in the schoolhouse, know their A and B and C, and one, two, three. Our baby, the girl, goes for the first time this year. She's the one sitting at the bass viol player's feet. We'll be proud to measure you for boots when Thea declares you're all healed. You'll need a pair for everyday, one for riding, and one for Jubilee. Would you like your Jubilee pair walking or riding?"

Muran looked with embarrassment at Leon. "You are so generous. So generous that I feel bold to ask a favor. Could you make one of your offered pairs for my student, Leon, whatever sort he'd choose?"

Jeremy's response had nothing to do with Muran's request. He asked Muran about his feet. Before his accident which one had been the biggest? Did he think his feet had changed since walking so far?

He talked over every aspect of Muran's answers at great length. Becky occasionally interjected an adoring exclamation for her man's brilliant words.

The Governor's brother-in-law was a handsome man and undoubtedly King of boot makers. Leon rather suspected none of Jeremy's children were going to follow in their dad's bootsteps. He'd been looking at the stage. Every once in a while, through the intoxicating sight of Saquave's beauties, he saw a small, enraptured face, whose body was curled next to the bass viol.

Muran said, "You will excuse me, friends, but I must seek my bed. Gather my strength, you know, to begin teaching after Jubilee. Coming, Leon?"

Restless, dissatisfied with himself and everything else, Leon wasn't at all sleepy.

Becky softly put out her hand to Leon before leaving. "Orangehair doesn't suit you at all. The brush on your head glows more like that stone in your ear, when the light shines through it. I'd like to find a dye or stone here that would give such a color."

These people didn't miss a bloody thing.

The Governor's relatives insisted upon escorting Muran out of the hall and steering him through the maze of passages behind it to the Big House room temporarily given to him and Leon. He thought Jeremy had probably put Muran asleep long before the tutor was delivered to his bed.

Leon leaned back against the wall and beat time with the music. If he acted like he was enjoying himself, maybe he would. He had reason enough to feel good, didn't he? He was alive and safe.

Now that he'd come to a stop he thought constantly about his mother, Queen Sharissa, and Nolan. Was Sharissa safe? Was she even alive? It had been a very great risk, sending him away. If those opposed to his coronation thought he was dead, surely they'd do away with Sharissa too?

"Survival isn't enough to make some of us satisfied with ourselves, is it?"

He'd never heard her approach. Leon leaped to his feet, made a short bow, and took her hand for the kiss his mother had trained him to believe, King-in-waiting though he be, was every lady's right to receive from him. Then, her sister's recoil went through his mind.

But Glennys's hand lay in his. It was a large hand, with very long fingers. It was rough and calloused. A shock dilated all the fibers of his being as his lips barely dared touch the smoother skin on top of her hand.

He was sharply aware that all the eyes at this end of the Hall were locked upon this obscure corner.

"My lady," he said.

"May I sit with you awhile?" Glennys asked.

There was no distance to be covered to the splintery bench, but together they made her seating a homage proferred to the Governor of the SSC by Nolan's heir.

She was without finery. Her silver band wasn't on her brow tonight. She'd pushed it up like a headband to hold back the shorter front hair that didn't fit into the long braid hanging over one shoulder.

"You're staring," she said.

"I apologize. You're the most beautiful woman I've ever seen, except for Sharissa."

He waved a hand toward the women dancing. "I thought them stupendous, and I still do," he stumbled.

He gave it up and shrugged. "You're—more."

"Your compliment," Glennys said, "waters my dry heart."

She really did seem to like his words, and understand them as he meant them, he thought. The proof was her choice of acceptance words, words a well-bred lady, some of which Sharissa had managed to insinuate into her court life in spite of Roald, would have said, or not said, if they didn't accept his compliment.

He carefully selected a plate of tidbits from the food tables. An old woman, hunched, crippled, and missing teeth, whispered, "Tonight the Gov's only drinking mint tea, not anything stronger. She's got lots of work yet before she sleeps. Tomorrow's another day, worse than this one too."

They talked about Nolan. She'd covered a lot of this ground during their ride from the bat cave to Hometown. Nathan Drake rallying St. Lucien to drive out the mob and the Alaminites. Roald's wedding of his mother under the auspices of both Wheel and Aristo factions to conclude Nolan's Civil Wars and unite for the desperate campaign against the invasion from the Shipper King of Andacac. The forced labor that rebuilt St.

Lucien even during the Andacac war. The execution of Nathan Drake after his brilliant work against Andacac for the treason of leaving the Outremere campaign against Sace-Cothberg and sailing back to Nolan. The anarchy throughout Nolan after so many years of licensed brutality and thuggery.

Her questions this time around were more personal. He'd been a child through most of the events she asked about, and had lived in St. Lucien only since Sharissa had married Roald.

He asked her about his father, King Leon. She said they should save that for another time, but there was a lot she'd like to tell him.

They talked of his grandmother, the Baroness Ely, who as far as he knew also still lived. She was a member of the old line blood Aristos after all, the source blood of Nolan's royalty. Old Blood Aristos had had long, vigorous lives. He confessed Grandma was the inspiration for the oath he'd started with his class at the Equine Academy.

Glennys threw back her head and laughed. "The Baroness does have great titties. I heard a description of them once from Duke Albany, when I was his concubine. He was more familiar with them than either you or I could ever be."

She asked, "Does Roald treat Sharissa decently?"

This time she'd stepped further than he wanted to go right now.

Leon's face went hard. "He crawls on her constantly trying for an heir. But he can't do it. He flaunts the Baroness Waterford, Thurlow Fulk, in front of her always."

Glennys said, "Sharissa told you, a child, all this?"

Leon said, "She didn't have to. Thurlow told me herself."

"And went after you too, no doubt," Hengst said. "Ho, Leon. Quite a night, ain't it? Hope you're having fun. Glenn's bloody proud of Solstice Jubilee. Every year we've been here she's worked to make it a big deal for both Valley and Wilderness. This one's the best yet."

Leon got up again and saluted the Chief. "Allow me to get you something to eat, Sir. I'll be back in a flash."

This time the crippled lady introduced herself as the Keeper of SSC's Big House. She gave him a skin of Sidewinder for the Chief. "Take him this jar too. Tell him I mixed the MaMa myself, with him in mind." Then she winked.

"Hengst," Glennys said, "Leon reminds me of you that first

winter on Three Trees when you got a case of hero-worship on one of our Baron Fulk's aides, Wildan."

Hengst disagreed. "Leon's the same age as Wildan was then." A look of sadness crossed his face. "He was the first man I saw die."

Glennys said, "No he wasn't. Remember the Alaminite who burned Three Trees' barn that same winter?"

"We didn't *see* it happen, we only saw the results of my dad's war stallion's work," Hengst said.

When Jeremy and Becky were talking with Muran, Leon could hardly stifle his yawns.

Leon asked Hengst, "Sir, how did you know Thurlow got me?"

Hengst looked at Glennys first before answering. "Because she wouldn't be Thurlow otherwise. Please excuse our bad manners for talking of matters and people meaningless to you. Shoot, you either weren't born or were a babe when we lived over there. But your presence here is bringing back to us what we'd nearly forgotten."

"Sir, my lady, please, I beg you, tell me more, if you can bear it," Leon said.

Hengst said, "Thurlow, me, Glenn, we all grew up together. All of us have the same father, so Glenn's a Fulk, therefore an Aristo, too, though her sisters are not. Some Fulks are good ones, like Glenn, and some of us are not."

Leon said, "Like Thurlow and Stogar the Troll."

Glennys reached for Hengst's hand. He gripped it hard.

Hengst said, "Is Stogar still alive?"

"Alive and sticking to Roald tight as a tick," Leon said. "I despise Roald, but I hate, I hate, Stogar."

Hengst said, "We got reports from over there often in the earlier years, until it got too hot for our people after the Civil Wars got good and going. But we never heard a whisper Stogar was still alive."

Glennys said, "I'm so sorry, Hengst. I let you down. I thought sure I'd killed him. I saw Stogar go down. I still see it when I'm remembering, the knife in his chest, on the floor of the St. Lucien Fortune House, the mob and Alaminites pouring in over his body."

Leon said, "Stogar can't walk and has lost an eye. He's the richest man in Nolan."

Hengst and Glennys took silent conference together. She stood up and said, "Thank you, Leon, for your company. We must talk together again, soon. Now it's time to dance."

Hengst said, "Me too. May I have the honor?"

He put out his arm and conducted his sister into the dance.

Clapping and cheers went up as the two of them, on the beat, gracefully inserted themselves into the patterned lines on the floor. The musicians whooped on their stage.

The caller yelled, "Let's go to town!"

She was ready to be seen. She attracted all eyes, all the available light to her. Hengst, as her partner, was part of her brilliance. She swung, swooped, and pranced. No one sat or stood. Everyone danced, including the old wheezers. A bunch of pozeem leaped into the Hall and joined in, cutting loose with a whole new Wilderness range of movements, trying to shut down the Valley men.

"Ho! Ho! Confusion to Nolan!" raised the rafters of the Hall.

The only person not dancing was himself, Leon, the only one here for whom Nolan meant more than escaped misery and a looming threat of oppression.

Sharissa had told him that Glennys had worked upon the stage of Queen's Theater in Nolan. He could see there was a lot of theatrical sense of timing in the Governor. She danced, flirted, and joshed with Valley and Wilderness. Hengst had more partners than he knew what do with.

He saw Becky pick up her daughter from the stage. Jeremy collected their two boys. It seemed a signal. Soon all the older people and the children were gone.

Then at the right moment, when everyone was filled with themselves, *She* was gone too.

Some younger folks came in, bringing a breath of fresh, cold air with them. They weren't in finery.

"Last set," was called from the stage. "So our friends relieved from watch can at least pull the tail of our fun. But we expect you to do your duty on the floor tomorrow."

Hastily the newcomers gulped down whatever was left on the food tables and swallowed some Sidewinder. Swiftly they lost their stiffness and were dancing.

One of them hung back. Leon watched with interest as she slowly divested herself of her dark outer clothing, took down her hair and shook out the dust. Hatice helped her pull back the cascade of flossy strands, and tied it behind her ears with a beaded thong.

Leon heard Hatice say, "Ronnie, go dance. There's a boy here who hasn't stood up all night except to serve your mother and Hengst."

The light was guttering down, but he was sure that the young woman looked his way with strong interest. His heart began to flip-flop when it seemed she was coming over to him. So this is how women they call wallflowers at court balls feel, he thought. Would Cameron, the Stallion Queen's foster daughter, dance with him, the one with whom nobody wanted anything to do?

She made something like a curtsy and asked him, "Do I call you Prince Leon or is it Your Highness, or are you King, and therefore Your Majesty?"

He stumbled out quickly, "Orangehair or Leon, my lady Cameron."

Her eyes widened with delight. "You know my name! Would you like to dance?"

Leon felt like killing himself. "I want to dance with you more than anything in the world but I don't know how."

A low purr slowly escaped from the lovely, round column of her throat through the delectable fullness of her lips. "It will take no time for the hero the pozeem call the Young Wolf to learn something this easy. But first you've got to get to your feet. This is a two-step. We'll practice back here for a minute first."

He took her in his arms and floated away into roseland. Their feet moved in perfect time together. He didn't have to listen to her instructions. Her body told his how to move.

"Last dance! Last dance!" broke into his paradise.

Two men stood there. One was a stranger and the other was Kazimir. "I've saved the last dance for you, Cameron, and it will be my only dance tonight," he said to her in the most flattering tones a woman can hear.

She looked deeply into his eyes with her green ones. She squeezed his hand and stepped, he thought reluctantly, from his arms. Before she moved into Kazimir's she whispered in his ear.

"I have duty all during the day, but I'm free for tomorrow

night's dance. I'll see you then? Yes, please?"

"Oh, yes," Leon said. "Yes. Yes."

That Kazimir stared at him with such open hostility almost made up for her going with the Badger Chief. Kazimir wouldn't bother to show such dislike unless he felt the man from Nolan was a rival.

Hatice and Deborah were clearing away the debris from the food tables. Deborah complained loudly, "Where's our help, that's what I want to know. Leave all the jobs for us, the most overworked of any, to do! They treat us like scullery slaves."

Hatice said, "It's late for the little ones, they're asleep, and the others have something else on their minds now. Remember what it was like when you were young, Deborah?"

"I was never young. Glennys saw to that! And now I'm old before my time," Deborah said.

Leon came over. "Let me do the trestles, my ladies. I've done nothing but sit on my bum all night. And many compliments for the food. It was delicious!"

Under their direction he scrubbed down the boards with scalding water that he lugged from the kitchen fires. He carried the heaviest things for them and banked the kitchen fires under Hatice's critical eye.

"You really understand how to save a fire," Hatice observed. "Not everyone does."

Leon said, "Thank you. Saquave taught me that."

Hatice said, "I think you've mastered all the lessons Saquave's given you so far. You have nice manners too."

A pang shot through him. "My mother taught me those."

He hadn't thought about Sharissa since he learned the two-step.

· Twelve ·

MURAN'S SNORING WOKE Leon very early. He shook out his pants and buskins before getting dressed, in case scorpions had strayed into them. Shivering, he lathered as best he could in the cold water on the laving stand, and shaved by feel in the dark. He dumped his used water into the chamber pot.

As he'd done every morning in the few days since they'd arrived in Hometown, he hurried to the warmth and light of the Big House's kitchen to replenish the pitcher for Muran's use.

Knowing her name and position now, he greeted Hatice and offered to help her. "It's time this man did something to earn his keep," he said.

"Bet your bohotchie on that, buckeroo," Hatice replied sharply. She gave him a utensil with a handle as long as his arm. The scrape spoon on the end was big as a trowel.

"Stir the corn porridge. Don't let it lump or stick to the sides of the kettle or at the bottom. It'll burn otherwise. When it thickens up no matter how hard you stir, swing the kettle to the edge of the fire."

That was just the beginning. He ran for firewood. He got blisters from overheated bacon drippings set to melt that splattered and popped. Platters and breakfast bowls were picked up from the drain board as soon as he'd rinsed them, filled again, and sent to the Hall. It was midmorning before the fires died down, he'd finished dumping the hearths' ashes in big jars outside, and the kitchen floor had been sprinkled, swept, and rubbed to Hatice's satisfaction.

Hatice sat down on a chair constructed to accommodate

her hump. "A sip and bite before meeting Glennys in the storerooms. The noon shift will have it easy today. Most will eat elsewhere, be too busy watching our exchange with the council women, or too sick, to show up. After the exchange I don't have to do anything except get going for tomorrow's Solstice Eve banquet. The tribes are hosting an outside feast today from their share of the Valley's harvest."

Leon set to with hearty appetite over corncakes, beans, and bacon.

He asked, "Too sick? You mean from Sidewinder and dancing?"

"From the Governor's Justice. There's a hanging," Hatice said sadly. "One of the Valley's own, not an outlaw from over there. I know he's guilty, but I need to rest more than the SSC needs me to witness for that one's Justice again."

She changed the subject quickly. "You should go to the pasture tonight. The tribe women make music that's something to hear. Their dancing is as much fun as ours."

Leon said, "It's for everybody?"

"Yes indeed," Hatice said.

"Then I'll go," Leon said. "As for dancing, I'll watch, maybe learn something."

"Why would a young man who is as starved for the companionship of young females as you are want to sit out?" Hatice demanded.

Her eyes were so knowing it came out in spite of himself. "I've nothing fine to wear."

"The pozeem and Hengst have said you're a hero, so that should be enough for anyone. You've done your share to earn your food today. Shoo, shoo."

He said awkwardly, "Would you have me on your breakfast shift every morning? Give me other jobs too? You run the Big House. There must be work for one who needs anything he can get."

Hatice said gently, "I'd be pleased to have someone on breakfast shift who is as awake in the morning as you, and as clean-shaven."

Then she got sharp again. "I'll have ya. Until ya find sompin' else. Aristos always do. Now outta my House."

As he took to his heels, to his relief he heard her say, "See you tomorrow morning, if not sooner."

The bazaar was deserted. He thought he might find Muran at the schoolhouse. Nothing was going on there either. As far as he could see, the Wilderness people who'd come to collect the tithes, or only to participate in the Valley's Jubilee, were keeping to the pasture across the River. Where were the settlers?

Leon wandered through the Rambles. The dog at the bottom of the watchtower ladder got up barking at his approach. A blue-and-orange wool scarf fluttered to his feet. He looked up.

Cameron hung dangerously over the palisade at the top. "Young Wolf!" she shouted down.

"Where's everyone?" he asked.

"At Glennys's Justice, outside the stockade by the Big Gates, south. Want to come up?" Cameron asked.

"I think I'll attend the Justice," Leon said.

"Another time. Sky's reminded me that visitors up here is against regulations," Cameron said ruefully. "But it's so dull! Alaminites won't come down today when they must know there's so many Wilderness friends about."

Kazimir had strolled up and stood with hands upon his slim hips staring at Cameron's hair, which had fallen out of its knot and whipped wildly in the wind.

The Gates were open. Everyone of the SSC including, horribly to Leon's mind, children, were present standing in front of a gibbet. Then he realized the children were Becky and Jeremy's two boys, who'd climbed to the top of the Gates to see.

"Don't tell, please," they hissed at him.

The man standing under the noose was Breevor, the herder at the SSC sheep station who'd told him the sad tale of how he'd escaped evil Nolan and come to the free and equal land of the Saquave.

He was flanked by two men in black hoods. In front of the herder stood Glennys.

Her voice was so low that he could hear the soughing of the eternal wind. Her words carried cleanly through it, however, to enter his own ears far to the rear of the gathering.

"When Breevor first came to Hometown it was summer, and he was sponsored by those over there that vouch refugees. He worked with Hatice in the kitchens, where so many of us begin in Hometown. He stole corn to make likker. We explained that corn is too precious for likker or even horses in this dry country where it is our staff of life, and our coin. He begged pardon manfully, and spoke of what he'd endured in Nolan. It was winter then. We put him to guard the poultry yards. He stole the little corn we give our few winter laying hens so the sick can have eggs, and Hometown can have a variety in winter's dull diet. He fed the corn to our roosters, so they'd be restless and strong, and tempted others into cock fights. Again, he begged pardon. Jeremy took him in to help in his shop. He stole tools, leather, and silver. Breevor said living in a house with a couple and their children brought so many unhappy memories that he'd lost control over his wits. He asked to be a weaver again, as he'd been over there. We gave him a herder's place with the opportunity to raise his own wool for his goods. Now Breevor's been caught red-handed selling sheep to Silver City. They were not his sheep, but those belonging to our Saquave Settlement Company."

Everyone knew Breevor's story already, but Hometown listened attentively to Glennys's recital of what seemed the bare facts.

Glennys turned her back to Hometown, to face Breevor directly. Leon could still hear her.

"What did the Alaminites give you in exchange for a few sheep that the SSC did not?" the SSC Governor asked.

"Nothing but their respectful gratitude for helping fill their stomachs and clothe their limbs, which is what the SSC stands for!" Breevor cried.

Breevor's possessions were heaped at one side of the gibbet. Glennys leaned over and chose a heavy bag from among them. She opened the top and dumped a pile of shining silver disks and very old jewelry studded with turquoise stones upon the planks. In its own way this was a trial, Leon saw, not necessarily an execution.

"Is this how Silver City expressed its gratitude for your freely given gifts?" Glennys asked.

"Out of respect I accepted their gifts, as any man would do," Breevor said.

"Were you unaware that the silver mines the Alaminites have made up there had been used carefully time out of mind by our Tongue Kindred, the Wilderness tribes? Were you ignorant that the Alaminites have robbed tribal burial kurgans of the possessions of the dead? Did you not know that these same Alaminites come down here burning Valley steadings, robbing Valley harvests, slaying Valley people, and kidnapping Valley women, condemning them to labor for that same silver they, with their firearms, have stolen from the tribes?" Glennys asked.

Breevor cried, "Yes! No! I didn't know any of that. If I'd known I'd never have given them the sheep. But Governor, you're so fair, decent, and compassionate. You stress the need to share food. The Alaminites often go hungry, which means the Valley women do too, if, as you say, some are in Silver City. They told me they'd share the sheep with the Elk tribe, whose luck has been bad these Rains, as you know. The Elks are Wilderness, Tongue Kindred. I only gave them what you would give them yourself. Please, let me have another chance. Let me join the Rangers. I'd be your first Ranger who has friendly relations with Silver City, which can be very useful to the SSC."

Breevor rested his case.

Glennys turned to face the SSC. "Shareholders, what do you say?"

The people shuffled back. Long minutes of silence passed. Finally another sheepherder stepped to the front, out of the anonymity of the gathering.

"Out with the flocks, herders work in pairs with their dogs. We talk under the stars, between sandstorms, and during the Black Blizzards. We talk over food in the burning heat of summer sun. We talk of whatever we can until we're sick of the sound of each other and talk no more. Breevor talked with us, and listened too. He knows about Alaminites. He lies if he says else."

Several other herders who'd been with Breevor at the SSC station reluctantly stepped out to corroborate the words of the first.

While they spoke Breevor shifted uneasily on the scaffold, first looking nervous, then hangdog, then very meek and humble. Tears began to run down his face.

"Do you have an explanation for why your fellows witness the accusations against you?" Glennys asked.

Breevor assumed bravado, as he'd previously put on sincerity, humility, and regret.

He shouted, "You all blather about sharing good and bad equally among yourselves! But the Governor takes the lion's share and lords it over us all, her and her relatives. The only way a woman gets on top is on her back with legs wide open. Over there this so-called Governor was nothing but a whore. Old Duke Albany gave her all the money that he stole from the likes of me and all the rest of you down there staring at me. She took that money stolen from us and started her own little kingdom in the desert, making us her slaves, and whoring for the savages. There's others of you that agree with me and I know who you are!"

That last sounded like a threat. Leon's eyes searched the crowd. Breevor had struck chords familiar to some of them, or at least believed he had.

Glennys asked quietly, "Does anyone wish to witness Breevor's defense?"

No one stepped forward.

Glennys asked Breevor, "Do you have anything else to say defending your crime of stealing from the SSC in exchange for the Alaminites' stolen goods?"

Breevor's eyes searched desperately the people in front of him. "Revolt against the Nolanese Aristo bitch! Take what's rightly your own. Put the tribes to work! They're savages, unfit for anything but to be slaves of civilized people like us from Nolan!"

Kazimir had come up during Breevor's last defense. He joined Leon where he stood back and apart from Hometown.

Glennys asked, "Hometown, what do you say? Shall Breevor have another chance to live equal and free among us, as a Ranger, carrying weapons, guarding our communication lines, keeping watch on the stockade against Silver City's winter ski army? Or shall he hang?"

One by one those before the scaffold, in the short, wan light of approaching Winter Solstice, filed past a jar sitting on the ground. Earlier, each adult had been given a stone painted white and one painted black. After the last wheezer put his hand deep in the jar's neck so no one could see his vote, the stones were counted.

Glennys and Hengst counted them out in front of everyone.

Kazimir said, "If there are more than ten white stones the thief gets another chance."

There were only seven.

Glennys and Hengst climbed down from the gibbet.

Breevor was hung.

Both executioners grabbed his kicking legs, jerked expertly with all their weight, and Breevor's neck snapped.

In silence the executioners climbed down and took off their masks. Hometown linked hands. The wind picked up swirls of sand. The grains ticked against the stockade. Anything that sprouted here for three bowshots, other than what grew thorns, spines, and burrs, was plucked out. It was a bare, bleak, poor prospect.

Glennys said, "Breevor betrayed home and hospitality. Who steals from one steals from us all, including our Tongue Kindred, the twelve tribes, who have named us the thirteenth tribe. We are not only SSC, Hometown, and the Valley. We are also the Snakes, sharing the Saquave with Badgers, Wolves, Rabbits, Elks, Owls, Crows, Beavers, Coyotes, Cougars, Bats, Gazelles, and Scorpions. What diminishes one diminishes us all. Breevor is cast out. He is not one of us."

Stella said, "Breevor, may you rest in peace, and find consolation in the everloving, all forgiving arms of Alma."

Everyone but Glennys, Hengst, the ones who'd worn the executioner's masks, and Stella departed quickly. Leon watched those left take down Breevor's body. Stella took off the body's clothes and washed it. After the shroud-wrapped body was loaded on a mule, he followed. The body was walked up the eastern ridge among the dwarf pines. They built a burial cairn outside the cemetery up on the ridge.

There was quiet for another hour; then the Rambles were full of children throwing balls, running, leaping, shrieking, and tussling. The bazaar went back to business. Wherever Leon's wandering feet took him, he found the SSC's Governor.

Glennys, in company with Hatice, Deborah, Thea Bohn, Captain Michaela, and several other women, gathered on the wide veranda in front of the Hall of the Big House. Banked around them, and behind, just inside the Hall, were the Valley's domestic manufactures. Sacks of corn, beans, sun-dried tomatoes, and bolts of cotton cloth went as exchange for the Snakes' use of the Valley. Dyes, honey, and other small, valuable things like needles were bargained for dates and tobacco. The council women bartered feathers, coral, kikkuli and hemp fibers, spices, and other goods brought back from the Green People in the trading caravan.

Counters were passed over, one for each ten of stock the tribes were entitled to out of the SSC's flocks and herds pastured on tribal lands. Only a few animals, chosen to make the best impression, actually changed hands. Except for the horses, most of those would be eaten at the feast hosted by the Wilderness.

There were no counters for Brecca's herd. He defended his own without human assistance, and he grazed where he chose. He was the Sovereign, who brought Saquave's luck wherever he stepped.

The women exchanged impatient glances when Chief Sepul of the Elks, and his Owl and Beaver peers, appeared to take their share, instead of representatives from their women's councils. Courteously Glennys gave each of the three men corn, beans, tomatoes, and cotton, and then waited for them to leave.

Chief Sepul said, "You have forgotten my counters for sheep, goats, and horses. I would like to exchange the goats for pigs and turkeys, for the goats eat even the cactus, allowing the wind to eat the earth. So also would the Owls and Beavers."

Glennys said, politely, "You have no Rains, so the Valley runs no herds, no flocks on your pastures. Nor do we ever put the swine or poultry outside the Valley. We have made no deal with any of you for six Rains. You cannot share with us what you do not have. Surely your women's councils explained this to you?"

Sepul looked bewildered and angry, as if he had never known that the Valley had to use his tribal pastures in order for him to share in the Valley's animals. "We want our counters. Everyone else has them," he said stubbornly.

Kazimir's mother, Konya, a long-legged, broad-shouldered woman with a magnificent mane of dark hair said, "You will excuse us, please, Elk, Owl, Beaver? This is a time when we are doing business that's not of interest to men. However, we are regrettably missing the women of your councils. Please take them our compliments and say we look forward to seeing them again soon. Otherwise Elk, Owl, and Beaver business will be hopelessly behind."

"We want our counters," Sepul maintained firmly. "Without the Rains our people are hungry."

Konya said, "That is a different piece of business, and one the women's councils can only take up with yours. The women must join us first, Sepul. That is how business is done. Now go away and leave us to our work."

Leon took the hint more quickly than the Chiefs did. He carefully crossed the Planks, following his nose to the cook pits dug in the pasture where an entire buffalo roasted among other game and domestic meats. The buffalo had been cooking for two days already.

Informal contests were going on everywhere, without any prize other than the acclaim of one's peers. Wrestling, knife fighting, trick riding, archery, roping, passed the time until the qualifying races.

He felt the dervishes and the rug diviners staring at him from where they prepared for tomorrow's rites.

Hulaff found him there. "Come with me and take a look at the favorites, Young Wolf."

Those were the words of a born wagerer. Hearing them put Leon into a thoroughly comfortable and familiar state of mind. He grew up with the manners of the track, of horses, and betting.

There were thirteen races this afternoon and each of the three favorites were in a different one. They were Hengst's Catclaw, Kazimir's Dervish, and Black Blizzard, owned by Azal, a woman riding in the tail of the Scorpions' council representatives. Sepul had entered his Cayugan, and he wasn't in any of the heats with the favorites either.

"If Cayugan qualifies, tomorrow's going to be real interesting. Sepul's riding himself, like Hengst, Kazimir and Azal, but he's not in their class, though his horse is. This is going to be one real horse race," Hulaff said.

Hulaff went off to get one of his own horses so he'd a have good seat from which to see in the crowd.

Leon saw Glennys stride through the jostle of bodies surrounding the riders warming up their horses and putting their outfits in order. There were over a hundred hopefuls, which explained the need for qualifying preliminaries.

Glennys made her way over to the Scorpion rider. Her Black Blizzard had drawn the first race. Azal discarded her outwear.

A sleeveless black underjerkin revealed powerful muscles in her arms and shoulders. The heads and stingers of red and black scorpion tattoos running across her deltoids crawled over the tops of her shoulders.

"I like Azal and her Black Blizzard," Glennys said to Leon.

"More than Brecca's own child, Catclaw? More than your own brother and Chief?" Hengst asked in mock dismay. "How disloyal! But you've always had a weakness for the black ones, hey, Glenn?" he teased.

"We'll worry about divided interests tomorrow," Glennys said, serenely ignoring his jibe. "Blizzard's the only horse Azal has, unlike you or Kazimir or most of the contenders. In fact, Blizzard's just about all Azal's got. She grew up in the orphans' camp, and that's rough. She got him by keeping his mother alive during a very complicated foaling. The mare's owner gave her the colt as a skill respect gift. Yes, I like this one a lot. Much intelligence, guts, and bottom to her."

Her eyes snapped with excitement as she talked points of the contenders, mounts, and riders with Hengst. She looked about sixteen, and completely at ease. This was the first Glennys Eve, the one whose happiness was horses and everything to do with them, Leon thought. He felt a sense of mournfulness as she moved off to wish luck to other riders and their horses. He recognized there wasn't much room in the life of a leader for happiness.

Kazimir came up, leading Dervish, a bright bay four-year-old filly. "They're going to dump a lot of rocks on the field for Catclaw. He likes climbing better than galloping, from what I hear."

Hengst said, "He won last Solstice. Is that why you're riding a filly this time out? Hope Dervish will distract Cat tomorrow?"

Kazimir ran his fingers through Dervish's silky mane, a gentle, sensuous caress. "Dervish is the same color as Cameron, daughter of the Stallion Queen. Like Cameron, Dervish moves like the wind, she refuses to mate until she finds one worthy of her, and she carries Saquave in her heart. Smart bets will go on her."

A reek of Sidewinder invaded the circle. Sepul led Cayugan, a tough, big-jawed dun stallion. "You wear women's blinders, Kazimir, like too many Chiefs. The women's councils are blocking the winds of change. Since that one calling herself by the name of Stallion Queen arrived, their arrogance has become intolerable. But the wind blows nevertheless and one day it will be too strong for women's weaker strength to hold off."

A roll of drums and call of flutes created a scramble of people on foot and others on horseback rushing off to get positions along the ropes marking the track in the prairie meadow beyond the pasture. The first preliminary race was about to begin.

For Glennys's sake Leon was glad to see Black Blizzard come in first. He cheered Catclaw's victory wildly. Because there was a quality about Dervish that reminded him of Cameron, he applauded her win too. But it was all for the filly, not for Chief Kazimir. He had no joy at all watching Sepul strut about after Cayugan's qualification.

Afterwards he went to Jeremy to ask his advice. Muran used a cane to walk farther than the Hall. It was a long trek from the Big House to the pasture, and it was impossible for him to cross the swaying, narrow Planks.

There was a ford further down the River that patrollers used, when the spring cascade wasn't running. Jeremy had patrol duty that night. As often as Becky assured him that she was surrounded by friends and relatives, Jeremy fussed at great length over her going alone with three children to look after. The man therefore was very happy after Leon explained his problem.

Muran went to the pasture behind Becky, her daughter between them, on the long, swayed back of an old mare, the only horse Jeremy's lady would ride. Leon learned what it was like fording a river with two very rambunctious little boys riding behind him. One service in exchange for another, that was the Hometown way.

The women's wagons made a loose circle, with painted hides hanging between them to break the wind. Inside the circle were many fires, with carpets spread over the ground, liberally scattered with cushions.

Leon spent a good deal of the time he could have been eating, listening, and getting acquainted checking on the children's whereabouts. The girl was easy enough. She was where the women making music were.

Becky told Leon, "Thea insisted I shouldn't have any more children after Harl, who came after JerJer, was born. I wanted a daughter so much that we took the risk. I named her Delight, for she is that to her mother."

What a horrible thing to do to a child, Leon started to think. Then he caught sight of JerJer burrowing under the hide painted with Bat signs. It was closest to the River.

His heart thumped. He had visions which had never previously engaged him of a child lost, drowned, burned, or trampled. He jumped up and pulled the boy back, who kicked out and squealed like a pig going to slaughter.

Everyone had eaten so much that not enough people were ready to dance. "Konya!" the shout went up. "A story, Konya!"

The big woman had dressed her hair. The shorter lengths around her face stood out, the ends skillfully bleached and dyed to imitate the silver tips of a dowager badger. She was not one to eat too much. In one light spring she took the wagon's tailgates where the musicians had arranged themselves. Absently she stroked Delight's hair while making a short conference with the musicians.

During the palaver JerJer and Harl curled up, the younger in Becky's lap, the older next to Thea. Glennys and Hengst sat down with them, as did Stella and Deborah.

An oud played a series of sad, long notes, joined on a lower scale by several others. Tambourines jangled and divided the sweeter, higher notes of the flutes, forcing attention to lower ones of the ouds.

Konya took her place in front of the players. Her head was bowed. She raised it, revealing her hands placed one on top of the other before her high breasts. The silver hanging in her ears, and between her breasts, winked in the firelight.

"Noloani and Ableir," she announced.

Muran's hot breath tickled Leon's ear. "Please listen with all you've got, and remember what you hear, so we can compare. I'm going to write this down first chance."

Eve, after a hard labor, birthed two sons.

The first, whose name the tribes remember, was Ableir, was like any child of Eve, male or female. He was wild and gentle in turn, respecting all the animals above, on, and below Saquave, bending them to his will when appropriate, hunting them as needed. He was strong, as were all Eve's children.

He became pozeem in his time. Then he became Chief. He killed men when it was needful, sad though this was for him. But the tribes had increased and covered Saquave. Disputes over range and pasture would break out where there were so many persons who had good luck.

The other son, whose name the tribes remember, was Noloani. In every way Noloani was Ableir's equal. There was no significance to the circumstance that he came after Ableir. Eve found delight in him as much as Ableir. Women's eyes followed him as often as they followed Ableir. They were equal in everything, until Ableir was chosen Chief.

It was as difficult a decision choosing between them as it had been for the Stallion Queen to give birth to both at once. The council's only solution was to choose Ableir, for he entered Saquave first.

Noloani spent more of his time in the Wilderness. He found the places where other tribes' ranges met his. He challenged the Chiefs of other tribes for graze rights in those places, and he always won. For this he requested to be made Chief in place of Ableir.

No one wanted to do this.

Noloani killed Ableir, though no one knew that for a long time. He became Chief.

The pozeem of Eve's tribe divided, for their lives became exclusively that of a warrior. There was no time for herding, making songs, painting stones, or hunting. They had many women but they had no loving of woman or child.

Eve's pozeem drove out Noloani and made a new Chief. Noloani should be part of no tribe now, a no person. But many pozeem went with Noloani, and with them all the women who loved them, their children, and their things. They made a new tribe, the tribe of Noloani.

Their tribe grew, and became many other tribes of Noloani. They ate everything in the valley. They took our things. They killed many of us, all the time, for seeing the blood come from a person was their greatest delight. Many of the pozeem who preferred the way of Ableir joined Noloani, some from choice, others because they resembled Noloani too strongly and were driven out, as Noloani had been first.

Then Saquave forgot all us persons. We were not interesting. Volcanoes lived. The Rains went away. The river went away.

Noloani's people stopped being persons forever, now that there was no luck for anyone.

Ableir's persons came together in council. All the Stallion Queens were there. They said they'd take Noloani's people away from the Saquave, for there were too many of us all, Noloani's and ours, to live while Saquave was occupied with itself.

"Where will you take those others, Stallion Queens?" we asked. "We must know the boundaries between their range and ours."

"Over there," the Stallion Queens said, "across the Rain Shadows. It is Eve who brought this upon us, for only Stallion Queens make Noloani."

The people mourned. They had lost the Stallion Queens to Noloani.

The Stallion Queen Eve rode back in the night. "A shaman has said there is an important thing that you should hear. A dervish told him, and a rug diviner knotted it. A Stallion Queen will return. There will be a time, different than this, but as terrible. A Stallion Queen named Eve will come from over there to help you."

The Stallion Queens rode to Noloani's people. The men were of Noloani, but their stallions knew the Queens. They went away, over there, across the Rain Shadow Mountains. That is the boundary line. All the rest is Saquave, and it is Saquave's own, that which belongs under, on, and above Saquave. Anything else must go away.

Muran whispered, "Do you think this is a version of 'Noloani and Ableir' particularly tailored to this audience?"

Leon thought carefully. Something in Muran's question resembled what he would ask in certain lessons back in St. Lucien.

"It could be tailored for Sepul, of course. Or for their own Chiefs. Or for Glennys," he said.

He thought a little harder. "It could be pointed at me too, I think."

Muran rocked a little in excitement. "What a diplomat Konya is. I must remember this!"

A large variety of drinks were passed around and shared, but under them all Leon could taste Sidewinder. Muran stretched out, oblivious of it all, going over what he'd heard, fixing as much of it in his memory as he could.

The children, who'd been quiet long enough, were up and screaming, grabbing anything sweet offered from the wagons.

Just as the dancing began Cameron came to sit with them. She smelled as clean as a newly peeled willow wand, and of a scent that Leon would swear was perfume, if he thought there was any out here. Bats went first, and Cameron was asked to join them immediately. "Ronnie knows all the tribes' dances," Glennys said proudly.

Thea said, as the two of them got up to stroll about, "Cameron should know all the dances. You taught her."

Soon Leon realized that Becky wanted to go home. Muran wanted to leave also.

With difficulty he collected Jeremy's offspring, and herded his party under the hides to their horses. He was sure he'd drown at least two of the children going across the ford.

After putting up Jeremy's horses in the shed adjoining the workshop, he helped Muran hobble down to the Big House. "We've lessons to do," Muran declared joyfully.

The only warm, well-lighted place was the kitchen. With great respect Leon cleared a corner of cooling baked goods so they could have a place for the tutor to spread out a vellum scroll. Between them they reconstructed what they remembered of Konya's 'Noloani and Ableir' story. During that process they discussed the events of the day.

Muran's mind was snapping and crackling, making connections that illuminated the relationships of the tribes with each other and to Hometown.

"The checks and balances here are neat, natural, and powerful," he said. "Because the rains fall so erratically over here, the snowfalls in the Mountains vary year to year, no tribe can be dominant for too long, when a tribe's prosperity depends upon flocks and herds. Decisions governing trade and grazing are made in the women's councils, which make it difficult for the warrior hunters, the pozeem and the Chief, to plunge any tribe into warfare. When a Chief, like Sepul, has destroyed his tribe's council, he's shut out from what the other tribes share, and any assistance they may decide to give those who are having bad luck, because the councils only deal with each other in intertribal matters. Glennys must have instinctively mimicked those patterns."

Leon said, "She was well set up to do so. A prophecy among the tribes foretelling the return of a Stallion Queen, for one. Coming with her own Chief, one as war-experienced as Hengst, one that other Chiefs and pozeem recognize as manly as themselves, had to help, I think."

Muran thought for a while. He said, "So how can a refugee Leon from the brother-slaying Noloani, seeking a base from which he can claim the throne that is his by right, use this Saquave power? That's the task before you."

Leon said, "At the moment the task before me is breakfast shift. I would like to get a little sleep before then, if possible."

Under the compulsion of the savory, sweet odors surrounding them, Muran's fingers began to hover over a tray of honey pastries filled with dates.

Leon drew Muran's hand back. "Don't take even a crumb without asking somebody first. Food is freely shared, but stealing it is a hanging offense."

· Thirteen ·

WHILE LEON WAS shaving he heard a low whistle outside the hanging on their doorway. The Ranger, Captain Michaela, was outside. As the Captain spoke it gradually dawned on Leon that it was Muran in his professional capacity that was wanted, and that it was the Governor who wanted the tutor.

Without remorse he rousted Muran out of bed. "Glennys wants you to copy out the winners of yesterday's races for the messenger pigeons she's sending off to the SSC forts and stations, so they can wager too. You're going to do the same this afternoon after the big race."

Leon took pleasure at the sight of Muran's heavy-lidded eyes and the bristle of his heavy beard. Since Muran chose last night to resume his tutorial position, Leon never got to dance with Cameron, as he'd promised.

Hatice cocked an eye when Leon stumbled into the kitchen. "A man of his word. A few cuts on your face from shaving, but you're clean, and you're here."

Breakfast, the preparation and serving of it, was given short shrift this morning. Hatice and Deborah chivvied everyone out of the Hall as fast as possible. Latecomers were out of luck.

Leon was set to heavy lifting and carrying. First they dismantled the trestle table in the Hall, then set up as many smaller tables and shorter benches as could be fit in. Tables were also put up on the veranda and down in the little square where the Rambles converged upon the Big House. The inner courtyard adjoining the Hall was filled with tables too.

After that, Leon's bunch followed Deborah to the storerooms

many times where their arms were filled with heavy table coverings. He learned everything he never knew about the difficulties, and the skills, of laundering tablecloths after a banquet.

He pushed one wheelbarrow, borrowed from latrine duty, after another to the Big House from the lumber yard up the Ridge. Rangers were doing heavy duty in the sawyer pits.

It took four hands to keep the barrow on keel coming down. His partner, Ricold, told him that Rangers chopped down trees all this last summer in the Mountains so there would be enough seasoned wood, not only for the winter, but for Solstice Jubilee.

"There's some as think the Governor shouldn't pay out to the tribes at Solstice Jubilee, since they insist on hosting a feast in return. We're the ones that provide the firewood as hosts," Ricold said.

"What do you think about it?" Leon gasped, manhandling the stinking barrow down the Ridge.

"Saquave likes its children to have fun. The Wilderness folks don't have to join us. They've got their own celebrations out on their home ranges. But like us, some of them enjoy fresh faces," he said, giving Leon a friendly grin.

Ricold wore heavy gauntlets. "This work must be blistering your hands," he said.

When they braced the barrow before the last turn down the Rambles, Leon showed him his hands, thick with calluses and scars.

"Saquave gave me its own gauntlets," Leon said. "Good thing too, since I don't have any others."

Ricold said, "A man at least needs gloves to dance properly. Like I said, the tribes, and that's us too, the Snakes, know how to have a good time. You should dance."

When Hatice declared there was enough wood, it was noon, and he still hadn't eaten breakfast. Like the others he gobbled what was left for them in a manner too reminiscent of the bad days wandering in the Wilderness. He forced himself to slow down.

"Now that you've eaten, I suppose breakfast shift is relieved of duty," Hatice announced to her crew, it seemed reluctantly.

She nodded when he asked for hot water to clean himself up.

He wasn't cold after all those hours of labor. He stripped to the waist, and took off his buskins in order to wash his feet.

There was another whistle outside the door. Thinking it was Hatice, Leon flung aside the hanging, wishing she'd thought of another job before he'd washed.

Hatice's eyes widened at the sight of Leon's wetly gleaming scarred torso, trews clinging below his navel, and strong arm holding the hanging against the doorway. Due to her hump, the lift of the threshold, and his own height, Hatice felt very small.

Hatice turned to Hengst, whose arms were laden. "Good thing you volunteered to help me instead of one of the girls."

Hengst kissed Hatice on the cheek. "Everyone receives gifts during Solstice banquet. Hatice thought you would enjoy seeing yours a little early."

They pressed clothes upon him. A fringed jacket came from Glennys herself. Jeremy sent boots, Becky, a long earring of twisted silver set with turquoise stones and coral. There was a pair of soft trousers from Hatice matching the Governor's jacket, and three shirts beautifully embroidered with Stella's work. Deborah had contributed socks. A beaded belt with a sheath that fit his longest knife finished the outfit.

Hengst said, "I tried to trade the Wolf council for the sheath," he said. "When they found out for whom it was intended they insisted on gifting it to the Young Wolf."

Hatice said, "Ricold, an apprentice to Jeremy, wants you to have these."

Ricold had given him a pair of thin, flexible gloves, beautifully sewn, with cuffs ample enough to cover his wrists. Such generosity from one who, if he also worked for Hatice and Deborah, couldn't be very prosperous, brought tears to Leon's eyes.

He stammered his gratitude. "So much kindness, from so many, overwhelms me. I can't wear all these things right away. Just one of these beautiful shirts for the race. I'm pulling for Catclaw, Sir."

Cheerfully, Hengst said, "I need all the luck wishes I can get. Glenn's counting Cat out because of condition, and his rider out because of stupidity. The Governor's not letting me forget that I didn't send a pigeon from the sheep station, and lost three horses by taking the canyon shortcut."

Hatice said, "Hengst, allow this man to get decent instead of begging his sympathies for your bad judgment."

Disregarding entirely the chill of his rapidly drying body, Leon spread out his gifts on Muran's bed, which he'd made up as taught in the Equine Academy.

He pulled one of the shirts over his head, the one Stella had embroidered with emblematic representations of the thirteen tribes. His fingers trembled a little as he removed the garnet, sign of the Eidel Kings of Nolan, from his ear. He replaced it with the earring that represented nothing but the handiwork of Hometown.

The shirt was homespun, the embroidery threads of cotton. He felt resplendent. Hatice had said he was a man, twice.

The race course had changed since yesterday. Others besides himself had been laboring all morning. The track was broken with jumps and obstacles. The first one was a rock slide.

A horse bored through the press of people around him, the rider's hand outstretched. "Come ride with me, Leon," Cameron caroled.

He got up behind Cameron. The feel of her supple waist moving in his hands made it difficult to breathe easily.

Her horse shoved through the crowd, past the slide. Ahead of them was Glennys, mounted upon a young grey stallion. Under her direction other riders planted flags by each obstacle and took up positions all the way around the course.

"There's been no rain since the Day of the Dead. Dust will fly, obscuring the distant field and turn from us here at Home. The flaggers ride back, tell us what happens. It's a good way of learning who has talent for the Flying Companies. It's a big responsibility. I know, I've done it. You've got to see and hear accurately, and pass on the information clearly and quickly, while riding like loco. When the last horse still running makes the turn, wagering freezes. But those still on track must take the obstacles again to get back Home. So anything can happen up to the last minute," Cameron told him.

Leon's blood was running fast, not only from the feel of Cameron under his hands. Race fever had him, like everyone else. More than anything he wanted to be part of the course.

"What's the prize?" Leon asked.

Cameron said, "Four fillies of Brecca's get, a cask of date wine from the Big House, and a pair of Becky's silver spurs. Winner takes all. If a mare wins, like Dervish, it's three fillies and a colt. If someone rides for another, the owner splits according to his or her own interpretation of fairness."

The prize was rich, especially for someone like Azal or Sepul. Or himself, Leon thought. He might get mounted, riding for someone else. But he couldn't afford to wait until next year to get a horse of his own.

He ached to bet, but had nothing to wager but the gifts he'd received that morning. No gentleman would stoop so low as to back his bets with free-given gifts.

"Which one are you backing?" he asked Cameron.

She answered, "Any win, except Sepul's, will be good for the Valley."

She added thoughtfully, "Sepul's loss might drive him closer to the Alaminites, may their bones rot, or maybe, if he's smart, and the Elks are lucky, force him to recognize the authority of the Elks women's council."

Leon's blood surged. She hadn't declared for Kazimir in particular. The way she stiffened whenever he moved his grasp from her waist up higher suggested Cameron had yet to bed anyone. She had other qualities though, that were nearly as exciting to him as awakened sensuality, such as a deep understanding of Saquave politics.

The thirteen were up at the Home line. Peremptorily, Cameron removed his hands altogether.

They were off, in a full-career break of speed in a calculated approach to the rocks, each rider's strategy to scramble up first. The slide's footing was extraordinarily insecure, as it had been in place only an hour or two, so there'd been little settling.

Cat struck the rocks first and took them in three leaps, all four hooves grabbing like claws in wood. From the top Cat made one long spring to the open track between the slide and the next obstacle.

Second was Cayugan, who walked deliberately up the rocks, choosing each step. Dervish's hooves spun on the tumbling surface, as she danced at speed next to Cayugan. Yet Cayugan made it to the top in hardly less time than Kazimir's filly.

Beaver and Crow contestants collided on the upside, one galloping recklessly, the one ahead stepping delicately. The whole edifice was rolling and clattering. A Coyote horse broke its foreleg jimming down the other side. The race had barely begun and three were out.

Blizzard cut to the off side, where the slide was low. He jumped over without ever climbing at all, picking up speed and ground at once.

It was a good decision only if Blizzard was able to catch up with the others, and keep the pounding pace that making up ground forced on him.

Halfway up the track Dervish and Cayugan were closing in on Cat. A Ranger, riding another filly named Silver Leaf, was coming up from the outside, Blizzard trailing, but ahead of the rest. The five behind disappeared after the others into the dust kicked up by the front runners, and Home could see nothing at all.

The flag riders raced now, galloping back to keep Home abreast. A stallion named Echo, under a Bat rider, had broken out of the back runners. A Gazelle's stallion was down, knees broken, tangling the brush-and-ditch jump for the others.

A flagger tore up to Home. "The turn," she announced, "the turn! Cat ahead, Dervish and Cayugan neck and neck and tail to Cat, Silver Leaf on the outside, Blizzard trailing, Echo coming up, the rest nowhere! Freeze bets, freeze bets!"

Some minutes later a roar of disappointment went up from the Rangers. Cat had lost his lead. Little by little Dervish and Cayugan pulled ahead. Silver Leaf passed Cat, then shortened the distance between her, Dervish, and Cayugan.

At the same time that Hengst decided there was no reason to keep Cat in the rest of the race at punishing speed when there was no hope of winning, Echo's rider pulled up the Bat stallion for the same reason.

Blizzard was still gathering momentum, only a length behind the three front runners. Everyone at Home could see them now. The Rangers screamed. Silver Leaf still gave them a chance.

The rock slide loomed ahead, not as steep on this approach because the start had brought so much of it down. Rocks and stones, however, had scattered in all directions, and therefore it was equally dangerous getting Home. There was no way for Blizzard to use the same strategy as before.

They could hear the harsh, bellowing gasps of breath from the horses under the thunder rolls of their hooves.

At the first touch of his hooves upon the rocks Cayugan threw up his head, and wisely decided to slow down. Sepul tried to force him back to speed, but the stallion refused.

Dervish and Silver Leaf also slowed stride by stride as they covered the treacherous footing.

Behind, Azal asked more speed from Blizzard. He gave it to her, passing the balked Cayugan, then pulling ahead of Dervish, coming even with Silver Leaf.

Blizzard speared the air with his red-flared nostrils, drank air in great gulps. He lifted over the rocks and stones, scrambling them with the force of his passing, like his namesake, driven by the wind.

Blizzard and Azal crossed Home a length ahead of Silver Leaf, and three lengths ahead of Dervish.

The stallion was mostly red mud from the sandy soil mixed with sweat, lather, and blood from scratches and gouges from the thorns in the brush-and-ditch obstacle. Azal's nostrils streamed bright red blood. Either a stone had flown up and hit her, or it was the velocity of her ride. Her gloves were cut through by the reins. By nightfall her arms would be a mass of bruises, her face covered with lumps and bumps.

The winning horse and rider disappeared from sight under the press of the congratulatory crowd. Cameron twisted in the saddle and beat her fists on Leon's chest.

"The winning rider's a woman, who came up with no family behind her, the runner-ups are both fillies, and the second placer a Snake! A great race, fair and square too, no questioning this year what the flaggers told Home. A great, great race!" she screamed in Leon's ear.

Unceremoniously, she slid out of the saddle and ran to lend her shoulder to Azal's triumphal hoist.

Leon was left in the saddle of Cameron's horse, and was glad to be there. It was pandemonium on the ground, and nothing to do with him.

The girl children under puberty were taunting the boys in their age group. Even Delight had come out of her dreamy otherworld.

The six-year-old turned in a circle by herself away from the others. She clapped her hands softly and chanted to the percussion she provided herself.

> "The girls went running,
> And the boys fell behind.
> A girl came second,

A girl came third,
The girls rode 'em down."

There was so much power out here it made Leon yearn to put it under direction, his direction.

With a touch and a breath Glennys greeted Cameron's gelding, Sarissa.

"You think with a few thousand of these at your back you can take St. Lucien and get the crown safely on your head. Please bury such ideas. None of Saquave will go over there."

Leon looked down at her. "Nolan will come over here, though. The SSC is a company with deep investors, and a colony of the throne, illegal at that. Over there, Justin Sharp, speaking for himself and the Fortune Houses, instructed Muran to investigate the investment."

Glennys said, "Muran is welcome to look at our accounting scrolls, and see those parts of the storerooms where the SSC keeps the investors' shares. The investors may be disappointed, but by Saquave's lights, they hold great wealth. It's what we have. I'm not afraid of the investors. And we're a fact now, illegal or not. So Nolan would deal, except for one other overwhelming fact. *You*. What will we do with you?"

He didn't know the answer.

She threw up her head then, catching something in the air. "Please give me Cameron's Sarissa, Sir. I have need."

Glennys was on Sarissa before Leon had his foot out of the stirrup.

She inserted Sarissa into the mob. "Elk pozeem, Elks! Separate your Chief from Cayugan before one kills the other! That stallion deserves all respect for running an honest hard race, not a beating."

Sepul and Cayugan bloodied several Elk pozeem. They were forced to put Chief and stallion under rope constraint in order to separate them.

Leon noticed that the SSC Governor, instead of interfering personally in this internal affair of Elk honor, rode through the mass and kissed Azal's battered visage.

"Excuse my withdrawal, but I must send dispatches of your great race to our other people whose duties keep them from joining in your victory," she announced. "Muran, where are you?" she called.

Leon pushed his way to Sarissa. He put his hand on the Governor's thigh to get her attention. She looked down at him.

"Muran's up at the House. Any sort of horse race bores him past endurance," Leon told her.

She dropped her hand over his, where it still rested on her warm, hard muscles, as acknowledgment, and rode off to the Planks.

Preparations for clearing the race track had begun. Leon carefully removed his shirt and pitched in. Before they finished, the night patrollers were gathering their horses.

He and Ricold worked together. "Who is in charge of the Valley patrols?" Leon asked.

"Colonel Wheatly Lubbock and Captain Michaela," Ricold said. He volunteered the information that Wheatly Lubbock was his father.

"My distance vision is so poor I can't hit a target unless standing right in front of it, or ride anywhere at night unless the horse knows the territory. As Wheatly has one eye and a bad arm, he can't see why my vision handicaps me. But it's all right. The close work leather requires, and work calling for a strong back, keep me out of trouble."

That morning all fires, except those in the Big House kitchen and Hall, had been put out. Chimneys and outdoor cook ovens had been cleaned before the race. When the dancing began, bonfires would be set from the Hall's fireplace. At dawn, Hometown's cleaned hearths would be rekindled from the bonfires.

Muran, catching a pre-feast nap in his warm bed, heard Leon swearing softly in the dark as he tried to bathe in cold water and put on his new clothes.

"Between you and Glennys, a man can't catch up on his sleep. You shouldn't complain about a little dark and cold. This dousing of fires is a practical ritual for Winter Solstice, since there's no one tending private ones in Hometown tonight," Muran instructed.

Food, celebration, closely packed bodies, and the Hall's roaring fireplace warmed up everyone. Little by little all the careful placing of tables and seating arrangements changed. People moved tables and benches to suit themselves. Many, like Glennys and Hengst, never perched anywhere for long.

The children shrieked, "The Bogeyman, the Bogeyman." The littlest ran to bury their heads in laps.

The Bogeyman carried a sack over one shoulder, and leaned on a very long crutch. It was a grotesquely tall figure with half a face that smiled and half that frowned.

The sack had gifts and sweeties. On the Bogeyman's first pass through the Hall, Leon rejoiced to see that JerJer and Harl not only received acorns, as Stella had threatened the night before last, but a few nicely placed whacks with the crutch. On another pass, though, the boys, displaying immense remorse, promised better behavior in the future, and please, could they have some?

The Bogeyman came and went mysteriously in the smoky din of the Hall, but a pattern of gift-giving emerged.

Toys and clothing went to the poorest-looking children, many of whom were missing one or both birth parents. Older members of Hometown who were without families, or families with bad luck, received tools and implements to help develop skills and interests they'd displayed during the year.

Gifts were also presented to those who were able to provide for themselves and their own. Hengst got a messenger pigeon. Glennys, who never sewed even a square for a quilt, was given needle and thread. Deborah got a small jar of honey, which everyone understood was a comment upon her disposition. Captain Michaela, who brought dogs into the House, received a neat package of dog turds. Except for Deborah, these recipients laughed at least as hard as everyone else. Becky and Jeremy, however, only looked bewildered when presented with a paddle and two sets of hobbles. Everyone else hooted uproarious appreciation.

In another pass through the Hall the Bogeyman tugged a two-part cage cart behind him. A small, pregnant sow squealed indignantly, joined by the gobbling of a turkey cock and hen. The cart came to a stop in front of Chief Sepul.

Cameron was flirting with both Kazimir and Leon at that moment. "That is a bad move," Cameron said. "Making fun of our shortcomings is good, but this time the Bogeyman's gone too far."

Kazimir said, "That's not the Valley's Bogeyman. That's my mother on the stilts. Laughing at bad luck, which comes to us all sooner or later, is something Konya knows Sepul cannot do. She should have known better."

Sepul stood up. "First the witch puts a word on Cayugan to make him throw the race. Now she insults me in her own kurgan during the gift of salt. I challenge her Chief. His blood will cleanse the Elks' dishonor."

Hengst had been sharing a large jug of unmixed date wine with several laughing women. He went to stand at Glennys's side.

Konya stripped off her mask and came down from the stilts. "Accept my apologies, Chief Sepul, for my poor judgment. I mistakenly had tried to save your honor, not insult you. You requested pigs and turkeys. These were gifted to me, and in turn, I gifted them to you."

Sepul never took his eyes from Hengst. "Men do not recognize the words of interfering, underhanded women. Challenge, Snake Chief."

Sepul kicked tables and benches away.

Playing for time in which Sepul might cool off, Glennys assumed the position that said she was going to make a speech.

"The rain is in Saquave's breath, not that of Saquave's Stallion Queen, who cannot dishonor horsekind by throwing a race. Cayugan behaved as Cayugan does. He is a stallion that takes his rider safely to the tops of mountains, time and again, under heavy saddle, carrying gear, and comes down again, packed with the meat and racks of elks, and carrying his honored rider, Elk Chief Sepul. Everyone recognizes no stallion is finer on rocks and inclines than Cayugan. And everyone knows that Cayugan, wise as horses are wise, never gallops on rocks when he feels no necessity from fear or danger. Only a rider can unwise a horse to be so foolish, and only if the horse consents. Cayugan did not consent to his rider's unwisdom, as Blizzard consented to Azal's. The Stallion Queen says the Snake's Chief hears no challenge."

Konya immediately filled the silence that followed Glennys's words.

"Please, Chief Kazimir, give this jar of date wine to the Elk Chief Sepul, on behalf of this befuddled old woman, who has burdened you with her motherhood. Together, drink her foolishness away."

Alternately Konya babied Sepul, and humbled herself on the

anvil of his masculine pride to save Glennys's Jubilee. As soon as Kazimir took the wine, she removed the sow and turkeys, and herself, from Sepul's sight.

With a glance from Kazimir, Hulaff gathered Sepul's pozeem. Badger and Elk men went outside to drink together, and to rank the idiocy of women who weren't able to hold their liquor.

Before the men were out the door, Cameron called, "Cousin Delight, I need you to shake your new tambourine and help me teach our new friend how to do the Snake Dance."

Delight's eyes lived up to her name. "Oh, yes, Cousin Ronnie."

"We got to teach this boy to *dance!*" Cameron announced loudly. "Come on, JerJer, Harl. Show Leon what the boys do. Can't somebody clear this lumber out of my way?" she demanded.

Instantly the tables and benches Sepul had kicked over were righted and moved back.

Cameron and the boys did indeed teach him the Snake Dance, and incidentally, gave the Hall back its festival spirit. The boys were very hard on Leon, paying him back for last night.

Later, when the dancing started in earnest, and Glennys made the calls, Leon was ready.

> "Rattles on their bohotchies,
> Diamond Back Jimm now slither,
> Now crawl along the log!
> All you lady snakes join in,
> And squirm around the bog.
> Rub your scales together,
> But don't you shed your skins!
> Oh, the music is a'sighin',
> Oh, it's wailin' in the Hall.
> It's gettin' mighty lively here
> At the Snake's ole Jubilee Ball!"

Leon rattled his bohotchie, and lowered it to the floor. His pelvis crawled up against his lady Snake with admirable enthusiasm. His hot tongue flickered with the most versatile lewdness.

> "Snakes do it the kitchen,
> Snakes do it the Hall,
> Oh, them slippery Snakes,
> They do it anywhere at all!"

Though he lost Cameron to others, she frequently returned
to his arms. The Sidewinder, neat and burning, came round and
round. And when it came time for the other dances Leon was
never wanting a partner to guide him through the first time.

Much, much later he found himself dancing in a line on
the swaying, creaking Planks. Dancing among the wagons,
he caught a glimpse of Glennys sitting among the spinning
dervishes and the rug diviners. They were staring at him.

Cameron was his partner. It was the Wolf Dance. Leon
alternately licked her eyelids and swallowed more Sidewinder.
Then Cameron was swept off into the pack.

He sank upon his haunches and threw up his head to howl
the Wolf chorus. Getting back to his feet took a little time.
The pack swirled around Cameron. He was alone.

He stumbled over to Glennys and the diviners. His tongue
flickered.

"I am a Snake. I am a Wolf. I am everything. I know what's
in store for me all right. I'm going to wash tablecloths with
Deborah. But not tonight."

There was the parade through the Rambles, and the relight-
ing of fires.

The last thing he remembered clearly was sitting in the Hot
Springs, surrounded by bare-breasted women. Cameron was
certainly one of them. Wasn't she? He held out a palm. Steam
flickered like snake tongues in the cold air.

He thought he remembered holding Cameron's head while
she sicked up Sidewinder, date wine, and honey pastries.

He woke up surrounded by bodies, a carpet or two, and
some cushions. There was a lot of hay. It took him some time
to figure out they were in the stables.

Getting out of there taught him why they called it Sidewinder.

· Fourteen ·

GAUGING BY THE bit of sky he could see, snow was going to fall again upon Fort Cloud. Leon was colder than he'd ever known a person could get, and not be laid out in a burial kurgan. He wore several pairs of Deborah's wool socks inside his clumsy brogans, but his feet felt no more sensation than ice did.

He tugged on the line, then rested against the rock. The bucket filled with rock fragments went up, an empty bucket came down.

Leon took off his gloves and warmed his hands in the heat coming from a smoking butt of creosote. The things a man would do to prove himself good enough to be a Ranger and earn horses of his own.

He squinted out tears against the fumes gathered in the hole. He ran his fingers against the rock wall. He yelled, "My grandma's big titties!"

Yes, indeed, there was a webbing of lines here telling him of a cluster of natural faults in the rock.

He put on his gauntlets, picked up chisel and hammer, and went back to work with enormous will, opening and expanding those natural flaws and cracks. After he'd opened them deep enough, at the right plane and angle, he'd pack them with mud. When the mud froze and expanded, so would the faults.

They called it bridge building. In those droning afternoon lectures and calculations he'd endured at the Equine Academy, before Muran's evening tuition in more elegant subjects at home in the palace, *they* called it engineering. What it was,

was labor worthy of a chain gang, and taking about as much training.

Though Sharissa had sent him off on this wild goose chase before he'd finished the Academy's courses, he had learned the rudiments of trigonometry, geometry, algebra, and, more deeply, the rules of arithmetic.

Exactly the argument Hengst had used with the Governor when Captain Michaela and Colonel Lubbock told them Leon had requested Valley patrol duty. They needed bridges so reinforcements could reach Fort Cloud faster. The Snake's course forced two crossings in the mountains before reaching the Fort. Leon had the great good fortune to arrive in Fort Cloud the year work started on the first of two bridges. This winter's big project was to sink holes in the rock for the trusses' foundation.

"Listen to what he's told me," Hengst had urged them, "and remember, I went through the Academy myself. Our disastrous Nemourian Mountain campaign, in the wake of the assassination of Leon's father, forced the Academy war horses to learn new tricks. They teach mountain bridge building now. Let's use what the boy learned. He can join the Rangers as a novice under me, and be taken out of your hair, Glenn."

That was Hengst's brilliant argument, done on behalf of the Young Wolf, as he confided to Leon on the winter ride up to the Hammers with the winter rotation of Rangers. Leon envisioned himself with planes and triangles, seated at a desk, making calculations, overseeing others carry out his ideas. There had been very little calculation, at least on his part. Instead he broke frozen rock with the strength of his body.

Like young soldiers of any time and place, he boasted he was stranded in the armpit of the universe, pulling mean, hard duty. Leon cursed his superiors, long, loudly, deeply, and sincerely, if not imaginatively.

The cursing had nothing to do with the bone-deep conviction that he'd gladly protect Chief Hengst's back, or stand in front of him as a human shield. The cursing had nothing to do with the fact that he was going to give, to the last breath in his body, everything he had to make this the best bridge ever built.

"Ho!" he shouted up. "Is this snow going to be only another dump out of the mountain's ass or a real storm?"

All light from above was cut off. Bari, a huge, enormously strong woman, shouted down.

"A dump, after supper, I think," Bari told him.

"Then I'd like to keep at this ball-buster until the shadows skate across Lake Umbel's ice, if you agree. Good lines here to pack with mud."

Bari's girth descended the ladder. Leon ascended a few rungs to leave room for her examination of the stone. She accepted his assessment.

She said, "I'm going to tour the other pits now, before going in. Learn if we've the luck to have the rock be the same in them, and webbed with the same faults, at the same level, as you've discovered in this hole."

He worked in solitude, silence and cold, losing all track of time down in first site, pit number one. Then Bari returned.

She called down, "We got new faces here. From Hometown. Came up the trail not long ago."

Leon said, "So what? We'll be as sick of them as we are of everybody else in no time."

Bari and Leon were the last of the Rangers to flounder over the icy ruts that twined up from the bridge site to the Fortress trail. One day those ruts, and the trail, would be a road, bending and winding, broad enough for six-wheeled wagons, as well as horses and pack mules.

The brief, mountain winter daylight had long gone by the time Bari and Leon sighted the gatehouse's beacon torches. They clumped over the drawbridge as fast their frostbitten feet would carry them to put the stone ramparts between them and the wind.

The mountain wind was razor-edged as a sabre blade sharpened by Evart, Bari's man, himself. He was Fort Cloud's cutler as well as blacksmith and farrier. Bari went on to the forge, Leon into the gatehouse.

Bari was a stone mason, equal in bulk and strength to her husband. Over there, in Nolan, she'd owned a quarry. She was her family's only child, and she'd grown up with stone. Before buying the quarry, her father had been a mason. Soon after his death, the quarry had been underhandedly wrested from her by a powerful Wheel banker.

Always a large woman, at that time she was also beautiful. A bunch of King's Guards had deliberately destroyed her physical beauty over a period of days. After she picked the locks of her manacles and gotten free, Bari killed three of her captors.

Bari and Evart came together during the SSC Crossing. They stayed at Fort Cloud through all rotations of duty, year after year, raising Evart's sons born in Nolan, and a second family, in their private quarters behind the forge. Hengst's authority over anything within the walls and ramparts of Fort Cloud was complete and final, but the walls and ramparts belonged to Bari and Evart.

Blue and white with cold, barely able to make his fingers work, Leon took off his engineering clothes and left them on the gatehouse floor. He hunched on a bench a safe distance from the fire to thaw out.

Feeling returned in agonizing degrees to his hands and feet. It was a matter of pride not to show it, and as soon as possible, hang his mud-encrusted coveralls on the pegs, and change the brogans for boots. The gatehouse kept hot water for the Rangers returning from their work down at the site. He carefully put his hands and feet into the water and washed up before heading to the mess hall in the keep.

Poppy red, tiger lily orange, and dandelion yellow flames streamed their colors briefly out of the smithy over the stones of the inner ward. Someone had gone in. Even from this distance he could hear Bari whoop with glee at the visitor. Exhaustion and cold took up all the room in him where curiosity would have been.

He grunted. A Ranger who'd pulled duty inside the rampart walls gave up a chair near one of the roaring fires in mess. Leon's red eyes, still running from the creosote fumes trapped inside his pit, closed before he finished settling into the cushions.

He fell into a stupor vacant of anything except a wish for a hot beaker of yarrow tea. Wrestling mountain rock all day left him good for nothing else until after supper.

His wish came true. Someone wrapped his limp fingers around a hot beaker.

"Open my mouth and pour it down my throat please? And swallow for me, would you?" he requested drowsily.

"A neat trick, that. You'll have to teach me," his benefactor said.

Leon's eyelids popped open. "Cameron, what are you doing here?"

She quirked her lips. "Why is it 'what are you doing here' instead of 'how wonderful to see you here,' and 'how kind you are to join us here'?"

Heat and vitality had surged back into him the moment he heard her voice. The dim illumination and her winter wear made it ticklish to determine such things, but she looked drawn and nervous, quite different from her Solstice self.

"How did you get here?" he asked stupidly.

She lifted an eyebrow in the manner he remembered from Solstice. "On horseback, silly, how else? On a young stallion, trained by Glennys Eve herself, Stallion Queen, or as others not so far from here say, witch. Trained, she assures everyone, especially with me in mind to nurture my burgeoning Horse Sense."

He must have looked as puzzled as he felt.

"Oh, don't get me wrong. Mirage is magnificent. Carries more Saquave blood than the three-quarter Saquave Brecca, the stinking old billy goat himself, carries. Mirage is out of three generations of Brecca's daughters. There is a big difference though. Mirage's rider is only a Stallion Queen's fosterling, not another!"

She settled on cushions at his side. She said with soft amazement, "I'd planned to leave Mirage down there, but hard as I tried he refused to be given back. Or I couldn't give him up. One or the other, damn her. *She*'s determined to make me into another of *her*. I won't have it, you hear? I don't have Horse Sense!"

Leon shook his head. "I apologize for not following this. But I don't understand much of anything before supper call when I've been breaking mountain all day."

The other Cameron came back, the one he could understand.

"Why don't you pray to Alam, then? The Alaminites swear prayers move mountains," she suggested mockingly.

That was the Cameron he liked.

"So what are you doing up here? It was your first Solstice Jubilee in Hometown in three years. Which, you did say, was your reason for getting sick drunk, if I recall, which I can't swear. On my honor as a gentleman," he finished.

Even in the high-raftered mess hall that ate all light, he saw her blush.

Hengst ambled over to them. Both of them got to their feet and saluted the Chief.

He kissed Cameron heartily on both cheeks.

"Ronnie," Hengst said, indicating they were to be at ease, and this was friendly, not official. The broadly egalitarian manners of Hometown didn't apply in Fort Cloud. "What are you doing here?"

Cameron pulled her hair. "You too, uncle! I already told you when reporting in. Dispatches had to go up. It's too cold now for pigeons. Hometown felt closed in, so I volunteered to be another guard for the Flying Company's rider, and requested another Fort Cloud tour."

Hengst said, "You expect me to believe that? Last winter all you talked about was how much you looked forward to Hometown, the Valley, and riding the open ranges with Glennys, and how you liked the mountains no more than she."

Cameron said sharply, "I am *not* like the Stallion Queen! I wanted to have a mountain spring, which is beautiful, instead of a Saquave one, which is hideous. The only way a Ranger earns mountain spring is by winter tour. I requested it from Captain Michaela and Colonel Lubbock."

Hengst said, "I'm surprised the Governor consented, even if Michaela and Wheatly did. She looked forward to visiting the tribes this winter with you on your leave. She must have been very disappointed."

Cameron said, "Oh, you know. I had Thea talk to her. What would *she* do without Thea to show her how to mimic human behavior? Then the Governor gave me a horse that she believed would change my mind. That's her solution to everything."

Hengst's laughter was short, slight, and forced. "That's Glennys all right, but whoa! Up here she's the Governor, not your mother, so she's not to be spoken of without respect. If she thinks you have Horse Sense, you likely do."

Cameron said quietly, "My mother died a long time ago, and she was no Stallion Queen."

"Glennys's mother is no Stallion Queen either. She didn't have the tribes to help her learn how to use it either. If they'd consulted me in this, I'd have refused your request. Four winters in a row up here is no good for anyone your age except those in Evart and Bari's quarters," Hengst said.

Disapproval of his niece showed in every line of his body as he left them.

Supper call.

A savory fish stew was on the boards, heavily laced with the dried hot peppers of the Valley. The fish had been caught that day from holes cut in the ice of Lake Umbel. An elk had been shot a few days back and put up to hang. Roasts had simmered slowly until they fell apart in a sauce made from the same peppers as in the fish stew, and thickened with cornmeal. Peppers were in everything, even infused in the Sidewinder that went around in ponies during the meal, though never before or after. There was no cornbread tonight, nothing honied. But there were steaming bowls of sweet-sour cabbage and rehydrated pumpkin.

Leon wondered if he'd ever eat rice, potatoes, or wheat bread, have the pleasure of mulled wine when he was cold, or cold ale when he was hot, again. Instantly he buried such thoughts as less than useless, and gave his attention to available pleasures.

"Cameron, come and sit next to me," he suggested.

"Glad to," she said.

Hengst, on his way to his canopied chair at the head of his table, stopped. He put a hand on Cameron's shoulder.

"You've forgotten, Lieutenant Cameron Eve, the tables at this end belong to novice Rangers. You find another place in the middle, all right?" he ordered very quietly.

As the winter progressed Leon was frequently excused from breaking rock to hunt. The perimeters of Fort Cloud had been fairly cleaned out in the years since it first began going up, and hunters had to go further and further afield. By mid-winter game was wary and scarce. Every night they heard the wolf packs howling.

Wolves didn't intimidate Leon. Unlike many of the others, Leon quickly became skilled going on foot, snowshoe and ski, rather than horseback, which was impossible in the mountain snow. Everyone warned him, however, that his abilities were nothing compared to those of the Alaminites, who seemed to have been born in snow, wearing skis.

Wisely, like everyone else, he was wary of Alaminites. They were uncanny mountain trackers. They seldom closed hand-to-hand, preferring to set off explosions and bury a hunting party alive in an avalanche.

During quiet, windless drops of snow, they'd send fire arrows against Fort Cloud's ramparts. That was of less use these days, now that all the half-timbered walls had been replaced by stone.

But they had a quiver of tricks, all of them nasty. Other than the keep, the buildings within the ward were timber. Many a night the Rangers were blown out of bed to fight fires while the snow fell so thickly they couldn't see the buckets passed along the line from the wells.

Fort Cloud's position was very strong, however, built upon a cliff promontory protected by Lake Umbel on three sides, and Bari and Evart's handiwork. So the Alaminites preferred to concentrate on the Rangers. It was a terrible thing when a Ranger didn't return from outside the walls. Had there been an accident? Had the Ranger fallen to an animal? Or had the Ranger been taken by a party of Alaminite Coals of the Lord?

Ranger women sent them into a frenzy of hunting perseverance. The Coals of the Lord and the Prophets who led them could not bear the knowledge that a woman carried weapons and knew how to use them, and lived under equal discipline with fighting men, subordinate to no masculine order but that of her superior, who might possibly be another woman. Such a being was unnatural. Such a being must be destroyed whenever discovered.

The Alaminite frenzy justified Hengst's own reluctance to take women into Fort Cloud, though he knew there was no choice. He didn't want female members of the Flying Company riding dispatches up to him. He refused to allow women to hunt at all.

That was one reason he was unhappy to see Cameron this winter.

Another reason, Leon soon discovered, was himself. He and Cameron were never assigned any duties that brought them together. They never saw each other except during storms, or after supper, when everyone inside the walls or not keeping watch came together in mess hall.

There are no songs sung, or tales told, of a woman who agreed with her friends when they declared her suitor unsuitable. But stories teach that a young man and a young woman can fall in love without seeing each other, or even speaking. These two were not running under that handicap.

Leon was popular with the others. He had a supply of new card games to play with painted leather stiffened with bark. He was better than any of the younger Rangers using his weapons during practice, or in earnest. He was a fine rider. Any hunting party that included him came back with a bag. He mustered out first of any of them when the alarms sounded. And week after week he busted his ass breaking rock for their bridge. If his heart's desire had been to become a Ranger Chief someday, anyone would have put money on his chances.

As winter rolled over them, burying them more deeply under snow, it seemed that Leon was one of them. When Hengst learned that Bari was giving Leon extra treats out of her own kitchen, he suspected that no one except himself remembered that Leon was the disputed heir to the crown of Nolan. Nothing but Leon's death could change that irreversible fact. Against all odds he'd appeared out of the Saquave once, when he was too young to remember, to throw Nolan into civil war. It could happen again, but this time a civil war in Nolan might drag along the Saquave, because it had sheltered Leon.

Winter was falling off. Leon didn't believe it, but everyone else assured him that down in the Valley, and upon the Wilderness, the temperature was rising. Sandstorms kicked with cruel extravagance, slamming into the spew of the Mountains, the coupling of the two birthing Black Blizzards, a roaring blowing of snow, black mountain topsoil, and the sand that was everywhere.

Bari said, with comfortable smugness, "I'll take mountain winter, long as it is, anytime, over spring down there. The foals, lambs, kids, chicks, piglets, buffalo calves, all come into the world in choking dust and sand. The first breath of my babies was clean, clear mountain air, perfumed with mountain flowers, the best air in the world."

A Bat pozeem, escorting the head of their council, brought much-appreciated variation to winter's hind end. They were finishing their winter bargaining tour directly with the Snakes' largest forge.

The Bats differed from the other tribes because, like the Snakes, they lived in towns. Their towns were caves far southwest in the forest- and iron-rich Windsong Hills.

In most other parts of the world the Windsongs would be called mountains. The Bats guarded the secrets of ore and smelting for Saquave. They made very fine weapons.

Their prideful boast was that no Bat pozeem went on the Noloani Crossing. However, Bats had remembered the fate of the first Snakes, who also had lived in towns, at the hands of the Noloani in the Snake River Valley, destroying Saquave's balance. So Bats played politics as much as any other tribe. They were very powerful players too, controlling the metal out of which weapons were forged.

The council woman, Moria, set up her travel kurgan behind Bari and Evart's forge. It was Bari with whom Moria dealt here, and whatever other Ranger women were present. Evart and Bari had shared so much for so long that he felt it was natural that she speak on his behalf.

Fort Cloud's smithy was growing. Evart's two oldest sons were part of it now. His third son born in Nolan specialized in wheelwright work. They needed more metal than ever, for banding the bridge trusses and rimming wheels, as well as their usual work.

After they concluded the last bargaining session, Bari grasped hands with Moria. "I am sorry that this time of playing is finished. I enjoyed myself greatly."

Moria said, "I always look forward to playing with you, for you play hard. Your pozeem know how to treat our iron so its songs are released. I will send our pigeons home to Windsong as soon as we descend to warmer air. The wagons bearing your iron will be below by the time the trails are dry enough for their weight. And as you bargained, our pozeem will assist packing the mules up here. You will have to inform me next year what new curses the Bat pozeem play against the mules."

Moria was a tiny, dark-haired woman with piquant features, and long nails, so they looked like fragile claws. Like many of the Bat women, her riding style was high up on her horse's withers, hiding herself under the long swath of her mount's mane.

The other Ranger women departed, leaving Bari and her napping three-year-old daughter behind with Moria.

While refreshments were brought, Moria nursed her baby boy. "Tell me about the Stallion Queen's daughter, please. It is common for mothers to be resented by their daughters for a time after their own womanhood blossoms. The only solution is to send those daughters to live with the women of another kurgan. It seems that the Stallion Queen wisely has sent her daughter to your kurgan," Moria said.

Bari's daughter woke up from her nap. Moria gestured to a screened corner. Bari took the little girl to pee, welcoming the moment to devise her answer.

Settling the child among the warm fleeces, carpets and cushions, Bari gave her a handful of peanuts to shell. That would keep her occupied for a short time, at least.

Bari said, "Cameron does not want to be a Stallion Queen, and thinks that Glennys is trying to force her into becoming one. She has said Glennys is not a person, that her nature is that of an animal. Stallion Queen business is hard for this person to follow."

Moria said, "This is not gossip we do here. If the Stallion Queen and her daughter are divided, this is business of all the councils. Cameron is at the age when her place is with her mother, learning all she can. It has been going about the tribes this winter that Cameron has Horse Sense, and that Mirage has matched her in the proving of it. However, Horse Sense is a small thing. Many persons have it, though not to the degree of a Stallion Queen. A Stallion Queen is much more than one who understands horses, and she is certainly a person. All the best animals, like the best people, are persons. My horses are persons."

Sighing, Bari said, "Glennys, when very young, still over there, had as her first lover the man who was her father. Neither of them knew until nearly the moment of his death. Cameron does not like it that Glennys appears to have no sorrow over mating with her sire."

Moria said indignantly, "Here such a thing could never happen. The Noloani always were shockingly barbaric unpersons, giving no memory to offspring of casual mating. That is hardly the fault of the Stallion Queen. There is nothing like that among the Snakes!"

Bari continued, "Nevertheless, Cameron holds that only an animal would not sorrow every day over such a thing. That

Glennys never weeps after her Justice calls for hanging, she finds grievous. Only animals don't weep over the deaths they make."

Moria shifted impatiently. A squall came from the baby, stifled instantly by the other nipple.

"Pah! A hunter will beg pardon for life taken, but those who eat what the hunter brings only thank the hunter. Does Cameron weep over the meat set in front of her? If she thinks hunting and giving justice are the same, Cameron is still a child."

Bari said, "Cameron got caught up in a Weirding Ride taken by the Stallion Queen before Solstice. It frightened her very much, because she went into many of Saquave's children, and they were all hunting. I think that is honest fear. We all know that Cameron is a brave person."

Moria thought a bit. "I know nothing of the Weirding Rides of Stallion Queens, because there were none in my mothers' time. But the stories say Weirding Rides are terrible, which is why only Stallion Queens are strong enough to take them."

Bari's daughter threw her peanuts at her mother. Bari bent over her to show once again how to get the nuts out of the shells.

Moria spoke. "The truth of this is, Cameron's self is divided. And the division is worsened by that Noloani from over there that she moons at with the curiosity of a gazelle in season for the first time. Once she learns what's between his legs is what every other pozeem has, she'll get over that and be her mother's joy again. That Leon must go away," she concluded.

Bari said, "Leon's mother sent him to the Snakes because the Noloani want to kill him. He's Tongue Kindred, and a person. By the end of the winter Chief Hengst will make him a Ranger, a Snake pozeem."

Moria snorted. "He will go away, sometime. He may be a person, a pozeem, he may even be a Snake. But he will always be a Noloani, and his true heart is over there with his Noloani mother, who has the impertinence to call herself Queen. Cameron is Saquave and ours. The Horse Sense proves it. There is only one thing to be done, Bari. See to it that he beds Cameron as soon as possible so she can get over it and begin learning business."

The women looked sharply at each other after Moria's last words. One face moon-shaped, one pointed, both wore identical expressions of lascivious complicity, sharing memories of what all women remember.

Moria burped the baby and put him down. Rising to stretch her legs, she pushed back the hide to look outside. Leon and Cameron were standing next to each other in the stable yard with Mirage.

"He is a male person of fine appearance," Moria said. "He fought heroically against those Skulls who polluted a Bat cave kurgan. So he is partly one of ours now, as he's partly of the Wolves. If I wasn't going away in the morning, I might try him myself. But that would cause trouble that I am now too wise to provoke."

Bari said, "I like him too. He has a feel for stone, which not all of these Ranger persons do."

Moria let the hide drop. "Kazimir wants Cameron. She likes him, I know. Now that Chief is one who believes what he carries between his legs is so much better than another pozeem's that any woman he puts his desire on will fall on her back at one look from him. It is only fair that the one he wants most takes another first. She should take many before giving herself to one who walked like this in front of my girls when we were with the Badgers."

Moria strutted over the kurgan carpets, hands on hips, thrusting out her pelvis, preening her hair, legs wide apart as though what was between was too large and heavy to allow a normal person's walk.

The two women laughed hugely. Bari leaped up. "This is how Chief Hengst walks when he carries his jug of date wine in front of women."

Infant and toddler both began to cry, furious that their mothers were thinking of anything but their most important little selves.

· Fifteen ·

CAMERON WAS BREAKING Saquave's fundamental law. She was being stupid, and she gloried in it. This was the most wonderful day of her life. There could never be another one like this one.

Glennys had given her Mirage. She declared Cameron another possessor of Horse Sense. Everyone knew that Glennys used Horse Sense when she wanted to be left alone, or didn't want to be seen.

So be it.

Cameron would use this unasked-for ability to be herself, not a smaller, shadow Glennys Eve.

She opened her mind, and matched with Mirage. In spite of her haste, Cameron was able to wait patiently. As her mind had opened and grown this new sense, so had the rest of her life opened and blossomed. She was going to ride a trail never dreamed of. A Stallion Queen, no, never. But a Queen, nevertheless.

A mountainous cloud sailed between the warm sun and the lake. Mist spumed and billowed around the ice melting into Lake Umbel's waters. The mist was picked up by the fresh wind and thrown up to Fort Cloud. Before the day resumed its brightness, Mirage carried his rider over the drawbridge out into spring's gorgeous fresh mud and silvery green with no one any the wiser.

Concealed among the trees belting the Fort's bare perimeter, Cameron halted Mirage. Reverently she took the stone glowing like blood from the poke at her belt. Leon had given her his father's garnet this morning, with a bouquet of tiny violets, snowberries, and pussy toes, sparkling with drops of water. The words declaring his love turned her weak, made her tremble, put her on fire.

She worked the garnet into her earlobe. The post was thicker than the ring wires of her own earrings. The resulting drops of blood eased the insertion.

Tonight Leon would be inducted into the Rangers. Then, when it was all over, then he, then she, then they, they would go together, to the little tent that Bari promised she'd make ready for them behind the forge.

There were no rules or regulations against it. She had the right. He had the right, if she gave it to him. She would give it to him. Yes, she would, she would.

It was too wonderful, too good, to hold in without bursting, and she wanted to keep it all to herself. She couldn't breathe in Fort Cloud, where winter chill and smell lingered. She felt too precious to be looked at by other eyes.

Mirage carried her through the beeches, up into the cedar grove. Squirrels chattered from every branch. Birdsong poured down the mountain, its exuberance merging with the rilling, rushing song of snow melt. A small cottontail bounded over a patch of snow.

She had to look at it, she had to see it, feel it. Again she halted Mirage. The young stallion turned his head back to her, confused by his rider who had her head in the clouds, and not on him, or with him, or in him. He was as unused to matching in Horse Sense as she.

"I care nothing for horses today, Mirage, not even you. Be grateful I took you with me, instead of leaving you behind with Rastil," she told her horse.

She took the garnet out of her ear, rolled it in her fingers, played it among the shafts and lozenges of shifty sunlight. She pressed the stone to her breast, then kissed it.

It was very pretty up here, and utterly private. She dismounted. Fearing more than anything to lose the garnet, she fastened it in Mirage's soft wisp of halter underneath the bridle straps.

Below the trees, smoke tails blew toward them out of Fort Cloud's chimneys, bending and swaying in the updrafts coming off the warming lake. She saw without seeing.

She hiked up to the higher snow pack, wading sometimes in water, hearing Leon's words of love in every gurgle, every crash of melting snow. She caressed delicate ferns and tiny cresses, marveling at their strong delicacy, ruminating how much like her they were.

"I shall be crushed tonight, in his strong arms," she whispered to a honeytuft blossom. "I shall grow all the stronger for it."

She kept climbing, following the trail of her future in which she would ride into Nolan at Leon's side, his Queen, who would win his crown for him. "I am at the top of the world!" she said voicelessly. She threw her arms open under the herd of clouds racing through the sky. She arched her throat to swallow the sun.

Mirage was so noisy, blowing his stallion trumpet. Well, spring was no doubt moving in him too, she thought generously. The whole world was like her, fevered with the heat of spring and love.

Out of nowhere mighty arms folded around her and she was crushed from behind in an embrace. "Leon, how did you get up here without me seeing?"

Foul breath blew into her nostrils. She was thrown belly down into the thin, lacy ice that carapaced the snow pack. Her arms were yanked over her head, ice scraping her face. Her ankles and arms were bound.

"Gabriel, git that horse, take him out, now," a harsh voice ordered.

"Leon, Leon, Leon!" she cried. The mud and ice in her mouth gagged her. She saw, so clearly, Fort Cloud, where Leon and safety were, where she wanted desperately to be.

"He's turned tail and taken off downhill."

"Git him, I say!"

The snow pack heaved and broke under the glide of a pair of skis. Yelps and swearing. "Damn mountain bones breaking through the rotten snow. Fouled my skis!"

Silence, as the weight on her body never shifted, as the pressure keeping her face down in the melting snow pack never relented.

"I cain't see through the damn trees. That Satan's spawn's gone. Gone, I say. Cain't see him nohow. We gotta git outa here now."

Cameron was brought face up. All she saw before everything exploded into blackness was a bare fist coming at her face.

Snow, mixed with grit, rubbed over her face. It was night. There was a small fire. Her ankles were free, though her hands were bound now in front of her. She was on her back, lying on a sled, under a cover of some kind, bare from the waist down.

Her face hurt badly. There was a taste of blood in her mouth from biting her tongue. But the blow had been an expert one, delivered to knock her out while doing no damage. There was a soreness between her legs.

Her pants were thrown at her. "Git dressed. We cain't pull you no more. You're still intact. Had to feel it to believe it. A heathen female that ain't hored herself by your age might could be called a miracle."

Violated, humiliated, and hurt, she maneuvered awkwardly to pull on her pants under the cover. Incongruously, the cover was a patchwork quilt. Her chin was a massive crag of pain. Slowly she wriggled her legs into her pants, pulled them up with her tied hands, and got them fastened.

The one who'd spoken, the man who had determined her virginity, tossed over her socks and boots. After swinging her legs over the edge of the sled, she bent over to put on her footwear. She stood up, but her knees gave way. She fell in the slush made by the fire. She was very sick.

"You two young ones can turn around now. And keep your four eyes peeled. Tell us who you are," the one in charge ordered.

She bit down on her aching tongue. She didn't say, "Someone who is going to kill you first chance I get, with great pleasure."

From her sickness Cameron's head was already bowed. Her answer was as meek as possible.

"My name is—Deborah, a poor, lowly woman who, by the grace of the Lord, has been put into Alam's hand."

Her interrogator hit her two open-handed blows across her face. Blood poured out of her nose.

"Thou shalt not lie," he said. "Look at me."

He jangled spurs in the firelight. Her spurs. Their little chains made a sad, little music in the cold air.

"Women graced with a decent, godly name don't wear spurs."

He hit her again, this time with such force she fell over upon the rotting snow. He pulled her up, and hit her again, and again. He completed the beating with a kick in her stomach.

The worst was understanding that he was knowingly hurting her, while holding himself back from breaking her bones.

He said, "Everyone knows that the daughter of the witch has hair the color of gold cedar and is named Cameron Eve. Think of that the next time you are asked questions."

She'd been given the Alaminite's chastisement of a woman. Glennys had suffered it more than once, when younger than Cameron, and worse too. But Glennys never had suffered them digging between her legs. Cameron gagged and retched. A weapon. A weapon. She choked, unable to breathe through the loathsomeness of it.

The other two hung the sled in a tree. Then in the dark began the long, cold hike up and down the sides of mountains, and along meadow rims. She was dropped down one canyon wall, and dragged up another before they stopped. There was no chance that Rangers on horses could catch them up on that trail.

There was no chance for rescue unless Glennys came after her on Brecca. Brecca was in the Wilderness, with his mares now. Brecca had guided his mares and their babies to water, to grass. Brecca, and his boss mares, were leading the herd to hollows and downs safe from the Black Blizzards and the hunters who lived on newborn life and the mares who brought it into being.

While the new foals were born, down in Hometown Glennys was training Brecca's children, the children of Saquave's sovereignty. Glennys was already wagering and guessing, thinking of which tribe woman or man she would choose to ride upon those born out of Brecca's loins.

Daytime was warm and sunny. The men made her pack their skis like a mule under yoke. They carried everything else themselves. The skis were of no use now that everything was melting below the permanent snow line.

Gabriel and Silas were brothers. They were much younger than the one in charge, but very strong. They were ugly. They smelled bad. She loathed the manner in which they regarded her, as though she was something they were going to eat. The older one evidently held them in high regard, and despised them at the same time.

Only three of them. If, instead of being heinously stupid, she'd kept Mirage next to her, she and her horse might have taken them. If she'd been paying attention to anything but love, she might have been able to fight them off long enough for Mirage to reach her.

Then she learned, by keeping her ears open, that the older, third man was Hans Rigg, Prophet of the Lord, so filled with Alam's light that he'd successfully led an attack on St. Lucien, capital of Nolan, itself. She and Mirage, as inexperienced at working together in the Horse Sense as they were, could not have taken him, with two of his own kind at his back.

Cameron had heard accounts over the years about Hans Rigg from Thea, Glennys, and Hengst. Thea, who hated nothing and no one, hated Hans Rigg. He was a murderer.

Hans never spoke directly to her again during the hike to Silver City, except once. He asked about Thea. "Does she have a man, a family? Who does she live with?"

Cameron answered truthfully, "Thea's family is everyone, and the healer's welcome everywhere. If she lives with anyone in particular, it's the family of the Saquave Settlement Company's Governor."

Hans swung one of his ski poles, which was now a hiking staff, with a mighty crack against a tree.

"Thea is an angel of the Lord, who has been bound by the power of the horse witch. Alam handfasted Thea to *me*. And I will have her. Alam has revealed it."

Cameron's skin crawled. The only chance out of this was ransom, the same ransom the Alaminites had asked before. An exchange of women. Glennys must give Thea to Hans Rigg to get back a woman taken from the Valley. The Governor had always refused. She'd refuse now. She would, if she were Governor. Thea was her mother's only real friend. Thea was more essential to Hometown than anyone—except Glennys herself.

More essential was the Governor's belief in women. They were persons, not to be bargained over.

Cameron thought her hostility toward Glennys had begun on the night the Stallion Queen took the Weirding Ride, that ended in Glennys's rescue of the man who'd become the point and reason of her all her days and nights. Only now, having been taken prisoner by Alaminite men did she understand herself. Somehow, in spite of the love and admiration she felt for her foster mother, she'd also harbored jealousy and resentment. She wanted the honor for herself that was given to Glennys by the Valley and the tribes. How preposterous she had been. In light of her capture even remorse for her hostility was valueless.

There was little time, and less use, to think about this now. She had to cook supper for the three Alaminites out of what little they gave her to prepare.

There was meat, thin to be sure, all around them, careless with spring's ravenous hunger. These men were easy in the mountains too. Yet their hunt bagged nothing more than a skinny brace of rabbits. They were moving fast and in high terrain. But a Bat, an Elk, a Ranger, even she, given time to make a hunt out of what she'd possessed when captured, could have caught bigger meat than two rib-showing rabbits.

She learned to think of food since she was always hungry. This afternoon they'd descended to make camp in a meadow so tiny that as they looked at it from above, the little place was nothing but an overflowing cup of sun. By the stream, where they watched her wash and fill the cook pot, she spied some cresses and picked them. In the grass there were other budding leaves she added to the simmering rabbit. The two brothers inexpertly dismembered the carcasses. She preferred to be the cook. Her hands were clean.

She'd learned Hans was served first. He took the lion's share. The other two ate everything that remained except a bit of broth and the vertebrae. That was her meal.

Silas said, with halting astonishment, "She cooks good. Good for us, hey, Gabe? How come a heathen female can cook?"

She answered, "I was raised by women who believe only Alaminite women know how to keep house."

Silas and Gabe stared at her across the fire. Their mouths hung open, giving her an excellent view of what was inside.

"Hans, is that why she's a virgin and no hore?"

Without thinking she said wistfully, "In the Valley everyone learns to make a decent meal—men, women, children old enough to trust around a fire."

Hans threw rabbit bones at the two brothers.

"Huh?" said Silas.

"Wah?" said Gabe.

"She talked without you telling her to," Hans said.

"That's right." They got up, and each of them, Silas first, hit her mouth.

Silas said, "You cain't open 'less Gabe and me say so. We caught you so we git to marry you when we git back to Silver City. Our first wife ain't good for much anymore but cookin' and cleanin'."

Cameron's hands went up, an involuntary gesture of revulsion.

All the rest of the hike to Silver City her mind twisted and turned, trying to think of anything that would get her back across the chasms that irrevocably divided her from the life she'd always known. Once confined in Silver City she'd never get out. The Alaminites had taken SSC women before. Not one of them had ever returned. Rescues weren't possible because of Silver City's horse-hostile terrain, cannon, and firepower.

Silver City was an enormous enclave of stone houses, straight roads, and square gardens. Everything was within stone walls. Pens holding mules were of stone. Far off she saw chimneys belching into the pristine mountain clarity. That must be the site of the mines. The central, dominating city edifice, built within and upon a craggy upthrust of rock, was the kirk.

Alam's sanctuary sat behind high, thick walls, its towers covered with sheets of silver. Workers crawled about it like ants in their hill, digging out more rock, adding more silver, building more spires, more walls.

Hans Rigg said, "In praise of the Lord, the Alaminites have created his own mountain of godliness in the midst of heathen mountains. He has poured his grace down upon his men, and given each of us his divine revelation. From God's Mountain we will conquer the world! Praise the Lord!"

Nothing in the worst nightmares Cameron had suffered since her capture was as bad as this. There was nothing further from Hometown in the world.

Her clothes were taken away. The night after their arrival in Silver City, Beula, the brothers' first wife, put her in a tight-waisted dress with very full skirts. It had been Beula's own marriage outfit. Cameron's hair was covered. Her name was taken away, and she was given a new one—Modesty.

In the kirk she was hastily bound in Alam's sight to Silas and Gabriel. The ancient Reverend Tuescher, Glennys's old enemy, performed the ceremony.

Reverend Tuescher concluded the ceremony by telling her, "As soon as you give Gabriel and Silas Abram their first son, you will be sealed to Alam in his silver wedding tower, your name written on his silver tablets in the kirk, the highest honor a woman can achieve, the only honor to which a decent woman aspires."

She was taken back to the Abram house, escorted by a pack of howling Coals of the Lord. She was given to Silas first, because he was the oldest.

"I like it you never been used. You'll be tight. Never had a tight one before. You kin make all the noise you want now," he said, tearing her open.

She forced her mind into nothingness, willed herself to feel nothing, know nothing, not even hatred. The only power she had was hatred and anger. She had to hoard her power until she found the chance to use it.

Through the night they took their turns with her, sending her back and forth between their rooms.

After a sparse breakfast at dawn, Beula locked a pair of hobbles on Cameron's ankles. They went to work in the Abram gardens.

Beula said, "Most of Abram's plots got no water so you gotta haul it from the well, while I do the weedin' and plantin'."

Cameron's body was a mass of aches and pains, but it was the anguish and terror in her mind that made her stumble to her knees after her first trip under the water yoke. She wept until she was sick. She continued to weep while Beula beat her with a stick to get up and work. She wept while other born and bred Alaminite women came to join the beating, forcing her to her feet and to work.

At noon she hauled more water to the Abram house. She chopped wood to feed the fire under boiling kettles, and washed the men's filthy clothes. It seemed that though Beula was strong enough to beat the new wife, she had no strength for anything that needed heavy lifting and carrying.

The day was waning. "The floors ain't been done properly in a coon's age. You scrub 'em now while I go fetch honey for supper. The men always want it ever night. Plenty of hot water in the kitchen for your job."

Cameron's heart leaped. She remembered exactly where the axe was kept. But it was locked away. It seemed anything that could take a lock had one.

Cameron heard the buzzing of bees under the honeypot cover when Beula returned. Maliciously Beula ordered, "Sit out back and separate the honey from the wax and bees. You gonna do this job every night."

"Yes, mam," Cameron said.

"You call me Sister Beula," the first wife said.

Cameron sucked up smoke from the dying laundry fire with a tube she rolled from bark. Gently she blew the smoke into the honeypot until the angry buzzing stopped. Carefully she separated the stunned bees from the honey and their wax and set them with a few drops upon more bark.

Moss grew around the stone foundation of the woodshed where tools were kept, and where in winter they did the wash. Rapidly she formed moss, wax, and honey into a set of plugs. She dipped a forefinger into the honey and worked it up inside of her, along with one of the plugs. Oh, she hurt bad. It was going to happen again tonight, and every night.

She'd been allowed to tie up the voluminous skirt, which was another set of hobbles, while she worked. There was a lot of room in it to conceal what she'd made.

"What disgusting thing are you doing? How can you feel yourself there?" Beula screamed.

Very humbly Cameron said, "Sister Beula, I am still bleeding. See my knickers?"

"I don't want to see your knickers." Then, with the first trace of kindness Cameron had experienced since her capture, Beula said sadly, "They're gonna use you up as fast as they did me, and I cain't stand any more road building or take another winter workin' in the mine. I told 'em that's why my eight babies were born dead."

Cameron couldn't help but say, "I'm so sorry about your babies. I don't know how you bear it."

"The Lord gave women their burden in the world, and Alam helps us carry it. Best you learn that right quick."

· Sixteen ·

THE ALAMINITES, SILAS and Gabriel, and Sister Beula called Cameron's violation marriage. It was never anything but rape. Being in Silver City, enduring what the men did to her, was not Cameron's will, it was not her choice, it was not her desire. Her own desire, choice, will was sin, a manifestation of woman's insubordination. What she wanted meant nothing. She was only a woman, the weak, animal side of man.

As the spring waned, Cameron learned her violation by the brothers was walled about by Alaminite fear of animal power. Sex, like everything else in Silver City, had rules. Alaminite fear provided her some respite.

One brother at a time exercised his rights, instead of sending her back and forth between their rooms as had been allowed on the night of her marriage defloration. It was a sin to have connection with woman's polluted body the nights before and after Lord's Day. The congregation regarded sexual congress in the daytime as self-indulgent, so close to sin it was the same as sin. In the manner of closely knit communities, everyone knew who indulged and who didn't. The brothers cared about rising in the kirk hierarchy more than they cared about anything else.

Then her monthly courses began to flow. She doubled over in a relief from pregnancy so great that it was agony.

For five nights in a row she slept in the wife room. Beula, not one of them, was her companion in the bed. Alam, who regulated everything, had decreed women to be more polluted at such times than usual, and forbidden to touch men.

Beula never stopped bleeding now. Only a little, but the

seepage from between her legs never stopped.

Cameron hoped to recoup some of the strength she'd lost by sleeping through the night. But many times during those five nights Beula slapped her awake out of nightmare screaming.

After the marriage, before summer had arrived, the Abram household had the outward appearance of a decent, two-wived, two-husband Alaminite household, where one wife was older and the other a new bride. The men wore clean clothes. The floors sparkled. The garden plots were well attended. The men were highly regarded by the kirk hierarchy because Hans Rigg loved them, and in return, the kirk and the Prophet provided the Abram's house with all those necessary items it couldn't provide for itself.

Not many Alaminites had their own private house and garden plots. Alaminite converts did not live as well as those born and bred in Alam's light, such as Silas and Gabriel.

Beula was weak, though never so weak she couldn't chastise Cameron or remember to fasten her hobbles, or never put a knife in her hand while meals were prepared.

Cameron's hatred and loathing of the men who raped her waxed greater with the next phase of the moon. The Abram household might have been decent. It might, by Alaminite standards, be prosperous, showing all the favor of their god, and their god's representatives on earth. The house was not a pleasant place to visit or to live, with one wife dying a slow death from overbearing and overwork, and another hiding her desire to kill them all.

At night Cameron laid herself down in the rough nightgown upon one brother's bed or the other as if in her burial shroud. Before the first grab at her breasts, Sister Modesty went away.

Cameron was a spring foal in Brecca's herd. Grey and silver, she learned to nibble grass, surrounded by the protection of the herd of mares and foals, watched over by the stallion who sired her. She was Mirage, growing up on the plains, coming under Glennys's hands before Mirage found his own power and Brecca drove him away.

One night Silas braced himself over her.

"Talk, you witch bitch, say something. I expect more from you, raised heathen and all. The witches in the mines were better than you until they got so ugly. Do something!"

Mirage learned to wear a saddle. He learned to take the bit.

He learned what a horse can learn under the mind and hand of
one who understands how hard it is to give up freedom for the
bonds of love. Under Glennys's hands Mirage learned interesting things. Two different natures joined. Love and respect
matched sympathies. Cameron and Mirage rode away in the
summer into the wild, into the ranges of the tribes, her mother
with her, teaching her all the things which, like Mirage at first,
Cameron had been afraid to learn.

Silas hit her. His abuse pulled Sister Modesty back out of
Cameron's defense against Silas's forced entry of her body.

"You heathen bitches is all alike, you want it rough?"

Cameron put fingers to her bruised jaw. Tears leaked out of
her eyes, though she didn't want them to. He would like that.

Then he said, "I git it now. You like Gabe better'n me! Our
ma did. Ya keep it all for Gabe!"

Sister Modesty screamed as Silas beat her. She shrieked,
and shrieked, and shrieked. She rolled off Silas's bed while
he rained blows upon her.

Suddenly Gabe was there, and Beula.

"Stop it, stop it, stop it!" Beula cried weakly. "If a wife
must be chastised, it should be by the older wife's hand when
it's a household matter and not kirk business."

Beula needed the second wife strong. If the second wife
was badly damaged, or removed, she would have to do the
heavy work. Beula's wasting health wasn't up to the tasks that
gratefully she'd given over to Sister Modesty.

Silas threw Beula against a wall. "It is kirk business, because
the witch makes me clobber her. Git outta here and leave
me to it."

Beula's shrieks joined those of Cameron.

Gabe set his strength against his older brother too late to
keep away the nosy neighbors who had their own interests in
seeing the Abram brothers appear foolish in the sight of the
congregation. They poured into the Abram's house. Some of
them ran up to the kirk, and for Hans Rigg.

The Prophet cleared out the neighbors, then made himself
comfortable while Beula crept into the kitchen to fix him
something hot to drink and their supper leftovers.

Cameron needed to lean on Beula in order to get off the
floor of Silas's bedroom and into the presence of the Lord's
Prophet when he ordered.

Hans looked at her. He said, "The witch's daughter ain't so pretty anymore, I see. What did ya do to get my man here so riled?"

Cameron kept her head down. This, in its own way, was as unutterably awful as what she was forced to endure in the brothers' beds. She realized Hans Rigg found great pleasure knowing to what she was subject at the hands of the Abram brothers, and had given her to them particularly because they were stupid, dirty, and brutal.

"Silas beat me because he thinks I care more for Gabriel than for him," Cameron said very softly.

Under her eyelashes she saw Gabriel swell with satisfaction. Beula wrung her hands, more distressed than ever.

Sister Beula cried, "She doesn't mean that!"

"Do you?" asked Hans Rigg.

"You gave me to both brothers. My feelings for each of them are what they should be," Cameron answered.

Hans regarded her for a very long time through the huge amount of hair on his face. "Got a long way to go before ya break and see the Light. Sister Beula, put the hobbles on Sister Modesty. You two boys, come with me. We need to do some tall prayin' together up at the kirk."

When the Prophet of the Lord wanted to pray with the Abram brothers, it meant drinking mountain mead, and some other Alaminite high in the kirk's business disappearing.

In the wife room Beula said, "You listen up good. You set Silas and Gabriel against each other over your young body, the Prophet will put it on your own head right quick. Brothers quarrel over a woman because she's a witch, only a witch woman could make a good Alaminite man hate another because of her. Hans Rigg gives such a woman to the Coals of the Lord, and they burn her."

Cameron said wearily, "I am going to wash the blood off my face now, Sister Beula." She hobbled off to the kitchen.

While she waited for the water to heat, she stood out in the dark porch in the front of the house, nursing her bruises with cold air. The only night life in Silver City was up in the kirk, among the men who were high rulers over the congregations. On Lord's Day the women were allowed into the kirk to be assaulted by endless sermons from Reverend Tuescher about their weakness, their inferiority to the perfect being, man.

It was amazing to Cameron, standing on the porch in the night to see the moon, which was waxing again. The moon was portent, filled with aspect. The edge, instead of sharp and clean, was jagged. That was the edge she wanted on the knife that she'd plunge into the brothers. Then she'd twist and saw the blade. Instead of Alaminite silver the moon was orange, set in a cobalt blue sky. Orange and blue were the colors of the Valley, the SSC, of Glennys, her mother.

The air moved, soothing her outraged flesh, opening her spirit, as women were not allowed to open in Silver City. The air smelled of what she dared not remember, for the anguish of loss was too great. She felt the same as when very young, when Glennys had allowed her to stay in her lap, made her a daughter once again, wrapped her up in strong arms, put upon Brecca's back in front of her.

"Brecca does not want to hurt you. Most of the time animals don't want to hurt you, unless they are very hungry or very afraid. Don't be afraid, Ronnie, don't be afraid. If I put you here, he will allow it. Most of all, Ronnie, you want it. You must remember that."

Cameron stood on the porch, breathing great, deep breaths, the first honest breathing she'd done since her capture. She ignored how each inhalation pained her ribs. The freshening wind carried down to her the wolves' driving song. Bats swooped past the porch. A badger came out from under the steps. He shuffled off in the direction of the gardens. The gardens had sprouted in the last few days, filled with tender shoots pushing up above the shallow dirt.

Badger claws would care nothing for garden walls. A rabbit doe, followed by her family, leaped across the road in front of the Abram house, heading for the bee gardens, where flowers from over there had come up with the vegetables.

There were few trees left on the mountainsides above Silver City. They'd been cut down for fuel and the mines. Nothing had been replanted in their place. Glennys insisted the Rangers could never log much on any one slope. The trees, with small exceptions directly around Hometown and Fort Cloud, could endure only very careful harvest.

Cameron saw why Glennys made that rule. The mountainside was falling down on Silver City. She was going to be buried with the people she hated. She couldn't move.

The falling mountain was only elk. They drifted like smoke down their old trails. Sister Beula had told her the Alaminites had slaughtered all the elk up here years ago, because at the end of spring they walked down over Silver City. So there should be no elk. Yet they had come again. The Wild still endured. The Wild remembered the ways it walked to graze on sweet feed.

Where the elks' tall legs didn't leap over Silver City's walls, the pressure of their combined weight broke them down. They spread like irrigation water over the gardens. Their huge bodies trampled the scarecrows.

In the night silence, where the only ones allowed to stay awake were drinking and praying in the fortress of Alam, no one heard the elks' eager grazing upon the sprouting barley, the pawing of their big hooves uncovering tiny carrots and radishes, but Cameron. She raised no alarm.

Very quickly there was no more to eat. The elk flowed away, following paths Alaminites never recognized. It was only the Wild, which belonged to them by Alam's law, to wrestle from evil, and make docile. The elk left nothing behind in the gardens where they'd paused for refreshment.

At dawn a mountain thunderstorm broke over Silver City. When it was over, all the topsoil, dug out of the surrounding mountain meadows, carried to Silver City, and spread out in the gardens, done by back-breaking female labor over many years, had washed through the broken walls and run down the mountains.

The gardens had to be made again. Though gardens could be reconstructed, there was no time in the short mountain growing season for a replanting. The only food Alaminites believed fit for the Lord-fearing to eat was what they'd eaten in Soudaka County, back over there. This winter the only supply of decent food would be what came back from the silver caravan going down to Nolan. Only Alaminite family men high up in the kirk, those who lived in the stone houses, could afford imported food.

There was a lot of praying up in the kirk. In the end Reverend Tuescher and Hans Rigg received the same revelation. The women bought from Chief Sepul, the Elk slaves, would be taken out of the mines, and they would resoil Silver City's gardens. While the men received revelation, Cameron received her monthly bleeding. Gratefully she slept in the wife room.

The second morning of her bleeding, Gabe sneaked back to the Abram house and spoke to Cameron over the laundry tubs. He shuffled and hemmed and hawed. He put out one big hand to touch her. She flinched away.

"Me in my blood, in the daytime too!" she cried. "What will the congregation say!"

"No, wife, I jist wanta talk to ya. I want ya to know I don't want ya to go out where wild beasts might git ya, where ya'll have to live and work with the damned heathen slaves. It ain't my idea, but Rigg's and Silas's. They think puttin' ya to work with the the slaves will teach ya not to like me better'n Silas. Alam don't hold with women likin' on their own. But ya poor, frail things, ya cain't ever help likin' the best man best."

Cameron stood with a pair of his heavy, filthy pants in her hands, the scrub tub between them. "I don't understand," she said.

She was dumbfounded at the depth of male vanity. She couldn't comprehend why he believed she nursed passion for a man who repeatedly raped her.

Gabriel said, "Silas and me are goin' off with Rigg for the summer like we do. Ya are goin' to dig and carry for the gardens in the slave coffle with them creatures we bought off that Chief Sepul. You're goin' out in the morning with 'em. Silas and me, we're takin' mules at noon, goin' off first with the silver caravan, and then with Rigg to meet some big shots from over there."

Cameron's breast heaved. She tried to blink back tears of relief.

Gabriel rushed around the tub and embraced her. "Little sweetheart, don't cry. I'll be back faster than a fly you swat away. I'll git rid of Silas, and git Rigg to take you off the coffle. Then ya'll be back in my house and seein' me, only me, ever' night."

Cameron's eyes spied the heavy stick with which she beat soap into the clothes infested with her rapists' stink. She rubbed her free hand furiously against her bundled-up skirts, trying to get rid of the soap. If she got a good grasp on the stick, she could break his head open.

"I gotta git back to the boys. But I'll see ya sooner'n ya think. Remember, this time it'll be only me. And I won't let Sister Beula hit you so hard. You were the purtiest thing I ever saw up there on the snow pack. I ain't lettin' 'em keep you slave 'cause you like me best."

He escaped before she could get the stick.

The women were chained together at the waist, about four feet between each of them. They were beasts, creatures, as the Alaminites called the tribeswomen, their humanity denied. Even so their legs, feet, and hands had to be free to climb up and down the mountainsides.

The Alaminite wives were very swift to administer the whip, the stick, the switch. They were even quicker to pinch and slap.

The men left such overseer tasks to their wives. They stared around from the height of muleback, firearms cocked at all times. They shot off their guns at cloud shadows, telling each other they had seen a bear or a wolf in broad daylight at the beginning of summer. The men's every movement proclaimed their absolute, essential importance in the universal scheme of all things.

The first night they shot an Elk woman, who went for the eyes of the man who had the key while he shifted her shackles from waist to ankles.

The others were allowed to minister to her. She would live, or she wouldn't. If she died, it would teach the rest. The Saquave woman was pregnant.

"I die happy, not forced to bear what was forced into my womb," she said.

An Elk woman, like the others dressed only in the tatters of what she'd had on when sold to the Alaminites, closed her tribeswoman's eyes.

Cameron, ashamed of her whole clothing and less starved ribs, wept and hated. Her belief, that once united with her own kind, together they'd be strong and become free, died before the Elk woman. Her shacklemate, Sigune, had whispered during the day the ordeals the tribeswomen suffered in the mines.

"Slave, that is the word they use for us, with heathen, and beast. We do not know these words. These are not Tongue Kindred. In the mines the men forced us, to make us bear slaves. Our wombs will not deliver persons, only more like us, to be bred and raised slave for them. We persons are bad slaves, they say. In the mines we have nothing but our tools to remove what they forced into us. Many persons died forcing out what they

forced into us. Now they leave us alone, for we are ugly and
dirty. They say they are buying new slaves from the Owls and
the Beavers, because Sepul, may his bones rot, will help them.
May Sepul's thing weep, rot in long agony. I request only one
boon of Saquave. May Sepul live, may I live long enough to
creep among the kurgans in the wastelands he has made. I will
take him and dig a hole in Saquave and put him in it to never
see the sun, to never smell the wind, to never hear a mare call
to her foal. I will slowly, slowly cut off his thing, a tiny piece
at a time. I will make him eat every bit of his rotten thing, and
then bury him, still breathing. This dream came to me first,
before all the others. It is mine. I will live that long."

Cameron had believed her hatred for Silas and Gabriel was
like no hatred ever loosed upon the world. She believed her suffering like no suffering ever endured. Her hatred, her suffering
were nothing to what the tribal women possessed and endured.

She had been captured. They had been sold by one of their
own, one they themselves had helped become Chief.

Over four hundred of them had been sold to the Alaminites.
After illness, disease, accident, and the pregnant women who'd
died by their own hands, eighty-three had survived the underground winter. They'd been provided little food, no clothing,
and much hard labor, and had been raped many times.

The slaves were driven over washed-out trails, through
despoiled forest and meadow. Wherever the Alaminites had
dug before, seeking fuel, more silver or other valuable minerals,
or simply topsoil, the trees had been cut down and burned to
make it easier and quicker. The rains and runoff had washed
away the mountain's flesh.

Alaminite devastation was part of Valley lore. It had begun
around Lake Umbel when the SSC claimed the Valley. Glennys
studied the charred logjams damming the Snake and determined
there was more to it than the usual spring washout. Chief
Hengst had taken the Rangers and driven the Alaminites
out. The building of Fort Cloud had begun that summer,
and the site had been defended ever since. Fort Cloud took
an enormous share of the Valley's resources, that they could
have put to more productive use, but there was no other
choice.

It was incomprehensible to Cameron and the other women
that the Alaminites were blind to the consequences of their

stripping and deforestation. The evidence of cause and effect were there for anyone to interpret.

But to the Alaminites it was all the endless Wild, given to them by Alam to tame to his will. It had no reason to exist, no right to itself. If it could not be tamed, then it must be destroyed. If they used up the lumber and soil in one area, there were a thousand more places to cut and dig.

The slaves were forbidden to talk. Cameron joined the coffle already knowing the slaves' secret language. It had grown out of the way a trainer or rider communicated with a horse. They also practiced a very old sign language known by all the tribes.

The coffle was driven through one wasteland after another. A moan went up from the women.

They broke silence. They sat down and wept. "It was not Saquave's loss of favor that made our summer lands barren. It is the loss of the Rain Shadows' trees. There is nothing left to catch and direct Saquave's breath and bring the rains."

They poured dust over their heads, and would not get up.

One of the Alaminite men fastened the chain to the mules and dragged the slaves down the ruined landscape until his wife talked him into stopping.

"Ya'll kill 'em all, and then what, Jake? I'll have to take their place and ya'll hafta do for yourself."

The women were essentially naked now, under the hot sun of day and the frigid air of night. The summer flies hatched out, the giant mountain flies that bit until the blood came. The little the slaves had been fed was cut in half as punishment for their noise and refusal to walk. They got no water at all. Cameron's eyes were nearly swollen shut from the dragging and the flies. The sun spun in a white circle directly over her feet.

The sun spoke to her, giving revelation. She was dead. She'd died that early spring day up on the snow pack above Fort Cloud. She was walking on the path of her death journey. Since Alaminites killed her, she'd been sent to Alaminite hell. It had to be Alaminite hell, because everything was just one damned thing after another.

"Sun, you're not fair. I was never a believer in Alam," Cameron told the sun through broken, dry lips. "I don't believe in hell. So I shouldn't be here."

Then, miraculously, there was relief. Water ran through a wide meadow filled with tall grass and flowers. Bees buzzed

busily, and the flies were not there. The slaves were allowed
to bathe their torn bodies, wash their filthy nit-filled hair, as
best they could.

"We cain't have this. Heathens and beasts they are, and the
devil put them in female form. We got to cover 'em up."

The Alaminite wives' reluctance to provide heathens with
the human dignity of clothing was overcome by their fear
and disgust of naked bodies in human female form. There
were more Alaminite men than women. Even a filthy, heathen
female skeleton had the witch power to tempt Alam's most
perfect holy men.

The Alaminite women ripped the patchwork covering off
their quilts, looked to their trade cloth out of which they
were continuing their female tasks of providing clothes for
their men. Quickly they sewed shifts for the women.

With the donning of their brief clothing, their eyesight once
again used to light, the women regained a measure of strength
and spirit. They were in the open, not underground. They had
lost everything, but they were alive, and they wanted to live
to get their revenge.

They found roots, leaves, wild things like grasshoppers they
could add clandestinely to their small food allotment. They set
snares around the area designated for their latrine, their only
place of privacy.

The tough grass had to be scythed down before they could
begin work with pick and spade. The men covered the slaves
with loaded guns every step when the sharp blades were put
in their hands.

Guards covered them whatever they did, wherever they
went, except inside the latrine screen. The Alaminites were
terrified the women would attack them or run away. That
meant the Alaminites had to watch sharp and move with the
slaves.

It was much hotter and drier down here. Silver City was far
away, above them. The signs told these women, who spent a
good part of their lives in the lower mountains and the foothills,
that true Saquave Wilderness was only a couple of hard days'
travel below. Like the others, Cameron felt hope growing in her,
the most dangerous weapon masters can hand over to slaves.

The Alaminites, used to the dogma of their belief, the pressure of the congregation, to keep their own in check, were,

after all, inexperienced slave masters. Slaves learn the conditions of their slavery instantly, for, after all, their immediate survival depends upon what they know.

Alaminites, by the nature of their belief and the community it had created, had a place for everything and everything in its place. The chain was broken roughly into nine coffles for sleeping. There were keys for the leg hobbles and keys for the waist. The chains were lengthened or shortened, depending upon the work. Scything needed a lot of room. At any moment each slave knew who carried the keys to her chain. Orderly in their method, the Alaminites never switched overseers for the coffles.

Bright, bright day in true summer. Cameron's hands trenched the sod with a pick. Her foot pressed down upon a spade.

She dreamed of the Valley when the heat of afternoon was so fierce almost everyone worked under roof, inside the cool dimness of mudbrick walls. Her tongue savored beakers of sun tea. Her ears heard the hum and hiss of spinning and weaving. She smelled the sharp, clean odor of wood being made into furniture. Those who found it necessary to carry their work on outside, like the dyers, sawyers, tanners, were swearing under the awnings, their sweat drying upon them instantly. Their laughter was heard faintly within, as the outside workers broke again in a dash down to the refreshing waters of the Snake.

"Sst, sst, Cameron," Sigune whispered out of the corner of her mouth. "Look!"

Her spade pointed among the scythed grass at their feet. A scorpion trundled over the broken grass, stinger raised over her back. This was not scorpion country.

A crow swooped back and forth across the meadow. It cawed three times before flying away.

Cautiously, the women alerted each other. Some saw a gazelle standing in the trees. This was far too high up for gazelle range.

Along each strip line of the meadow, the slave women signed to each other wordlessly. They heard the yip of coyote in broad daylight, the howl of wolf, and the cough of cougar. Some had seen bats, a set of creatures looked for with the coming of night.

A rabbit bounded along the strip, raising a small dust storm in its wake. A badger rolled behind the rabbit, already putting on fat lost over winter.

At dark, as they went two by two in their partner shackles to the latrine, they whispered to each other. Back to the coffle, locked into their leg hobbles, while joining in their forced Alaminite prayer of thanksgiving for the sorry food given them, while listening to their evil, heathen ways being prayed over, their excited eyes in the firelight spoke back and forth.

They were too excited to sleep. They huddled close together, for the fires were mainly for the benefit of their guards in the cold nights.

"Aspects from all the tribes excepting Elks, Owls, and Beavers. Owl Chief and Beaver Chief must have followed Sepul and betrayed their women's councils as Sepul has done. Something is going to happen. There will be rescue!"

Very carefully, among the women, they told off which Alaminite carried which key, to be certain nothing had changed.

There was a snap among her fellow slaves that wasn't there before Sigune sighted the scorpion. Cameron hardly dared believed they were right. If they were, excited as their anticipation made them, suspicion would be aroused in the Alaminites before whatever these signs portended came about. If these were signals of rescue, they weren't complete. What happened today was to prepare them to move fast when the time came.

"There was no snake," she sent through the chains. "We must be very careful. I think until there is a snake, nothing will happen. Sleep, so we may be as alert as we may be."

The others did not want to let go of their first hope since slavery. The chains rattled restlessly. Usually after they ate, went again to the latrine, they fell into their exhausted sleep.

"Settle down now, ya witches, or we'll come among ya with the lash! Maybe we should burn a few of yas on a mountain top as sweet savor to Alam. Them elk never came into the gardens until you was in Silver City."

During the next day's labor Cameron tried to think. How fast her mind had lost its usual active manner. It was terrifying to move outside the thick walls she'd built to hide from what was done to her.

It was painful to recall action directed by her own will, almost impossible to think of attack rather than defense. She began to think like a Ranger.

The Stallion Queen, Glennys, her mother, was the only one

who could unite the tribes for one action. Her mother was the only one who could care enough about her own stupid, lovesick child, to risk all she'd built with the tribes to bring her daughter out of Alaminite bondage.

Cameron thought of what her considerations as a Ranger would be if she were to mount an operation like this. Gather information first. The Stallion Queen's Weirding Ride had taught Cameron that Glennys had means for this no one else did.

Yet, Saquave's sovereignty did not run in the mountains, which was why they had never been able to move against Silver City. Fort Cloud's power came from walls, speed, and vigilance, and almost all its supply came from Hometown. Fort Cloud contained Silver City, and defended. It could not attack.

Now the Alaminites had brought their slaves very close to Saquave's power, which flowed through Saquave's chosen Stallion and Queen.

There were fifty Alaminites whose task was to make their slaves work. Twenty of them were women. The men were always armed, and their slaves were always in chains.

Their guns' effective range wasn't that of tribal arrows. However, they were perfectly adequate to kill, or at the very least, dreadfully damage a slave, from anywhere in this mountain meadow. They manufactured their own powder, they made their own weapons. They'd learned all the most modern techniques from Nolan's own gunpowder manufacturer. There had been Alaminites involved all along the line in Nolan's development of these weapons.

But if it were very wet, their firearms might not be so effective as arrows coming from many different directions at once.

·Seventeen·

"COVER ME! HOLD me down!" Glennys pleaded.

Kazimir's sinewy arms wrapped around Leon from behind.

"Keep away from them! We've had days looking at what the Alaminites have done to Cameron, and keeping ourselves under bit. Except for Bari and the Stallion Queen, none of them have ever seen such a thing. Women's rage could rip us from throat to balls before they remembered we're on their side, and not a maggot."

Konya, Moria, and Bari grappled with the Stallion Queen. Glennys's face contorted in a horror more hideous than the tragic masks painted upon King's Dramatic Theater's drapery. She was a mother forced to swallow her fury over men's treatment of her daughter.

Lower than the mountain meadow where the slaves, pregnant or not, did their labor under the lash, the day was still bright upon the Benches, a lower range of mountains below the Hammers. The Hammers were crowned by Silver City. Below the Benches were the Sweet Grass Hills, a summer range divided by the Owls and Beavers, where the women had gathered without Owl or Beaver permission to seek their own.

"Get Thea!" Bari ordered. Her voice was the same as that of the Stallion Queen, a jagged whisper that ripped out her throat.

The women held down the Stallion Queen, who had seen with her own eyes, for the first time, what the Alaminites had made of Cameron. Her need to strike now, when it was the wrong time, helped them to control their own need.

Bari sat upon the Stallion Queen. Konya held her legs, and Moria laid herself over the Stallion Queen's mouth.

The Gazelle woman, Dream, leaped down the Benches, returning with Thea, the healer.

Thea put her hands upon the Stallion Queen's head, murmured into her ears.

"You must wait! Do not break your own training now. You must wait for the Hammer thunderstorm. It is coming. Keep us hidden from Hans Rigg and his men. Our persons know their friends have come. Trust Cameron. She has seen what you've loosed, she has heard the animals call. We must wait. All us persons must wait, until the Snakes and the storm. The storm always comes. Cameron knows this! We will take Cameron back. You will free your child. Cameron will be free, if her mother is quiet now. There are so many more than *your* child, which is why the women are here *now*. It is not your child, but all mothers' daughters made for Saquave's future. The silence and cunning of Saquave, Glennys. Quiet. Quiet."

Bari was the first to heft her weight off the Stallion Queen, at Thea's nod. Surrounded, held, comforted by other strong women, the Governor of the SSC, head of the Snakes' women's council, Stallion Queen, crawled down the Benches on her hands and knees, dizzy, nearly blind, to the Sweet Grass Hills below.

Bari and Moria brought up the rear. "The Gov is a person of the wide open spaces. Every time she comes into the mountains she's sicker than the last," Bari observed.

Kazimir said to Leon, "You and I must walk soft, even when they take our persons back. Our women go loco when a man forces a woman. Nothing but force made our women persons bear for Alaminites. When they are ridden by such hatred, like an unbroken horse, they will lash out at any man. I've seen it. Our rage, yours and mine, is terrible. It is only a shadow of what these, not to say those up there, feel."

The memory of Sharissa, his mother, made Leon shiver under the hot sun. So many times after she'd come back from Roald's bed he'd seen Sharissa crawl into her bath looking as stupefied from brutality, and as ugly with hatred, as the Alaminite slaves.

After Mirage had plunged over Fort Cloud's drawbridge Leon had led the party looking for Cameron. Reading the signs in the show, Hengst had said, "Alaminites got her."

Fort Cloud couldn't afford to divide its strength to go after her. It was a law of Hometown as well as the Fort. Hengst had the awful responsibility himself to write the terrible news to Glennys. He stripped Fort Cloud's mews of pigeons, loosing one after another to Hometown, hoping the Governor would send by return a negation of their own law. But Chief Hengst believed his sister would not give to her foster daughter what had been denied to every other woman taken by Alaminites.

Before the first pigeons were thrown to the skies, Leon renounced his intention to join the Rangers. He was no longer under Hengst's command.

Hengst gave Leon every support Fort Cloud could provide him, which was little enough in such terrain. Horses were useless. Rangers would be needlessly sacrificed before Silver City's wall cannon.

Before nightfall Leon set off alone up the mountains on Cameron's trail. At first light the next day he found Cameron's spurs in an iced-over puddle of melt, next to the remains of a small fire. Leon dogged, panting, behind the sign of the four, sometimes three. He closed behind them enough to hope he'd catch them asleep.

But he wasn't fast enough. His first sight of the Alaminite aerie was the morning after Silas and Gabriel had taken Cameron to wife.

Kazimir had made his way up from the Sweet Grass, over the Benches, into the Hammers. He found Leon's barren camp the day after Silver City's gardens had been eaten by the elk. Leon had never seen a glimpse of Cameron in all that time, for he couldn't get into the place without being recognized as a stranger, an enemy.

Leon's and Muran's survival last year upon the Wilderness proved Leon's ability to track. Kazimir, all thoughts of rivalry set aside, believed Leon when he said Cameron had been brought here.

Leon told Cameron's other suitor, "I don't think they raped her on the trail, though I'd give almost anything but the chance of getting her out of there safe and sound to know," Leon said bitterly. "At each place they spent the night, there were four sleeping places. Their haste proclaims an overwhelming inter-est in getting her to their aerie, more than having themselves a good time. From what I've heard I think Alaminites believe in holding off their good times. Once they got Cameron inside Silver City the worst no doubt happened, and like with my mother, they call it marriage."

Except for being better armed and clothed, Leon was as dirty and desperate as when Kazimir first saw him. He'd eaten only what he could catch, after his light supplies had gone. He dared not have much of a fire at all, for fear of discovery by the Alaminites.

"It's up to us, Young Wolf," said Kazimir. "Hometown and the Rangers cannot do anything because Silver City is too strong. This has always been the Valley's policy. My pozeem cannot attack the cannon any more than the Rangers. Only in winter could all the pozeem leave Saquave's work and mass up here. Then the snow and the Hammers give the Alaminites greater advantage than ever. She is only one Snake woman, and those others are the Elks, here from their own pozeem's filthy betrayal. That is not enough of a reason for all the tribes' pozeem to unite in war upon Silver City."

Fiercely Leon retorted, "Then Silver City will destroy every tribe, one by one, by raping the women and devastating Saquave's summer grasslands. Look at what they've done up here already! Water dammed and diverted, trees burned and logged, soil run away."

Carefully, not wanting the younger man to get excited, Kazimir said, "It appears the women's councils have come to your thought, Young Wolf. Some are coming from all the tribes excepting the Elks, Owls, and Beavers. These are women who have won or been gifted horses out of Brecca, or are the wisest of all the councils. They have gathered to the Stallion Queen, come up the Valley to the Flying Company post of Windgate. They left the horses and most of their force at Windgate. A few have come with the Stallion Queen and my mother to wait for me and news in the Sweet Grass Hills."

Leon said with relief, "Then we will succeed. The Stallion Queen can do anything."

"It's very dangerous. The Sweet Grass Hills belong to the Owls and Beavers, whose Chiefs seem to think like Sepul. It is the closest approach up from Saquave to Silver City by horseback. But after climbing the Benches, there are few horses that can go higher and do riders any good. The loss to the tribes of these women would strengthen Sepul's ideas among pozeem of all tribes when they hear, and immediately in his Owl and Beaver friends. If I'm caught, after killing many of them, I will be tortured and killed and another pozeem will be Chief. But there's no one to take my mother's place, or that of Moria, or the Stallion Queen, or Bari in Fort Cloud, who has taken to muleback and joined them. If found and caught by Beaver or Owl pozeem, the women will be sold like the Elks to Silver City."

Leon said, "The Alaminites will burn the Stallion Queen as a witch if they get her. That will be the end of Hometown."

"It's her own daughter, this time, and the women's councils fear that it will be them next, as happened with the Elks," Kazimir said. "For the honor of all women, they have come together."

When the slave coffle went out of Silver City, the two men didn't recognize at first that Cameron was part of it. Finally, the better state of her clothing, and that she didn't stumble, as if unused to sunlight like the rest, brought their attention upon her.

It was her hair—for, unlike that of the other slaves, it was clean at the start of the journey—that called to Kazimir's spying eyes, as it had first drawn his attention when she became nubile. Cameron's hair netted the sunshine of the bright day. It shone with the deep glow of cedar wood touched by the sun. Once Kazimir pointed, Leon knew that stark, miserable creature was Cameron, the woman who had taught him to dance.

A slave among other slaves, Cameron, only a little less than the others, was stripped of her proud carriage, her open stride, her bright-eyed interest in the world by her captivity. The two men, each risking a life that was sweet, in a deeper desire to deliver Cameron from captivity, couldn't find the woman they both loved in the body shuffling at the front of the chain, her head drooping in hopelessness. All that brought up her head was hatred. Hatred radiated out from the chain with heat so great it seemed it must melt their shackles from their bodies.

"At least she's out from behind the cannon mouths," Leon said grimly. "Now we have a chance."

Kazimir said, "Now we must do the hardest thing in the world. We may not strike a blow for her. We must track her more softly than you ever tracked anything in your deepest hunger. We must learn where they're going. If they stay in the open, we will call on the women in the Sweet Grass. Only if they look to put her behind cannon again, will we risk moving against them before having our friends at our back. We are the only ones who can tell Eve where her daughter will be found."

After the slaves were put to labor, and the two men reasoned out the work, Kazimir left Leon to watch. The Badger Chief went down the Benches to lead the Stallion Queen to her daughter.

With the Stallion Queen came a few carefully chosen women, all possessed by the Queen's feel for the weirding way. One by one they'd released a sign of their own tribe, which could only be read by other women of the Wilderness. It was very hard for them to depart after Glennys and Dream had called the gazelle up from the Saquave. They had to wait for the mountain storm, the element which would tip the odds against the Alaminite guns more in their favor.

Kazimir and Leon came down into the Sweet Grass Hills far behind the women.

"For a long time this was the richest grass in summer anywhere on Saquave," Kazimir said. "These days the Rain Shadows have refused the snow melt which had always filled the streams and rivers in spring, so they never had to care for Saquave's rain breath. Saquave's luck is gone from the Owls, Beavers, Elks. We have learned Saquave's laws to survive our bad luck, always remembering that luck turns around again. Sometime."

Leon said, "Drought is drought. How can you have laws about rain?"

Kazimir said harshly, "I'd forgotten in our common cause that you're a Noloani, bred out of those who first broke Saquave's laws. Of course you don't know the important things that distinguish persons from Noloani."

Leon said, "I have proved that I am capable of learning what a person must know. As a person I have the right to be instructed in Saquave laws, in order not to break them in my turn."

The two men halted in their progress through a dried-up Sweet Grass stream bed torn up by gazelle, antelope, and buffalo hooves in a desperate search for water. The land was pitiless in its splendor of blinding glare.

It was hard for Leon to believe that grass that had grown tall and thick here, where he saw only cactus and creosote bushes. Red dust lifted and fell in tattered veils over the sun wheeling in brilliant spokes of crimson and orange. The wind was like the poison breath of a lion, drying out their eyeballs.

They dropped the hems of their robes, tucked up in their knife belts. They pulled down part of their turbans to cover their faces.

Through the veil over his eyes, Kazimir studied Leon. He was as dark, hard, and lean as the Chief himself. A knife hung on either hip. He carried the rest of his gear on his back, bow case and quiver at the top, available instantly to his need.

He said, "Very well. Listen most carefully to the laws of rain. When Saquave's breath does not open upon your lands, the persons must slaughter their sheep, goats, and mules. They must kill half of their horses, turn half of the rest free. Only the best of their horses, sheep, and goats can be kept from the knives. Only one woman in five may bear a new child in the year. The women's councils from the watered tribes must take the youngest children into their tribe's orphan wagons when asked. The watered tribes will share food in the winter, when asked by the dry council. They will allow, when respectfully requested, grass and water to be shared with the breeding stock of the unlucky. The lucky ones must give all the best back, with half their increase, when the rains return, making the unlucky lucky again."

Leon scuffed the red, sandy dirt under his feet. He scratched his beard. "I vowed never to look like this, feel like this again, or to walk. But I have done all these things of my own free will, for I am a person. Saquave's rain laws are sensible. But it is hard to believe that any persons will give up their wealth in an unlucky time, no matter how sensible the law."

Kazimir answered, "The law keeps us very strong, which is why Saquave created us to keep the law. Badgers had years of bad luck soon after Konya bore me. Konya gave me to the Elks when I'd lived four rounds of seasons. I survived in the Elk orphan wagons. My father was a pozeem to the Badger Chief. My father, and my brothers, obeying the law, were the mule skinners in the trade caravan that crosses the

Dead Lands to the Green People. That also is part of the rain laws. The big men must earn their right to make more children. The pozeem cannot kill the buffalo and Saquave's other herd children, for all the tribes will suffer, even as the neighboring tribes have to share their grass with the buffalo, antelope, and gazelle that invade, fleeing the waterless ranges. All of Konya's clansmen, one year after another, died in the Dead Lands. Konya dealt wisely with her dead men's share out of the caravan. When the Badgers' water returned, Konya's wisdom brought our tribe swift recovery. She, even before Moria of the Bats, was the first to recognize Brecca was ridden by a Stallion Queen, and began trading with the Snakes."

Leon said, "Shouldn't Sepul and his pozeem have gone on the caravan this winter, then?"

Kazimir said bitterly, "Sepul breaks Saquave's laws. The Elk Chief, Sepul's father, never gave back our breeding stock until the Wolves and Scorpions came to our back. Offend the Scorpions at your risk! Their luck, with range bordering the Dead Lands, is always so little they are stronger, though smaller, than all rest of us. The Owls and the Beavers don't want to risk themselves in the Dead Lands. The water has not failed here in many, many generations. This has made them selfish. Children in the orphan wagons get little to eat at best. The Elks provided less. Now in their bad luck the Elk pozeem refuse to slaughter their herds or turn out their horses. The pozeem refuse to believe their luck has turned. Insisting the water will come, they've overgrazed, making the dry lands bigger instead of containing them until the rains come. Instead of fostering their children, they sell the women. Without wise women, without their children learning how to survive bad luck in honor, these tribes will birth a desire for war loot. The stories tell us that."

Dark was falling before they sighted the women's camp. The wind was dropping, and with it the dervishes' spin decayed. Dust rained upon their heads. On the horizon, where lavender hills and blue tables unfolded like an endless, carelessly unrolled bolt of cloth, evening stars poked through the haze. With the deepening darkness the flies retreated.

Kazimir said, "Since I've waited so long to bring my manly self among the female persons, perhaps Konya has cooled, and will share the gift of salt. Water too. I'm as thirsty and hungry as I've ever been, and more unhappy than either."

Leon said, "Kazimir, I'm here because my mother, Sharissa, who lived upon Saquave for a little while, who birthed me here, whose bloodline first bred upon Saquave, recognizes Saquave law. Over there my mother saw no future for her own tribe, of which, except for her mother, a wise woman fit for any council, and my father's bad Noloani brother, I am the last living. She sent me to be among the orphans of the Saquave, to wait until our luck returns."

They were close to the camp. The women had propped up their outer robes upon spears, creating tiny tents to break the wind. On the ground they'd put down their saddle blankets, which now served for a carpet. There were no fires.

Kazimir pulled away Leon's veil from his eyes and stared into them. He gripped Leon on his shoulders with his strong, hard hands.

He said, "Sepul refuses to obey Saquave laws. The Alaminites cannot see Saquave law. You have eaten Saquave's law, twisted the law in your guts, then shit it out. Like a child, you are playing with it, believing because it came out of you it is a treasure recognized by everyone. We know persons who ran away from over there, from your mother's tribal range of Blue Fields, where they worked as slaves. My Noloani brother, your words made shit upon the kurgan carpets of the horse people. Only an honorable life gives light in the eternal darkness of our burial kurgan."

Kazimir loosed his grip and walked away to his mother's place, leaving Leon alone.

He eased the pack off his back, left his knives strapped on his hips. He spread out his buffalo robe, mangy by now from the weeks it served as ground cover and greatcoat against the mountain cold and wet. There wasn't much left to eat out of his last mountain kill, a small elk buck.

He settled himself upon his back to look up to the sky. It was so soft that, near as he was to them, it took a long time before he realized the lowing of the wind and hissing of the dust was the women, singing. He couldn't make out any words. Perhaps there weren't any.

It raised an expectant prickle along his flesh. He sat up and crossed his legs. There was a hypnotic rhythm in their music. It put Leon's head, neck, and shoulders swaying.

Slowly he felt all his anger, disappointment, and unhappiness, along with the gnawing of hunger and bruised body hurts drain out of him. It went on and on. The moon rose fair and clear, dazzling the land with light. In place of his hurts of mind and body, he felt a melancholy yearning, flickering now and again with a charge of excitement.

He was in the fabled, mysterious desert lands from where his forebears had come a long age ago past. He was in the midst of an adventure more true than any he'd watched avidly upon the stage. All his early life had fallen from him. He had tasks to do, upon which, perhaps, the fate of this land hung. There was an innocent, beautiful woman, who loved him, and whom he loved, to rescue back to the life that was rightfully hers. It didn't matter, after all, whether they loved or not. It was the right thing to do, in this place, and this time. The light a man can take into death is the deed he does.

Jackals barked under the stars.

His senses twined among the questing, twisting, falling voices of the women. The sound never rose more than a few inches above the ground. He felt, rather than saw, something moving in a long, dry passage close to the place where he sat swaying. It delicately went on to where the women sat together. The music looped upon itself, an extended, soft, satisfied spell-binding hiss of welcome.

The singing continued. It rose now, seeking the currents of air. The women no longer beat their palms upon the earth, but upon their thighs. There was the clicking of tongues riding upon breath that snorted and blew. They loosed, "Huh, huh, saa, saa." Leon's body rocked loosely to their rhythm.

The moon was high overhead when he realized the women were silent. He unkinked his legs, stretched out and rolled himself up in the buffalo robe. His sleep was very deep.

Before dawn he was awakened by Azal. She brought him mare's skin to eat, long, thin, flat pieces of dry paste made of pounded buffalo meat and dates. Huge black clouds hung over the Hammers.

"The storm is coming. The Stallion Queen has four fine rattlesnakes. Now we only wait for our friends coming with the horses."

· Eighteen ·

FOR TIME OUT of human mind the bowl out of which the Alaminites scythed, pickaxed, spaded, dug, stripped, carried, and dumped turf had been a beautiful place that eyes of persons never saw. That persons had not seen it didn't matter in the large patterns that overlay mountain and Saquave, holding each necessary to each.

Here grew mixed grasses, spotted with wildflowers, spring through fall. The stream course carried runoff of rain and snow safely down the Hammers. The pools provided cool coverts for trout to sport at insects, and bears to sport at fish. The meadow nourished and watered bees, birds, meat-eater and grass-eater alike in all seasons. Before Silver City began to grow under the Claw, the meadow's water would have merged with the others that watered the Sweet Grass Hills, which in turn, on a larger scale than the meadow, sheltered and fed a host of life.

Today, while the air hung with heavy weight under the black boil of clouds overspilling the Hammers, the big meadow's water course was sluggish with sediment. On the rim, birch, beech, aspen, and high pine lay dead, or if not quite killed, the wood's mutilation bled sap and resin.

In the center of this good place grew a man's mountain of dirt, naked of protecting roots to hold the mountain's skin to its bone.

The squirrels never ceased their furious territorial chatter of bared teeth. They darted into everything, confused by loss of home, their young taken by hawk, falcon, crow, and raven. The squirrels' tails flowed like water after their ever-scavenging small bodies. Small they were, nothing but vermin in the Alaminite pattern of things, but squirrels protested loss of their life as they'd been created to lead it.

The Alaminites shot the squirrels, angered by the squirrels' ceaseless racket as much as if they'd been babies screaming with colic. Their whips struck the slaves often and bit flesh hard.

"My work will be nothin' if ya don't get the dump covered up before the storm. No use keepin' ya at all then, if there ain't nothin' to haul back to Silver City," Jake warned.

The slaves were as bewildered as the squirrels. Any person knew that when a mountain storm hit, no canvas, no tarp could hold free, open dirt. The wind was already so strong they could hardly stand. The black mounds lifted and beat in their faces like the wings of the black angels serving the hell to which the Alaminites had condemned their heathen slaves.

Cameron said, "Sir, Mr. Jake, nothing we've got here can hold against mountain nature."

Jake kicked Cameron, and then her shackle mate, Sigune, for emphasis.

"I didn't ask for mouth. If ya weren't so damned lazy we'd a had this here all loaded and home by now. If ya lose it in the rain I'm gonna shoot each and every one of ya myself, starting with you, daughter of the witch."

Screams, so high, so penetratingly sharp that they cut through the winds, came from the Alaminite food tent.

"Shit! The damned squirrels are at the supplies again," Jake swore.

The squirrels had taken cover long ago, all the slaves had noticed.

"Snakes! Snakes! Rattlers in everything!"

Jake and several other men left the chains to take care of the snakes.

At the first scream of "snake" those watching at the rim saw the slaves stiffen with alert attention out of their futile task of covering dirt from a storm.

Alaminite women were trained to believe from birth that anything not under man's control, and given by man's hand to them to care for, was from the devil, and they needed their men to stand between it and them. They scattered in all directions, screaming.

"Come back, you female fools!" Jake yelled. "Did ya git our food lashed down, stored away?"

"Snakes! Snakes!" For once the Alaminite women couldn't be made to obey.

The slaves knew that the Snake told Eve, the first Stallion Queen, where to find Torgut, the First Stallion. That was how Eve found the daughter for whom she yearned, and the horse people were created.

The mules brayed wilder than before. They plunged and kicked. Their hobbles, strong as Alaminite shackles for their slaves, but made of leather, not chains, gave way. The mules ripped from their picket line. Most of the men grabbed for flying mule leads.

Mules can buck, legs hobbled or not. Like horses, mules go loco over snakes. Unlike Alaminites and horses, though, mules knew the difference between poisonous and unpoisonous serpents.

The Stallion Queen placed the pretty little ones that glowed in colors bright as jewels among the Alaminite supplies. She freed rattlers and sidewinders among the mule picket, slashing their hobbles at the same time, at great risk of head and limb.

Heraldic storm drops smashed down, as bruisingly hard as stones thrown by Alaminites in the Ceremony of Defiance, which served to teach woman never, never to question man's will. The storm clouds obscured the sun; all was darkening as though night were falling. Hail came first, then piledrivers, sledgehammers, whiplashes of rain.

The Wilderness was strong, hard, and enduring. So were Alaminites. The Stallion Queen did not underestimate Alaminites, whom she had known from her childhood. But the Wilderness was better at finding its way in dark and storm, when godly folk stayed under roofs or went to ground in cellars, waiting for the devil's force to recede.

With the larger number of the Alaminites alarmed, fighting to save supplies, catch women and mules, the slaves were guarded by fewer men than at any time since they'd come out of the walls of Silver City.

Bari waded through the dark, hail, and rain, Moria at her back, directing, to the slave chain trapped by their shackles between and at the bottom of the liquefying hills their labor had built. The black mud slipped down in slick sheets, sticky and suffocating as quicksand. Moria told Bari where the women were. Bari pulled them out of what was rapidly becoming their graves.

Azal's blades stung one Alaminite guard after another.

Dream flew free, like the gazelles her tribe honored and matched, bound neither by earth nor air. The Gazelle tribe's curiosity moved them between worlds, and brought back to the other tribes, on their painted stones and hides, what the Gazelles learned.

Dream rounded up the Alaminite women with rope, lash, and net, so they would not fall lost forever in a chasm. One of them might hold a key to the chains. Dream killed, more than once. She remembered where the body fell, washed clean and white under the storm. She stored away the sensation, the feel, of killing.

Mules out of their hobbles used their sense to get under cover of the Alaminite tents. Mules and storm brought the shelter down. Mules and Alaminites tangled.

The Hammers pounded mercilessly. By blistering sheets of lightning, Moria counted, as best she could, the slave chains. Bari retreated to high ground in the uncut trees, carrying, dragging, pulling, the slave chains behind her.

Kazimir put his mouth to Leon's ear between cracks and rolls of thunder. "This water rushing out of here down to the Grass Lands will be chased by the Owls and Beavers. We've got to get to the horses and off their range as fast as we can."

Glennys slid through the water as if a part of it. "We must finish all of it here, unless we want to be tracked, carrying women still in chains, by Alaminite men with guns, down the Benches to the Sweet Grass."

Unlike the cold, bruising rain, *her* lips on his ear were soft and warm. Leon's flesh grew hot, swelled, under that touch.

Konya wriggled around to where Glennys squatted between the two men. "The light's coming back, the storm's moving on down. Killing time, I think."

Glennys slithered away to see for herself that they all had dry arrows and strings.

The Wilderness force didn't wait until the birds began to speak or the squirrels began to chatter. By then the Alaminites would be able to see quite well under their dripping shelter. They shouldn't be allowed that advantage.

The Alaminites were stupid only as to certain things. Under the arrows they retreated into the tangled pile of their belongings. Out of their possessions they built very quickly a circle of defense.

As the light returned two Elk women could be seen, half-submerged in one of the dirt mound's mud slides. The Alaminites shot them in the head, without bothering to learn if the women were alive or already dead. Such brutality showed the Saquave force that the Alaminite powder, like their guns, was of very high quality, and not much affected by the wet.

Saquave was outnumbered. Eight of them against some twenty with firearms. Glennys had insisted they gather upon the high ground, between the Alaminites and their route up to Silver City.

Only one of the rounded-up Alaminite women carried a key. Now there were nine more on Saquave's side, but unarmed. Armed or not, the slaves took charge of the women overseers, and were adequate to do so.

Mountain evening spilled across the destruction of the meadow before Saquave arrows took out the last Alaminite man. One of the nine chains could not wait any longer. Giving the Elk battle cry, the women ran down the washed-out gradients to the Alaminite position. At least one Alaminite was alive but the gunfire abruptly stopped when the Elks reached the snarl of tarps and canvas, at the price of one dead upon the threshold of freedom. She was heavily swollen with pregnancy.

The keys were found. The Alaminite women were chained waist to waist by those who'd lived in chains for so very long. Fires were lit, while the war women traced the mules and brought them back.

The camp was stripped with all the swift expertise of raiders, food piled and made into bundles for the mules. The freed slaves began to attack the tools which they'd been forced to wield.

Glennys stopped them. "Everything here, including the mules, belongs to you. Destroy it all, if you wish. But what is here is all you possess at this time. You cannot return to your tribe. The Snakes will help you, and so will the Badgers. The Alaminites make good tools. Moria's people, who can make use of them, and mine, will trade you weapons, maybe horses, for these things if you can get them down from here."

As the night came on Glennys hugged herself close. Cool as it was, her face was beaded with sweat, as though she had a fever.

Bari said, "Governor, I know that the mountains make you suffer, where you cannot see from horizon to horizon, so far from your horses. You should go on ahead. We'll clean up here."

Glennys said, shivering, "Brecca will be very angry that I've gone away. I can't touch him up here, and he can't find me. But I must stay, otherwise the Elks will do as the tribes do when prisoners are set free among their unarmed enemy. Once the Elks begin upon the Alaminite women, Cameron will become a part of it."

Bari said, "I think it's time, Glenn, you give up standing between Cameron and the hardest parts of life. You've always treated her as your pretty kitten, to give you amusement when worn out from the hardness of life. But Cameron left kittenhood behind a long time ago. She's a cat now, and must hunt her own way into life."

Glennys said, "If I allow the Elks to torture, Cameron, whose first loyalty right now is with them, will suffer in the future from the memories. She's got more than enough evil to remember as it is."

Azal and Dream, with some of the Elks, kept guard over the chained Alaminite wives. The fire flashed brightly from the blades of their knives, with which they made suggestive, cruel displays.

Glennys asked Bari and Konya to take their place.

"Azal, Dream, please collect the arrows, and remove any signs from which Silver City could learn who was here," Glennys requested.

These were necessary tasks, and they put the young women's minds on something other than blood.

Leon dug through the Alaminite possessions.

Kazimir and Moria watched with impatient puzzlement.

"What are you looking for, Young Wolf?" Konya demanded.

"I want to take the guns and powder with me. There's never been a chance to get any before."

He piled up some small barrels and a cord of weapons on a canvas.

His companions were not the sort who believed in bearing burdens by free choice any more than by slavery. Glennys was appealed to. She didn't like it at all, that was clear.

"All right, we can put this stuff on the mules with the prisoners. This horror is coming to Saquave, it seems, no matter what I do. It's the next step. Silver City will arm the Elks, Owls, and Beavers. The upper tribes will then have the advantage, water or not, against the lower eight. The only solution is to disarm Silver City, and I cannot see how to do that."

Everything useful was loaded upon the mules, while the dead Elk women were put under stones. The Alaminites were left wherever they'd fallen.

A sobbing wife begged to be allowed to burn her husband's body. Sigune slapped her silent. She stood back, contempt and hatred on her face, holding her big belly.

"Go down into the mines, then you might have something to sob about. Your Jake shoved his shit into my womb down there, where *we* had to grub for the silver *you* desire so much that you steal, kill, and slave. You say Sir Mr. Jake will not find your heaven when left for vultures, coyotes, and jackals? We say the scavengers are far too clean for him and all the rest. I think we should leave you with them, after we've made Jubilee with knife and fire."

Glennys went among the Elk women, calming and arguing.

"These women are what Sepul and his pozeem are trying to make you be. It is their men who have done this to you, not them, just as you must remember it is Sepul who is your true enemy."

"The women helped," Sigune stated. "They whipped, punched, and kicked, while their men held us down, had us in chains, kept us under weapon guard."

Cameron came to stand at Sigune's back. It was the first time either Kazimir or Leon had seen her clearly. Gaunt, in rags, all the soft roundness they'd both loved to watch was gone. Her face was hard and set.

Bari yelled, "We ain't got time for this shit. I'm hungry. So move out. We got one mean journey ahead of us to keep the Elks and Beavers off our tails. The sooner we start, the sooner we come."

She went to the lead mule. "Get over here, you whining gals. Expecting to sit on your asses now we got you out of Alaminite hands? Hee! Haw! Make yourselves useful. Skin these bastards down to the Benches where the horses are waiting. You do remember horses, don't you?" Bari concluded derisively.

Leon took in everything that occurred. He understood now that Glennys had considered every angle of the mission, including the possibility of prisoners, and that the slaves would want to torture them. No man would have the ability to force the freed women as Bari had done. When the big woman told them to jump, by Saquave, the Elk women jumped. They still had the slave responses lashed into their bones enough to obey Bari. No doubt, if their mission had failed, Glennys had several contingencies for that too.

Control over yourself first, knowing your people, and realistic planning ahead, was what made a good leader. Glennys possessed all the elements. She had earned her authority among the tribes. He had a long way to go to ever match her.

A slippery, greasy, nasty piece of business in the dark it was too, getting down to the Benches, through all the mud that had run out from the ruined meadow.

Shortly before midnight the war band met up with Thea and several other women waiting upon the bare, rocky Bench Legs wind-carved out of the Hammers. With the exception of Dervish and Black Blizzard, the horses were all Brecca's children. They made a close-bunched, shifting, shimmer, hard to see among the moon-shadowed rocks.

No time for rest, reunion, or celebration. The prisoners were lashed upon the mules, the Saquave women mounted double. Thea rode behind Glennys upon Hengst's Catclaw. Cameron was handed the reins of Mirage. Sigune rode behind her. Kazimir and Leon were given charge of the mule train of plunder and prisoners.

All night the horses were given their heads among the rocks, allowed to jimm slightly downwards until dawn. The horses were given a short breather, a handful of corn and beans, a suck of water out of the travel skins. Only then did their riders take a little water themselves, swallow a few hasty bites of mare's skin. Thea saw to it that the prisoners got a share. Foolishly, most of them refused the mare's skin as strange and revolting, though they drank the water.

The band was headed for Windgate, situated among the upper canyons of the Valley, where Rangers and an SSC patrol waited. That was a hard ride in the licking heat of day, many hours away.

"Kazimir, Leon, over the morning the mule train will fall behind. The two of you stay with the prisoners. Deal with them as humanely as possible. But if Owl or Beaver pozeem show up, ride to save yourselves. Leave the mules and prisoners for the pozeem to plunder."

Thea objected. She wanted to stay with the prisoners.

"Thea, Cameron and the others need your attention more than these. There's no time to stay here for that," Glennys said.

Leon marveled at the Elk women's endurance. They'd not ridden in nearly a year. They were starved, covered with sores and bruises. Most of them carried the hated burden of pregnancy. They never complained about themselves. They jeered at the prisoners. Their hands and feet lashed astride muleback, in the heat of the Wilderness that they feared as much as hell, hungry and thirsty, having no idea of their eventual fate, the Alaminites were an utterly miserable, hopeless bunch.

Kazimir and Leon perforce had to share their misery as the mule train fell ever further behind. Their prisoners prayed and tried to sing hymns, until the two men could no longer bear it, and forced them, under threat of gag, to be silent. The terrible, dry heat of Saquave summer was more effective than the men's threats. The women lapsed into a stupor.

This wasn't the way it had been in poetry and opera, Leon meditated. This was no thrilling, wild ride into freedom, yelling and shouting in exaltation, with the woman he loved gratefully hugging his waist. It was heat and thirst so strong his stomach cramped with nausea. It was the burden of women for whom he had nothing but contempt as the mates of men he burned to kill. The woman he loved had never addressed him one word of greeting, much less gratitude. Silver City had done that to her, and took her away from him, maybe forever. He rode with his rival, and that was his only consolation. Cameron had given Kazimir no more than she'd given him.

Time and again they had to stop, to water the prisoners. They had to beat the mules, whose legs greatly outnumbered theirs, from chasing up into the Benches, where the flies weren't so bad, and there was some grazing to be had. They had to allow the prisoners to relieve themselves, which they then couldn't accomplish with others, two of them men, watching. Then they had to remount them.

"If it were up to me, I'd just leave them," Leon said to Kazimir. "I don't think they're going to make it anyway. They refuse to rip up their skirts to cover their faces. The sun, sand, and flies have blistered them as if they'd fallen into boiling water."

Kazimir agreed. "It's worse than skinning the trade caravan in the Dead Lands. Then at least I was with my own kind who knows what it's doing. But the Stallion Queen is in charge of this operation. I believe she regards this as the opening battle in the war we're being forced into making upon Silver City."

Kazimir squashed a handful of flies that made a crawling mask, in spite of her forelock, lashes, and tasseled bridle, upon Dervish's face.

"Battle?" Leon spat. "The forces on either side were too small to make it a battle."

Kazimir snorted. "Noloani must possess men in the number of these flies, then. It was a battle up there."

It was long after dark when the men delivered the prisoners to Windgate, a stoutly stockaded SSC Flying Company station, built up around a cliff town deserted ages ago by the people who had made it.

"This is the worst duty I've ever pulled," Leon said to Glennys. "Tell Sigune that the prisoners have suffered enough torture to gratify even her bloodthirsty desires."

· Nineteen ·

THE SSC FLYING COMPANY station named Windgate was positioned high up, where the River ran wild in its youthful, newly gathered strength. The ancient people who had first lived there, carved out the rocky canyon rooms, and covered the walls with paintings of Saquave's creatures, had been a good-sized group. There were chambers, and to spare, for everyone, including the prisoners.

Below, the Snake River sidewinded against the chasm's jutting abutments in furious energy, smashing, crashing, tumbling, grinding stone. The water power poured out of Lake Umbel, greatest catchment for the Rain Shadows' drainage system, in torrents of falls, cataracts, and cascades. White foam boiled and bubbled. Where wind out of the Mountains funneled into the chasm and struck the River, flumes reared so high that the station's decks, built of cedar wood upon a wide landing between the River and the canyon town, were misted in moisture.

Rainbows materialized and evaporated on either side of the River, and under the feet of those leaning over the Windgate deck stockade. The River's drama was endless. A person had to be vigilant in her marveling, for one would begin to think she was able to walk from one side of the canyon to other upon the sparkling, many-hued arches.

Windgate was a permanent station, with a small stable built upon the decks. The soil wasn't deep enough for crops, and the growing season was much shorter than farther down the Valley where the River widened, matured, and spread out the pulverized riches it gathered out of the mountain runoff. The gardens were at the canyon rim, where the horses grazed.

Windgate had its own seasons and climate, separate from the Wilderness, the lower Valley, and the Rain Shadows. The station was cool, pleasant, and beautiful in the summer, without either flies or mosquitos. Protected by the River's power and the canyon walls, Windgate was a safe, secure place where they could catch their breath and decide what to do next.

Konya and Moria sent pigeons to their tribes, telling them they were alive, the mission successful. Behind their own pigeons, Flying Company riders went up to Fort Cloud and down to Hometown with written dispatches of what the Governor had seen up in the Hammers, and her conclusion that Silver City's strategy was to arm the pozeem of the three Sweet Grass tribes. In return for the guns that would give the upper Saquave advantage over the other tribes, the Sweet Grass would strike at the SSC.

The Governor wrote, "Indeed, the rains overleap Elk country, in the eternal Saquave cycle of rain. However, the Owls and Beavers don't lack rain. They suffer from the consequence of Alaminite diversion of the watercourses that have always watered their hill ranges during all seasons of the year through erosion and damming. The Bat and Gazelle women, who played their parts in our mission to rescue Cameron and the Elk women, will witness this to their neighboring Crows and Cougars, the Scorpions to the Wolves.

"More—Moria has chosen to request her Bat Chief, with his pozeem, call upon the Beaver and Owl Chiefs to make a long talk about erosion and diversion.

"Konya of the Badgers will witness to the Rabbits and the Coyotes. I believe the Elk women who survived their enslavement will provide the solution to the threat Sepul is to our security. The Valley will outfit the women with what they need. Badger Chief Kazimir has chosen upon his own to lend the Elk women strength from his chosen pozeem.

"I like this very much. When there is fighting, as there will be, no one from the SSC will be upon Elk range. We will not play any role in the torture-executions that will happen, and no Elk son, in the future, will be able to say so."

There was much more Glennys put into her Fort Cloud and Hometown dispatches. She detailed the ruin she foresaw if some tribes had firearms, and the others didn't. Hometown was at a dangerously critical junction. They either had to destroy Silver City or get possession of firearms themselves. If the tribes were armed, they had to be armed equally. Perhaps that way the tribal balance would remain in effect.

From whatever angle Glennys looked at the situation she saw firearms in the future, the future she had hoped to keep from the SSC as long as she was alive. She couldn't see any way around this dilemma, for only with the tribes living in unity and cooperation, allied to the Valley, could the SSC hope to keep its independence from Nolan. The SSC was too small alone.

Glennys doubted that Hometown, even backed by the lower tribes, could pacify or destroy Silver City.

Leon woke after sleeping a full day and a half. Even before thoroughly awake he heard Windgate discussing the Governor's postulations and premises. Kazimir had been correct in calling Cameron's rescue the first battle of what, to the young heir of Nolan's crown, looked like a long, hopeless war.

"You don't hide anything of what you think or know," Leon said when invited to eat with Glennys in her rocky room.

Soft sand was spread over the floor and covered with rugs and cushions. Woven, patterned, dyed wool from the SSC hung on the walls. The fireplace drew clean. The candle flames had no drafts to fight. The old people had dug and carved to good effect. The place they had left behind, with painted walls and ceilings as their only history, was a comfortable room in which to sleep, eat, and talk strategy.

"I don't hug what I know or guess about the future to myself. My mother concealed my true father's identity from me because she was hiding it from herself. Duke Albany went so far as to hide Sharissa and your existence here from me and many others, without a word to anyone. He thought that gave him power. Both pieces of information were my right. Those secrets Stella and Albany kept were so important to me, that if I'd known them when I should have, likely I wouldn't be sitting here in Windgate tonight," Glennys said soberly.

In a quick change of attitude she said, "On the other hand, who knows that if I'd known, any difference would have been made at all? Let's get over being hungry and thirsty, and have some fun."

"Fun? When you're getting ready for war?" Leon asked.

Glennys answered, "There are no kings here. What can be accomplished among the tribes will be done, in its own time, after tribes delight themselves in a summer made of talk, battles, and kills. I declare a leave of absence for myself from the SSC to go out and talk with them, though not to fight or kill. These recent events have provided an excellent excuse to get out of Hometown and ride on Saquave. You were smart to take the Alaminite weapons. I'm distributing them to the tribes so they can learn, before Nolan comes, how Nolan's weapons work."

Leon said doubtfully, "You want to teach Badgers and Scorpions how guns work? When did you last sleep?"

Glennys laughed. "I slept on Catclaw on our ride to Windgate. What I'm suffering from is a heavy head from thinking and writer's cramp, after putting my thoughts down in an orderly manner in long dispatches."

Leon asked, "What are you going to do with the Silver City women?"

Through big, greedy mouthfuls of trout and greens, Glennys said, "They are one big pain in the ass. Wasn't counting on women brought up to believe they were born only for men's convenience. Much as I'd like to, I can't make myself turn 'em out on the Wilderness. That's murder. What they are, what they've done, is the fault of their men. Got to keep them prisoners in Windgate. Alaminites can't be allowed to see Hometown's defenses from the inside. Any tribal representative who wants to test my words against theirs can talk to them here. Maybe we can convert the women from Alam's way to ours. By evidence of my sister, Deborah, I doubt the women will turn, though."

Leon ate as heartily as Glennys. He felt more cheerful with every mouthful of fresh-caught, grilled fish he ate. Her warm, frank conversation garnished the meal so enjoyably that he'd have been satisfied with corn mush.

They talked of war. She was prepared to gamble a lot of the Valley's resources upon Sigune and her Elk companions in tribulation. Removing Sepul was the first step to bringing the upper tribes back into Saquave's fold.

"You don't think war is the glorious crown of a man's life?" Leon asked.

She answered, "I'm smarter than men. Ask any woman. War is nothing but waste and destruction, at the very best. I've worked my ass off to save what I loved from it. As I said earlier, if I'd known Sharissa, still carrying you, had survived your father's assassination by the Wheel-Spur faction, maybe St. Lucien wouldn't have been sacked by Hans Rigg and his prophets leading the poor. Maybe there'd never have been a Silver City here, or a Civil War over there. War's coming to me and mine now. I can't wear blinders, or hope to outgallop what's on my tail. I know better than to believe that if I turn over on my back and show my belly, Alaminites and Nolan will treat me and mine with honor, or even fairness."

Leon carefully separated the little bones from the fish. He didn't quite understand the question she asked him.

She repeated, "In St. Lucien, did you ever hear a musician named Jonathan Reed play?"

Leon thought about the name. He barely remembered anything from St. Lucien now, except his mother, and his uncle's friends, all of whom, no doubt, hoped he was dead.

Slowly he said, "Jonathan Reed. He had a bunch of children. He used to come and play for Sharissa, when she was so unhappy she wanted to die. She didn't like Reed to console her, as Roald had Reed play music to help him sleep. Sharissa feared that if Roald discovered Reed, one of his own favorites, came to her he'd get in trouble, but sometimes she needed what he gave her too much. I vaguely recall Reed lost his position running the Opera. I just don't know much about people so much older than me."

Glennys had a very faraway look upon her face. "Johnny was always best pleased when his music was needed by someone in distress. He must have been very happy playing for the Queen of Nolan."

Leon held up the wooden spoon with which he was putting honey upon his cornbread. "You knew Jonathan Reed?"

"He was the great love of my life," Glennys said. "He said I was his, until he understood that horses did more to take away my despair than his music."

Cameron came up the ladder from the decks. She half-hauled Rastil in with her. Now that Rastil had his mistress back, he wouldn't allow her out of his sight.

Cameron startled perceptively to his eyes when she saw Leon was with Glennys.

Glennys immediately got to her feet. "Come in, darlin'."

Leon's stomach flip-flopped. His grandmother, the Baroness Ely, often called Sharissa darlin'.

"Sit down by me. The Fliers have been waiting to grill more fish. They got so many this evening Windgate's pride will be sore if we don't eat 'em up."

More food appeared shortly. Cameron stayed very close to Glennys while she ate. It wasn't just him, Leon saw, that made her nervous. It was the presence of any man. Yes, Leon thought, he had a very good reason to hate Alaminites.

Other people joined them one at a time. Under cover of their talk Glennys and Cameron carried on a low, private conversation. Leon's hearing was extremely acute. He eavesdropped.

"Sigune come through it all right?" Glennys asked.

"She did. Sigune's so strong, so much stronger than me. She'd only have me, not Thea, to help or comfort her. Thea couldn't have stood it. Sigune's decision went against everything that Thea is, except Thea's belief that the choice was Sigune's, and there was no other choice. Before Sigune started, Thea asked Jake's wife if she'd take it. She wouldn't. There was no place for it in the world."

"How?" Glennys asked.

"A bath of warm water," Cameron answered.

Cameron talked about the upper tribes and Silver City. "You're giving Sigune and the other Elk women the horses they came in on, aren't you? I told them you would."

"Oh, yes, and others beside so they won't have to ride double. But," Glennys asked, "does Sigune know that you are needed to bear witness to the tribes about Silver City and the rest?"

"Sigune knows. She doesn't think I'm letting her down, either. She is so strong! I wish I had half of what she's got in her. I'd never have lived through the mines," Cameron said fiercely.

Glennys said, "There's no point in comparing suffering. You suffered. She suffered. You're both alive and going to act on what you've learned, so that other women don't have to endure what you did."

Slowly Leon realized that Cameron had drowned what Jake had put into Sigune as soon as it came out of the womb.

If Sharissa had gotten pregnant from Roald, and she'd asked him to do the same with what came out of her, could he have served his mother the same way? Surely Sharissa would have hated Roald's get as much as Sigune hated Jake's. Maybe women were stronger than men because they had children. And men, like Alaminites, and his own kind, had betrayed that strength, called it weakness. These speculations were unwieldy, as hard for Leon to catch hold of as a thrashing fish upon the hook.

The River was a crashing water symphony below, looping and twining among all their words and his thoughts. He was worn out. It was hard for him to understand anything except that he'd lost Cameron, the first woman for whom he'd felt love as well as lust. It was what other men had done to her, nothing that he'd done, which had changed her.

Leon's earlier cheer deserted him. He'd lost his love. The paintings upon the ceiling moved in the firelight as if they were true animals, alive with blood and bone, though small. A cougar, what he would have thought of as a lion, but her color was all wrong, seemed to roar at him like a lioness, then hiss like any cat disturbed by a stranger.

He was an unwanted, uninvited, foreign, orphan intruder upon strange people and their unknown land. He got up from the rugs and wished everyone a good night.

He climbed down to the decks. He hung over the palisade. Down below, water and rock battered each other in their endless conflict. The clean, aromatic scent of pine resin and cedar wood touched his nose, along with grilled fish, and the smell of the stable close by. He was so tired.

The River broke the moonlight into cold, shivering, silver lances. Bats swooped across the decks. Owls hooted. Over the rim drifted the hunting cry of wolves. A coyote yipped. The horses pastured above neighed nervously. The dogs up with them barked reassurance to the pigs and sheep. Behind him he heard the sentries making for the rim trail to relieve the others upon the watchtowers. Buckets of fresh water bumped up alongside the sentries by weight and tackle.

In the River's rampage he saw his life. The desires and hatreds he nurtured were without meaning. He confronted the inexorable condition of being human. He was nothing, and he was alone in the nothingness.

An agitation shook the ladders. A small, choked sound was with it, as though it were a laugh that didn't know how to make itself. An anxious barking.

"I'm coming, Rastil, I'm coming."

Dog claws ticked upon the deck planks. A cold, wet nose shoved into the hand hanging listlessly at Leon's side. A warm tongue licked his fingers.

All of Leon's senses strained. She was wearing soft-soled buskins. His sharp ears could hear every step she made anyway. She came to stand next to him. Carefully he made no move to shorten the distance between them. He gripped the palisade to keep his hands from touching her.

"Rastil is kinder, and more courteous, to my friends than I am," Cameron said.

Resolutely he kept his face down to the River. He looked at her out of the corner of his eye. She too was staring down at the water's tumult.

"It's hard to put what I feel into words. But I am grateful to you from the bottom of my heart."

Again came that choked sound, upon "heart."

Cameron cleared her throat. "Let me try again. There's no one else I'd rather be grateful to."

Leon whispered, the River taking his words. "Did you ever doubt that I would come, that I'd give my life to get you out of their hands?"

Rastil shoved between them. He stood up on his hind legs, bracing his front paws upon the palisade, tried to lick both their faces at once.

The man and woman had to answer the dog's demand for affection. They patted Rastil, ruffled his neck fur, scratched behind his ears, under his chin, crooned loving words to him.

"Good Rastil, smart dog, loyal dog, strong dog, we love you, Rastil, yes we love this good old dog."

He squirmed with delight, bounced like a puppy, rolled over on his back, begging to have his belly rubbed.

Inevitably their hands and fingers touched, then pulled away.

Out of the stable came swearing. "What the crescent are you doing? Think you're Brecca, and can go wherever you like when you feel like?" Hooves thudded out of the stable, over the deck.

Mirage came to them shining bright and clean. He carried his head high. His prancing progress spoke clearly of his wicked delight in his own strength and cleverness in getting loose to be with his people. Mirage thrust his nose into Cameron's ear, blew slobber down her neck. Mirage shared the pleasure of himself with woman, man, and dog, as he'd done during Fort Cloud's winter.

It wasn't the same as at Fort Cloud. Too much had happened to Cameron. But it was very good.

As dog and horse settled down, Leon and Cameron stood at Mirage's head, stroking his neck.

Shyly, Cameron reached out to touch the garnet in Leon's ear. "I'm glad you got it back."

"I still want you to have the stone," Leon said.

Cameron shook her head. "Please, not yet. That stone meant everything to me, which was why, even in my stupidity, I was wise enough to put it upon Mirage's halter."

Glennys had come silently down the ladder. What Mirage could hear, so could she. Leon was speaking to Cameron of Kazimir.

"As soon as the Badger Chief heard you were taken, he bent every power he possessed, dropped every concern, aided your mother in every way. I'd have made some bad mistakes up there if Kazimir hadn't been with me to show me the wise course, to make me wait."

Glennys came up to them. "Saquave gives you, Cameron, both stallion and dog. You have not one, which is rare enough, but two wise, strong, and generous men in your service. One of them is so honorable that he praised the Chief who had to collect his pozeem for Sigune's mission, leaving him alone with his rival."

Before Cameron or Leon could feel embarrassed by the Governor's observations, Mirage and Rastil demanded the Stallion Queen's attention. Glennys rubbed first one, then the other.

"I wonder what it's like to be so lucky that the men I love are loved by my horse and dog too. Well, I'll never know."

Leon's heart leaped. Cameron loved him. The Stallion Queen said so. She would know, if anyone did.

Cameron put her arms around Glennys. "It's mothers who love best, I think. I don't want to go away from you for a long, long time."

Glennys took a hand of Cameron's and one of Leon's. The three stood there linked.

"I think all of us deserve some fun. It's time for Brecca to learn how to work again at something other than his studly pleasure. Leon, will you go with Ronnie and me for a round of summer visits?"

Leon's tongue stuck to the roof of his mouth. "I would love to. But since I never was inducted into the Rangers, I have no horses."

Glennys said, "I have a couple of fine young stallions out of Brecca I've been saving. You can have them as the first of your string."

Cameron began to laugh. She laughed until tears ran out of her eyes, and she doubled over with cramps. It was horrible, more like howling, nothing of amusement in it. The convulsion went on and on, accompanied by huge, wracking hiccups.

"Leon," Glennys cried, "Get Thea. Cameron's having a fit."

Cameron straightened up and pulled herself together.

"No, I'm fine, much better than I've been in a long, long time."

Glennys demanded, "Well, then what is it, my love?"

"It's you. This is twice in one night I've heard you give away some horses," Cameron said, her laughter mild this time, honestly amused.

Glennys and Leon were still bewildered.

"Oh, mother, horse giver, this time it's not a dream. I'm really home again."

· Twenty ·

THE HEAT OF Thirst Moon baked the mantle of Saquave hard and brittle. The wind of Saquave's breath was feverish, sucking all dry. The tight-bunched grass curled upon itself, to preserve roots and runners so stems might wave again when, if, with the arrival of Honey Moon the rains returned to Saquave's breath.

The Coyote clan's stud stallions were tethered distant from each other. Mares and their foals covered the grass, color of a cougar's pelt. Particular friends grazed together, head to tail, swatting pests. A few sheep and goats bleated among the mares, pets of the horses.

This Coyote clan, though their luck had been good for several cycles, like all wise persons should, kept their goat herd, which provided milk and cheese, whose hair made their tents, small. They had grass, and their water holes were half full.

But who knew if the Honey Moon rains would come? Who knew what this winter, or next year, would bring? The Stallion Queen, backed by Badgers and Bats, was riding the Wilderness to say that next year would bring war.

Among their own marked animals ran many painted with the red-orange raddle of the Valley's Snakes. As well as taking in some of the youngest Elk children, the Coyotes had promised to foster part of the Elks' breeding stock. The children and animals were being slowly herded down from the burned-out Sweet Grass by Kazimir and his pozeem.

Sigune and the Elk women, with aid from Kazimir and pozeem out of the Badgers, Rabbits, and Wolves, had taken back the Elk tribe. The rain laws were in effect upon the Elk lands, as right and proper.

Slender threads of green cut through the Coyotes' tawny plain, showing where the intermittent courses of water ran in their seasons. Shadowy paths were the washes, breaks, and gullies cut by thunderstorms. This clan's summer range was south of those claimed by the Badgers and Rabbits. Konya had made the arrangements, in company with the Rabbits' council, requesting hospitality for the Stallion Queen's tail. Their luck allowed these Coyotes the supreme pleasure of generous hospitality.

On the windward slope of a ridge Schoolmaster Muran sat next to Glennys. He'd requested the opportunity to ride upon the Wilderness instead of walking on it. The only shade was under their spear-propped kiftas. For that reason alone Muran consented to carry a lance.

Close by were Konya and the Rabbits' wise woman, Kicker. Konya had brought the Stallion Queen and her display of new weapons to the Rabbits. Kicker and her tribe were convinced that a very bad new thing was coming on Saquave. This thing was Noloani. Noloani would try sooner, if not later, to use this disgusting thing upon Saquave's good persons.

Kicker said with disgust, "Something perverted like this is exactly what a person has to expect out of Noloani. You are right, Konya. We must show everyone, so we can be prepared."

Next Kicker and Konya had approached the Coyotes for an invitation to visit their lands and confabulate. The head of the Coyotes' council, a woman named Rogan, kept a suspicious eye upon everything.

The Coyotes were noted for their inclination to play malicious jokes. Rogan, true to Coyote nature, wasn't sure the Stallion Queen, in company with the other two wise women, wasn't putting over an elaborate joke upon her people.

The ridge was covered with Badger, Rabbit, and Coyote women, pozeem of all three tribes, and their favorite war stallions. No one had brought their children, which was another sign that the women considered this very serious business indeed.

Cameron sat further down among the Crescents, the young, unattached women, Rastil at her side. These visits among the tribes involved a great deal of hospitable eating. Ronnie no

longer looked like the starved rabbit they'd brought out of
the Hammers. Better, her face glowed with a healthy, sleek
confidence in herself. Glennys had worried that Cameron's
recovery from the Alaminite marriage would either take a very
long time or only be a partial one.

The tribes called a rapist "soul stealer." The crime was very
rare, and punished heavily.

Glennys's instinctive response, taking both Cameron and
Leon with her to visit the Wilderness, where they would be
close together, had been the right one. Sharissa had done something right with her son, if he was able to make Cameron look
like that so soon after her ordeal. Glennys knew that no matter
what she was able to do for her daughter, she could never have
given her back to herself alone, at least not this quickly.

Glennys was deeply grateful to Leon. He gave this work
he was doing for her among the tribes the best he had. She
suspected that Leon didn't believe that Nolan would come
here with an army. In any case he was too much distracted
by the respect of pozeem, the admiration of the Crescents, and
Cameron's love to think very clearly about the future.

Like the Badger, Rabbit, and Wolf Crescents, the Coyotes
teased Cameron about Leon as mercilessly as the dry wind
drank moisture. Cameron knew this was good manners, Saquave
fashion. It was a way for those who envied her the most because
Young Wolf slept in her kurgan to vent their envy.

Leon was upon the plain. The herders had been warned
and were mounted. Their dogs trotted around the sheep, their
tongues hanging in the heat. Pozeem of the other tribes they'd
visited earlier, their horses, and their dogs had gotten used to
this testing of what Silver City's guns could and could not do
against arrows. They'd already tested it to their own satisfaction,
so they took over the task of herding from the Coyote pozeem.
Runaways were more of a danger than predators during these
demonstrations.

Away in the distance was a small herd of buffalo. Wild ass
stallions hung about the horse herd, hoping to steal a mare. Too
close for their own good was a small group of gazelle does and
their young, drawn by gazelle curiosity. Time and again the
guns went off, and the gazelle bounded away. Time and again
they, or another group, showed up, attracted by the pozeem's
brilliantly colored banners fluttering from planted spears.

Leon had drilled the Coyote Chief and his pozeem long and carefully. This afternoon Chief Guleir practiced his mastery of this strange weapon upon targets stuffed with grass in the shape of pozeem lashed upon running mules. His pozeem loosed their arrows at the same time. That way they got a feel for the difference in the killing range between guns and arrows. The hosting clans lost a lot of mules that way, but death was the only teacher with which not even a Chief could disagree.

Hopefully, the tribes learned that guns didn't have the effective range of arrows. Reloading was slower than nocking another arrow in the bowstring. Leon had already proved that guns weren't good enough to kill a buffalo with one shot. A strong pozeem could bring down a buffalo with one correctly placed arrow. That was one of the skills that proved a pozeem was a pozeem.

Showing the tribes all this had been Glennys's idea, sprung from the strongest premonition Saquave had sent her since her search for Leon in the Weirding Ride. Next spring, at the latest, Nolan would be on Saquave.

Being introduced to firearms by Leon, who'd trained with them at the Equine Academy, should save the tribes from surprise and panic when confronted by the Nolanese weapons. Such introduction should prevent them from believing firearms to be all-powerful. Hopefully, the pozeem would remember what they saw, what they did this summer.

Glennys's method in all things was to make carefully thought through, thorough preparation before any action was attempted. Long ago men had accused her of feminine cowardice because of her method. Everything that had occurred subsequently confirmed that her way worked. The SSC, Hometown, and the Valley were the proof.

Pozeem were willing to be instructed by Young Wolf, Noloani or not. He'd proved himself a person to other pozeem by surviving on foot for so long in the Saquave. Chief Kazimir had helped him bring the Stallion Queen's daughter out of the Hammers. Chief Hengst was willing to make him a Ranger.

Leon repeated that Noloani trained gunners worked in lines of one, two, and three. As one line shot, the gunners fell to reload, and the one behind shot. By the time the third line shot, the first line had reloaded. There were cannon too, much bigger, which demanded at least three men to fire.

He didn't have enough guns or charge to make an authentic demonstration of the deployment's tactics. In the evenings, sitting in the light shining out of a tribal wagon, he covered hides with colored paints in the configurations in which Noloani armies marched, emplaced, charged, defended, and attacked.

Faced with a Noloani army gone to earth with gunnery and cannoneers, the deal for Saquave was to ride break for leather just short of killing range, sheer off either side, prepared for any opportunity to roll up the Noloani flanks. Another, slower riding line was to take their place, and another after that, like the wind waves in the grass, against their ammunition. The tactic, a word unknown among the tribes, was never to ride into the killing range. They must never charge an emplacement until they were sure the ammunition was spent.

If the Noloani used their cavalry, well, then it was charge against charge. There was no hope of convincing the tribes to change that, any more than anyone had persuaded the Nolanese cavalry to change. They were warned, however, that Nolan's war stallions were heavier and bigger than theirs.

The likely result would be a standoff, a siege—if the tribes remembered, if they were lucky. They had to learn to wait until a storm, especially a sandstorm, struck. Waiting, when battle excited, was not a skill that proved a pozeem a pozeem.

Sandstorms, Black Blizzards, thunderstorms, these the pozeem did understand. They were of Saquave. Silver City and Nolan didn't understand the Wilderness laws. Sandstorms carried, with larger grit, dust finer than silt, that got into everything. That dust immobilized cocks and triggers, chewed up the action.

Unless, of course, Nolan had improved their weaponry greatly since Leon's days at the Equine Academy. Stogar was still alive, and he loved gunpowder and guns. The Alaminites believed these weapons had appeared by Alam's own revelation. They worked like ants, or beavers, to improve what they loved.

While the Stallion Queen's company acted to teach Saquave new rules for battle against new weapons, Kazimir, with pozeem from the Wolves and Rabbits, had ridden with wise women and Crescents. They had gathered by their own choice from all the tribes, at the back of Sigune and the Elks.

Kazimir and Konya had been outraged from the first rumor of it by Sepul's sale of the Elk women. Sepul had made that criminal bargain to get for himself the power within the Elks held by the women. Control of the pozeem wasn't enough to change the traditional balance of power within the tribe. Sepul had gambled that without the women to feed he could ignore Saquave's rain laws without suffering the consequences.

Sepul had not understood the place of the women in the tribe, or the place of their relationship within the larger tribal patterns of Saquave. A tribe with bad luck had to be assisted by the women of the others, if it was to survive at all.

Hengst's Fort Cloud Rangers had been reinforced by Bat pozeem. Accustomed to mountain travel by their home in the Wind Songs, they spied upon Silver City. When Coals of the Lord went out on their mission, carrying firearms for Chief Sepul's pozeem as payment for another slave coffle of Elk women, Fort Cloud knew.

They refined and expanded the tactics of the Stallion Queen's band. Under cover of a storm they hit the Alaminites.

The booty belonged to the Bats, except for the weapons. Those were divided among the women's councils west of the Valley: Bats, Crows, Gazelles, and Cougars.

In the meantime Moria and the Gazelles invited Owl and Beaver women to visit for a long confabulation. There were three subjects to be talked over: Alaminite thievery of Owl and Beaver water, Alaminite desire to buy Owl and Beaver women in exchange for guns, and an invasion of Saquave by Noloani armed with these guns.

Kazimir, backed by Konya, who was head of the Badger women's council, dared leave his own tribe to enforce Saquave's law upon another Chief's range. The Badgers' council was not incensed by Cameron's abduction. That was the Snakes' business, not anyone else's. Chief Sepul's sale of Elk women to the Alaminites had turned Silver City into a danger perceived by all the tribes.

Only the authority of the women's councils could sway their Chiefs into releasing their own pozeem to support one Chief against another. Sepul had frightened women throughout Saquave. They bent all their powerful means of persuasion upon their Chiefs to give assistance to Kazimir.

The guns' powerful ability, carefully displayed, served Glennys and Leon to frighten everyone further. This perversion was what the Alaminites had wanted to give the upper tribes, so they would turn them upon the lower. The Alaminites learned of guns from the exiled Noloani.

Saquave's power was on the move all summer. Saquave had done all of it through its chosen representative, the Stallion Queen who had returned from over there, out of Noloani exile.

Puffs of gunsmoke drifted over the plain. Whenever Coyote Chief Guleir missed the grass man target, he did hit a mule. The mules brayed in anguish, from shattered shoulders, torn chests. The damage was so great that if the mules had been men, not any of the most skilled tribal bone-setters could put all the pieces back together again.

It was a cruel manner in which to make a point. Cruel sights were familiar to the tribes.

Everyone had expected Sigune and the Elk women who'd survived to punish Sepul for a long time. His torture pleased them. The tribes felt it helped restore the balance Sepul had upset. Glennys turned her mind from that.

The mules were different. Mules were nothing that Brecca or the other horses cared for, but the mules' suffering touched their senses. They were agitated, and she kept her Horse Sense quiescent so she didn't have to feel it.

As soon as the bone-setters finished their examination, they put the mules out of their misery. Glennys untensed. These days, no matter how many sentries were posted, she was uneasy whenever parted for long from Brecca's senses, through which Saquave would give her due warning of approaching danger.

Matching shallowly with Brecca, she learned that Cameron had matched just as shallowly with Mirage. Cameron too was relieved that the mules' part was over. Mirage caught Glennys's affectionate regard of Cameron from Brecca. She turned around briefly and smiled.

When the new moon came up, Glennys and Cameron rode away from the kurgans out into the night. The shared affection and purpose of their riders kept the two stallions, natural rivals, at peace.

The stallions' shared curiosity about their riders, their approval of their riders, was the bridge that Glennys used to begin Cameron's lessons in the Horse Sense.

Glennys's method had been imprinted deeply within Cameron long, long ago. "I've been watching you train horses to be ridden, and people to ride them, almost my whole life. Never work at too much too soon, and never continue past the moment of accomplishment."

Cameron's Horse Sense carried the smaller skills she could do alone matched with Mirage. She knew how to enter his senses of sight, hearing, and smell, flow with them to learn what other horses learned from these senses. Matched with Mirage, she could ride over a command given by another horse's rider, and turn the horse to her own purpose. Matched with Mirage, she could call another horse or send it away.

Unlike Glennys, who didn't need Brecca for these small skills, Cameron had to match with Mirage first. Cameron's Horse Sense declined in effectiveness the farther she was away from her own stallion.

They were learning to partner Glennys and Brecca in the higher skills. Cameron and Mirage's effective field was expanded when they matched with the Stallion Queen and Brecca, much like spyglasses enhance sight.

They halted in a wind-scoured groove separating neighboring yardangs. Here was a trickle of water so small only a hint of dampness hung in the air. Mirage and Brecca scented stems from which grew pods of Locust Beans, somehow overlooked by the voracious forging of the goats. Horses loved the sweet Locust Beans.

There was no need for words. The two women dismounted and divided up the pods, fed them one at a time to Brecca and Mirage.

Cameron's senses dilated. It was as though they were partnered in an intricate riding figure. The stallions' gait was matched, a steady, even canter over the plain. The riders held phantom hands.

The tang of Saquave air-borne dust was stronger than the herds' and flocks' defecations scattered everywhere. They rode an ascending spiral, spun out of Saquave, channeled by Brecca, navigated through Glennys. They went up among Saquave's night fliers. The moon hadn't risen yet. Under them the patterns of the plain were slightly hazed. Their sense of tip, tilt, incline, decline, twist, and turn of water lines, and ancient herd migration paths had to be interpreted through a filter of minute sparkling particles of air-borne mica, quartz, feldspar, calcite and dolomite, all the elements that made up Saquave's mantle.

The fliers navigated by the same forces that wrote upon Saquave's mantle. The fliers found their bearings by the force of other vectors as well. The location of the mountains, the pull of the moon upon them, provided direction and dimension for movement.

They were on a pleasure ride, not the energy-consuming Weirding Ride of the Stallion Queen. They were out to see what there was to see. They flew north of the Coyote ridge. The night-flier spotted a hop mouse nibbling upon the grass.

Before it swooped, Glennys and Brecca cantered down the spiral to ride among a band of gazelles. The gazelles' delicate hooves, the slender bones of their long legs, sent information of an agitation upon Saquave's mantle. They sorted the wind; turned their ears to hear the north. When buffalo moved in a herd, all else had to give way.

It was too small for buffalo, but the gazelles bounded off to the east, partly in gazelle delight of soaring between earth and sky. For their own delight Glennys and Cameron stayed with the swift, graceful animals, until they stopped to lick their young and graze again.

Glennys was curious about what the gazelles had sensed. Saquave loaned more force to the spiral, set it spinning, spreading out slowly in a web to cover as much territory at once as possible. An owl took them, its flight lower than other night-fliers.

Dust thickened the texture of the air, in spite of the weight of night. It was raised by a slow night drive of horses and sheep, followed by mounted herders and three wagons.

Kazimir was escorting a group of Elk younglings and breed stock to the Coyotes. The recognition of him jolted Cameron's senses unexpectedly. He was riding Roxolani, and Mirage caught from the stallion that his rider was in pain.

Her phantom body lost its balance upon Mirage's back, her phantom hand lost hold of Glennys. She fell. Her stomach turned over.

She waited, unafraid. She had learned in Silver City what a woman truly needed to fear. Glennys and Brecca swooped under and caught her neatly. A phantom lariat noosed out from Glennys's arm and brought Mirage in.

Cameron blinked. Stirred by the night wind blowing among the rocks where she leaned, Locust bean stems tickled her hand.

Rastil sat quietly, panting in the heat of the night. The moon had come up. Glennys looked at her quizzically. The two horses stamped impatiently.

"You may as well tell Konya and Rogan that Kazimir's bringing in the Coyote fosterlings. He's about another day's travel from here. Brecca's in the mood to run, and so am I," Glennys said.

"I'd rather you did it," Cameron said.

"Leon's going to have to get used to hearing you use Kazimir's name sometime, just as Kazimir will have to get used to some other things," Glennys said.

The Coyotes delayed moving their kurgans and wagons for another day, though the animals were drifting off this pasture, seeking fresh forage.

Konya was the first to greet Kazimir when he rode in ahead of the fosterling drive. Then, as proper, he was greeted by Chief Guleir and Rogan.

The Stallion Queen's tail stayed out of this business, as these fosterlings weren't theirs. The reception for the ones Hometown had taken in, under the direction of Thea, had surely been more welcoming than this.

They weren't fed or given a chance to refresh themselves at the waterholes. They were given no time to rest. Like the Elk breed stock, they were divided up briskly, handed out whatever little food and possessions had come in the three wagons. The very smallest were put up behind the pozeem who were conducting them, with pairs of breed stock, among the clans. The others had to run beside the horses, or more likely behind.

There were nearly one hundred children between the ages of three and twelve. They were starved and dirty. They tried hard not to show their fright and their shame. The older ones each had taken responsibility for some of the littlest, sibling kin or not. Those bonds were ignored by the hosting tribe.

Kazimir went among them before they had to begin the next, and hardest, portion of their journey away from everything they'd known. He grasped the shoulders of the oldest boys, a gesture of respect from one pozeem to another, kissed the girls, took the smallest in his arms.

"This is very hard, but don't be afraid. You are Saquave's own, and will survive. You still have a tribe and are a part of it. Your mothers, sisters, sibs hold horses for you and work for you. Some of you are even lucky enough to have a father or uncle living. The rains will return. I was a rain law fosterling too. I grew up to be Chief. My mother, like yours, lost her man and all her children but me. Now she's head of Badger council and all the councils look to her."

The children stood around Kazimir, swallowing hard so they wouldn't cry. He was the only friend they had.

"Do you remember the four important things for getting along with the Coyotes?" he asked.

"Take good care of our breeding pairs. Make friends with the Crescents. Offer to help with anything going. When a Coyote plays a trick, make sure when we give it back it's so funny that the one on whom it's played laughs first."

Rogan said, "That's enough petting, Kazimir. You've delayed me from my own children and my own clan as it is. You and Konya are welcome to visit us whenever you like. Now, fosterlings, those of you hosted by my clan, move along."

Bravely, all the children not staying with the Coyote clan upon the ridge walked behind the horses. Those staying tried to match the courage of the departing friends.

Twenty children were apart from those parceled out among the Coyote clans. Konya took a deep breath of surprise when Kazimir told her these were going to their own clan of the Badgers. For one thing, they'd already received a quota of Elk children. For another, this batch was the dirtiest, raggedest, and most starved of them all.

"These are absolute orphans. They've no sib, no mother to hold horses for them. They had no one before we came, so there was no one to give them even a spoon before we left. I knew you'd be willing for our clan to take them among our orphan wagons, mother. Thanks to your wisdom, the Badgers are rich enough to do this," Kazimir said.

"If that's what you've decided, Badger Chief, that is what is done," Konya said.

She didn't look too happy about it, Glennys thought. Along with the other fosterlings, these orphans presented Konya's clan with over forty more mouths to feed. It was her duty to find the extra food.

Konya looked over the children. To Cameron she said, "Kazimir's fostering among the Elks during the cycles of Badger bad luck hurt him more than I ever guessed."

Kazimir went off alone to bathe. Cameron told Konya that she would see to Kazimir's horses.

"Such a service is the least I can do in return for what your son did for me," Cameron said.

Konya saw that the girl was blushing from the depth of the sincerity in her words combined with embarrassment about her connection to the Noloani. Her hopes for Kazimir's luck with Cameron revived, which was good luck for the orphans.

Konya smiled at the children. "I'll see what I can find you to eat. You can rest until tomorrow, when we start for home."

Glennys donated a couple of the Snake sheep running with the Coyotes' flocks.

Kazimir's mounts were as thin as the Elk children, though the horses were in better spirits than their master. Cameron couldn't get Kazimir's face out of her mind.

Leon and Muran helped her groom Kazimir's string. Salt from their sweat, mixed with dust and dried lather, crusted their coats. They'd been worked hard without time for a thorough grooming in many weeks. They needed water to do this properly. They led Kazimir's war stallions to a waterhole.

Muran said, "Kazimir has the appearance of a man who has seen horrible things that he wants to forget, but can't."

Cameron remembered with utter clarity what Sigune had planned for Sepul.

"I will put him in a hole in the ground where he will never see the sun. I will feed him his thing, one tiny slice at a time. I shall do this for a long, long time."

There were other Elk women riding with Sigune. Their hatred was no less fierce. Sepul wouldn't have been able to sell any of them without the help of the Elk pozeem.

Kazimir, as the Chief in charge of the pozeem who had volunteered to help Sigune, had to have seen everything.

· Twenty-one ·

THE LAST DAYS of Honey Moon dripped, gold and sweet, over the Valley. Saquave autumn was opening in all its splendor, a prolonged season of harvest beauty and moderate temperatures. In autumn, Saquave redeemed the violent extremes of its other seasons.

Tomatoes burst with juice. Peppers in all their varieties turned from green to scarlet. Pumpkins, squash, and melons ripened, one crop after another, along the irrigation ditches. They'd get at least one more picking off the bean vines. The corn was in, as well as the cotton. The tedious, finger-tearing work of separating the white puffs from bolls and seeds was over, and the trash was thrown to the pigs foraging upon the west side of the canyon.

The bleaching hours didn't begin until late morning, and relented soon after noon. The leaching aridity was balmed by a breath of moist freshness, though the rains had overleaped the Elks' summer lands once again. The middle west between the Mountains and the steppes falling to the Valley remained the same empty wasteland of thornscrub through which, this time last year, Leon and Muran had painfully quested for Hometown.

Sigune and her band of warrior women had handed back Elk tribal governance to the wise women who'd been sidewinded by Sepul's authority. The women had tasted battle blood, and there were few, if any, men, Elk or otherwise, these women cared for. Living under rain law, the Elk Crescents couldn't begin child-bearing years. There were no herds or flocks for them to follow and tend.

The middle-aged and younger pozeem who'd backed Sepul's law-breaking had been executed. Their surviving pozeem were gathering their meager resources for the Saquave caravan over the Dead Lands to the Green People.

Women had to perform the duties and obligations of pozeem. Writhing under the shame Sepul had put upon the Elks, preferring earning their keep to accepting charity, Elk women volunteered to patrol the Crossing Pass for signs of Nolan. A Nolanese invasion provided the hope of plunder. For the sake of adventure or booty, other Crescents asked to join Sigune, particularly those from the Scorpions.

Sweat beaded Glennys's face. Her hair was tangled, her homespun shirt clung to her back, big wet patches under her arms. Rattler, the young silver stallion under her, changed leads in a pattern of figure-eights around the training ring made close to the bosky. Rattler was getting the hang of what leg, rein, and spur were asking of him. She took him through the exercise one more time.

"Mab," Glennys asked, dismounting, "do you agree that Jer could take a try on Rattler?"

Jer swelled with anticipation, but he checked his rush over the rails of the ring, and waited for Mab's permission.

"All right, I think he's quiet enough in his mind to listen to you. Jer, ride Rattler through the gaits that the Gov calls out to you," Mab said.

JerJer was old enough to join Hometown's children who were passionate about horses, and old enough to object to the babyish "JerJer." He'd cooled down greatly, much to his younger brother's disgust, since he'd enlisted for horse duty under Mab. The addition of the oldest of the Elk fosterlings to Mab's roster, who already rode so much better than he, gave Jer's competitive instincts all the outlet they needed. If he couldn't outdo the Elk fosterlings in skill, he'd beat them in obedience. The day's long work of grooming, caring for tack, and exercising the horses left him too tired to make mischief for mischief's sake.

At nineteen, Mab wasn't a Hometown beauty, but her brown eyes were intelligent, and the planes of her face were strong. Her wispy hair was an undistinctive color. On horseback, however, it was as if she and the horse were one. In addition, she had a good memory, and figures came easily to her. She possessed an authority that kept the younger, inexperienced ones in line, and taught them what they generally never previously believed they had to learn about horses.

She'd integrated the Elk fosterlings among the Hometown younglings so quickly that black eyes and bloody noses were minimal. If Hometown could have afforded labor, room, and material for stables, Mab would have been Glennys's first candidate for Stablemistress.

Jer and Rattler moved with some uncertainty, but both rider and horse obeyed the commands they were given. If Rattler could be worked by Jer, then the stallion was ready for another, better-skilled rider to take over. As soon as one of Brecca's children was provided with a minimum of training, Glennys gifted the horse to a pozeem or a Crescent.

The sun's rays were longer and lower at summer's finish. Here in the pasture, close to the River, it was pleasantly cool. Jer brought Rattler to rest in front of her.

Glennys took the young stallion's head into her hands, blew into his nostrils, then placed her cheek upon the horse's for an expanded moment in time. She penetrated Rattler's senses with her own, so that he'd always know her, and she'd know him, whoever his rider might be.

"Mab, I think Rattler will enjoy carrying Feliks, youngest son of Woetzle, Chief of the Wolves," Glennys said.

Mab asked, "Is Feliks, like the other pozeem to whom you're gifting Brecca's children, reckless and hot-headed?"

Glennys answered, "Feliks was made pozeem only this summer. He is in a very big hurry to prove himself."

Mab watched critically while the youngsters gathered up the reins of the other horses standing outside the ring. She was one of the best riders, Hometown or Wilderness, skilled at management and teaching, but Rangering was another story. Like anyone brought up in Hometown, she could skin and butcher. She could hunt if she had to. But unlike Cameron or Jer, for instance, Mab was without desire to learn fighting skills.

Hometown needed people like Mab at least as much as they needed Rangers. Confronted by a Nolanese soldier, Glennys would bet on Mab, rather than on many others. Mab would band her hair off her wide forehead, then perform quickly, intelligently, and effectively face-to-face with an enemy, whatever needed to be done, then leave it behind if she could.

The older members of the SSC had accepted at first the likelihood of Nolanese armed invasion with a depression of spirits dangerously close to despair. The younger ones, on the other hand, thought at first an invasion would be a prolonged Jubilee.

But Glennys had opened to young and old alike the oppression Nolanese victory would bring, and her strategy to counter the army. That she had a strategy, and had begun to implement it during her summer with the tribes, raised the elders' spirits considerably. They were ready to gird their loins and remember their courage, of which they had a plentiful supply, or they wouldn't be part of the SSC. The young ones settled, much as had Jer.

"Take off their gear, but just wipe the horses off, and turn them out in the pasture," Mab instructed her charges. "Clean the bits and saddles and stow them away proper, before you start thinking about supper."

Glennys slouched against the rails of the ring. The sun's movement to the southern quadrant of the horizon provided deep modulation in the play of light and shadow. She pulled up a long stem of grass and chewed on it, empty for the moment of anything but the sense that she knew who she was, why she was here, and that her work was not only good, but well worth the doing.

Brecca led some of his mares through the cottonwoods and willows along the riverbank to drink. During the hot hours the stallion liked to browse and rest along the riverbank under her cave-den. Thea had told her that since Cameron's abduction, all the children's whispers about Glennys's den being the cave of a witch had stopped. Authentic threats had driven out the need for imaginary ones.

Mab collected the long lines on which the younglings had drilled the horses in hand. She coiled them up to hang upon their pegs in the tack shed.

"You look like that cat, Boxer, after she's whipped another passel of puppies," Mab observed.

"Hard not to, after Cameron's last dispatches concerning the northwestern tribes' choice to get rid of their old Chiefs who had been working with the Alaminites. We can have some security this winter with Chief Stasio directing the Owl pozeem, and Chief Ugew in charge of the Beavers."

Glennys's own obligations to her strategy returned her to Hometown after their visit with the Coyotes. Leon and Cameron, in company with Moria, Konya, Kazimir, the tutor Muran, and an increasing intertribal escort, had continued instruction in firearms and Nolanese battle deployment among the tribes west of the Valley. The younger members of the tribes were no different from those of Hometown. They too looked forward to the excitement of battle.

Mab asked, "Will you explain again, just for me, why you think Nolan's army is coming, and why it will come from the east, through the Crossing Pass?"

Glennys had been repeating a version of her premonitions all summer to Hometown, the women's councils, the Chiefs, and their pozeem. Moria, Konya, Kazimir, Muran, Cameron, and Leon had been convinced first, and spent the summer saying it for her to those she hadn't been able to see face-to-face. Glennys was willing to talk about her premonitions, hunches, and plans until, as they said in Nolan, the cows came home.

Glennys said, "Nolan will invade Saquave with an army because the crown has been given to a weakling who is the stalking horse behind which Nolan's strong men rule. Those men have deep suspicions that Young Wolf, our Leon, the Prince, and rightful bearer of that crown, is alive and well, and harbored by SSC. His mother, the Queen, sent him here for that very reason, for she and Muran discovered a plot against Leon by the same people who assassinated her husband, the King of Nolan, and our Leon's father. A living, rightful heir to a crown is always a threat to those who have usurped it, especially an heir whose father was so popular."

Mab asked, "Why are you certain that an army will come from the east instead of northwest through Silver City?"

Glennys answered, "Only the Crossing Pass can accommodate an army, and all that travels with it. You're too young to remember, but when the SSC left Nolan, Hengst and our Rangers made improvements ahead of us throughout the Pass. And before us, the old Duke Albany's original Rangers did work too. We're too few and too busy to afford to maintain the route. The bridges have come down, the trails and roads have filled with avalanche and rockslide. But the foundation work remains, making it much easier for those coming after us."

Mab said, "I still don't understand why you are so pleased at the idea of Nolan coming from that direction."

Glennys explained. "The Pass defiles into Saquave upon the wasteland of the Elk summer range. Nolan will come in spring, expecting a season much like over there, only hotter. Until you've experienced it, you cannot imagine spring on the wastelands of Saquave. The word for spring on Saquave is 'sand,' and it will blast Nolan. Leon and Muran were bloody lucky to be only two when they came into it. Leon and Muran didn't have Sigune and Azal on their tail either. They'll have maps, but Saquave, especially east of the Valley, changes its face from day to day. You have to live on it to learn it. I expect Sigune and the Scorpions will confuse and frighten the army from the moment it begins to march on Saquave. Saquave is our greatest weapon."

Mab said, "I think battles and wars are the most foolish, wasteful, cruel occupation ever devised by man. And I know you do, too. So why are you determined to have a battle?"

Glennys answered, "If the SSC wants to preserve its way of life, if the tribes want to, we've got to whip Nolan in a battle so decisive that Nolan knows it's whipped. We've got to hit them the first time, and beat them the first time. Otherwise Nolan will return every year, with more complete knowledge and better prepared."

Mab listened as intently as she had done the first time she'd heard this.

Mab said, "Then you and the Prince hope that the whipped army will recognize Leon as the rightful heir to the crown, and that it will want to go away with him to claim the crown for him. If the King who sits upon Nolan's throne is Saquave's friend, at least during his reign, we'll be safe."

Glennys grinned. "See, I finally found a use for him, and one that fits in with his own needs. Leon is having fun this summer."

Her smile disappeared. "There's still Silver City sitting on top of the upper tribes. Alaminites in the west, and Nolan in the east. The Valley's position is that of a peanut between two strong fingers posed to crack our shell and eat us up. Our friendship with the tribes is our only real weapon, that and Saquave itself. We are otherwise vastly outnumbered."

Suddenly the ram's horn on Hometown's watchtower blasted. Alert! Alert! Alert!

Glennys ran for the Planks, scrambled up the watchtower ladder faster than a cat. She grabbed the spyglass from Sky's hand.

Without the aid of the spyglass, the white puffs sailing close to the shoreline of the blue horizon couldn't be seen. With the glass, the eye had to be very sharp to distinguish them from cloudly white.

Three puffs, a pause, then two. Three, pause, two. Three-pause-two was the agreed-upon signal that the Alaminites had left Silver City for the Beaver range. This was the time of the year the Chief previous to Ugew had chosen to exchange women for firearms.

Glennys prepared to meet the Windgate Rangers. Instead of Beaver women, the Alaminites would get back their own wives.

Stella and Thea, in company with Deborah, came to her in Hatice's kitchen, where they were packing Glennys's travel supplies.

Thea said, "Deborah has a request, which she's afraid you won't listen to without our support."

Deborah seldom asked permission for anything. She did as she chose, and usually complained later that there hadn't been any appreciation for her efforts. What could her sister possibly want?

Thea explained. "Deborah has volunteered to go with you on muleback to escort the Alaminite wives back to their congregation. She's pointed out that these poor women know you for a witch. They've been living all this time under close imprisonment, with little other occupation than fear. They're going to believe you're taking them to the Wilderness to sacrifice them in some ceremonial witchcraft. Deborah respects their religion, and will be able to give them reassurance. She'll have more patience dealing with them than you, too. Her company will make your task easier."

Glennys rubbed her forehead. She'd scrubbed herself only a few minutes before. Surprisingly, it felt greasy under her fingers. She wiped them on her trousers.

"Do you, Mother, Thea, think this idea of Deb's is a good one?"

Thea said, "Maybe once Debbie's been able to spend some time with the women of Silver City, she'll learn how much Hans Rigg and Reverend Tuescher have perverted her religion. Debbie's gotten it into her head that Cameron's lied about her abduction and her forced marriage in Silver City to two men who were nothing more than brutal, murdering thugs."

Stella added, "Deborah refuses to open her heart to the knowledge that Alam is really Alma, the great all-loving mother goddess. She insists that my wits are scrambled when I tell her that the men changed everything. Let her speak with the poor bewildered women, and Alma's joyful being will enter her soul, displacing forever that cruel, heartless invention of the men."

Glennys was sick of religion. In all these years Deborah and Stella never stopped arguing about Alam versus Alma. She disliked Deb's humorlessness, her rigidity, everything about her, if the truth be told, and Glennys always told the truth to herself. Deborah was one of the few members of the SSC who was actively disliked by nearly everyone. She publicly accused Glennys of using the pressure of separation from Becky and Stella, her only family, forever. Without such separation Glennys would never have been able to drag her out to Saquave. Though that wasn't the entire story, there was a great deal of truth in Deborah's accusations. As Governor and, worse, as sister, Glennys had acted unjustly to her.

It was her awareness of failure in her own principles that made her consent, against her immediate inclination to deny Deborah's request.

When they rendezvoused with the Windgate Rangers, Deborah did make handling the Alaminite women much easier. The women had been well treated but were convinced it was only to fatten them up for sacrifice. They hated wearing dust kibba and veil, the riding leggings that went under. In such clothing no one could tell that they weren't heathen tribe-women. Deb kept out of Glennys's and the Rangers' way. She rode with the Alaminites, ate with them, and slept with them.

Thea and Stella's hopes for revelation over the falsity of Alam had been for naught, Glennys thought. Deb prayed with the Alaminites without ceasing. When they weren't praying, they were singing hymns.

Bari rode with them, along with her young children. With the uncertainty of the future, she preferred her daughters to be with her dear friend, Moria, in the relatively more secure Wind Song Hills.

Bari said, "All this caterwauling to Alam makes my skin crawl. But the prayers and hymns are an improvement over the wails and howls before Deb arrived. I've never heard anything like it in my life. You'd think Sigune had them."

They were very happy to arrive at the Beaver camp. After the prolonged, first courtesies were performed, the next order of business was to hobble the prisoners out of sight in a very large tent.

Auja was head of the Beaver Council. Her kurgan filled with tribal council women and pozeem. Bari's children were duly admired, then sent off with one of Moria's Crescents to find children their own age to play with. The walls were rolled up partway in order to enjoy the late afternoon air and light.

The sharp eyes of Glennys and Chief Ugew spotted the dust streamers rising up from the Benches at the same moment.

Glennys announced, "They are Young Wolf on Farhold, Kazimir on Antar, and Cameron on Mirage."

"Not even Moria can see that far," Chief Ugew said.

"Riders mounted on Brecca's children must be farther away than this for me not to know them," Glennys said.

The three galloped through the camp straight to Auja's kurgan. Eager Beaver Crescents led their horses away for attendance. Chief Ugew conducted them into the kurgan, seated them upon the carpet. Other Crescents removed their veils, wiped their faces with a damp cloth, held out a silver basin and poured water over their hands. Once they'd rinsed their mouths and spat out the dust, and drunk, they could report.

"Silver City will be here in the morning. They've camped on the lower Benches. They are well armed, and there are ten Noloani on horseback with them," Kazimir said.

"Stallion Queen, one of the Noloani is the High Judiciar Skiller of Nolan's Fortune Houses," Leon told her. "I read his presence here as a sign that your premonitions of Nolan's invasion are true ones. Fortune House officiates foresee and gather their strength like scavengers around strife, looking for first share of the pickings."

The evening meal was brought in upon an enormous platter and set upon a low platform in the center of Auja's kurgan.

The conversation was of treatment of the ills horses suffered and other polite subjects.

After Chief Ugew passed around the pipes he said, "Silver City will be displeased when they receive their own women instead of ours. They've been angry with us since Beavers and Owls took out the dams so our own waters could run again in the Sweet Grass. Will you be with us if they attack?"

Chief Kazimir gestured with his pipe to include all those within Auja's kurgan and those outside. He spoke with complete assurance.

"Wise women, Crescents, pozeem, and Rangers from all parts of Saquave swell your forces. None of us can stand alone against Silver City or Noloani, but together we can. Already the Stallion Queen has been proved right. Though they are still few, Noloani is here."

Before dawn Chief Ugew rode point of a representative confederation of Saquave over the cold, green-hazed ground of the Sweet Grass Hills. With the rains and the return of their mountain water, grass had covered the red, baked Hills. At the rear, conducted by the SSC, were the Alaminite wives, gagged and veiled, but generously mounted upon mules.

They moved so early in order to reach the bargaining ground before Silver City and scout the area for signs of treachery. A bargaining ground was neutral territory, but the tribes had learned that Silver City, like the Noloani, had no honor. All appeared quiet and undisturbed. The yardangs' incline showed no signs of anything but small animal tracks. It seemed no one had come here in months.

When the Alaminites came into sight, several Beaver pozeem, chosen for their calm temperaments, were detached to greet Silver City. Their condition was that of heralds, which was dangerous. The Beaver pozeem conducted the Alaminite leader and his chosen to the center of the bargaining ground, where they would meet face-to-face with Ugew and Stasio at an equal distance from their persons. As a matter of courtesy and to indicate their own honorable intentions, the Beavers gave the security of the rocky yardangs to the backs of their visitors.

Glennys Eve's attention divided among several lines. One of them was Cameron. She'd been silent and tight with a nervous energy ever since coming in yesterday. It was the proximity of Alaminites.

Another part of Glennys was given over to the Alaminites. They were mounted—mules, to be sure, not horses, but large, well-bred, well-trained, glossy animals, with full battle riding tack and armor. The answer to where and how they'd acquired them was provided by the Nolanese in their company.

Glennys examined the horse-mounted Nolanese carefully. They were ten, dressed in rich journey gear. Their horses showed some loss of condition from traveling, but far less than one would expect. Evidently they'd come to Silver City in easy stages, with time for graining and rest along the way. That filled her with unease. The routes out of Silver City down into Nolan must be vastly improved during these last years while she'd been occupied with confederating Saquave tribes, fighting off the Silver City, and doing her best to make the Valley a good place for the SSC settlers.

Hans Rigg and twenty of his bodyguards met in the center with the Chiefs and an equal party. Like the Ugew band, the Alaminites were unarmed. Before any words were exchanged, those witnessing for Saquave, so used to horses, noticed how the Alaminites held their bodies. Their contempt for the Beavers was great.

Chief Ugew greeted Hans Rigg courteously, though his courtesies were not returned. He explained that the old Chief had broken Saquave laws by bargaining women in exchange for weapons. He himself did not hold with breaking Saquave laws. But they had unviolated, well-fed Alaminite wives to give back to Silver City to make the journey down the Hammers a joyful one.

"We will accept those females, but we demand the property we were promised last winter. We will not go away until we have in hand the five hundred chattel from Beaver, and five hundred from Owl," Rigg said.

Chief Ugew said, "It is against Saquave law to deal or trade persons. Saquave punished the Elks harshly for breaking this law, among others. You cannot ask us to suffer Chief Sepul's fate."

As Chief Ugew had foreseen, the broken dams and Alaminites slaughtered during the release of the Elk women were thrown into the bargaining ground.

"We've held back our punishment for those dreadful sins you heathen committed against the great God Alam. Unless you earn Alam's mercy with the bargain made by your old Chief, we will hold back Alam's wrath no longer."

Chief Ugew said quietly, "Until a deal is made final, any party can withdraw. An exchange for women is no longer in effect, for Beavers and Owls do not break Saquave laws."

Hans Rigg said, "We do not permit heathens to chisel out of the bargain made with Alam."

"How can a bargain be made by only one side?" Chief Ugew asked.

Under his beard and sun color, Hans Rigg was white. His body was stiff from keeping his rage in check. No one had disagreed with him, or refused to perform his will, in so long he no longer believed such a thing could happen.

Rigg's hand clenched in a fist on his thigh. Gabe Abram, Rigg's favorite, most trusted bodyguard, was on that side. Gabe had seen that clench many times in his long association with Hans. It meant "We're gonna take 'em out."

Hans began a long harangue to put all eyes upon him. His men were familiar with this tactic. His left arm raised in the air. Its fall would be the signal to come in and fire at will.

His arm dropped and he pulled out his own concealed pistol at the same time.

Glennys watched and listened with all that was in her. Out of her long-distant past, Rigg's exhortation about pollution of the light put her on guard. The cadences of sermons like this one, coming out of an Alaminite preacher, preceded and followed Alam's punishment.

She put her will upon the horses, making them dance backwards, which wasn't so difficult to accomplish as their riders were beginning to fall under the spell of practiced, rhythmic, mesmerizing exhortation. The horses were immune to the Alaminite spell which was pitched to human ears. The horses followed another will laid upon their own. They backed, step by step.

Moments before Rigg's arm dropped, the tribes' riders were outside of the very short range of the pistols carried by the twenty men who'd come into the bargaining ground with Rigg. The longer guns fired by the Alaminites backed by the yardangs were short of the killing range by several yards.

Their charges blown, the Alaminites stared into one line after another of mounted men with drawn bows, arrows nocked. They were greatly outnumbered.

The Alaminite women were driven to the front of the line. "You have proved all your intentions against Owls and Beavers are treacherous. Take your own women, Silver City. Leave ours to us!" Chief Ugew shouted.

The Alaminites herded the women through the yardangs' grooves up to the Benches. Ugew's young pozeem charged their mounts in front of their Chief, just out of killing range of the long guns. The young pozeem spread out in a long line. To show their contempt of the foe, to demonstrate their own bravery, and their horsemanship to the Crescents behind, the pozeem had their horses rear, dance, and cavort in place.

At the moment the last Alaminites disappeared into the grooves between the yardangs, though the sky was bright blue, thunder roared. Beaver pozeem and horses were hit all down the line. It was an eruption of blood, guts, and shattered bones. And screams. Such screams.

The cannon had been dug in, emplaced, and artfully concealed by Alaminite skill long before Chief Ugew had taken the place of the old one. The cannon performed their evil work until Rigg and his favorites, driving the Alaminite women, shoved their mules up into the Hammers.

Grimly the Beavers went to work to circle behind the yardang pile and flood through the grooves. The gunners were Coals of the Lord, whose purpose in life was die for Alam and Hans Rigg. They knew they were going to die. They knew they would go straight to heaven. Kazimir and Leon were close to the head of the attack. Each Coal of the Lord fought until the Beavers put an end to his life. None allowed himself to be taken alive.

In the confusion of the dead, the dying, the fighting, and the later scavenging of the cannon, only Glennys saw Cameron racing Mirage on the back trail of the Alaminites.

Glennys thought to bring Mirage back. She could do it. But Cameron had a purpose. Her mother had no right to interfere.

· Twenty-two ·

IT WAS NEARLY noon by the sun. They were far up on the Benches now. Unless she caught up with the retreating Alaminites soon, she and Mirage would not be able to outflank them and ride to a place where she could make a good shot and get home free. Only if she got out free would her vengeance be successful.

Ahead Cameron heard a protesting whinny, the sound of a horse whose rider is forcing him into motion while someone else is holding both horse and rider in place.

"Jist gimme yer clothes and yer horse and I won't kill ya!" the Alaminite said. One arm hung on the bit, pulling the horse's head down with all the man's great strength. The other hand held a cocked pistol aimed for the rider's chest.

"Many pardons," said the Nolanese, "but I cannot comply with your request. I have ridden back down this carnage trail under your duress, but now you are become ridiculous. This is my horse and these are my clothes."

Cameron's heart beat its normal steady rate. Her breathing was calm. She studied the disposition of the scene. Saquave's law was that the victim of a soul stealer had the right to execute sentence upon the criminal. She kept in mind that soul stealers were twisted growths, unfit to live, for they could not believe that what they did was wrong. She intended to execute sentence without dragging it out either by accusation or torture. But the criminal must hear the reason for his execution, whether he understands or not.

"Gabe! Gabe Abram! Turn around."

Gabe's attention left the Nolanese as if he'd been dropped by an arrow. "Modesty? Modesty. Ya escaped from them heathen! Good gal. I was comin' back to rescue ya."

She nudged Mirage out of the rocks with her knees, and Gabriel saw her again as she'd first appeared in his life, wearing her Ranger gear. This time she was armed, and her face reminded him of a hawk's rather than of the pretty girl who'd turned up her face to the early spring sun on a mountain side. An arrow was aimed firmly at his heart.

"Modesty? What be wrong with ya? This is me, Gabe."

"You thieved my soul. You took me against my will from my people and my love. You and your brother raped me. Saquave's sentence upon a soul stealer is death," she said.

"Rape? You're my wife. Ya liked me better'n Silas. I dumped him down a cliff fer ya so ya could be alone with me like ya wanted," Gabriel Abram protested.

The arrow loosed and went into his chest. He plucked feebly at his death, unbelieving that a woman had right of choice, that a woman did not love brutality.

She nocked another arrow before the first one had reached its target and pointed it at the Nolanese.

"So ends the Abram house," Cameron said. She rode up to the body and spit on it without taking her eyes off the Nolanese. "Would I could do this to them all. What are you doing on the backtrail, Sir Justin Sharp?"

"You know me?" he asked.

She looked at him sourly. "Answer my question."

This is how it is for Glennys when she deals Justice, Cameron thought. No sooner is that nasty job of work completed than there's another one clamoring for immediate attention.

The man answered, "I was abducted by that man in the confusion down there. He thought with my horse and my clothes he could assume my identity and penetrate the strong-hold of Albany City, though he gave it the uncouth name of Hometown. As I fight with intelligence and he with brawn, I doubt he'd have found his scheme a success. Are you familiar with Albany City? He was convinced a female that belonged to him is held captive there. I gather that you're the woman of his dreams, and you have a somewhat different interpretation of events?"

Cameron considered. Sooner or later they were going to have

to deal with the SSC investors. Sharp had aided and assisted Leon's flight from his would-be assassins.

"If you want to get to Hometown, you can ride with me. But that means you won't be going back up to Silver City to join your friends. Likely you won't see them again for a long time. Hometown and Silver City are enemies. Which do you choose? Pick quick because I'm getting out of here now."

Justin Sharp grinned at her. "I've already seen Silver City," he said. "I didn't much like it," he added.

Sharp's intelligence swiftly grasped that he couldn't trick this woman into answering any of the questions he longed to ask her. Consequent to that realization, he prudently kept silence. Watching her, the landscape, and thinking his own thoughts were adequate occupations for his active mind during the ride down the Benches and over the Sweet Grass to the Beaver camp.

It was after sunset before they reached the Beavers. They could hear the wild outpouring of grief for the dead. The Rangers who were keeping watch greeted Cameron with great relief.

"Your safe return will make up for a lot with the Governor. We'll tell her you're back."

She put Sharp under the Rangers' guard. "Give him food and water, but don't let him go wandering, until the Governor decides what we should do with him. He is an SSC investor, and he did help Leon, but he was riding with Silver City," she said.

Cameron unsaddled Mirage and gave him a quick grooming.

"Tell the Noloani he's got to take care of his horse himself," Cameron added. "He may as well get used to it."

Glennys, Leon, and Muran were alone in her tent. Kazimir and the others were at the wake.

"Ronnie, at least you're safe. I know you had a reason to chase after them, but couldn't you have told me first?" Glennys reproached her.

Cameron said, "One of the soul stealers was with Hans Rigg. I passed sentence on him."

Glennys blew her hair out of her eyes. "Oh, my dear." She took Cameron into her arms. "I feared it was something like that. Are you all right?"

Leon said, "You killed him? Yourself? With your own hands? A woman shouldn't do that. A woman shouldn't have to do that."

Glennys interjected, "Saquave law. The victim takes back the power the soul stealer took from her."

Cameron spoke in sharper tones than she'd intended. Her head felt thick and heavy. She longed to fall upon the carpet and sleep for a thousand years.

"I did it, and learned that the other one is dead by his brother's own hand. Now what else has gone wrong besides that cannon emplacement we stupidly suspected but didn't find?"

Glennys ground her teeth. "Another piece of stupidity, and every bit of it my own. Deborah concealed herself among the Alaminite wives. She's with them up there in the Hammers."

Cameron said, "Just as well. It's her own choice. Maybe now our family can live peacefully for a change."

Glennys said, "Stella and Becky, Thea, will never forgive me."

Cameron said, "Thea will be asking you to forgive her! She's the one who convinced you to bring Deborah. The last time you went against your own judgment because Thea asked you, I went to Fort Cloud, and look what happened to me. Stella will find solace in Alma the next time somebody dies, and now that Jer's old enough to look at girls, Becky's not going to be thinking of anything else!"

A snort of laughter escaped from Glennys in spite of herself. It turned immediately into something suspiciously like a sob. "Cameron, Deborah is my sister! The Alaminites are going to wring her out dry and then work her to death while they sell what she's told them to Nolan."

Cameron sank down to the carpets across from Glennys. Leon's arm, the one not in a sling, reached out to her. She smiled wanly at him, but stayed where she was. There was a thick dressing on the side of his face that had been slashed, a bruise on his forehead. Both of his eyes were swollen. The Coals of the Lord had forced Saquave into close-quarter fighting before they died.

Cameron buried her head in her hands. She was so tired. Her words were slow and muffled, as if she didn't want to think them, or say them.

"Shit with hair in it. Deborah knows Leon is the heir apparent of Nolan. She knows everything about the Valley. She knows our strategy for meeting Nolan."

Leon said, "I think at this point our strategy has more to

gain by deepening the credibility in Nolan of my continued existence."

Glennys said, "I fear this morning's bad work will shake the credibility of our strategy among those on whom it depends most."

Kazimir hailed them softly from outside before coming in. "No, our confidence in you hasn't been shaken, Stallion Queen. This morning proved what Young Wolf told us about cannon. And now Saquave possesses three cannon that sometime we may be able to turn against Silver City."

Then he looked to Cameron. "I was told you'd returned, Cameron. Are you well? Why did you follow the Alaminites?"

"One of *them* rode with Hans Rigg. I gave him the justice of a soul stealer," Cameron answered again.

Seeing his face blanch, she added, "Justice the SSC way, Kazimir, not Sigune's. As much as I hated him, that I had no stomach for."

Kazimir sank to the cushions next to her after kissing her hand. "I'm very glad, Cameron, that it was SSC justice, and not Sigune's. I saw enough of that this summer to learn that the SSC's way in these things is better. I know this is woman's business, but I'd like to hear what happened."

Haltingly, Cameron began. She finished by telling them Justin Sharp was under Ranger guard.

"He's got the investor's right to enter Hometown. Though he helped Leon escape from over there, he appears to be friendly with our enemy. I wanted to discuss the problem with you before bringing him among us."

Muran spoke up. "There's only one way to decide. We must bring him in front of Leon."

Justin Sharp gracefully stepped into Glennys's tent. Kazimir actually saw the man's self-possession leak away, to be replaced with questioning wonder, rapidly followed by certainty. His face opened into joy. He knelt in front of Leon.

"My Prince, how wonderful, how stupendous to see you alive. I'd hoped against hope to find you, or at least hear word of you."

Immediately his surge of joy changed to anxiety. "Alive, yes, but not well. How serious are his injuries?" he demanded of the company.

Leon said, "Minor enough that I can answer for myself. I am alive *and* well."

Sharp drank in Leon's face. "So like your father's face, but you know, I think there's more in yours than ever was in his."

He reached out and touched the silver, turquoise, and feathers dangling from his left ear. "Where's your father's garnet? Have you gone and given it to some little native girl with a fine figure and many horses?"

Sharp didn't miss how the eyes of Leon and Cameron locked together in response to his question, and mentally he kicked himself hard. That clearly had been a bad gaffe.

Muran said, "It is in the same safe place that the Governor of the Saquave Settlement Company keeps the charters and contracts."

Sharp bowed to Muran, then threw his arms around him. "You did it, Mr. Muran. You got him here! How many others are with you?"

Muran said quietly, "It was the other way around. He kept me alive until the Governor saved our lives at the last minute. There are no others from our party. You should greet the Governor of SSC, Glennys Eve."

Sharp kissed Glennys's hand. "It's been a long time. I believe I saw some horses out there upon the field with a strong resemblance to the one I brought you from Duke Albany many years ago."

Muran said, "The Governor's honors include that of being Saquave's Stallion Queen. She is also head of the women's council of the Snake tribe, which is how the other twelve tribes refer to the SSC."

Among them, Glennys, Leon, and Muran did an excellent job in turning Sharp inside out, beginning with Sharissa's well-being. Finally they were satisfied he was telling the truth, as far as a High Judiciar Skiller could tell the truth. The Fortune Houses were under siege by the Wheels. The Roald faction had forced Sharissa into confessing that Sharp had helped her send Leon to the Saquave.

The Fortune House spy planted among Sharissa's ladies got to Sharp barely in time for him to escape arrest. His life was at stake. He had no choice but to flee and join the Prince in exile. There was nowhere in Nolan where he could safely hide. He needed assistance that could be turned into hard cash.

Glennys said, "So Albany's first idea for his Company

has come to pass after all—a bolt hole for old blood-line refugees."

Silver City had been a safer route for his small party than the one through the Crossing Pass. You could bribe Alaminites as long as the matter had nothing to do with their religion. During the Andacac invasion of Nolan, Duke Colfax had ridden shoulder-to-shoulder with Blood Chief Nathan Drake, and emerged in his own right as a great military leader. Nolan's military and the King's Guards of his own generation were deeply loyal to Colfax. Sharp hadn't dared to try and corrupt them.

By the time they'd arrived in the foothills of the Rain Shadows, the country below the trail through the Crossing Pass crawled with Nolanese soldiers, spies, and King's Guards for supply dumps. After the Alaminites concluded their bargain with the primitives, he'd hoped to hire some of those primitives to guide him to Albany City.

"Glennys, your people have performed a notable work in teaching the primitives our language," Sharp said.

Kazimir narrowed his eyes at "primitives."

Leon said, "The tribes are Tongue Kindred, not primitives, Lord Sharp. Chief Kazimir, I apologize for this Noloani insult. Now please, tell us, in your opinion, does this gathering below the Crossing Pass indicate that Duke Colfax is bringing an army to Saquave?"

Cameron couldn't take any more discussion. They were going to continue until dawn, and she had to lie down, if not sleep. Leon hardly noticed when she slipped out of the tent.

Kazimir followed her. He put out his arms and kept her from falling when she stumbled.

"Let me help you to wherever you're going," he said.

"Your mother's tent. I must sleep. I'm so afraid that I won't be able to, and I must."

"There are children and Crescents and persons coming and going in Konya's tent because of the wake. My own tent is empty and quiet. It's yours, if you'll accept it," Kazimir offered.

She could hardly get her boots off. Kazimir helped her, and gave her water to drink. She toppled like a dead tree upon his bed.

He wrapped himself in a buffalo robe and lay down by the

entrance. His eyes stared into the darkness. He listened to her tossing restlessly on the furs for a long time.

She sat up. "I'm sorry, Kazimir. That I can't sleep is no reason to keep you awake."

Kazimir asked, "I think you are cold. Nor have you eaten anything since before dawn."

He kindled a fire and went to his mother's tent for some food. He fed it to Cameron as though she were a small child.

She had eaten half a bowl of stew when, to her surprise, tears spilled over her face. Her body shook, hot and cold, at the same time. Her teeth chattered.

He wrapped her in his buffalo robe and held her close to him, trying to make her warm.

The fire died out.

He felt her lips searching his face. For a long time her kisses were like porcupine quills, sharp and biting. By degrees her lips softened, and with them her limbs loosened.

He opened her clothes and touched her from hair to toes, gentling her as one does a frightened horse that has been ill-used. He stroked her until she began to lean into him, as a horse will do when it begins to trust that the hands would not give hurt.

With her fingers Cameron traced his lips, and his brows, both of which were swollen and lumpy from the morning's battle.

"Who held Sigune after she did what she had to do?" Cameron whispered.

"Her women. They have each other, which is little enough, Saquave knows," Kazimir said.

"And Glennys, who holds her?"

"I think Saquave holds the Stallion Queen. She's not like us."

"And you, Kazimir, who held you after witnessing for the tribes the Elk women's justice upon the pozeem who sold them?"

She felt his eyelids flutter under her feather-touch. There was moisture on his cheeks. He clung to her. Cameron held him close and rocked him in her arms.

"You. Only you. With you I can bury what I saw and heard. But I cannnot forget it," Kazimir said.

Kazimir lifted the tendrils of her hair that spilled over his face and kissed them. "The Stallion Queen has not played us

false. She is true to Saquave's purpose for her. Change is upon
the land whether it or the tribes wish change or not. Some
matters should change I think, and she's opened the way for
us. Accusation, justice, then the sentence executed quick and
clean is better for the one who was hurt than prolonged torture
of the law-breaker. Orphans and children suffering the sentence
of the rain laws need a gentler care. There's so much we can do
for Saquave."

Cameron slipped one hand inside Kazimir's kibba. She felt
his heart beating against her flesh. She placed one of his hands
over her own heart.

They listened to their blood speaking in the dark.

In wonder they discovered that their hearts beat in the same
rhythm.

His mouth found hers. Together they made tender and generous love to the land they shared.

He felt, rather than heard, a tiny sigh.

"It's really over now, all of it," Cameron said.

Kazimir parted the veil of her hair. It smelled of the cedar
wood shavings that had been wrapped within the folds of her
turban.

"It will not be truly over until Saquave whips that Noloani
army and Leon is seated upon that throne over there," Kazimir
said. "Only then can we begin the work that Saquave has made
us for."

Rangers and pozeem prowled the Benches, alert for Silver
City vengeance and slavers. In their scouting they discovered
Sharp's party retreating from the pursuit of Alaminites. The
Fortune House men were bloody, and several more died before
the Alaminites were driven off by the bows' superior range.

Sharp and his men settled down in Hometown to wait for winter
to pass. After inspection of SSC's accounts and the investors'
share of the Valley's goods, a shareholders meeting was held
in the Hall. Sharp words were exchanged between the settlers
and the investors.

Glennys recognized Hatice. Hatice stood as straight as her
hump allowed.

"You Nolanese seem to believe we've cheated you somehow
because your share is in kind, not in silver. The Alaminites
stole the big silver load from the tribes. The other mines are

in the Wind Song Hills and are part of the Bat tribe's range. You want us to steal and slave like those over there and Silver City?"

Whatever Sharp's private preferences were, he knew well enough to agree that business on Saquave couldn't be conducted in that manner, at least until he got his power base back in Nolan.

"One more thing, Lord Sharp," Hatice said. "Why is it you and your people are the only ones in the Valley who don't work to earn your keep?"

Sharp said, puzzled, "Whatever are you getting at?"

Hatice said, "Everyone works here, even Prince Leon. What's been held back for the investors is what you live on. You're living off our sweat and our blood. What's there is more than you and yours can use up on Saquave even if you stay for the rest of your lives."

That was a novel way of interpreting contracts, Sharp thought.

Hatice added, "Now, on the other hand, if you choose to put this wealth to work, which is always better than letting it sit, myself and others will be pleased to advise you, for a share, of course."

Sharp realized that this hump-backed woman with missing teeth and callused hands had neatly turned the tables on him. Of course, she was right. In Hatice he'd met his match, and he suspected that she wasn't the only one.

· Twenty-three ·

AT END OF winter, like the bears waking out of hibernation, Black Blizzards roared claim on eastern Saquave's middle. Spring's sandstorms abraded, corroded, and galled what the Blizzards had rended.

In the canyons of the Crossing Pass, Nolan's invasion corps inhaled the scents of wildflowers and fresh pine resin. Rivers flashed with fish. The thin, clear air went to the leaders' heads like crisp champagne sipped from a sparkling crystal goblet.

To the watchful eyes of the Elks looking down upon its advance, Nolan appeared an enormous army. According to the civilized, cultured experience of war, the forces led by Blood Chief Duke Stogar Fulk from the litter in which he was carried, and Blood Chief Duke Colfax from the backs of the war stallions on which he rode, were so small as to hardly warrant the appellation "army."

The fighting members of this force, particularly the infantry and the gunners, had been carefully handpicked. At the conclusion of the Civil War and the Andacac invasion, Nolan's armies had enlisted men and conscripts they no longer needed. Certainly Nolan's purse no longer desired to support these ferocious and lawless killers. Most of the enlistees had homes and families absorb them. The conscripts, being the sort of men they were, did not. If they were turned off, Nolan would again be overrun with murderers, brigands, and thieves.

Stogar and Colfax devised an excellent solution to this problem, after hearing Queen Sharissa's forced confession as to the whereabouts of Prince Leon. Battle Chiefs as well as co-Council Chiefs, the two of them pulled out the conscripts from Nolan's military and made of them a special force. That force would be their armor in the Saquave Wilderness while they stalked their unhappy suspicion that Prince Leon was alive over the Mountains among the savages. When they'd concluded that issue, in one way or another, they would dump this well-honed fighting scum of infantry and cannoneers upon the Saquave Settlement Company. The conscripts were promised land there of their own, land that they could take easily by force from the nomadic savages, and force the savages to work for them.

In accordance with the two purposes of their plan, last winter Stogar and Colfax announced to Nolan's House of Assembly an innocuous "Royal Progress throughout Nolan's Domain." The Progress was to reassure Nolan that the crown was in good hands after the sudden death and funeral of the heir apparent. A Progress provided an innocent explanation for the inclusion of so many of the highest-ranking and most wealthy Aristos from Queen Sharissa herself, to the daughters of Duke Colfax, sired upon his wife by Leon's father, the previous King of Nolan.

The true reason for the presence of so many powerful and highly pedigreed members in this company was that no member of the Royal Council trusted the others enough to leave his rivals behind in St. Lucien, with or without Queen Sharissa and the Duke Colfax's daughters who carried the blood of the dead King in their veins. The Queen, the young women, and girls were Nolan's most important figures. Marriage to one of them, successful penetration of their groins, and planting in the womb by a Stogar or another Aristo, Spur Blood or Wheel banker, was a giant's stride toward usurping Nolan's crown. The second step was the removal of King Roald. That could be accomplished any time they wished. His usefulness was nearly finished.

The Queen and the Duke's daughters, all of whom were a part of her court, knew themselves to be of primary importance. They also knew themselves to be utterly powerless in their own right. The Royal Council had them under intimate surveillance by rapidly rotated guards. Their jewels were locked safely away except upon public occasions. They were allowed nothing more than pin money. They had no opportunities of conversing in private or public with anyone who might be out of sympathy with any member of the Royal Council.

Once the small army reached the foothills of the Rain Shadows, it was announced throughout Nolan that the Progress would continue to the Wilderness on the other side of the Mountains, from where, history instructed, the Old Blood Nolanese Aristos and their war stallions hailed. The heirs of the first Old Bloods, on behalf of all the people of Nolan, were going to pay their homage to the lands of their origin. Below the Crossing Pass they absorbed those who'd been sent ahead with cannon, the infantry, and the supply trains.

The Blood Chiefs' efficient planning made the spring Crossing as enjoyable a jaunt as such mountain traveling in primitive conditions could be.

Waited on hand and foot, the male Aristos found it delightful. There was new and interesting game to hunt, new fish to catch, new things to see and wonder over. The Aristos' greatest pleasure was the interruption in their intrigue against each other. Until their quest to settle once and for all the survival of Prince Leon was completed, they were all on the same side.

The Alaminite representatives from Silver City had sold the information regarding Prince Leon's existence dearly. They received the promise of control over the Snake River Valley, favorable trade agreements with Nolan, and a hundred years' relief from taxation. The Valley's Governor was to be handed over to them alive, to be burned as a witch. The SSC's healer, Thea Bohn, was to be given to Hans Rigg for a wife.

Stogar and Colfax, following the principles of the Wheels, knew any agreement made could always be broken. They cared nothing for the burning of Glennys Eve or the forced marriage of a healer. Control of the Valley, and any profits out of the Wilderness, were entirely different matters. That was going to stay in their own hands through those of their scum.

Colfax would have preferred to disbelieve Silver City's information. Stogar, who had a history of dealing in both alliance and betrayal with Alaminites, was inclined to believe they told the truth. Hans Rigg provided proofs. He'd learned of Leon from a Deborah who was sister of the witch, as he called the Governor of the Saquave Settlement Company. Stogar's knowledge of Glennys and her family included the names of her sisters.

Stogar and Colfax agreed upon one thing. The information they'd bought from the Alaminites regarding Leon living among

the settlers of the SSC was their own. No one else was to hear
about it, particularly Queen Sharissa.

Queen Sharissa's existence was a daily sweat of terror. Every
night when she put herself down to sleep she wondered if she'd
awake the next morning. When she woke she wondered if she'd
live long enough to sleep that night. Her chances of surviving
past the summer were so meager that she'd advise anyone to
wager against it. Her only hope, and that was faint as a whisper,
was that her son lived and had found Glennys Eve, Governor
of the Saquave Settlement Company and Stallion Queen, and
forged an alliance.

Glennys had rescued her a long time ago. That rescue allowed
Sharissa to experience the only days of happiness she'd ever
known after her childhood was over. Sharissa had to believe
that this woman could also save her son, the only evidence
that her life was something more than the miserable burden
of a pedigreed pawn that it had been ever since in Nolan's
games among powerful, ambitious, scheming men.

East of the Valley, in a lull between storms, Glennys, Leon,
Ricold, and Elk Crescents struggled across the devastated
wastelands that had been the Elks' summer grazing grounds.
The fluctuant air was compressed by the particulate suspension
flowing over the thornscrub. The fibers of their clothing were
impregnated with fine, red dust that dyed their kibbas the same
color as the aimless ripples sidewinding across their buskins.

Breath came to Skinners and mules through water-soaked
wraps over nose and mouth. The Skinners dug holes and piled
rocks over the water and mares' skin. The mules got the biggest
share of water allotted to the use of the caravan from the pottery
barrels under the stone cairns. The rest of the water and other
supplies were cached for the summer war against Nolan.

When Leon and Muran had searched for the Valley, most of
the larger animals had already deserted the thornscrub for better
country. Two more years of drought had driven out everything
but the ants, wasps, flies, and cactus.

The prairie dog town where Leon had taken the little King
was a ghost town. There were no more rabbits. The ravine
where they'd found sweet water trickled dust. The smaller life
on which he and Muran had fed had either died of thirst and
starvation, or had followed the buffalo to a better place. The

thornscrub was so deserted that even the vultures had gone.

Ricold dropped back to walk with Leon awhile. "Wish I had the eyes to be a fighting man. Battle against Nolan's got to beat this shitty job."

In spite of the wraps concealing his face, Ricold managed to convey a cheerful willingness that belied his words.

Leon swore at the drag mules of the train. Glennys whacked the leaders. He tried to distract his body's misery with a choice of which, among the many hard jobs he'd taken on in the last two years, he'd hated most. Skinning mules between sandstorms was worse than digging foundations in mountain winter for Fort Cloud's bridge.

Skinning mules in wind-driven sand was better than facing Alaminite Coals of the Lord, determined to take him with them into death before he'd had the chance to strike a blow on his own behalf to gain his crown. Fighting fanatics had been better than wandering the Wilderness two years ago never knowing if there was going to be a next meal.

The most terrible of his jobs had been tracking Cameron to Silver City. Now she was off with Sigune in the Benches under the Crossing Pass looking for Nolan. She was going to get to strike the first blow, not he. But Sigune wasn't ready to allow any men to ride in her company of women.

He punched Ricold lightly on the shoulder as the short-sighted man moved up ahead again, to shove his mules into line.

Caching food and water against the summer's invasion had fallen to him in the natural course of things because everyone else had their seasonal work to do, which the threat of invasion couldn't stop. The tribes' herds were on the move from their winter grounds. Lambs were dropping, and the predators were hungry. Every carnivore haunted the birthing and newborn meat that couldn't fight back. Pozeem needed to penetrate into the Dead Lands with food and water for the trading caravan returning from the Green People. Soon it would be time for shearing, followed by the breeding season. In the Valley and the Wind Songs the fields had to be prepared for planting, the seeds had to be sprouted.

Spring came later to the northern Hammers than it did to the Crossing Pass in the east. Throughout the winter the Alaminites sent one troop after another of Coals of the Lord raiding the camps of the upper tribes. Bat, Crow, and Gazelle pozeem had loaned their own prowess to the Owls and Beavers who bore the brunt of the attacks. The Rangers were equally hard pressed as Silver City made one strike after another at Fort Cloud and Windgate Station. This time they'd leveled cannon against the walls.

Creating supply caches fell to those without other obligations or those who had nothing better that earned their keep. Glennys had every reason to be excused on that ground, but she, more than anyone in the Valley or the tribes, except Leon himself, felt herself most responsible for turning back the Nolanese invasion. No one believed in that invasion more than herself, not even Leon. The two of them took out the cache caravans, assisted by whoever was available and willing. This was the last one. Spring's promise for summer in the east was nothing but more drought, more wind, more sand, and dust.

Then, breaking Saquave's patterns for both spring and drought, the brilliant blue sky clouded over. One gullywasher after another pounded the thornscrub between the Crossing Pass and the Valley. In between were long, soft, veils of misting moisture that drifted day and night over the land.

The thornscrub turned green. Cactus flowers opened, covered with bees. The cracked mud playas were mirrors of water reflecting the hanging clouds. Every ravine, every depression was filled with rushing, foaming, tumbling cataracts.

The first skirmishing actions between Nolan's cavalry parties scouting out the country and Sigune's women took place on the lower Benches covered with grass and the evergreen cypress. The Crescents lost three of their number and the horses as well. Without their superior knowledge of the country, and the pigskin armor their own horses wore against the cactus, none of them would have escaped except Cameron. She'd refused to participate in the wild, ululating charge against the cavalry scouts.

"How long before Noloani learns to protect their horses?" Sigune mourned. They'd not been able to recover the bodies of their dead companions.

"Whoever would have dreamed that horses could be so big? Noloani stallions cover in one stride what ours do in two. They will be through the thornscrub by early summer, and devouring the Valley."

Cameron said, "Sigune, pull yourself up! None of the stories persons tell ever said the Noloani weren't cunning or brave fighters. This is only the first round. We've learned their firepower isn't hurt by the wet, and to respect their ability. Now we begin teaching them to respect us. Their stallions are used to living on corn, that's why they're so big. Without corn they will weaken. This is Coyote Rain, a Saquave trick to lure Nolan far enough away from the Crossing Pass that they cannot retreat into the safety of the Rain Shadows when they finally realize they are both thirsty and under attack."

Cameron believed what she said, but her state of mind was grim. She'd been shaken by her first encounter against men whose entire life was made for killing others. They approached fighting very differently from the pozeem. They preferred to kill than to drive away. They killed horses without compunction, not caring for loot. Without Brecca and Glennys's Saquave power behind her to hold back more than part of the horses, the women had flown at the enemy without plan, lusting for blood and plunder. Maybe next time they'd listen to her when she gave the order to hold a line.

At the side of Duke Stogar's litter, Duke Colfax's horse snuffed the air rising off Saquave with eager interest. All the horses under the first columns of the army danced, entranced by the novel variety of smells out of wide-open country, where an enemy could be seen long before it was a danger, and a horse could easily do what it was made for, which was run away safely.

Colfax took the distance glasses from his eyes, and passed them down to Duke Stogar in his litter. Colfax found great satisfaction looking down at his partner. Stogar's crippled body made him appear like nothing so much but a heap of discarded clothes in the middle of the litter, though his upper body's strength was immense. If any Aristo's arrogance deserved the humiliation of maimed legs, it was the Fulk for certain. Stogar's sister, Thurlow, was more intolerable yet. As Roald's mistress she remained safe, for now. Her cruel manipulations of her petty power and nasty wit had made her more enemies than he and Stogar had together.

Stogar screwed the glasses into his one eye. The sunset was a spectacular display among the clouds lowering on the horizon in whichever direction he looked.

Stogar grunted. "Sharp's confiscated papers may have been deliberately misleading. It's mud bogging down the wheels of cannon limbers and our supply, and lightning strikes on our metal that's the danger, not thirst and heat. I won't bet on it, however. Every water wagon is to be filled to the brim before we deploy downslope, and every personal water skin. From now on all of us cut back by a quarter on what we eat and drink. The mules' and horses' rations will be cut by an eighth."

Baroness Thurlow Fulk Waterford, in company of King Roald, rode up to the Blood Chiefs. "The Wilderness, I see, has been, like everything else about this farcical hunting party, vastly overrated. No reason why the King and I can't have baths. See to it, Stogar. In this open country there's no excuse for the King and I to strain our groins in the saddle. We will have litters like yours."

Colfax said, in an attempt to goad Thurlow, "Queen Sharissa continues to ride. If she and her women do so, it isn't in your favor to do differently."

Thurlow shot King Roald a keen, threatening glance. Colfax considered that perhaps Thurlow's greatest enemy of all was Roald, because he was so afraid of her.

The King spoke up under the prodding of Thurlow's eyes. "The King and his dearest friend have no desire to participate in Sharissa's playacting the good little soldier. We expect litters in the morning. And a morning bath," the King ordered.

Stogar and Colfax never looked at each other. Roald feared the Blood Chiefs more than he feared Thurlow, who stubbornly refused to fear them herself. It suited her to have Roald shelter himself behind her when her brother and Colfax enraged him, and he was helpless to do anything about it.

Stogar and Colfax shared too much past not to understand each other's thoughts. Though each knew the other's ambition for the throne, they were as one in their contempt for Roald, and their loathing for Thurlow. One of the many pleasures they looked forward to in the near future, whichever of them came out on top, was never having to deal with the fatuous Roald and the vain, demanding, jeering Thurlow again.

Stogar sent one of his own aides to see to Thurlow's demands before resuming his sweep of the country with the viewing glasses. One functioning eye or not, Stogar's vision was the first to discover the returning cavalry scouts.

"They did run into some savages as we hoped. They're bringing back the bodies and their horses for us to examine, as I ordered. Too bad the horses are dead too. I've been hearing rumors all my life that Saquave horses are invisible to human sight. I'd like to check that out for myself," Stogar mused.

Upon examination, the dead bodies proved to be female, dirty, and scrawny. They also proved to be young and comely enough to be of interest to brothels in civilized cities. These days in St. Lucien, King's Daughters no longer were highly trained, highly skilled female practitioners of music, dance, and the other performing arts who had bought the right to negotiate good contracts for their sexual favors. Now, King's Daughters were whores, pure and simple, but the King's privy purse received the fees for their license to work just the same. Colfax knew how slender that privy purse was.

Additionally the women had worn silver ornaments. The horses shot out from under them by Nolan's cavalry, behind which they'd made their last defense before killing themselves, though small and rough-coated, were very interesting. The horses were certainly swift.

Horses and women both were promising commodities to be picked up here and turned into profit somewhere else. Perhaps there were others of these strange female creatures who presumed to men's fighting skills. They might make good shock troops when Nolan mobilized to take back her Outremere Domains. No doubt many other opportunities of profit would appear. With all this rain they should reach the Valley more quickly than anticipated, and the action for which they'd come would be finished soon. There'd be a little time before departing against winter's closing of the Pass for investigation into potential profit development.

Twenty-one days later there was no place in anyone's mind for profitable deals or litters and baths for the King, much less his unpopular mistress.

Four legs or two, Nolan's invasion force suffered festering sores from spines embedded in their flesh. They'd lost valuable time devising protection for their horses and the mule trains against the cactus that had no end. No matter how far in any direction the scouts went, those who returned found no signs of a way through the cactus jungle, and no sign that it would end anytime soon.

It hadn't rained for nine days. Within the first two days

without thunderstorms, open water disappeared. Within five days the green turned brown. By the seventh day everything was covered with a haze of red dust.

An army can read a map. An army's mind can understand that there are no towns in a country, no farms, nothing that an urban civilization has made armies accustomed to anywhere within any distance it looks, except a thousand miles behind it. However, until an army has marched in such a country it never learns that nothing literally means nothing, nothing to beg, buy, plunder, or steal to replace what was lost, broken, or used up.

At sun's westering the country turned buff brown, orange, silver, and black, witch colors. It was studded with the stark architecture of giant's tables, dead date palms, and bone-dry oasis.

Heat mirages played havoc with their vision. The water was tepid and horrible in the skins and barrels, and disappearing fast. The sun fried their brains, making them sizzle in their skulls. Everything jumped and buzzed. The flies were a torment. Above them black carrion birds circled endlessly, dropping the moment a horse, a mule, or man fell out of its formation.

Worst of all was the howling, beating, shrieking noise that went on ceaselessly day and night. The army's mind understood it came from human mouths, savages on light horse. They hung and stung at their flanks like the flies. They picked off horse, soldier, and mule here and there. They never attacked, the ranks were never broken. But the daily losses to riders they could barely see in day, and not at all at night, only hear because it was the riders' intention that they hear, became unnerving. They made moving at night a tense, frightening maneuver. They only did it because the sun took a higher toll than the enemy.

An army moves in hostile country on heart, trust, and full belly. It also must have water. Pounded by the sun, sucked on by the wind, Sigune's music wore at the army's spirit. The whispers about witches and witch country began among the rank and file. When overheard by a commissioned officer, such whispers were severely punished with the lash and triangle.

Stogar and Colfax were strong men, very strong men, and there was not one soldier who didn't know that. Most of the infantry and cannoneers had welts on their backs administered by one or the other, some many years ago. The army held steady ranks and performed its regulation tasks, and moved very fast.

To the eyes of Cameron and Sigune the army galloped over

the thornscrub. It made such good time that the Valley was less than two hundred miles away before summer, by Saquave stars, had properly opened. They couldn't delay, much less stop Nolan.

The army was approaching Spring Lake, the one dependable supply of water out here. Glennys and Leon were still fighting Alaminites in the northwest. Hengst was slowly, oh so slowly, driving others back to Silver City. The Alaminites had failed to establish a base for themselves during the winter on the other side of Fort Cloud. They'd lost this year's chance to get down the Benches to eastern Saquave, so they could come at the Valley from east and west.

The Nolanese army feared Saquave less than it feared Stogar and Colfax.

Though the Rabbit and Coyote pozeem were thoroughly occupied with their work of guarding, herding, trading, and breeding, Cameron rode to beg assistance from their women's councils.

They helped her drive up a small herd of mangy buffalo to lure the army away from discovery of Spring Lake.

Thurlow's highly polished boot under a scrim of red dust prodded the dead buffalo dragged back to the center of Nolan's bivouac. It was thoroughly unlike Thurlow's usual manner to show the slightest interest in ugly or gruesome things, Sharissa thought.

A shriek of anguish, directly followed by another, cut through the night. Thurlow noted the kill was on the near side of their central column again, or north by cardinal direction. The number of harassing arrows had increased over the last two days until the edges felt like they were marching through a swarm of witchly insects, unlike any known among natural, civilized human beings.

Colfax squatted next to the old bull. He used his whip to point where he wanted to examine the carcass. An aide did the actual handling of the flea-bitten body.

"About thirty of these you saw?" Stogar asked the cavalry scouts.

Upon their affirmative response Stogar presumed these buffalo were only representatives of those fabled beasts. The healthy, fat ones had driven these others out of the well-watered, richly grassed territory. If they continued down the backtrail of this little band of animals they too would come upon water.

Thurlow kicked the dead buffalo. "You are fools. All the attacks for the last two days have come from the north. South, the cavalry scouts find some ratty old animals. All of the scouts get back to us, without one skirmish going out or coming in. Those women may be savages, but they're women for all that. They're bloody good at making fools out of you men."

Between gritted teeth Stogar said, "The only woman who has ever made a fool out of me is you, sister, since you have succeeded in keeping me from putting you out of your misery through all these years."

Thurlow growled deep in her throat. Her eyes flashed. Roald moved out of her sight. He recognized those signs.

"There's something north they're afraid for us to find. It can only be water. Since I cannot go without bathing any longer, I'm going to find it. It can't be far."

Thinking Thurlow's death worth the loss of good cavalry men, Stogar and Colfax allowed her to pick fifty crack shots from horseback with both bow and gun. They donned armor and helmets in spite of the ferocious sun. They feared the skirmishers' arrows more than heat stroke.

Speed was the thing. Those who lived through it never forgot that wild ride, surrounded by howling witches who valiantly attempted to turn their own larger stallions back the way they'd come. Thurlow laid about her with a fine, rapier-thin whip lash. With each flick of her wrist, flesh opened on horse or skirmisher. She pushed wherever their opponents shoved the hardest. That was the direction of the water Thurlow's will had fastened upon.

Spring Lake was so close to the army that Thurlow's smoke explosives, signaling success, were seen on the northern horizon before dark. Her men drank in relays, while the others held off their attackers. Thurlow plunged, horse, clothes, all into the Lake. She immediately began washing her hair.

In spite of their dangerous situation the cavalry men had to admire this infamous, unpopular woman. Not only had she been right, she was fearless. There was something to be said for vanity, if it could breed such courage.

· Twenty-four ·

FROM THE TOP of a giant's table, Cameron looked across to Spring Lake. The gunners had succeeded in emplacing their cannon among the pillars and columns of the red sandstone Arches. Others had been dug in around the Lake. The infantry was camped in battle-ready squares and triangles. Cavalry columns were lined up.

During these terrible days and nights of clawing and biting at the fringes of Nolan's army, she'd learned to distinguish the sun-bleached, but still gay, arrogant banner marking Thurlow's tent, and the sad, limp rag outside of Queen Sharissa's.

She'd failed. She and Sigune's warrior Crescents had been too few, her own shadow of Glennys's Horse Sense too weak, to turn the enemy, or even delay it. She was only the foster daughter of the Stallion Queen, not a Stallion Queen herself.

She couldn't remember the last time she'd had enough water to quench her thirst. Between her thirst and her weariness, a feather touch could knock her irreversibly down the slope of despair.

Cameron squared her shoulders and straightened her back. She turned to their own horses and shared out among them their sparse allotment of water. She was free under the sky, to come and go as she pleased. She wasn't in Silver City. That was the place and time of despair. The Wild had saved her then. The Wild would save all of them now. But it had to be soon, or it would be too late.

She kept back her own share of water for Sigune. The Elk Crescent tossed in a fever. Her leg had been shattered by a shard of cannon shell. If Sigune had been only a few inches closer to the exploding shell, she and her horse would have been scattered in gobbets between the giant's table and Spring Lake. Down there, the flies and vultures swarmed over clots of flesh and blood that once had been her friends and their horses.

She wiped Sigune's face, forced her to drink. She spoke to her in words of hope and encouragement. "Kazimir and his pozeem will be here tomorrow. With them ride the Chiefs and their pozeem of Cougars, Scorpions, Wolves, Rabbits, and Coyotes. Your wounding wasn't for nothing, my dear sister. Our lines hold. The skirmish you led chased the enemy back to the Lake."

Kazimir and the first confederated tribal pozeem arrived that night, earlier than their messages had led the band of women to hope. The men brought fresh water, meat, and wood to cook the meat. The dervishes went to work upon Sigune's leg. It wasn't possible to save her leg, but they were able to save Sigune's life.

Chief Hengst and as many Rangers as could be spared from defending Fort Cloud arrived shortly before dawn. They carried, along with supplies, the good news that Glennys and Leon had left Hometown. The western tribal confederation, the sun, and attrition had defeated the Alaminite Coals of the Lord. They were forced to retreat all the way up to Silver City. The western campaign had been a long one, for the pozeem could only attack hand-to-hand when the Coals' ammunition gave out. The confederation possessed the greater number of warriors, and it was that which made the final difference.

There was no wood for the Nolanese army to cook with, much less with which to illuminate their camp. However, Kazimir could feel the army's spirit grow stronger as it watered from Spring Lake. At sunrise he looked for the first time upon an army of Noloani.

"Saquave," he breathed. "How could they carry water and food for so many across the Wilderness in this drought?"

Hengst said, "Nolan has a thousand years of experience at moving armies swiftly and successfully through hostile territory. Until the present day, Nolan had the added advantage of horses, which the peoples they conquered didn't have."

Long hot days and nights of charge and countercharge began. Keeping just beyond the killing range, the pozeem tried to draw fire. Nolan quickly understood their tactic and refused the bait, saving its ammunition.

A mule train sent ahead from Hometown brought the tribes all the firearms and ammunition captured from the Alaminites. The weapons were few, and there was less ammunition. Coals of the Lord fought until their last charge, then turned to knives, killing as many as they could before going down.

But the tribes' eyes were sharp, and their aim was accurate. They concentrated upon the gunnery teams around the cannon. Nolan's cavalry made charges, not to attack, but to escape from the opposing enemy that grew in numbers every day. After recovering from their long thirst, horses and men were hungry. The Snake River Valley, and food, was tantalizingly close.

The Chiefs and their pozeem managed each time to turn the Noloani back to the Lake. Their success entailed many deaths and more wounds.

Konya, and the women of the councils who were present to witness for those back upon their ranges, began to wonder. Others voiced doubts.

Rogan whispered among the Coyote women, "Why hasn't Saquave sent a sandstorm? Why aren't the Stallion Queen, and that Noloani Young Wolf with us? It is our pozeem who are dying. Have the Snakes played a trick upon us after all?"

When Glennys and Leon arrived with a large company that included Justin Sharp and his men, she saw which way the wind was blowing. She particularly requested Coyote assistance with unloading a large number of bundles from the mules.

Glennys told Rogan, "These are what have taken me so long. It is a Saquave trick upon the Noloani, better than a sandstorm. Cover all exposed parts of your bodies and wrap your mouths and noses."

Rogan asked, "What is it?"

"Bushels of Volcano Peppers ground into powder. Don't you think throwing this to a wind blowing toward Noloani might force the gunners away from the cannon in the Arches?" Glennys asked.

"Oh, Saquave," Rogan gasped. It was the first laughter Cameron had heard in many months. This was a nasty and very clever trick indeed. Rogan wished with all her might that she'd thought of it herself.

Volcanos were a sweet, tasty, fleshy variety of hot pepper. Ten minutes after eating one, the biter was helplessly erupting mucus and tears from the fire in mouth and throat. The eruption continued for at least an hour. The reaction to breathing the powder was even stronger and lasted longer. The Volcanos demanded protective handling, for in a few minutes their oil soaked into the skin, raising burning blisters as effectively as a flame. On Saquave the Volcanos were a valued crop. One tiny powdered pinch provided a wonderful tang and flavor to stews made when the only available meat was stringy, tough, tasteless, and perhaps hosting maggots.

At mid-morning the next day a fine, steady wind blew out of the west. Under Glennys's direction, protected pozeem tossed small bags made of the thinnest cotton, filled with Volcano powder, in the air downslope from their own people. Other pozeem broke the tossed bags open with stones from slingshots. The powder was a deep orange red. They could track the progress of powder, fine as Saquave dust in the clear, licking heat of the wind.

Through the spy glasses Glennys watched the effect on the gunner teams. One group after another deserted its post, running in a beeline to Spring Lake.

Then with Leon and Hengst at either side, Justin Sharp and his Fortune House men behind her, she rode Brecca safely through the Arches, carrying the white flag of parley. Pozeem labored to turn the cannon mouths toward the Nolanese army.

"Negotiate," Thurlow demanded of Stogar. "The first thing we want is roast chicken and rice."

"The only way I will negotiate with savages is over your dead body," Stogar snarled.

He and Colfax ordered a cavalry charge.

When Cameron heard the calls directing Nolan's cavalry charge, her heart pounded so hard her chest hurt. She grabbed the spy glass from Kazimir's hand and put it to her own eye.

"Saquave," she swore, "if I could do with Nolan's horses what Glennys is doing this minute, this mess could have been cleared up by now."

Kazimir lightly touched Cameron's shoulder in understanding, though he kept his eyes on the action. "Do not blame yourself for what Saquave chose not to provide," he said.

One unit of cavalry after another were mounted upon horses that snorted, plunged, danced, bucked, did anything but straighten out and move at the trot and into canter, then full-out gallop against Glennys's company.

Reluctantly, Colfax and Stogar agreed to the parley.

The Stallion Queen's party carefully remained out of the killing range. Hengst spoke first, well-accustomed to pitching his voice to be heard long distances. They had the wind in their favor too.

He spoke as the representative of Saquave. Nolan had come uninvited, and without permission. If the army surrendered to Saquave, their lives would be spared, but they had to go home.

Hengst knew this parley was only a time-out, but war and battles had rules, which like all games men played, had to be observed to satisfy men's honor.

Then Justin Sharp spoke, as the representative of Prince Leon, legitimate heir to Nolan's crown. At the age to wear the crown the Prince demanded it as his right. He then introduced Prince Leon as King Leon.

Leon declared himself. He rode Antar in a finely calculated gallop just beyond the killing range. Guns went off in a deafening explosion that went on for long minutes, until Colfax and Stogar ordered "hold fire."

After all that fire power had been expended, Leon still rode before the cavalry. The sun made a blaze of his hair, sparked the garnet in his ear, his father's famous jewel. The cavalry was noticeably impressed. That was how a King *should* declare himself to his own. It had been so long since the crowned head of Nolan had provided any display of a man's natural bravery, much less the dash that Royals owed their people, most particularly their riding warriors.

Roald's fingers clung like claws to Thurlow's hands. "It's him," Roald whimpered. "It's my brother come back from the dead."

Thurlow slapped the King. "That's no ghost, only your brother's brat. If Stogar and Colfax can't get rid of your nephew with a whole army aiming at him, I guess I'll have to do this job myself too."

Guns roared and the infantry advanced on the run.

Sharissa's face was blanched of all the color put there by wind and sun.

"My son. It is my son. He's alive," Sharissa whispered to herself.

She'd saved him by sending him here. He'd win. She knew it. She believed Stogar and Colfax would kill her momentarily, but she'd won and they'd lost. That was all that mattered.

But perhaps she could do something more, something that would strike back at those who'd tormented her for so long. She was an Old Blood. The lineage of her war stallion-riding, conquering forebears, moved richly in her, the first sensation of vitality she'd felt in a long time. Quickly she determined where her captors were in relation to her position.

Thurlow stood with Roald behind the Blood Chiefs. Her wardens' attention was upon the red-haired figure riding the stallion across the army's front.

Sharissa retreated into her tent. Because of the heat she wore nothing except riding trousers and blouse. She hacked off her hair short. She crawled under the back flaps. She moved slowly, carefully, deliberately. Without consciously willing it so, her hands took up a pike-gun from a rack among the infantry tents.

A true battle had started. Everyone was fighting, even the cavalry, though without their horses, which refused to obey orders. Colfax and Stogar forced them to provide backup for infantry. That was dishonor for the horse warriors.

Sharissa joined an infantry unit under the cover of confused disputation between cavalry and infantry officers.

Arrows mowed down the infantry charge. Sharissa fell on her belly before the first rain of arrows hit the line she'd joined. She squirmed across the deadly ground inch by imperceptible inch. Horses leaped over her body now and again.

The Saquave horse charges were under the commands of the tribal Chiefs. Leon could ride with any of them, and be welcome, but he, Noloani, was not allowed to lead any charge himself. He chose to ride with the Rangers under Hengst.

Whenever the pozeem or Rangers began to feel battle lust too strongly, felt the urge to leap ahead of their comrades, the Stallion Queen held back their horses.

The battle went on under the sun. Pouches of Volcano were tossed among the infantry whenever they attempted to rest. Sharissa crawled over a pouch that had split but not drifted. Her writhings were nothing more than one more gut-shot man hit by a savage's arrow. All through the day she burned, thirsted, and struggled. But her progress was always toward the west, to the Arches, that tumble of buttes and rocks that were the outermost boundary of the army. Late in the afternoon she reached her goal. She didn't know that the Arches were now territory of the savages.

A hand grabbed her ankle. A knife point nicked her throat. Sharissa croaked, "Leon. His mother. Mother."

Azal licked her knife in preparation to thrust into her prisoner's jugular. Her knives were having a fine day. As she shifted her grip, Azal's hand found the shrunken swell of what would be a good breast in times of water and food. So far, except for that Thurlow, the Noloani had proved without fighting women. This could be sport so good that it should be saved for later savor. Azal flipped her knife and knocked the woman out with the hilt. Then she dragged her captive deeper into the Arches.

Starving, exhausted, thirsty, Colfax and Stogar's scum kept up the fight until the other side gradually withdrew with the fall of darkness. The scum didn't think anymore of winning or losing, only enduring what must be endured. Their commanders' discipline held firm. They gave the order to their men to retreat so they could rest, drink, and eat the little food they still had.

Cameron worked her way through the Arches by light of a creosote torch. She stumbled upon Azal and a prisoner that Azal had touched so far only lightly with her sting.

Cameron said, "Azal, any of Saquave's children here must get up on the giant's table as soon as sooner. Stallion Queen's orders! Put your ear to the rock if you don't believe me."

Azal had ripped up the little clothing Sharissa was wearing to bind together her hands and feet.

"What have you here?" Cameron asked.

Sharissa raised her ravaged face. There was something in the voice of this other one that had penetrated.

"Leon, for his mother's sake. Leon," she rasped.

Cameron carried the torch to look at the prisoner. "Oh Saquave. Azal, I think you are playing with Young Wolf's mother."

Azal shrugged. "Nah. She keeps moaning that word, Leon. I don't hear that word, it is not one of the Tongue Kindred."

Cameron said, "Leon is only one of Young Wolf's names. This is his mother. Now cut her bonds."

Somewhat reluctantly, Azal complied. "Lucky for Young Wolf you came along then. I never knew a mother myself, but would have liked to have had one. Hope she don't hold it too hard against me. I think this one could make a fair and square fight."

Now that the woman was no longer the plaything of her knife Azal lost interest in her. Obeying the Stallion Queen's orders, she slipped into the dark up to the giant's table. She didn't need to put an ear to the rock. The soles of her feet felt the thunder rumbling under them.

That rumble was made by the stampede of a very large herd of buffalo. No one could huddle away from that in a shelter while it passed, as one could during a sandstorm. You got out of the way of the buffalo or you went under.

It was left to Cameron to get Sharissa away in time safely. The first storm of the buffalo surged below them as she tugged and dragged Nolan's crowned Queen up the steep sides of the giant's table. Sharissa's presence and her appearance came as a severe shock to Leon. After embraces and the first gush joy of learning his mother was alive, Leon left her care to Cameron and Thea.

The young King encountered Cameron making rounds of the wounded with Thea early the next morning.

"Please give my regard, compliments, and love to the Queen, my mother. Please explain that I am so occupied ordering what remains of Nolan's army that there is no time for personal business," he requested.

"You have earned that much from me at the very least," Cameron said.

Leon briefly thought she regarded him with a mild disapproval, then forgot about it in the press of his business.

To the relief of everyone Roald and Thurlow had perished. Against all odds, Stogar and Colfax were among the few

Nolanese who had survived the buffalo's passing. Hengst and Glennys, following the patterns by which they did Hometown Justice, requested permission of Leon to execute Stogar and Colfax immediately.

He graciously granted permission. Glennys and Hengst's own history with those two agreed with the young King's. Allow those men to live for another year, a month, an hour, and they'd come up smelling of roses and intriguing against him again. They had to die now.

However, as the two men were traitors to Nolan and had plotted his own death, Leon and Sharp agreed that by Nolan's laws of the Fortune Houses and the New Courts, Sharp's people had to perform the execution.

With no ceremony, no fine speeches, as soon as two axes were sharpened to razor edge, Stogar and Colfax lost their heads. The corpses were left to the vultures and coyotes.

In company with Justin Sharp, Leon set about making himself known to the remaining officers of infantry and cavalry. He brought food and water which got him his first hearing. His resemblance to his father, and his fighting abilities proven before the buffalo stampede, easily persuaded the soldiers that they would be better off under his command than without it. The Nolanese army was pitifully small. It hailed him as Leon, King of Nolan.

It was the most wonderful moment of Leon's life, standing upon the trampled remains of a water wagon under Saquave's stars, and listening to the hoarse Nolanese throats cheering him as the rightful ruler of Nolan. There were many proud and happy moments in his future, but none ever would ever be as good as this night, he was sure.

Leon sat in the Hall of the Big House. "I feel exceedingly embarrassed. Saquave has taught me to love you all. Your deaths and injuries have advanced my own desires. Instead of giving you all the proofs of my true regard, honor, and love, I'm riding away from you as fast as I can. But for Saquave's sake I must get over there and begin the long and arduous task of putting the tribe of Noloani in order."

Hatice, Koyna, Moria, and the other heads of the women's councils put in front of the Young King the vellum scrolls on which Muran had written out the relationship between Nolan

and Saquave. They came to agreement only after many long and
hard-headed negotiations with Justin Sharp and his group.

Somehow, after his winter with Hatice, Sharp hadn't been at
all surprised that the women of the tribal councils had learned to
read and write from Muran during the previous summer. Sharp
was just grateful that he wouldn't have to face opponents as
tough as these women back in Nolan.

Saquave's status was not that of a colony, but that of
Nolan's best friend. Nolan had no claims upon Saquave.
Saquave paid no taxes, but Saquave had favorable trade
agreements. Among other clauses were Nolan's assistance,
military and otherwise, to contain the Alaminite determination for domination over the Valley. That the SSC might pay
shares to some persons in Nolan was a separate issue, but
Hatice had managed in her dealings with Justin Sharp over
the winter to work that out to everyone's near satisfaction.

These articles of friendship were to be read into Nolan's rec-
ords in St. Lucien's Houses of Assembly, the Fortune Houses,
and the New Courts. To be sure all was written and spoken
correctly, certain representatives of Saquave would ride over
there with Leon.

Moria, Hatice, Konya, and surprisingly, Hulaff were among
those going to Nolan. Hulaff wanted to see with his own eyes
the Young Wolf fight for his own territory.

In the press of business Leon did manage to find a moment
in which to plead his cause with Cameron.

"For reasons of state I cannot marry you as my father married
my mother. But we can make another arrangement. We have an
institution of morganic marriage. My official wife's children
would be my heirs, but she would know from the beginning
that you are first in my heart," Leon told her.

Cameron said, "A Saquave woman does indeed love her
freedom, and does give her heart where she will. Therefore
I will not leave Saquave. A condition that would be good
and right here, over there will likely all too easily become
unbearable. I have no desire for that state of morganic wife.
I am the one, or no one."

"It's Kazimir, isn't it?" Leon asked. "He's the reason you
won't come with me." Leon frowned. "If I can't have you,
there's no one better than Kazimir, I suppose."

"Think as you like concerning my refusal," Cameron said.

She had reasons other than Kazimir and her love of home for refusing Leon's offer. She thought that some of those reasons would never be understood by Leon.

One worry of hers, however, he might understand. It was Glennys. She seemed only a shadow herself these hurried days before Leon's departure.

Glennys was healthy. She ate and drank like a normal person. But Glennys had never been like other persons. Cameron found Glennys's new state profoundly disturbing.

Something had gone out of Glennys, Cameron thought, the night she drove the buffalo against the Noloani. Having experience of the Weirding Ride in company with Glennys, Cameron knew that her foster mother had been the focus of more Saquave power than had ever poured through her before. Brecca and Glennys together had Saquave's gift of getting inside all of Saquave's children. But the Horse Sense was for horses, not others of Saquave's creatures. And Glennys had pulled up a herd of buffalo and driven it over Noloani. Perhaps that stampede had flattened her Horse Sense as it had flattened everything else in its path.

Sidewinder went around the Hall before Leon's departure. Valley and Wilderness alike were embarrassed in their turn. At a moment of celebration or coming together the toast was always, "Confusion to Nolan." That toast was not appropriate to this occasion.

Glennys came into the Hall. Strange, Cameron thought, how none of us had noticed that she wasn't with us all along. It's like she's done her work and has been taken off the duty roster.

Glennys took up a pottery thimble between two very thin fingers, and turned to the gathered company.

"We are all related!" she stated, and drank it off. "We are all related, whether the heritage of Ableir or Noloani. Now our division has been filled and we are friends."

There was time for only one more momentous announcement. Chief Hengst and Queen Sharissa had fallen in love. Hengst would travel to Nolan, where the marriage would be performed. They'd stay there until Leon's coronation. Then both he and Sharissa would return to Saquave for the rest of their days.

Those going to Nolan left Hometown and the Valley during the cooler hours of summer nights. The Saquave persons promised they'd be back next spring, or early summer at the latest.

*   *   *

Early in autumn Cameron found her feet taking her to Glennys's den in the Sandbank. Upon the gravelly beach she saw her foster mother sorting through all manner of travel gear, one piece after another which she rejected. The pile of acceptable objects was ridiculously tiny. Brecca snorted softly. He looked very old. For a horse, he was ancient, Cameron realized.

Tenderly Cameron asked, "Are you planning another sojourn in the Wilderness? You could use a little relaxation, I think."

Glennys peered at Cameron out of eyes that frightened her as much as getting caught up that cold night in the Weirding Ride. Cameron had been thinking that Glennys had lost what had made her different from other people. She'd only disguised it more carefully. There was nothing domestic in her eyes at all. Then they focused upon Cameron, and softened.

For a while Glennys said nothing. Cameron realized it was because it was difficult for her to use words.

Finally she said, "Have you ever wondered what was beyond the Wind Songs, beyond the ranges the tribes know? In the south we know about the Green People. What's in the farther west?"

Cameron said, "No, I haven't thought about that at all. Saquave's already too big for me to ever know it all."

The neigh of a mare came from the pasture. Brecca's ears pricked. The mare's neigh was answered by that of another stallion. Brecca walked to Glennys and put his heavy head on her shoulder. She stroked his cheeks.

"I wonder, though," Glennys said. "I've performed the purpose for which Saquave formed me. It will be able to keep itself, and change at its own choice now. For the first time in our lives Brecca and I are free to live as we choose. And we find that all we have are each other, and itchy feet."

Cameron began to feel shaky. "That can't be true. All of us, tribe and Valley, love you. We want you. We need you."

Glennys looked at her sidewise, much like an animal collecting itself for a dash away from those attempting to lure it into a cage with tasty bait.

"No," Glennys said. "Maybe some other time Saquave will need us again, but probably it will be too late for us to serve much purpose. I was the last Stallion Queen. I don't think Saquave will make another. The world changes, and so will Saquave, more slowly than many parts, which was why I was made. To give Saquave time. For generations Saquave will be a place for persons who find cities stifling, as long as those same persons are willing to learn what Saquave teaches. What every person who lives upon Saquave must understand—and that is your job, Cameron—is that human beings are made to keep the balance between land, sky, and what walks, or crawls, or swims, or flies. It has been forgotten everywhere except in Saquave."

It was eerie and edgy, this conversation. It wasn't at all like after that night Weirding Ride when her mother had tried so hard to be with her. Glennys was casting her off now, as mares, bitches, and other female animals did with their young when the time came.

"Saquave, Glennys. You're human, not an animal. You can stay with us. We won't demand too much from you." Cameron heard herself shouting.

Glennys raised one hand wearily. "Very soon Hometown's children will begin to call this place the witch cave again. You'll see."

Cameron retreated from the solitude that Glennys and Brecca had pulled over them like a cloak of invisibility.

Some days later Cameron, after a long day's work of training horses, and arbitrating disagreements among the SSC, happened to be standing upon Hometown's stockade. Kazimir had ridden in to be with her for a few days. Their arms around each other, they watched the sun go down and Saquave's magic spread over the western lands.

Suddenly Cameron stiffened. She groped for the distance glasses.

"It's Glennys on Brecca. They're riding away. They've already left the pasture behind. They're going into the sunset. Glennys hasn't said farewell. I must go after her and find out where she's going," she cried.

Kazimir in his turn took the glasses and gazed west. The sun had dropped just that much lower, and against its spill of glory he couldn't see a thing.

"If she hasn't said farewell, she means to return," Kazimir said with masculine reasonableness.

Throughout the rest of the autumn and into early winter news floated back from the west of the Stallion Queen and Brecca. Sometimes they spent the night and shared a meal. By the end of winter no more sightings had been reported.

The children of Hometown took to calling her old den of privacy in the Sandbank "the witch's cave." During a spring flood the Snake River dug itself a new channel, and that was the end of that.

After a time memories of the Stallion Queen disappeared altogether, except in stories told to children and during Hometown's Jubilees.